WOODBORN

HEATHER NIX

AUTHOR'S NOTE

This book contains some topics that historically have been used in different ways to vilify and wrongly persecute the Jewish people. As someone who grew up in a Jewish household, I wanted to be sure to handle these topics in a way that was not linked to the historical propaganda against Jewish people.

I worked closely with a group of people from various Jewish denominations to ensure that these topics were handled in a way that did not perpetuate harmful stereotypes or other antisemitic tropes. I designed my characters with great care to not be Jewish-coded. However, these topics may be difficult for some readers, so please refer to the content warnings found at www.booksbynix.com/ContentWarnings for a comprehensive list.

Please find a link below regarding Blood Libel and its origins in antisemitic propaganda.

https://encyclopedia.ushmm.org/content/en/article/blood-libel

AUTHOR'S NOTE

The characters contained within are inspired predominantly by Greek mythology—both the mythological creatures and the witches, who are based loosely on Hecate and her followers. I also drew inspiration from Norse mythology when creating the cloaks they wear.

PRONUNCIATION GUIDE

Characters -
    Cicerine - Sih-Sa-Reen / Ceci - seh-see
    Mamère - Mah-Mare
    Jynn - Jin
    Farragen - Fair-Uh-Gen
    Morwenna - More-Wen-Nuh
    Maelwen - Male-Wen
    Tuii - Twee
    Athros - Ath-Rows
    Jarrus - Jare-Us
    Kefleh - Kef-Luh
    Caelfry - Kale-free
    Cenna - sen-nuh
    Idyth - Ee-Dith
    Lafeine - La-fayn

Places -
    Kanitosh - Can-Ih-Tosh

PRONUNCIATION GUIDE

Athydis - Ath-Ih-Diss
Iowain - Yo-Wayn
Minos'Idyl - My-Nos-Eye-Dul

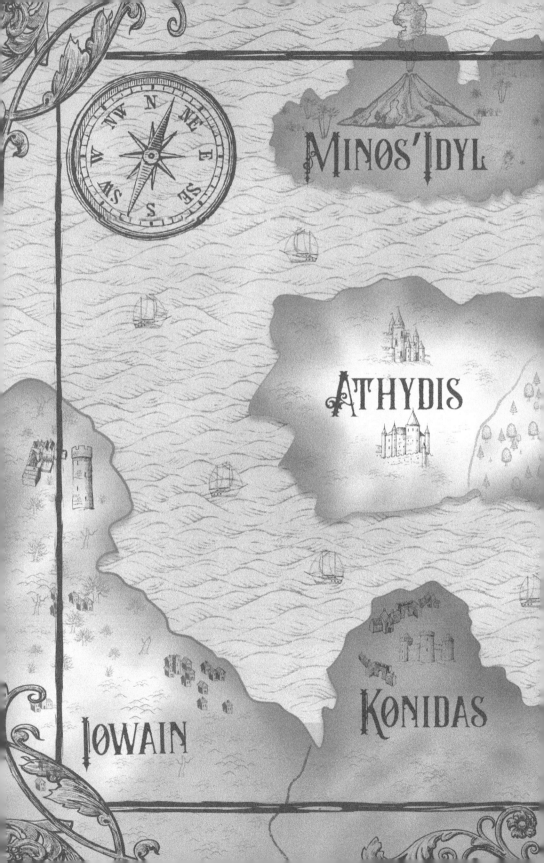

IDYTHIA

Kanitosh Woods

Copyright © 2022 by Heather Nix

All rights reserved. No part of this book may be reproduced or used in any manner without the prior written permission of the copyright owner, except for the use of brief quotations in a book review.

This book is a work of fiction. Names, characters, places and events are products of the author's imagination, and any resemblances to actual events or places or persons, living or dead, is entirely coincidental.

To request permissions, contact the publisher at authorheathernix@gmail.com

Paperback: 978-1-922936-06-6

First paperback edition January 2023.

Edited by Ambria Beal

Cover art by Anna (Newt) Doušová

Cover Layout and Chapter Headings by Eternal Geekery

Formatting by Amber Palmer

Printed in the USA.

www.booksbynix.com

For all the people who struggle to see themselves in stories, you are seen. And for those who still don't know who they are, it is never too late to find out.

CONTENT WARNINGS

The first three chapters of this novel contain some difficult scenes.

Please visit www.booksbynix.com/contentwarnings for a comprehensive list

This book contains a lot of my personal trauma, seen through a fantasy lens. Much of this story is about found family, and finding the people who take you as you are. The villains in this story are a group who believe that only one type of person is acceptable, which I hope will resonate with many others who grew up feeling like their identities were "wrong."

As a sexual assault and rape survivor, I wanted to write a novel in which rapists and abusers did NOT get away with their crimes. However, this is a fictional novel featuring mythological creatures and magic. I do not advocate for real-world violence, murder or assault.

CONTENTS

Prologue · 1
Morwenna · 3
Morwenna · 5
Morwenna · 7
Morwenna · 11
Mamère · 13

PART ONE

1. Maelwen · 19
   Year 989
2. Maelwen · 25
   Year 990
3. Cicerine · 31
   Year 993
4. Maelwen · 37
   Year 991
5. Cicerine · 47
   Year 993
6. Cicerine · 55
   Year 993
7. Shell · 67
   Year 992
8. Maelwen · 71
   Year 992
9. Shell · 81
   Year 993
10. Cicerine · 87
    Year 993
11. Shell · 93
    Year 993
12. Maelwen · 99
    Year 993
13. Cicerine · 103
    Year 993

14. Shell 113
Year 993
15. Cicerine 119
Year 993
16. Maelwen 123
Year 993
17. Mamère 129
Year 973
18. Shell 131
Year 993
19. Mamère 139
Year 974
20. Maelwen 141
Year 993
21. Mamère 147
Year 977
22. Shell 153
Year 993
23. Mamère 159
Year 977
24. Maelwen 161
Year 993
25. Cicerine 165
Year 993
26. Maelwen 173
Year 993
27. Jynn 179
Year 993
28. Shell 185
Year 993
29. Cicerine 191
Year 993
30. Maelwen 195
Year 993

PART TWO

31. The Crone 203
Year 981
32. Jynn 205
Year 993
33. Shell 211
Year 993

34. Cicerine *Year 993*	215
35. Jynn *Year 993*	219
36. Maelwen *Year 993*	227
37. Shell *Year 993*	237
38. Cicerine *Year 993*	243
39. Maelwen *Year 993*	249
40. Jynn *Year 993*	253
41. Cicerine *Year 993*	261
42. Jynn *Year 993*	265
43. Maelwen *Year 993*	271
44. Shell *Year 993*	279
45. Cicerine *Year 993*	285
46. Shell *Year 993*	291
47. Jynn *Year 993*	299
48. Maelwen *Year 993*	305
49. Cicerine *Year 993*	313
50. Jynn *Year 993*	319

PART THREE

51. The Crone *Year 993*	327
52. Maelwen *Year 993*	329
53. Cicerine *Year 993*	335

54. Jynn 343
Year 993

55. Shell 349
Year 993

56. Cicerine 353
Year 993

57. Maelwen 359
Year 993

58. The Crone 365
Year 993

59. Jynn 367
Year 993

60. Cicerine 373
Year 993

61. Maelwen 381
Year 993

62. Shell 391
Year 993

63. Jynn 397
Year 993

64. Cicerine 403
Year 993

65. Jynn 411
Year 993

66. Maelwen 419
Year 993

67. The Crone 431
Year 993

68. Shell 433
Year 993

69. Jynn 439
Year 993

70. Cicerine 445
Year 993

71. Maelwen 451
Year 993

72. Shell 457
Year 993

73. Jynn 463
Year 993

74. Maelwen 471
Year 993

75. Shell   479
Year 995
76. The Crone   487
Year 995
77. Cicerine   489
Year 995
78. Maelwen   491
Year 995
79. Jynn   495
Year 995

Acknowledgments   499
About the Author   501

PROLOGUE

IOWAIN

MORWENNA
YEAR 958

She aches—aches with the heaviness of her body, full with child and weighed down by knowledge. She feels as though all of Iowain rests upon her. At twenty-nine years, her swollen belly and the crushing pressure of her title to-be presses her down, down, down. She aches to escape this. She does not wish to be what she is. Morwenna mourns the child in her womb before it has even been born.

IOWAIN

MORWENNA
YEAR 959

Morwenna was born thirty years ago today, and on that day the Crone bore witness. The Crone heard that mewling cry from across the plain, from atop her tower—the edict that her era as the seventh Crone had come to an end.

All of witchkind chanted in unison, "Morwenna, Morwenna, Morwenna."

The plain shook with their stomping feet. The wind shivered with the weight of the command. It was decreed thirty years ago, and now it is time —Morwenna will begin her descent and become the next Crone.

It is done. In the morning, Morwenna bore her witchling onto the morning dew, the cave walls weeping moisture down their faces like tears in the early sun. She did not allow herself to look at the infant nor hear her cry. Like every Crone before her, Morwenna placed a trembling hand onto that small forehead and, with a resolute mind, cast her own flesh and blood into ashes—burning her baby into dust. With shaking fingers, she cupped the remains to her mouth, consuming her child with salty sorrow running down both cheeks.

She is stained with ash; it coats her face, her mouth, her hands. She will bear the stain forever. Already, her hair has begun to fade into a dusty gray;

her nails have begun to blacken. But this is how it is done, how it has always been done. The child must be consumed for the Crone to come to power.

IOWAIN

MORWENNA
YEAR 970

The man is dressed in rags, but his face is handsome. He looks as though he may have been a lord once, has the aristocratic tilt of the head. He does not know who she is, has no inkling of her power. All he sees is a beautiful woman on the plain, and she does not correct him. She is lovely, even now, as she nears her full descent. His eyes travel down her tall, slender, frame, seeing how gracefully her pale ash-colored hair falls in soft waves. Her eyes meet his, glacial, a pale aquamarine that reveals none of the darkness within. Her skin is cool-toned as if beneath perpetual moonlight, flawless and smooth save for small wrinkles beginning to settle around her eyes. His eyes catch on her hands. They are long and thin, tipped with claws as black as onyx, as sharp as obsidian. The claws no longer retract, forever extended. The lush red of her lips tempts most men, and he is no different. His breath goes ragged as her mouth curls into a smile.

It has been eleven years since she began her descent, twelve years since she has brought a man into her bed. She has gorged herself on them, but has not permitted herself to feel one's touch. She is forbidden to do so now. But as the former Crone nears her end and Morwenna approaches the start of her reign, she finds herself yearning for one more carnal moment. A single night to indulge in the pleasures of the flesh, to revel in the beauty of this body before it changes and curls into eternal age. One last night as a witch, before she becomes the Crone.

The wind whispers Morwenna's witchsong to him. His body does as it is beckoned, and he walks her way on silent, mindless feet—drawn inexorably to her. As he nears, her words flow into him like rich wine, intoxicating and dripping with sensual need. She sings in a steady cadence, each note bringing the man closer, rending away his ability to resist. This is but one of Morwenna's many gifts. Soon Morwenna will take her place as the Crone. Centuries from now, she will pass those gifts to another, as her reign comes to its end, and she returns to the sky.

The man's heartbeat is so loud; she can feel it thundering through her own veins. She scents his blood. Her mouth waters. Yes, she will consume him, but first, she wishes to be ravaged by his touch. She loosens her grip on his mind, and his eyes brighten as he beholds her face. He opens his mouth to speak, but she silences his tongue. She has no desire for his words. She needs only his hands, his mouth, his body. She needs only to feel once more the pleasure of flesh against flesh. She chose her prey well. Beneath the rags he wears, his body is well made. His arms flex with lean muscle as he pulls her to him, and his chest is firm beneath her hands. She loses herself in this moment. Tearing the tattered clothing from his form, she succumbs to carnal need. The hot slap of flesh on flesh is the only sound across the desolate plain. She cries out her release as he grunts into her neck like a chuffing pig. Human men are not graceful, but witches do not bear male children.

She feels no sadness or regret as she slides her black claw across his stubbled throat. He doesn't feel any pain. His mind is still tangled in her song, his skin still pulsing with pleasure. As his thick, crimson blood coats Morwenna's mouth, she smiles softly. His taste is sharp, flavored with the salt and tang of a life built from hard work. She is certain now that he was well born. She can taste the subtle sweetness of luxury and a memory of fine food and wine. She does not gloat herself upon him, just a taste. He has wandered far from the opulence which bore him, become yet another stinking human man. She neither knows nor cares how he ended up traveling the plains of Iowain. His traveling is done.

For some, this hellscape is a hideaway, a place to run from the actions of their past. Iowain harbors miscreants and criminals, violent and cruel men. For others, this place is a mystery. They seek to find fabled magic and gaze upon the tower of the Crone. Men are fools. The witches suffer most to live, to carry out their business in the city, but the worst of them are handled like cattle, led to slaughter with a promise of pleasure. They walk toward death on their own two feet. Witches do not need to hunt.

Sated, she leaves him to the scavengers. This is not cruel. It is simply the cycle of life. Everyone has a place in the hierarchy of existence in Iowain, witchkind is simply at the top. Witches have populated this cold desert for as long as history has been written. While they age no older than thirty, they live for centuries in this form. They do not succumb to disease and are difficult to kill. They come in every shade and size, united only by their retractable diamond sharp claws and seductive song.

The stain of sacrifice begins the Crone's descent, thirteen years of power accumulating within a rapidly aging body. From a lithe body of twenty-nine to one made ancient, bent and broken, in only thirteen years. The Crone loses her beauty, loses her freedom, loses her name, but in doing so, she gains incomparable power. No one save for the Crone herself knows the depths of the raw and untamed Chaos magic she wields. She lives in the tower in solitude, watching the ways of Idythia and guiding her kin from above. Morwenna did not wish to be the Crone, but it was never her choice to make. She was chosen, and so it shall be. Morwennaa, the eighth Crone.

IOWAIN

MORWENNA
YEAR 971

She has hidden herself for nearly a year, since the moment she felt the flutter of life and knew the mistake she had made. This was an unprecedented event, a child conceived during the descent. She knew she had taken a risk when she lay with that final man, but Morwenna had made that choice on her own. She was a fool. Now she lay concealed in this dusty cave, chilled to her bones as she births a witchling that should not exist.

For the first time in her forty-two years, she does not know what to do. From her birth until this point, her actions have been dictated by the title forced upon her. She has had so few true choices in her life. Now, she bears the consequence of the one choice she made for herself. This bloody infant in her hands seems so fragile, brittle as an eggshell. She can remember the cries of the baby before this one, though she tried not to hear. She remembers what she did. The dust between Morwenna's fingers, something forever shattered. A place in her which cannot be repaired. Her last shred of morality was left in tatters. It was the blackening of a soul.

On quick, quiet feet, she makes her way across the plain. Bundled in thick wool, the babe is silent as Morwenna glides through the night. It is not love driving her at this moment. Her ability to love died with a witchling twelve years ago. This is instinct, primal and unshakable—the need of a mother to keep her child from harm. Morwenna will not look at the witchling, will not nurse her, will not love her, but she will let this baby live. She will give her babe one thing—a chance.

The house she chooses is random. She knows nothing of the inhabitants, sees only a golden light seeping from the window to push back the stifling dark. She does not wait for an answer. After laying her burden before the door, she raps a single knock on the peeling wood and steals away into the night. She does not look back, does not permit herself a final glance. She leaves behind the last piece of Morwenna, the last piece of her that is not the Crone. This is the last time her feet will touch this ground. Tomorrow she will take the tower.

KANITOSH WOODS

MAMÈRE
YEAR 972

The glade is verdant, carpeted in sun dappled grass and scented by a soft breeze that flows through the trees. The sheer volume of green would be overwhelming were it not for the brilliance of the thousand different shades filling the space. Olive leaves and viridian stems, climbing vines of jade, emerald grass and swaying hunter stalks, the only other color littering the floor of the glade comes from small, purple flower blossoms. Mamère sniffs the air, sensing a shift in the breeze. Someone is coming.

As another strong contraction wracks her petite frame, her knees buckle, hooves digging into the earth. She places a hand on the gnarled bark of a nearby tree and attempts to breathe and steady herself. Five months, her pregnancy has lasted the full five months of a typical faun gestation. She has often wondered if she would make it this far. Stress is hard on a pregnancy, and saying goodbye to her lover after the thaw had nearly broken her. Trappers never stay long in the Kanitosh woods, but she had hoped that he'd be different. She had hoped that to him, she was different. But he had loaded his pack, kissed her one last time, and set off for Athydis as soon as the streams had swollen with melted snow. She takes another deep breath. It is not a man she scents now.

Mamère has never smelled an essence quite like this. It tastes slippery on her tongue, oily, as if it would slither down her throat. The scent is dark, smoky, somehow a blend of ember and rot. She shakes her head, her mousy brown curls ruffling around dainty curled horns, and tries to clear the wrongness from her nose. It seems thick, like it could drip from her nostrils. Another contraction comes suddenly, and she cries out as she falls to her knees. She presses her face to the grass and prays, "Gods save me."

She senses the shadow before she sees it. Again, that oily sensation seems to slide along her skin. When she raises her flushed face, a man stands at the edge of the glade. She supposes it is a man. The figure is tall and clothed in a dark cloak. His hair is stringy, the color of granite exposed to the wind. His eyes are deep set, ringed by dark circles. His skin is a sallow beige, untouched by color. He stands at the treeline, in a shadow where none should be. He says nothing, only watches. Too soon, far too soon, another contraction rips a cry from her lips and forces her forehead back to the earth. She feels the wetness as it slides down the soft hair of her legs. It is time; the baby is coming. She lifts her head and glances back toward the stranger, but he and his shadows are gone.

Mamère has attended plenty of births and knows what to expect, but that knowledge does nothing to ease her pain. Were her child a full faun, this would be easier. Baby fauns are soft, small and covered in downy hair. But Mamère had not laid with a faun that winter. Her trapper had been a man, a full-blooded human with a thick dark beard and bright dancing eyes. She had thought him the most majestic thing she had ever seen. He stood tall and proud as an oak, with rough, calloused hands that had seen a lifetime of hard use. He had caught her eye one morning as she gathered branches to stoke her humble fire, and for reasons she didn't quite understand, she beckoned for him to join her in her little thatched cottage. The winter was a harsh one, and a deep carpet of snow had fallen upon the glade. Like all trappers, he had come fully prepared to face the elements with a sturdy leather tent strapped to his back, but she saw the chapped red of his wind-bitten cheeks and raised her hand to him. The trapper had called himself Kovic, and he had heated his numb fingers at her hearth for the next month. He was kind and good-humored, and he filled her winter with the warmth of stories from his many travels. He warmed her bed, and she filled his belly with hearty vegetable stews and freshly baked bread. He once offered her braces of rabbits and wildfowl, but fauns do not eat flesh. He cooked his meat far from the glade, where she couldn't scent the smoke. He was considerate in wiping down his leathers with melted snow before returning to the cottage. His company made the winter days pass more quickly. She spent her afternoons milling flour and baking, checking the contents of her small winter food stores, and gathering nuts and seeds hidden beneath the bark of the nearby trees. She spent her nights in his arms, feeling his strong fingers gripping her thighs and feeling his lips along her neck. He was never bothered by the difference in their bodies. In fact, he seemed to revel in the feel of the smooth coat of chestnut hair which covered her legs. He nibbled her soft floppy ears and stared deeply into her warm brown eyes without even giving their slightly elongated pupils a second thought. She loved the feeling of her long lashes against his scruffy cheek, and the fullness of him within her—body and soul. She cared deeply for him, and when the leaves dripped in the sunshine, her heart fell, knowing her bed would soon be empty once more.

 She thinks of her trapper as she kneels in the glade, screaming her babe into life. She hopes he thinks of her too, and that maybe one day he will return to her. Breath after breath brings her babe closer to her arms. She bellows as the pressure rises, and she knows it will be only moments before she snuggles her soft infant. With a final cry she bears down, and her child comes to rest on the fine blades of spring grass. She reaches down and raises the babe into her arms. "I will call you Cicerine," she whispers to her sweet baby girl.

 The spring passes quickly as Mamère watches her squishy baby grow. Though she is half human, Cicerine has the same softly haired legs as the other faun children in the glade, ending in small glossy hooves. Her arms are smooth and hairless, and her ears are only slightly smaller than an *average faun, tipped in downy, white fuzz. She has no tail, and her head is a mop of warm brown curls with two tiny horn buds peeking through—the same cinnamon shade as her hair. Her eyes are golden, wide and bright, with impossibly long lashes, and a glint of merry mischief. Freckles spatter her rosy cheeks like a constellation of stars. Cicerine is the sweetest babe Mamère has ever seen.*

Part 1

IOWAIN

CHAPTER ONE
MAELWEN
YEAR 989

I spit blood onto the dusty floor of this stinking shack. The massive fist swinging toward my face misses by a hair's breadth as I dodge the strike. He howls in rage and lunges for me. My jaw is already beginning to swell, the throb of my blood a steady rhythm. He clomps over the creaking floorboards to me, grabbing my long, silver-streaked black hair, and flings me against the stone fireplace. My shoulder bears the brunt of the impact. I do not scream, but I do not consent. I let him drag me back into his bedroom, bile rising in my throat as I stop fighting. I cannot win against a creature twenty times my weight. A stronger witch than I could. I try not to make any sound as he lays his disgusting body over mine. I stare at the wall and imagine I am somewhere else. My dreaming continues long after he has cast me aside once again. It is all imagination; I have never been outside of Iowain. I imagine forests I have never seen.

His name is Jarrus. He is a minotaur, exiled from Minos'Idyl long before my birth. He had a wife once, Kefleh. She was neither kind nor cruel. My parents died while I was barely walking, and she took me in, giving me a sleeping mat in exchange for labor. I have worked my entire life. Even as a toddler, Kefleh gave me duties to earn my keep, sweeping the floors, washing the clothes. I did not have a childhood.

I am small, and my quick fingers are adept at sneaking into pockets. Jarrus is a laborer, shattering great boulders in the quarry to the east, but the pay is shit, and enough travelers pass through to make a pickpocket handy. He is absolutely massive, taller than me by double, his shoulders as broad as a human man is tall. His curling horns curve outward; his whiskered snout is wet and vile. His brown-haired, barrel-thick thighs end in hooves the width of my head. His wife was nearly his twin. Kefleh died three winters ago from a wasting sickness which came on quickly. She became a living corpse and passed in the evening as I made my rounds at the tavern. Jarrus had already buried her by the time I returned. I emptied my coat pockets onto the table, and he stuffed the coins into the pocket of his trousers as he unbuttoned them. He did not hit me the first time, but I did not fight him then.

I have been hiding coppers in the floorboards. This ramshackle house is falling apart, and it was easy enough to find a loose plank in the kitchen. My meager pile has grown steadily, and soon I hope it will be enough to pay my way out of this shithole. Konidas is a few day's ride if I can get a horse or pay my way into a caravan. I could pass for a performer with my sleight of hand. I just need to get out of this place. It chips away at me day by day, night after night.

Jarrus wakes me with a hoof to my side. "Get up," he growls in his low timbre. "Go to town. I need beer and grain."

It is assumed I will steal the coin needed for whatever he wants. He makes a wage at the quarry, but I have no idea what he does with it. He is certainly not paying a copper toward my keep. It is warm for the season, but the air still holds the chill Iowain is known for. My toes tingle in my boots as I walk the dirt path toward the rough town. It does not have a name; we just call it "town," and I suppose that is fitting. Iowain is mostly cold, parched earth littered with shoddy encampments and dry brush. The looming tower of the Crone sits to the North. I occasionally spot witches in the tavern, but they pay me no heed. I wear gloves as I work, keeping my head down, my ice-blue eyes well hidden. They do not seem to notice I am their kin. Jarrus does not seem to notice either. He is a drunken idiot. Were he to ever truly look at me, he would see that my fingertips end in sharp claws. I keep them drawn in most of the time, but with a flick of my wrist, they extend to a horrifying length, lethal and razor sharp. I will kill him one day. I just need a way to get out of here first.

Town is no different today than any other. The tavern is already busy as the sun begins its journey through the sky. It is only a few hours past dawn, but the night workers need their drink as well. I slither through the tavern patrons like an asp, my fingers light as air. I hum a little song to myself as I work, low notes that keep my mind steady and my hands moving. This place is full of large men. I barely reach their chests. I am thin and lithe, able to slip between them with ease.

I wear a ruddy brown coat as I slink among the tavern's chairs. My skin color is uncommon, but not unheard of. I draw no attention, just another beggar child looking for a meal. Most assume I am very young, but I am an adult, albeit a young one. My small stature works in my favor in most ways, but it also puts me at risk of leering men and groping hands. Today, I escape relatively unscathed with a handful of coins in my coat pocket, heading out toward the open stalls of the market.

I am familiar with many of the vendors, almost friendly with a few. The beermaker usually slips me a cup of ale to drink, and I know he always undercharges me. His daughter works alongside him in the busy season, perhaps he sees a bit of her in me. He gives me a generous smile from below his fat, red nose as he hands over the jug of beer for Jarrus and a small cup for me. I down the bitter beer in a few swigs and return his cup with a nod of gratitude, making my way down the market line with the beer warming my concave belly. After I have purchased my goods, a few coins still clink in my pocket, and I decide to grab a pasty for my daily meal. The price is low—I do not dare ask what variety of meat it is stuffed with. I savor the buttery crust and well-spiced meat, a small pleasure in an unpleasant life. I have a few hours before Jarrus will expect my return, so I head for the book vendor near the edge of the market. I toss him a brass coin and select a battered book with an illustrated cover and head for Jarrus's hovel once more.

 I drop off the beer and sack of barley and head to a rock near the edge of town. A large bare tree presses against its craggy surface, its branches like skeletal hands reaching for the sky. I often sit here to pass the time, watching people pass by or reading whatever I can dredge up from the market. The book I flip through today ends up being poetry, rather dull and overly romantic, but there are faded illustrations of beautiful landscapes and great cities. One couplet catches my attention—*The golden flow of Ichor goes through veins of mortal man. One taste, so sweet, the Gods entreat, that life begins again.* It must have come from Athydis; it's written in the common tongue. If only I could have such a blessing, a new life. I have spent an hour thumbing through its pages and committing the images to memory when the soft sound of footsteps draws my attention. Peering from behind my rock, I see a woman walking with an unearthly grace. I do not need to look at her hands to identify her as a witch. She wears a long cloak of deep sapphire, striking against the pale hair that hangs like a rippling, golden sheet down her back. Her voice carries on the wind as she sings a low, haunting melody that feels as though it flows between my ribs. She looks back as she steps into a small building, at the man who follows her inside.

 I sit back against my rock and sigh as I stare into the book.

Muffled sounds of sex come from the building where the witch and the man went, and my mouth twists in disgust. I have heard many whispered conversations about the ... tastes of witches. Many men have disappeared from town throughout my years here, and most of them likely fell prey to my estranged kin. They are known at times to kill men, draining their blood and feasting on their flesh. I cannot speak on their motives, but the men in this place are rarely men of any virtue. I eat normal food like anyone else. I cannot say that a man has ever looked appetizing to me in any way. They are smelly and crass, and my lip curls just thinking about them. I do not want to touch them at all, let alone eat them. They have touched me enough for a lifetime.

The noises pick up in pace, and I hope that they are nearly through. I enjoy the quiet of this place, and the rutting groans and grunts are distracting. A crash jerks me from my thoughts and I stand, peering toward the building from behind the rock. The witch tumbles out of the door with the man close behind, raining blows onto her head and face. She has her arms up to cover her head. If she were to extend her claws now, she would only succeed in slicing up her own flesh.

She is fast and darts out of his reach, revealing her claws. From my vantage point, I can see no one else nearby. I impulsively grab a rock and head toward them, shoving the book in my pocket. She does not need my assistance, but something within me savors the weight of the rock in my hands, craves this, wants to feel like I am *doing* something. I am exhausted by the seemingly constant abuse in this place. I strike him hard from behind. He crumples to the ground, blood pouring from the split skin at his hairline. The witch looks at me, wearing shock across her face.

"Witchling." Wide-eyed, she rasps, "I am in your debt."

I am not sure how to reply, so I nod my head and turn to leave. My heartbeat is a rapid drumming in my chest, I have never harmed anyone before. It feels...*good*. Her thin-boned wrist darts at me like the strike of a snake, and she grabs my upper arm with her clawed hand. Her golden hair is stained copper with blood, and she pushes it from her face with a satisfied smile. Reaching down, she drags a claw across his throat, never taking her gaze from mine.

She licks the claw clean with a flick of her tongue. "The kill is yours, witchling."

My brows furrow and my lips draw back in disgust as I realize what she offers. Surprise lights her eyes, and she lets go of my arm with a start.

"Where are you from?" she asks in a sultry rasp. "I do not know you, witchling."

"Here?" I answer with a shrug.

"And you do not feed? Have you no power?"

I look down at his dirt-smeared, bloody face and his shabby, stained clothes and nearly gag, disgust contorting my features.

"Another gift then." Pushing her long hair over one shoulder, she unclasps the rippling blue cloak and slides it from her shoulders. With a tender touch, she wraps it around me. The edges of her mouth lift in a soft smile. "This cloak will serve you well. Embrace what you are, and it will help you on your way."

I raise an eyebrow. "My way where?" I ask incredulously.

"Anywhere," she says, her voice low. She walks away with her shoulders back and head held high.

IOWAIN

CHAPTER TWO
MAELWEN
YEAR 990

J arrus has been drinking more than usual. My split lip throbs from last night's assault, when once again, he forced himself upon me. He passed out eventually, snoring in his bed. I slunk into the dark night and retched until my stomach was empty. My thoughts are crowded with images of his calloused, disgusting hands on my body, his massive head rutting, his foul spittle flying onto my face. My pile of copper seems to call to me from beneath the floor of the shack, beckoning me with the promise of freedom, of anything but this. The sapphire blue cloak lies folded beneath my crumbling pallet. I long to grab my coin and don the cloak—to escape into the waiting world.

The tavern was nearly empty this morning, and my pockets feel too light as I head back across the dusty path toward "home." I do not expect Jarrus to be here, but his bulk fills the space as I enter the doorway. His hot, yeasty breath already reeks of beer, and he grabs me by the throat before I can dart back outside. Hurling me against the wall, his thick fingers paw at my body and I kick at him wildly, trying to escape his grasp. His grip does not loosen. My vision begins to blur at the edges, stars shimmering and glinting before me. I cannot breathe, and I thrash beneath his powerful grip. His glassy eyes are inches from mine as he lowers his head, a drunken smirk on his crooked mouth. Instinct drives me and I choose to fight. I flick out my claws, shredding my glove, and I rake at his throat with all the strength I can muster. Air floods my lungs in a rush as he drops me to the floor, hands clutching his throat. Black blood seeps from between his fingers as a rattled wheeze shudders from his lips. And then he is falling, falling, and crashing through the thin wall. His horns knock twin holes into the wood paneling as he lands on the floor with a dense, deafening thud. I am frozen, immobilized by adrenaline and fear. I watch in tense silence as his breaths grow more shallow with each passing second, slow, and then stop altogether.

Splinters from the dilapidated floorboards sting my palms. I crawl as far from the body as I can and catch my breath, my eyes never leaving Jarrus's still form. Time slides like silk across the tangle of my mind. I have no idea how long I sit pressed against the peeling wall. I dare a glance down and find my claws smeared with the burgundy-black of drying bull's blood. I cannot explain the compulsion that brings my fingers to my mouth, but I suck his blood from my fingertips and loose a shuddering groan. It is salty and thick, tasting slightly of beer and boiled barley. As if I am watching someone else, I stare at my hands as they reach toward the dark pool of blood which has slowly spread across the floor. I lift my sticky hands to my mouth and lick them clean, over and over again. My heart races and my pace quickens, scooping handfuls of blood to my lips and slurping them down until the puddle is nothing more than a smear on splintered wood. Suddenly I am shaking, and my vision swims as I get to my feet on unsteady legs.

As though someone has wiped a damp cloth over the dust of my surroundings, everything is brighter, more vibrant. I can hear every single nearby sound, from the scurry of mice beneath the floor to the faint groan of the planks beneath Jarrus's heavy body.

I walk, dazed, to my meager pile of belongings and strip out of my bloodied clothes, dressing in a clean set of pants and a loose shirt. I only have one other change of clothes, and I shove them into a sack along with a waterskin and a small loaf of stale bread. Tearing up the floorboards, I grab my meager hoard of coin. Searching through the house I find Jarrus's own stash, which is more than I expected. I shove the lot into my pockets. There is enough silver here to last me months if I spend it wisely. One more reason to be glad that his corpse lies slumped in the other room. The drying blood on the floor makes a slight sticking sound as I step through it. A strange hum emanates from the other room, and I follow the soft buzzing, seeking its source. I lift my pallet and the cloak rustles as if tousled by an imagined wind. The sound buzzes in my ears, louder, insistent, and I lift the cloak toward my cocked head, listening. It tingles against my fingers, feeling like tiny bolts of lightning where my hands grip the smooth fabric. With newly steady hands, I wrap it around my shoulders and gasp as my mind explodes with light.

It is a sunrise, an inferno, a windstorm, a maelstrom. The moment the heavy blue fabric settles on my shoulders, I feel a tempest of energy swirling through my veins, dancing across my skin. I startle at a brief flash of tiny sharp pains as the cloak seems to stitch itself to my flesh, running from my neck down to my wrists on both sides. The feeling subsides the instant the cloak settles into my skin. I tug on the fabric and find it firmly attached, like an extension of my own body. My mind reels with power, a sensation I have never experienced. My outstretched claws clench and release, and I blink as I shake my head in an attempt to clear my racing thoughts. My heart thunders in my chest as reality settles upon me. I do not spare a glance around at the hovel I refuse to call a home as I make my way out the door into the murky dusk of the unknown.

I can feel each grain of sand and dirt beneath my feet. The

sensation is unnerving, like a teeming anthill underfoot. The cloak seems to pull at me, drawn to some unseen force. It is nearly dark outside, but I can see for miles, brighter than the midday sun. Did blood do this? What magic does a minotaur's blood hold? I can hear the melody of the breeze drifting through the air. Raising a slender hand skyward, I feel the wind slip between my fingers, now a tangible flow. The cloak flutters from where it is stitched into my flesh. The currents and eddies of air slide through the spaces between my fingers. Exhaling, I let my arm sink back to my side, close my eyes, and try to center myself. This is a sensory overload, and my mind struggles to process each sensation. As if I am a marionette, my hands rise skyward unbidden, and I feel a soft current of air shift beneath my feet. I look down. I am no longer earthbound.

The image of that golden witch appears before my mind's eye. Her words about this cloak, about my nature, flit around my mind and begin to make some sense. I hover inches above the cracked earth, and I understand. I have never seen a witch fly before, but I have heard about it all my life. I always wondered how it was done, and I suppose that now I know. This beautiful sapphire cloak, the blood of my captor, they have gifted me this freedom. If only I knew how to use it.

It takes nearly an hour for me to figure it out. I am clumsy and awkward, glad to be alone in this silent corner of the plain as I bob and weave through the sky like a gawky fledgling bird. I fall twice, skinning my knee through my pants and scraping the heel of my palm. To my surprise, they heal in moments. I quickly learn the flow of the air currents. I can catch one and ride it, the cloak rising to glide over the air like the wings of a seabird. Maneuvering becomes easier as the currents glow in my mind. I can trace their path like streams of water flowing over the earth. I can smell the cracked plain, the trees, the buildings, and I feel how the air flows over and between them. This is an awakening of another sense entirely, one buried deep within the tapestry of my blood. At first, I am wary of being too far from the ground. The last thing I want to do is plummet to my death just as I have gained my freedom, but the sky calls to me, and I let the air carry me upward. Iowain is so ugly from the ground, but from up here, it is almost beautiful. Barren trees dot the landscape in little constellations, buildings glow like faint stars. My hair trails behind me, and the wind brushes over my face with a cool grace. The air feels clean in my lungs, free at last from the choking dustiness of the plain. I can truly breathe for the very first time.

Kanitosh Woods

CHAPTER THREE
CICERINE
YEAR 993

Jynn is absolutely insufferable. I will never understand how I can love someone so fully while wanting to wring their Idyth-loving neck. I've known Jynn for as long as I can remember. She showed up in the glade when I was still in diapers, and we have been inseparable ever since. Jynn is quick-witted and smart as hell, but she's also a magnet for trouble. This morning I find myself stomping through the woods, trying my damnedest to lure Father Farragen away from the schoolhouse long enough for Jynn to fix the mess she made.

After our early worship service, Jynn thought it would be funny to steal a flask of apple mead. However, the knotted boards of the schoolhouse floor are a gnarled mess of ancient wood, and she managed to lose her footing and spill the entire flask. This would not be an issue for any other beverage, but the mead is sacred. Our glade has very few apple trees, and Mamère hiked nearly the entire length of the Kanitosh last summer to find enough apples to make a proper batch. We don't disrupt the bees to harvest honey more than once per season, so our honey store is limited. This batch took the full autumn to prepare, using nearly all of our honey and all but a few apples.

Father Farragen has told us time and again that without making the offering, Idyth will not see into our tree-hidden glade, and without his blessed light, none of us would thrive here as we have. It is only the third moon of spring, and we have less than ten bottles remaining in the cellar. The loss of even a single flask could leave us short for the months ahead. Father Farragen will be furious if he finds out, and I cannot allow him to punish Jynn.

By the time I reach the east edge of the glade, an ache throbs through my hooves. I'm panting, and I hope that the raspy sound of my breathing is loud enough for Father Farragen to find me. He's always had an uncanny sense of hearing, and I've almost never gotten away with deceiving him. His punishments can be swift and brutal. I am fortunate that his fondness for Mamère lightens his hand with me, but I still bear scars from the times I couldn't escape his wrath, like the thin white line on my left flank from when I was barely old enough to coax the flowers from the snow. I had mistakenly crushed a pennyway blossom after summoning it from the soil, and no amount of scrubbing faded the violet hue from my fingers.

Pennyway is the physical rebirth of the tears of Idyth, and to destroy a bloom is to insult Idyth himself. The gift of botanurgy is extremely rare, and the glade relies upon me to bring the flowers earthside when the winter frost has hardened the soil. To use my gift to call the blossoms forth, and to destroy one, is an unforgivable affront to Idyth. Father Farragen struck me so hard with a sun-dried liana vine that he split my hide in a single blow. The wound took a full moon to heal completely, and I can still feel a tinge of pain in it from time to time. I have never again allowed a single bloom to come to harm in my care.

After what feels like an eternity, I hear the sound of boots on stone, and I know Father Farragen has crossed the small boundary at this edge of the glade. I've practiced the story I plan to tell him over and over in my mind, but my voice is still thin and wavering as I softly say, "Forgiveness, Father. Mamère's birthday is in three days, and I wanted to grow some narcissus for her in celebration. I wanted it to be a surprise." I bow my head in what I hope is a penitent fashion, my curved cinnamon horns catching the light that filters through the trees.

His low voice is calm but clipped. "Abandoning your duties to sneak off and grow frivolous things disrespects Idyth, Cicerine. Was it your wish to disrespect our God?"

He looks like a column of stone—gray, solid, unfeeling. My gaze shoots up to his, locking eyes with his inky pupils. "No Father, I would never wish such a thing. Please, forgive me. How can I best atone? Should I pray? Make an offering?"

I'm beginning to panic. The words tumbling from my lips are nonsense, and he knows it. I'm certain he knows I am lying. I can only hope that he chooses to overlook it and makes me scrub some floors, gives me extra schoolhouse duties, anything. I have done nothing wrong, but I know he revels in the opportunity to punish the fauns of the glade.

His long pale hand slowly emerges from his robe. "No, Cicerine. I believe a more...*impactful* penance is in order."

Before his arrival in the glade, we knew little of sin, but Father Farragen has taken great pains to educate us. He has taught us that Idyth often demands sacrifice in the form of physical or emotional pain, a reminder that no sin is without consequence. I find the emotional punishments are usually much worse. Father Farragen says he takes no joy in their administration, but that does little to assuage the guilt and shame which accompany his terms of penance. He says he doesn't enjoy this, but I think maybe he does.

I feel my hands shake as I clasp them in front of me. Before I can move back, his bony fingers grip my wrist. He holds me firmly and takes another step toward me. *'Not today, please, not today,'* I can smell his skin from this distance, a strange acrid odor with an undercurrent of sickly sweetness, like something burnt and putrid.

His other hand reaches out to stroke the soft fur at the edge of my left ear. "Such a sweet girl you are, Cicerine. It pains me to see you darken yourself with sin like this. How can I help cleanse you of this stain?"

His fingernails, too long for his hands, feel like claws against my face. Every time he touches me, my skin crawls, and I can't help but flinch when he is nearby. I don't dare look up at him. It's best to remain demure. Maybe he will see the quiver in my hands and take pity upon me. He has before, but I realize I've led us too far from the village. There is no one here to stay his hand. His eyes slide down my body, and I can feel his gaze upon me as it lingers on my chest, down the curve of my hip. Idyth commands his chosen to live without many physical pleasures, but I've seen the way his eyes are drawn to Mamère, the extra notice he paid to Jynn last summer when her legs lengthened and her muscles lost the soft tone of childhood. I know he has forsaken intimate touch for his own enjoyment, but Idyth's penance calls for cleansing, and I believe he chooses these punishments for more than our atonement.

His too-long nail slides beneath the strap of my dress, and it slips from my shoulder. "The purity of Idyth's light shall burn away the smudge of your sin, Cicerine," he says so low that it is nearly a whisper.

My golden eyes fill with tears as I frantically look around us, searching for Jynn's bright red hair in the trees. Regret turns my stomach; I should have let Jynn handle her own mess. My sense of duty to my friend damns me every time. I see nothing but green all around. No one is coming to help.

His cold, damp fingers grip my wrist even tighter. "Make yourself ready for his light, my child."

My stomach roils. *No, no, no.* With shaking fingers, I raise my left hand and pull my other strap from my shoulder. The loose, rough-hewn fabric of my dress still covers my chest, but he reaches out and grasps the indigo linen and tugs it down past my breasts. It falls to the glade floor in a whisper, and a tear escapes down my cheek. I feel sick, swallowing down the bile in my throat.

Again, his skeletal hand reaches for my face and brushes the tear away. "I am glad to see you understand the gravity of your sin, dear one. Now remove the rest so that his rays may light upon you and make you clean once more."

This is no penance, it is simply forced shame. His gaze sickens me as I watch it rake down my form. He lets go of my wrist and steps back as I reach for my under garment. I pull the soft cotton down the length of my thigh and drop it in a puddle at my hooves. His eyes meet mine once before he looks upon my naked body, roaming from my shoulders to my waist. His attention slides from where my skin is as hairless as a human down to my thighs and my hooves, to my soft, brown coat. His eyes linger a few inches below my navel, where a patch of cinnamon curls hides the most private parts of me. The skin of my breasts pebbles as a cool spring breeze blows over them, and my knees tremble as I stand in my shame, bare before him among the trees.

"Step into the light, Cicerine," he commands, and I take a single step into the small patch of sunlight that has made its way through the canopy. I see him swallow as he takes me in, and another tear runs down my face and chest. His black eyes watch as it rolls down my flesh, and I shudder at the expression curling the edge of his lips. "May Idyth's light make you clean, my child," he says as he stares at me. "May you be forgiven."

KONIDAS

CHAPTER FOUR
MAELWEN
YEAR 991

My bare feet pad along the floor of my small apartment as I head toward the bedroom. The desolate and stark journey from Iowain to Konidas took three days' time, and I arrived two months ago today. I slept on the open ground, wrapped in my cloak beneath the wide sky, full of stars. I did not encounter a single living creature as I flew. The nights were silent but for the whistle of the wind and the soft rustle of my cloak, becoming as familiar to me as a part of my body. Tiny pinprick scars now run along my arms and back from wrist to wrist, where it stitches to my skin for flight, looking like a seam pulled undone. They are the only wounds which my body has not healed. It feels odd, like finding something I did not know belonged to me. The cloak currently lies draped over a chair in my sitting room, humming softly to me as I sit on my bed. Months ago, I only dreamed of freedom. Now, I have it.

This apartment sits over a tavern in Konidas. The owners are human, plump, and kind-hearted. The night I arrived here, the tavern was the first open business I found, and I shook off the chill at a barstool with a tankard of frothy ale. The barkeep made small talk, and after the ale loosened my tongue, I let slip that I had just arrived and had made no arrangements for housing. I had planned on renting a room at the inn by the docks, despite the cost—rooms were rented by the day or the hour, not monthly. Without renting one of the rickety, dilapidated homes in town or an apartment above one of the small businesses, the cost of living in a transient city like Konidas is high. However, by the end of the night, I had made my first friend, the barkeep, Shell. She is the daughter of the tavern owners who coincidentally, and conveniently, had an empty apartment upstairs. I can't help but feel like this is all too easy, too good. I have never had a home or a friend, and this comfort is unnerving. Some god or goddess must have been on my shoulder, guiding me toward complete strangers who somehow trusted me enough to offer up an apartment within hours of my arrival. I would say thanks if we still recalled the names of the gods. I paid them upfront for three months, a show of good faith that I can at least be counted on in that regard. I am not a friendly face, but money is just as good when it comes to trust. For the second time today, I pull out my sack of coin from beneath my mattress and count it. Jarrus's savings and my meager hoard made a fair sum, and I have a decent amount left, but soon I will need to come up with a way to make more. I slide beneath my blankets and with a small smile allow myself to drift to sleep—almost happy for the first time in my life.

 I wake with the dawn, the pale pink light of sunrise filtering through my small window. There is a marked quiet to the morning and my brow furrows as I look around. My cloak has gone quiet. The persistent hum has stopped, and my senses feel dulled. I am tired, despite my night of sleep, and my body aches. Hunger grabs onto the pit of my stomach with a twisting cramp and I stand, unsteady on my feet. I dress in a pair of charcoal gray pants and a silk blouse, and I pull my long hair back into a leather tie. The staircase down to the tavern seems to shift beneath my feet, and I grip the railing to keep from falling. Shell is busy wiping down the bar, and I can smell something cooking in the kitchen, but it makes my stomach turn. Nearly gagging, I push my way through the door and out into the morning bustle.

Konidas is more of a trading hub than a city, and it is busy no matter the time of day. The street is mostly well-packed, sandy dirt, but closer to the dock it turns to old cobblestones. Seedy men skulk about the docks and at the tavern, and very few people stick around for more than a couple days at a time. The small number of permanent residents live in peeling whitewashed homes further toward the city center. A general store, tannery, weapons shop, clothier and other various storefronts make up the main thoroughfare of the city, which is one street east of the docks. Passing by the clothier, one of the dark-eyed men lurking around the water leers at me, licking his lips as he stares. I sneer at him as I pass. I have learned to keep my distance and keep my gaze averted, lest they assume eye contact is an invitation to approach me. I have no interest in speaking to human men.

Shell warned me early on that the docks are a notoriously unsafe area for unaccompanied women. Men long at sea are known for taking women by force. After my experience with Jarrus, I assured her I can take care of myself, but I am no more comfortable with weaker human males than I was around a hulking minotaur. The dark-eyed man trails me as I walk, and I hate the uneasy feeling of his stare on my back. Even knowing my strength, I am uneasy around men. I can smell his sweaty musk from behind me, and I am not sure if my mouth is watering because I am about to vomit or because I am imagining the taste of his blood on my tongue. My pace quickens as I try to lose him, but without turning, I know he is still following. Lucky me. In my attempt to shake him, I have managed to walk nearly all the way to the docks, and my nose fills with the stink of salt and sea. The cobblestones click under my feet, and I look for some sort of shop or vendor. If this creep insists on following me, perhaps I can get chatty with a shopkeeper long enough for him to grow bored and abandon his endeavor. But there is nothing this close to the water except alleys leading to piles of rubbish and sun-bleached docks jutting out into the choppy water with ships and dinghies tied up to load and unload their wares. Nobody gives me a second glance. I am just a common woman walking by. Out of options, I stop walking and turn to face the man.

He is just as repulsive as I had anticipated. He looks like a sailor—a wool cap pulled over his head, scraggly beard and sunbaked red cheeks. He wears a thick coat over a ratty sweater, despite the mild temperature of the morning. His boots are worn, and his hands are in his pockets as he looks at me from under bushy, unkempt brows.

"Ey, ladie," he says with a bit of a mainland brogue. "Fancy a tumble?"

I bare my teeth at him as I grimace, "Fuck off."

He looks back with a sinister gleam in his watery blue eyes and the corner of his lips pulls up in a suggestive smile. "I were bein' polite. You see anyone 'ere who'll care if I help myself?" He gestures around us, still smiling, "Be a good girl."

My eye twitches, and I swear I can hear the thrum of his heartbeat. "I *said*, fuck off."

Turning to walk away, I spit on the ground and head back toward the busier part of town. His hand falls onto my shoulder with a heavy thud, and he spins me back to face him. His stinking breath hits my face and his thumbs press into my upper arms as he grabs me, but I knee him in the groin and shake out of his grasp. He is momentarily winded, but he quickly snatches me by the shirt and pulls me back toward him. The steady throb of his pulse increases in volume, and I can feel his heart rate pick up as he looks down at my body again and yanks me into the narrow alley.

It takes less than a second for me to rip his throat out. I do not even waste a breath attempting witchsong. There is no need to lure a man who has put himself on my plate. One moment he is breathing through spit-moistened lips, and the next his breath is wheezing from the hole where his throat had been. My hand comes up to my lips, and I lick his blood from my fingers while I watch him fall to his knees. The toe of my knee-high leather boot nudges him further into the alley, and I step towards closer.

"Do you see anyone here who will care if I help myself?" I ask with a sarcastic smirk, bending down to his throat and cupping my hand beneath the spray of blood gushing from the severed artery in his thick neck.

I can see the abject terror in his eyes, and it brings me a small amount of satisfaction. His blood tastes thin and weak compared to Jarrus's, but I drink it all the same. I lean forward so my overflowing palm splatters his pockmarked face rather than my shoes. Human blood, I find, has a different weight than the blood of a minotaur. It is lighter, more like beer than port. He lacks the richness and depth I tasted in Jarrus. The man gurgles once more before falling still, and I scoop a few more mouthfuls of his salty blood to my lips as the flow shifts from a spray to a trickle, before wiping my hands on his dirty coat and striding out of the alley.

The world is bright again. I hear seabirds in their nests from high above the docks, and the rustle of papers changing hands inside ships. Every footfall seems to echo, and the sun, just cresting the tallest of the masts, breathes warmth onto my cheeks. The ache and hunger and malaise I felt are gone, washed away with the blood of that repugnant human man. I take a deep breath of the ocean air and smile. Apparently, my meals of meat and bread in the tavern will not keep me satiated after all. I come across a barrel of rainwater and wash my hands quickly, the smeared blood on my palms disappearing as it turns the liquid a murky pink.

I am almost peppy as I walk the streets back into the shop quarter and step into the small tannery. The man at the counter eyes me warily, and I notice the tinge of blood on the visible tips of my claws. However, when I drop a silver coin on the counter, his wariness is replaced by a smile. Bloody money is money all the same in Konidas. He takes measurements and shows me various leathers as we discuss my needs. I settle on three pairs of gloves. They will all reach to the elbow, and be made of supple leather in black, brown, and deep maroon. I request small openings be left at the tips of each finger to allow for my claws. I have no interest in hiding what I am in this place, but leather is easier to clean than skin should I find my hands bloody again. When. *When* I find my hands bloody again.

I can hear my cloak's hum before I even reach the tavern. The frequency seems higher; it feels happy. I think my cloak enjoys the blood of men just as much as minotaurs.

THE TAVERN IS BUSY AND LOUD THIS EVENING. I SIP MY BEER from a corner of the bar as I watch the patrons come and go. Shell does not bother me; we understand each other, and she does not need to make small talk. Having a friend who understands my lack of warmth is something I never dreamed of for myself, and I am glad that it is Shell. She is assertive and dominant, curvy and loud—exactly my opposite—and I enjoy her company. There is a collection of tables to the side where men play some sort of card game, and I watch, intrigued.

Shell notices me watching and comes over. "You ever play Orakulua?" Apparently my expression is answer enough, and she goes on, "It's a very popular game in Konidas. There are six oracle cards which are called 'the Queens'—Life, Death, Love, Hate, Light, and Dark. The Death Queen is the highest value card, and the other Queens are ranked next. There's lots of other cards with various values too. There's Kings of all the same qualities, and cards like Trust, Honor, Fear, Jealousy and whatnot. The goal is to put together combinations, like a little story. There aren't really any 'bad' cards. You combine 'bad' qualities with other cards to spin them positive or tell a story. It's a bit tricky to learn, but the men here bet and make decent coin playing at the back tables."

I look at Shell with a conspiratorial smile. "Can you teach me?"

We stay up late into the night after Shell's shift is done. She laughs at me as I struggle to make sense of the values of human emotions. Growing up in the isolation of Iowain, coupled with my witch's nature, I lack the range of feelings I see on the cards before me. However, I figure it out pretty quickly, and before long, I am beating Shell in every hand. The premise is simple, but it takes a clever mind to match cards to amplify their meanings. I have always been good with stories. My years of solitary reading gave me plenty of time to craft tales of my own. It is the emotion that takes me time to grasp; humans have so many *feelings*. This game is storytelling in its simplest form—three cards to tell a powerful tale.

"How much do people make in these games?" I ask Shell as she packs up her deck.

"Fuck, hundreds of coppers a night, sometimes silver. I've even seen some folks walk away with palms full of gold."

My eyes widen. Gold? This silly card game could net me that kind of coin? "How do I get into the games?"

Shell chuckles and shakes her head. "You're an odd one, witch. Most men don't start betting 'til they've played for years."

"Well, I do not have years. My pockets grow lighter each day I spend sitting on my ass in your tavern."

Shell grins. "I can introduce you to the boss tomorrow. No

guarantee he'll let you play, but you can at least watch and get a handle on how the men play. We haven't had a lady contender in years, and never a witch, so I'm lookin' forward to it."

I smile back. "As am I."

The man running the games is a burly, stout man named Cartwright, who seems larger than he is. He has a commanding presence and speaks in a deep baritone, but I get the sense from Shell that he is kind behind the straight-faced exterior. His arms are thicker than my thighs, though he is only about a head taller than Shell. I can see strength ripple through corded muscle beneath his shirtsleeves.

After a brief conversation with Shell, he agrees to let me sit in on the games tonight as a spectator. So, I find a seat in the middle of the space against the wall where I can see two of the four tables clearly. The gameplay is quick, each player keeping seven cards in his hand at all times. Combo after combo is slapped onto the pile in the middle—Creativity, Vengeance, and The Dark King beating out Lust, Affection, and Modesty. Possessiveness, Contempt, and Success being beaten by Hope, Fear, and Truth.

The tables rarely disagree, but when a debate arises, Cartwright is quick to resolve it with a final decision. Men are simple, and their connections of emotions reflect this; they're predictable and nearly always try to group similar cards together rather than seek a higher meaning or attempt to tell a story. Within a few hours, I am certain I can easily win a game. With a subtle gesture to Cartwright, I request a game, and he makes space for me at the lower level table to my right.

The players are a group of younger men who all look down their noses at me when I step up to the table. I keep my face neutral and take my seat silently, holding out my thin hand to receive my cards. Round after round, I win. Honor, Death, and Peace beat out Disgust, Dismay, and Confusion. The Queen of Light combined with Closure and Compassion trounces Fear,

Darkness, and Spite. My plays are nuanced and tell meaningful tales with only my three cards. By the end of the night, half of the men at my table have quit to be replaced by others, and my pile of winnings is substantially higher than any other player on this side of the room. It would seem I have found a way to make some coin.

Kanitosh Woods

CHAPTER FIVE
CICERINE
YEAR 993

Father Farragen left me in the glade, naked and alone in the chilled spring sun. The rays of light should have warmed my bare skin, but I felt nothing save for shame. I watched his black robes slowly fade into the shadows of the trees and trembled where I stood. I don't know how long I stood there, head bowed and shoulders slumped, but at some point I shrugged my dress back on and returned to the village.

Our village is small, less than twenty dwellings in total. Most of the inhabitants are fauns, but we have occasionally housed a few woodfolk, and even a few land-bound seafolk. We don't turn anyone away. Our cottages are simply made, thatched roofs with clay or plank walls. A small line of half-buried stones rings the edge of our territory, though there is no one else in Kanitosh to challenge our claim. We have a schoolhouse, which also serves as our temple to Idyth, a large community cellar dug into the east side of the glade, a small apiary to the west, and many gardens scattered among the trees. The glade isn't large, and most of it is fairly shaded by the canopy of oak, olive and cedar trees. The fruit trees aren't as tall, but still provide both shade and seasonal food. Our bounty is large, and we are well fed. Fauns are all vegetarian, though we sometimes consume the eggs of the guinea fowl who live among the trees, and we care for a few domestic goats who share their milk with us when needed.

It is to this idyllic village calm that I return when I make my way back through the forest. We keep to ourselves, and nobody raises their gaze to look at me as I walk past. From the corner of my eye, I spot a flash of red hair disappearing into our home. I sigh before heading home to Jynn and Mamère, my shoulders slumping in an uncomfortable blend of relief and hurt. When I enter the cottage, Jynn's eyes are wide and full of fear. Mamère has stepped out into town, so it is only Jynn and me in the small space.

"Where have you been?" she whispers, the terror clear in her deep, familiar voice.

"I, I tried," I gulp out. "I tried to give you time." Before I can stop myself, a sob breaks from my throat. I hang my head, my sun-warmed horns pressing into my palms. "I took your punishment, Jynn."

I feel her tentative touch on my shoulder, and I lean into it. Jynn knows what that means, knows that none of the many options are pleasant or kind.

"I am so sorry, Ceci," she says in a low voice, her hand moving as if to pull me closer but settling back down around my arm. "I never meant to bring you harm. Are you all right? Did he…?" Her sentence fades into silence as she struggles to find the right word. I expect her to finish, but she doesn't.

"He made me undress and stand in the sun," I quietly admit. "He watched me."

Her strong arms wrap around my shoulders, and she holds me. We sit in silence and any resentment I felt towards her drifts away. I know Father Farragen would have been far harder on

Jynn. He has been close to my mother for my entire life, and I am a faun born of the glade. Jynn, however, is not from here.

Though she has lived in the glade since I was barely walking, Jynn is still seen as an outsider by some in the village. Nobody knows where she came from. She showed up on a frigid winter day, wearing only a diaper, nearly frozen by the snow. Mamère scooped her up, brought her home, and that was that. I think Father Farragen resents her presence. She is wild and unrestrained, lacking the quiet calm Mamère and I possess. She is loud and commands attention with her broad shoulders and vibrant red hair. From afar, Jynn has always refused to wear dresses, despite Father Farragen's insistence. She is tall and long-legged, with strong, muscled arms and large, rough hands. She means everything to me. Other than Mamère, I love her more than anything under Idyth. Jynn has been my constant companion and confidante, the fire to my cool nature. She is the daring one who drags me to action when I would stay behind.

Last summer, we hung a swing from the largest oak we could find. Jynn clambered up the massive trunk to hang a thick sisal rope. We spent half the scorching summer months swinging and climbing into the canopy, wild as lynxes, laughing loudly and shouting whoops of joy. When the leaves had just begun to yellow, we found our rope in pieces on the forest floor. I knew it was Father Farragen's doing. Jynn paid it little mind and instead grabbed my hand and danced with me around the curved bits of rope like it was a stage made only for us. When we finally collapsed onto the soft grass in a fit of giggles, Jynn reached her arm across my waist and pulled me closer to her sweat-slicked body. We laid there for what felt like an eon, my messy curls resting on her shoulder, our fingers interlaced, the last bit of summer in the air warming our smiling cheeks.

I think of that summer as we sit together quietly in the cottage. Jynn strokes my back with a slow, reassuring touch.

"I am so sorry, Ceci," she whispers against my ear. "I fucked up. I won't do it again. I have no idea why I even wanted the damn mead, Idyth knows it tastes like piss."

Despite myself, I laugh. Jynn always knows what to say to shake me from a somber mood. She's right though; it does taste like piss. "What is Mamère doing in town?" I ask.

"Probably helping Farragen with the bread for the school-house," Jynn answers. "Farragen couldn't possibly be bothered to do something as simple as bake his own damned bread."

I chuckle. Father Farragen uses my mother for nearly everything. She is his wife in every way but touch and title. She cooks his meals, cleans his home, sets up for offering, assists with schooling. She spends most of her days hard at work managing both his life and our own. It's no wonder she often falls into bed the moment she is finished with the dinner washing.

"Why are you asking, Ceci?" Jynn says in a tone I can't quite place.

"No reason," I say too quickly. "Just curious how long I can lay here and get away with doing nothing." Jynn chuckles at my joke.

I am rarely lazy. I do nearly as much around town as Mamère. I grow most of our gardens single handedly, thanks to my botanurgy skills. I teach the little ones a few mornings a week, help gather fruit for the storeroom, make jams and jellies, cook nearly all our meals, and bake bread—though mine is a shoddy imitation of Mamère's. But today, I am tired. The shame and disgust from my altercation with Father Farragen still coats my skin like a greasy smudge. All I want at this moment is to wash that feeling from my flesh. I shudder and rub my arms as if I could wipe it all away.

"I know it's early, but I really want a bath," I say half to myself, half to Jynn.

She stands and grabs my hand. "Well then, let's go."

Some of the villagers have wooden bathing tubs in their homes, while others use basins. We haul buckets of water from the quick-flowing stream just outside the glade and heat it at the hearth until it's lost its frigid bite. But I have always loved the feeling of the brisk water flowing over my skin, and Jynn knows it. Years ago, we found a deer path through the trees leading to a shallow bend of the stream, with a round-pebbled bottom and large bushes all around. It's the perfect place for a secret bath, and we've taken great lengths to keep it to ourselves. With a quick glance out the cottage door, Jynn pulls me outside, and we slip quietly into the woods. It's midday, and the sun hangs high in the sky, lighting up the leaves of the trees with an unbelievable emerald glow. The green reflects across Jynn's skin as she jogs her way through the woods. I follow, equally quick on my feet, and my hooves click against tree roots as we pass. In no time at all, we have found the trail and run parallel to it rather than along it, to keep it looking wild and unused. Jynn pops through the brambles first, hissing in a breath as a thorn grazes her arm.

I giggle quietly, "All these years and you still scratch yourself every time."

Jynn grumbles, but there's a smile quirking up the sides of her lips. The stream is just as cold as I expect, the water flowing down from the great mountain range to the north. I shrug out of my indigo dress and step into the flowing water. My skin tightens, and I take in a sharp breath as the cold water envelops me. I duck all the way down, submerging my head of tangled curls. I feel the current flow over my horns and close my eyes, wishing I had been born to a naiad so I could stay down here forever. Lungs burning, I stand and shake my head, taking a deep breath of the fresh woodland air. I feel invigorated, the water helping wash the feeling of violation from my mind.

I have nearly forgotten about Jynn when I hear her splash into the stream beside me. A spray of water hits my cheek as

Jynn playfully flings a handful at me. I'm laughing before I know it, glad Jynn is here to help remind me of the happiness in my life. I duck out of the way of another artfully aimed splash, and my hooves slip on the slick rocks. I land firmly on my furry backside, laughing hysterically despite its sting. Jynn appears above me, silhouetted against the sun and glowing green leaves. She holds out her broad hand, and I reach for her. She makes me feel nearly weightless as she pulls me up, and I stand—looking up into her warm, open face.

Jynn is nearly a head taller than me, and she looks down at me with a mischievous smile. Her face has lost the plush softness of youth, and her jawline is strong and well-defined. A smattering of freckles sits along her cheeks and across her nose, and her mouth is wide and full. She is a handsome woman, neither soft nor sharp, but gracefully formed. Her human ears have always fascinated me, so different from my own, and I fight the urge to run a finger along one's edge. I suddenly realize I've been staring and go crimson. I glance away, pressing my fingers to my brow in embarrassment. Just when I'm about to turn and jump back into the stream to hide from my awkwardness, I feel Jynn's hand beneath my chin.

She raises my face to look at her, and I forget to breathe. Jynn and I are no longer children. I know she's seen me shrug off the advances of the obnoxious young males in the village. They have never captured my interest. I've noticed her body changing, and I cannot pretend she hasn't noticed mine. I can smell the sunlight and sweat on her skin, so human and familiar. My heart races like a rabbit across a plain, and I stay absolutely still.

"See something you like, Sunbeam?" Jynn teases, dropping her hand and using the nickname she's used since childhood.

"Just wondering how your hair can possibly be that red." She lets out a laugh, throwing her head back, exposing her long pale throat. "What?" I giggle. "The last time I saw something that bright was when you set Mamère's bread towel on fire."

She laughs again. "It's been ten seasons, Ceci. Will you ever let me live that down?"

I shake my head and give her a devious smirk. Jynn looks at me and her gaze lingers on my mouth for just a second too long. I bite my lip subconsciously, a heavy heat blooming low in my belly. In an instant her hands are around my waist, and our stream soaked bodies are pressed together. I can't find my breath, captive in the feeling of my bare body against hers. A throbbing ache curls deep within me, longing to be soothed. A nervous giggle rises in my throat, but it dies the moment her lips touch mine.

It's a tentative kiss—asking for permission with its gentleness. I have never been kissed before, but I know the question in my bones. Answering, I rise on hoof-tip, close my eyes, and kiss her back. I feel as if the entire wood has gone silent. I can't hear over the pounding of my heartbeat. I don't dare open my eyes for fear this moment will end, as her hand slides slowly up the curve of my waist. Gently, almost reverently, her fingers caress the swell of my breast. Her touch is so light, yet it feels like fire racing over my flesh, setting me aflame. I shiver at the sensation. Finally opening my eyes, our gazes meet, and I can't define her expression. I kiss her again, more firmly, demanding. Her tongue slides between my lips, and I taste a hint of that damned apple mead. My mouth opens as I allow her to explore me, lost in the feeling of this small piece of her within my body. My hands get lost in her chaotic tumble of hair. A small moan escapes me as she pulls me closer. Her calloused palms grip my fleecy hip, and I arch my back—pressing into her.

"Idyth save me," she whispers against my mouth. "You have no idea how long I've wanted to do that."

Heat pools between my thighs, and I clench them together to ease the crushing need. With shaking fingers, I reach up to cup her cheek. I have no clue what to do with my hands. As if she can read my mind, she guides my other hand up her body. I feel her tremble as my fingertips touch her. Higher, higher, until my palm lies against her small chest. I caress her gently, as if I would cup a rose, and I let loose a quavering breath. Her skin is silk beneath my touch, smooth and cool as a breeze blows over her damp flesh. We stand there in the babbling stream, pressed together as if there is nothing else in the world.

KANITOSH WOODS

CHAPTER SIX
CICERINE
YEAR 993

We make our way back to the glade as the sun touches the treetops. I can't be late to return, lest Mamère think I'm shirking my evening duties. Luckily, she hasn't returned from Father Farragen's, and I busy myself tidying and setting out ingredients for dinner as Jynn goes to gather greens for a salad. We don't talk about what happened today at the stream, but I can't help grinning at her each time she looks my way. Mamère baked bread this morning, so I grab a crusty loaf and set it on our rough-hewn oak table. Our thick-walled glasses were imported from Athydis, and I fill them with fresh water and drop a sprig of mint in each. I grab one of our heavy cast-iron pots and boil some tubers and spices. Tonight I plan on making a root vegetable stew and adding in some of the wild onion and astragalus I gathered yesterday. We have lumpy little carrots in a rainbow of colors, pale sweet parsnips, squat purple turnips, and a handful of gangly chicory. I chop them all up and toss them in the pot. Already the cottage smells pleasant and inviting, and I add a sprig of fresh rosemary from the bush outside our door.

I love to cook—always have. My gifts work best on edible plants, and I suspect it is because they are the plants I feel most connected to. Mamère is the best baker in the village, a skill I wish I had inherited, but instead I make scorched loaves that never quite rise. I enjoy the way she and I work together to fill our small family's bellies. Between the two of us, we always have something warm on the stove and a hearty loaf to serve alongside it. Jynn, however, is completely hopeless in the kitchen, not for lack of trying. I've spent many afternoons in the woods trying to teach her which plants are best for soups and which are best for roasting. The last time she cooked we were all sick for days, thanks to the false chanterelles she mistakenly gathered. Luckily, she's strong, and she happily carries our buckets of water and helps to churn the goat's milk into butter. She's also not afraid of anything, so she helps at the apiary, which means we often get a little extra honey. There are few things in the whole of Kanitosh that taste better than fresh butter and honey smeared across a hunk of Mamère's bread.

Mamère walks through the door just as I take down our wooden bowls, and she smiles gently at me in greeting. She is absolutely lovely and barely appears to be older than me. Her kind eyes are a dark, rich brown. Her mousy hair falls over her forehead in a halo of tight curls from between her curling umber horns. Her ears are longer and floppier than mine, and they perk up whenever she hears my voice. The only signs of age on her face are the faint lines at the corners of her eyes that crinkle when she smiles.

"Hello, Cicerine, my love," she calls as she comes into the small kitchen, setting her bag on the table alongside her glass. "Where were you all day?"

I blush and turn back to the stove, hoping she doesn't notice. Fortunately for me, she is busy unloading her bag as I reply,

"After lessons, Jynn and I gathered some nettles and walked to the stream."

"How nice. It was a lovely day."

At that, my mind flashes back to standing naked before Father Farragen, and I shudder. Shaking it from my mind with a tight smile, I glance at Jynn, back from gathering salad greens. "It was, Mama."

We eat in a comfortable quiet, Jynn's knee lightly grazing mine beneath the table. After we finish, Jynn helps me gather our dishes, and she washes while I dry.

Mamère prepares fresh dough to bake in the morning. "Father Farragen mentioned there was an incident this morning. Is everything well, Ceci?" she asks me over the clink of dishes in the basin.

"Of course, Mama."

"I am glad to hear, dear one. Tomorrow morning, I have to be at the schoolhouse early to get everything ready. Will you and Jynn be all right with getting your own breakfast together?"

"Of course we will," I say with a smile. We put up the dishes and settle in with hot cups of spearmint and lavender tea. The soft sounds of evening fill our little home as we slip into sleep.

JYNN IS A SOUND SLEEPER, AND SHE DOESN'T STIR AS I GET UP and make my bed. Unbothered by the click of my hooves on wood, she snores peacefully. I spend a moment watching the steady rise and fall of her chest before making my way to the hearth to begin breakfast.

Yesterday was…a lot. Between the incident with Father Farragen and the kiss I shared with Jynn in the stream, I am a tangle of emotions. With a deep breath, I shake my head and try to center myself. I set about collecting the various things I need to make breakfast for Jynn and myself. I love sweets, and since Mamère is busy this morning, I decide on a rather indulgent porridge for breakfast. Jynn stashed a small square of honeycomb just for me, and I smile as I take it from the cupboard. I toss a handful of oats and buckwheat into a small pot and add in a bit of salt and water. We still have a bit of butter, and I picked some raspberries yesterday morning, so when the porridge is thick and hearty, I scoop it into bowls with a bit of each. I add a drizzle of honey and a sprinkle of cinnamon to each bowl before I head to our room to wake Jynn. With a rather forceful push on her shoulder, I rouse my slumbering friend and hand her a bowl. Today I don't have many duties to tend to, so I take my time with breakfast.

Our conversation is blundering as neither of us seems to have the courage to address what happened yesterday. I am not going to be the one to bring it up, and we chat mindlessly about silly things like the coming rainy season and whether I should make a new dress for winter. I've never felt awkward around Jynn, and a wave of relief washes over me as she sets our bowls in the sink and heads off to tend to the bees. I wish I knew the right words to say as she steps out the door.

I dress in a soft pink linen shift, enjoying the spring breeze blowing through the glade. I plan on checking the fruit trees today, growing some narcissus for Mamère, and canning some preserves to add to our winter stock. Most of the fruiting trees won't be ready for another few moons, but I gather some rosy-cheeked apricots and half a punnet of strawberries. I spot some asparagus as I walk and add them to my basket as well. A neighbor nods their head in greeting as I make my way around the village, and I feel more at ease. Yes, things are different after yesterday, but my life is good. I brush my fingers along the trees as I stroll and send my gift through them, encouraging blossoms and speeding up the ripening process. I could ripen all the fruit at once if I cared to, but using that much of my energy is tiring, and our glade does a lovely job without my help.

An oily smell hits my nostrils, and I pause. I don't like it at all. It smells wrong among the fresh green of the glade. Glancing around, I look to see if I can spot the source of the scent, but nothing seems amiss. With a huff of air from my nose, I carry on walking. I don't hear footsteps approaching, but I have the uncomfortable sense of being watched. Once again, I stop and look around, but all I see are trees and their shadows. My skin prickles with the uncanny sensation that I am not alone, and I start walking again at a much brisker pace. It's then that I spot a shadow that moves strangely. As if stepping from the darkness itself, Father Farragen appears from behind a tree.

"Hello, Father Farragen," I say without looking at his face.

"Cicerine," he nods his head in greeting. "I hoped to find you today."

"What did you need of me, Father?" I ask, trying to keep the unease from my voice.

"Would you be so kind as to lend your gifts to the pennyway garden this afternoon?"

There doesn't appear to be any malice in his eyes, and I admonish myself for feeling discomfort in his presence. Father Farragen serves our village and connects us to the great Idyth. It is not my place to dictate how he does so. My shame about yesterday was earned. I lied to him about Jynn. It was an insult to Idyth, and I deserved it. But knowing this doesn't change the fact that I felt violated. Perhaps Idyth's light needed to cleanse me, but Father Farragen's eyes are not Idyth's light.

"Of course!" I reply, trying to sound as bubbly as I usually am. "I would be happy to help."

I follow him quietly toward the pennyway garden. On the far west side of the glade, just past the Father's home, is a fenced patch of pennyway blooms, perhaps ten paces square. Legend tells us that when the old gods were defeated and the great Idyth fell, his body cleaved the land and the sea rushed in, forming the Idyl sea. It is then we forsook the names of the others, and raised Idyth above all. The peninsula is where his body fell to land, his mighty spear piercing the crust of the earth and forming the large volcanic island of Minos'Idyl. As he fell, he grieved, and his tears grew as pennyway flowers. The small, six-petaled blooms are deep plum with bright golden stamens. They are lovely flowers, but their significance makes them more precious than gold. I loved them as a small child, and I have vague recollections of picking bouquets of them with Mamère, though that could never happen now. To destroy or disrupt a pennyway blossom is a great sin.

Long before my birth, Father Farragen says that a man who came from Athydis once crushed an entire crop, and he was hanged for his transgression. I run my hand over the scar at my hip as I recall the story, and thank Idyth that I only crushed one bloom. I don't know what Father Farragen does with the flowers he harvests. No one else is permitted to pick them, and only Father Farragen and I are allowed to tend them. Even though Jynn has lived here nearly her entire life, she is forbidden like any other outsider from coming near the small space.

A couple times a week, I spend time with the flowers and use my gift to coax them from the soil. I wrap my gift around their seeds and warm them with my love. They split open, and tiny shoots spread from the cracks, making their way to the sun. Today when I arrive, I see only the smallest of leaves peeking from the ground. I sit near the fence in a patch of grass and reach my hands into the loamy earth. My gift feels like warm honey flowing from my heart to my fingertips. It can't be seen by the eye, but I can sense the tendrils of green power running into the rich earth like rivulets of warm water. The small light green leaves reach toward the sky and spread out, tiny purple buds appearing at their apex. As I watch and focus, the buds grow, and a few begin to bloom. My weight shifts between my hooves, I'm momentarily off-center from the expenditure of energy, and I take a deep breath. Father Farragen stands just outside the fence, and he gives me a slight smile before turning and walking into his cottage.

Days pass by with little excitement. The baby rabbits finally leave their homes, and Jynn and I watch their tiny hops with glee. We gather food, I work with the trees, and Jynn tends to the bees. Mamère bakes loaves of bread with soft spongy interiors and thick crunchy crusts, and we snack on sweet chestnuts. Spring is coming to an end, and I can feel a shift in the air as it grows heavy and warm. I don my shorter sleeveless dresses and pile my heavy curls on top of my head, wrapping them around my horns to keep them off my sweat-damp neck. Tonight I plan a cool soup for dinner made from sweet cucumbers and fresh dill. I even send Jynn to collect a small pitcher of goat's milk to swirl into each bowl as I serve us.

Jynn and I still haven't spoken about the stream. It's been days, and I wonder if it was a singular moment of weakness for us both. Jynn looks wonderful today in her loose white top, bright hair catching the light like carnelian. I can't help but brush her knee with my own, and her eyes widen before her lips quirk up. We share a secret grin, and I feel her fingers lightly graze my thigh as she pushes back her chair to stand. Something flutters low within me. We clear the table and clean up the dishes, our roles easy and practiced. She bumps me with her hip, and I smirk as I flick a drop of water at her in response. Mamère kisses my cheek as she heads to bed, and Jynn tells me she's going to check on the new bees. She'd discovered them in a swarm this afternoon, and wants to make sure they've settled into their new box. It feels strange to stand here alone, but Jynn catches my eye as she steps out the door, and I see hunger there. Perhaps it wasn't a moment of weakness.

I'm more nervous than I have ever been before. Since the stream, whenever Jynn is in the room, I can't help but be aware of my round belly, my wide hips and their fleecy brown coat, so unlike her narrow frame and smooth human skin. I am not thin, all round curves and softness, but I am strong and healthy. There are only subtle differences between me and a full-blooded faun, and I am rather fond of my smaller ears and smoother skin.

I slip on my nightgown as I hear Jynn's heavy-footed steps approaching and slide into bed. My palms are clammy beneath my light wool blanket, and I consider feigning sleep. It would be a wasted attempt; I could never fool Jynn. She closes the door behind her with a snick and pads across the rug towards her bed. Our room seems so small, only a few feet separate our beds, and I can hear her steady breathing as she sits on the edge of her mattress.

"Are you hiding, Sunbeam?" I can hear the amusement in her voice. Leave it to Jynn to never feel an ounce of bashfulness.

"Obviously I'm not doing a very good job if you're asking," I giggle from beneath the blanket.

I hear the floor creak as she stands and comes to sit next to me on my bed. "Did I cross a line at the stream?" she asks in a low voice.

"No!" It comes out louder, more shrill than I intended. "I have no regrets, Jynn. I'm just glad you were brave enough to do it. You know I never could." My cheeks are so hot. I don't understand how people can bear to have these kinds of conversations. I'm gulping down nervous laughter with every breath.

"I've been wondering, would it be all right if I did it again?"

My heart stops, and I go completely still. My floppy ears perk up as I listen for Mamère, and I hear the slide of silk as she ties a scarf around her halo of curls. I hold up one finger, listening intently. Mamère has never come into our room after bedtime. Still, an irrational worry tickles at the edges of my mind. But I hear her hooves tap across the floor, and her bed groans as she settles into it for the night. Looking up at Jynn, I lower my hand, pulling my blanket aside in reply. That sly smile slides across her face again, and she snuggles in next to me.

My bed is small, and there is no way to avoid pressing into her. My thin nightgown feels like nothing at all, and the warmth from her solid form sinks into my skin. That ache pulses between my thighs once more, and I nearly groan at the pressure as I press my legs together. My body reacts to her the instant we touch, my skin prickling and flushed. I put a tentative hand around her waist, and she makes a small affirmative sound.

She scoots down in the bed, her long legs dangling off the end as she brings herself nose to nose with me. "I don't want things to be weird between us, Ceci"

I huff a laugh out of my nose. "You make everything weird."

"You know what I mean. I've known you nearly my whole life. You're my closest friend. I don't want things to get messy between us. I would probably die, and not just because you wouldn't be able to save me from Farragen."

Her words tumble out, and I know she means it. Jynn is always so confident, but I can hear the uncertainty as she goes on.

"Don't ever let me lead you down a road you don't want to follow."

I touch my nose to hers. "You know I'd follow you anywhere, idiot. Now kiss me." And she does.

This time, our embrace is less tentative. Her hand slides to the back of my neck and pulls my face into hers. The warm scent of her surrounds me, like she's brought the sun itself into my bed. She is summer against my mouth. I meet her every movement with one of my own. Her tongue and mine explore one another with urgency, both of us breathless. The taste of her drives me mad, quenching a thirst I didn't know I had. Our bodies are linked together, her breath flowing through me as though we are one. Her other hand traces the broad curve of my hip, and I arch into her. I'm on fire with need, acting on instinct as I press into her with a demand which goes beyond my mind's comprehension. I sparkle beneath her touch, as her fingers graze the soft hair of my thighs. I can feel each fine hair move beneath her fingers, and shiver at the sensation.

"Ceci, you are perfect," she whispers against my mouth, and I grin.

I don't know the right words to reply, so I kiss her harder. My thick lips nip and suck at her mouth, wanting. My hand drifts down to clutch her hip, and I pull her body closer against my own. I grind into her, begging for her, wanting more than I have ever dared in my entire life. A deep sound escapes her throat as her hand slides from my thigh to the round curve of my backside. I shift back into her hand as her long fingers grip me firmly. The pool of fire between my legs burns as I press my body into her hands, igniting a flame of desire. I have never done this with anyone, and I'm all nerves as I carefully move my hand between us, gingerly caressing my fingertips along her sternum.

Jynn's chest isn't large, and I can feel the firm muscle beneath her breast, tensing at my touch. Her smooth skin pebbles beneath my gentle caress. I elicit a small appreciative sound from her elegant throat as my fingers whisper over her nipple. Carefully, unsure of how I'm supposed to do this, I lower my mouth to her breast and softly kiss the firm peak. The sound that rumbles beneath my lips nearly drives me over the edge. Her hand drags through my hair as she moves beneath my mouth. I kiss my way across her freckled skin, finding her other breast with my lips. My tongue slides across her, tasting the salt of her sweat as it explores her body. It feels right to savor her. I suck her hard nipple into my mouth, rolling it against my tongue, moaning into her flesh as I feel the need radiating from her. She grabs a thick handful of my hair and roughly pulls me back up to kiss her, as her other hand slides back around my body. I open my eyes, meeting hers and seeing the raging fire in her gaze. Slowly, and gently as a feather, her fingers come around between us and slide between my legs. She stills at the sound of the small gasp which escapes my heaving chest.

"Is this too much?" she breathes into my ear.

My reply belies none of the frantic, nervous energy I feel. This throbbing need is nearly unbearable, torturous in its demand. My voice comes out raspy and deep, "No."

Of their own accord, my hips rock forward against her. She deftly slips one finger deeper between my legs, and it moves across a place that pulls a breathy moan from my lips. I am slick beneath her fingers, aching with pleasure that pounds in my chest like a war drum. She circles with her finger, and my thighs grow damp as my body revels in her touch. That one small place sends sparks of shivering sensation over my skin; my whole body quaking with the intensity. With infinite care, she slowly slips that long finger into me, and I bite my lip to avoid crying out. Feeling her touch from inside me is like nothing I have ever imagined, my body quivering around her slim finger as it pulls soft noises from my lips. Nothing in my life has ever felt this good. I clench around her, my body out of my control. Her thumb makes lazy circles and that finger dips in and out of me as a nearly unbearable pressure builds inside of me. I am balanced on the edge and feel my mind slipping away as I lose myself. My breaths quicken as I approach this peak. I kiss her hard, demanding, and I moan quietly against her tongue as she touches me. My hips rock as she slides in and out, over and through the wet heat of my body. I feel her everywhere, no longer able to identify a single point of pleasure. She hits a place deep within me, and I push into her, wanting her deeper—wanting more–until I explode in a sea of stars. I am shaking, waves of indescribable ecstasy washing over me, and I am panting against her. Wave after wave crashes through me, ripping a groan from my lips as my head falls back. She holds me to her, gently kissing the corners of my mouth as small sounds flutter from me unbidden. Her fingers still slide over and in me, pulling each and every last drop of climax from my quivering body. When I at last stop shaking and regain control of my breath, she withdraws her hand, and my hips buck as I feel so abruptly empty. I can barely move, entirely spent from the intensity flowing through me. I look up to see her grinning, and I scrunch my nose up in teasing annoyance.

"Enjoy yourself?" She asks with a clever smile.

"Don't mock me," I laugh in response. I am undone, unable to move other than to slide my thighs together, eking out the last glittering shivers.

In a suddenly serious voice, she whispers, "Never," and kisses me deeply.

I lay my head against her chest and fall into a deep sleep, her arms wrapped around me like a heavy blanket.

KONIDAS

CHAPTER SEVEN
SHELL
YEAR 992

I think I look damn good for twenty. Turning in a circle in front of the mirror, I admire my thick hips, thick amber-blonde hair, thick lips. I'm never going to be called small, in any sense of the word—which is fine by me. I've got a loud mouth, but it serves me well as a barkeep in this mess of a tavern. Ma and Pap taught me to pour ale at seven, and I've held this bar together by my bootstrings since I turned sixteen. Even now, I'm smearin' a lick of rouge on my lips, gettin' ready to head back to the tavern without havin' nearly enough sleep. The street is pretty quiet as I stride from our home to the bar. A few scraggly men mill about, but nobody bugs me none. Konidas is a shitshow of a "city," but it's *my* shitshow. I can handle these folks with my eyes closed, and I'll admit that once or twice I have. Smugglers and shakeroot sellers don't bother messin' around in the tavern, Pap may be a sweetie, but folks know he can handle his own. It's exhaustin' runnin' this bar with just our small family. There's another girl named Martine who takes over for the mornin' shift, but I'm here from late afternoon all the way til dawn. I push the doors open with a grin, surveyin' my kingdom. Our house is only one street over, but this place is home.

I know this city better than anyone, who to watch, who to play. We don't post prices, and sometimes a man with a fancy waistcoat—well, his ale costs double. But unless he's keen to start brewin' his own, this is the only stop for a good drink 'til Athydis. Couple'a rich folks sittin' barside already this mornin', waitin' for the tables to open, and I give 'em a winning smile. It was my idea to open the tables, and we've made piles of coin off of it since they opened five years back. I saw folks playin' Orakulua and coin passin' hands and figured we might as well put our penny in the pot. That little witch who moved in last year has changed the damn game. I need to raise her cost to play, but I can't help but feel a little pride watchin' her trounce everyone night after night. I'm glad to call her my friend. I know under her hard exterior, she has a good heart.

Maelwen is a quiet girl, keeps to herself and doesn't bother anyone. I like her for that. She keeps her quarters clean, and she scares the fuck out of half the men who wander in here. She's a good girl to have on our side. I've heard that witches live five times the lifespan of a human, but she seems to be about my age. She's green as hell, though. I haven't asked about where she came from, but it sure wasn't good. She rolled up here with blood under those scary ass claws and circles the color of spilled wine under her eyes. But she's found a rhythm. I don't ask where she goes or what she does, but there's somethin' in her step which makes me think she's a lot scarier than we know. I like it.

This afternoon the heat is near unbearable. My tits are drippin' down my bodice, and my hair is stuck to my forehead in a way that surely looks atrocious. But I don't have the time to care about my face. A smuggler ship pulled in before dawn and word is their captain has more to trade than pilfered silverware. Nobody has seen or heard much from the royals in a couple years. Pap says they used to give decrees, talk to the people, but they just stopped doin' it awhile back. Papers come out, get read by stuffy nobles, and that's that. Rumors skate through about them bein' dead, or undead, or bespelled, but nobody knows a damn thing in truth. I keep an ear to the docks. I like knowin' what's been said and today what's bein' said is quite interestin' indeed.

I know the man who walks through the doors is the captain before he says a word. He's got that boss swagger some folks find intimidatin'. He stomps up to the bar and pushes me a silver. "Fer the day, lass." Very well then, he can drink all he'd like. I keep myself near enough to listen as he swaps papers with men who visit throughout the day. The man seated to his left at the moment is a portly fellow with a deep crimson coat and fluffy white shirt. He looks like a parrot from Minos'Idyl and has the squawky voice to match. When the captain's voice gets low, I make it a point to fill the glasses nearby and make sure the bar is *real* clean right where they sit.

He says a whole lot of nothin', but then I hear a sentence that raises the hair on my forearms—"The Crone was in the palace."

The Crone lives in that sky-high tower north of Iowain. It's far by land but quick by sea. The peninsula juts out in such a way that Athydis and the tower are only about two days on a sailship. She never leaves the tower, or so it's said, so this is an odd bit of news. The witches don't sail; they fly—but the Crone can do things the rest of the witches can only dream of. I've heard it said she can appear wherever she fancies with a blink of an eye. The last Crone was a wicked thing, prone to killin' whole towns by order of witchkind for no reason anyone could say. The new one took over twenty-some-odd years ago, and it has been a fairly quiet affair. They still kill folks, but it hasn't been much of a problem here. Iowain is a nasty place, and when people are wicked enough to flee Konidas? They probably deserve what they get on the plains. But the Crone in the castle? That's somethin' I didn't expect.

The captain speaks quietly, but I hear most of what he says over the din of the bar. His men met with a group of servants gone rogue, stealin' what they could and tryin' to palm some coin from under the royals' noses. I'm not one to judge. The castle is full of far more wealth than anyone could possibly need, so good on them for lightenin' the load. They showed up scared as possums, beggin' to be smuggled out in the bottom of the hull. The captain had no need for more mouths to feed, so he turned them down flat, but while they begged, they told him why they were so scared: an old witch with hair the color of ashes was stayin' in the palace, hangin' around the King and Queen and everyone was actin' weird. The Crone is easy to spot since she's old as dirt and scary as sin. They say she eats babies, but I don't know, ain't my business.

The only land I concern myself with is the dirt beneath my feet. Hell, Idythia is a big place, and there's an entire world beyond. Across the seas are deserts of jynn, jungles full of wild creatures, cities filled with strange men, continents teemin' with things we wouldn't know how to explain. The Crone with all her scary shit, seafolk, woodfolk…there's records of all of it. Hell, the first Crone slew the old gods with her own hands. It gives me the shivers to even think of. So the Crone in the castle? That's certainly somethin'.

The captain doesn't have much more to say, just the usual talk of smoke and coin. I hear they've got a crate of shakeroot coming through. It's just a drug, but it causes trouble when too many men bring it through my door, so I make a note to sniff a bit more and make sure nobody's gonna start some shit in my bar. I feel bad for those folks left behind in the city. Fear makes a person do some awful things. I sure as shit hope they're wrong.

Konidas

CHAPTER EIGHT
MAELWEN
YEAR 992

The air off the sea is brisk and smells of snow. There is a breeze coming down from Kanitosh, and I feel a shift in the air as the season heads toward spring. I have been here for a full year now and have finally lost the tingle of fear which sat at the edges of my mind for so many years. I am at peace. In this time, I have furnished my apartment with lovely pieces from Athydis, likely stolen from the castle and smuggled in —a wooden armoire carved from deep ebony wood with vines and flowers curving along its doors, a matching vanity with a large silver glass mirror, and a small couch. My bed is plush, covered in fluffy down pillows with a coverlet of handspun rabbit fur as soft as a cloud and dyed a deep cerulean. I clothe myself in finery, textiles I had never imagined in Iowain—slick silks and luscious velvets, deep colors in shades of gemstones and forest fruits. I have no trouble keeping myself here. I have become a successful Orakulua player, spoken of only in whispers. *"The Card Witch,"* they call me. I use no gift with the cards, just the woven tapestry of stories. I feed when I like, and I have, at last, mastered my witchsong.

There are plenty of men in this place to test my skills upon, vile creatures who do the world a service with their deaths. Their blood is thick, spiced and soured with sin. This winter I spent the frigid mornings strolling the docks in fur-lined boots and my bespoke gloves. I worked at pulling the same haunting melodies from my throat that the witch in Iowain sang to lure that man into her bed. At first I struggled. I tried to recall the notes she sang, and I could only hold a man for mere moments. Certain notes seemed to thrum in my chest in the same way my cloak hums, and I slowly sensed the song as it came. I had thought it a song to learn, when in truth, it is a song of my own making. I can hear the tone of each man's heartbeat, sing harmonies to his breath. The notes lie upon one another in fluid layers of sound, weaving a trap as I sing. My songs are quiet and low, my tone richer and deeper than that of the blonde witch. My voice feels like molten brass flowing from my lips, ensnaring men easily. I have only fed from one woman, and I will likely not repeat the action. The song of her heartbeat was ever-shifting, more difficult to grasp. Her song had too many layers for me to hold at once, slipping through my fingers like water. I lost her twice before my voice captured her, but my fully extended claws were more difficult for her to evade. She was a cruel person; lovely to look at, but with a wicked, dark soul. I witnessed her kill a courier boy, no older than eight. She saw the coin his master tasked him to carry, and with a smile on her face, she stabbed him between the ribs. I left the coin in the street. I had no desire to line my pockets with that bloodied silver. I feel no pity for human men, but I cannot see value in the death of a child.

The streets have been full of whispers. I have smelled witch-blood on the wind, and I am not alone in noticing the veil of darkness which seems to be slowly spreading. Rumors pass through of something nefarious in the castle. Shell has been talkative, peppering me with questions about the Crone, but I have no answers to tell. Growing up in the village in Iowain kept me from my kin. I have met only a few other witches in my life and spoken only to the one who gifted me my cloak. The witches who cross through Konidas do so quietly, slipping through the city night on their way to other destinations. But I can sense it, the darkness. There is a thickness to the air, to the sound of the breeze. I know something is shifting, growing. I cannot help but feel as if this will affect us all. I will keep an ear toward the skies. It is all I can do.

The tables are busy this evening with men seeking solace from the whims of the wind. There is a palpable tension as I take my seat and hand my coin to Cartwright. It takes no magic to feel the animosity rolling off of the man before me. He is dark and tall. His teeth are cracked and yellowed with age, though he appears to be no older than forty. He smells like moldy paper, a strange powdery smell. He cocks his head and raises a wiry brow as I lay down my first hand, slapping his cards down an instant later. His play feels like a threat—Foreboding, Fear, and the King of Darkness. He takes the round. I raise a hand for Shell, and she brings me a glass of wine, a deep red that shines like blood in the dim lighting of the tavern. Taking a long sip, I play my hand with a smile—Confidence, Victory, and the Queen of Life. He scowls as he lays down a weak hand, and I continue to sip my wine in silence. We battle throughout the night. I am genuinely surprised to see him win a few hands, but as usual, I am the ultimate victor. I collect my winnings with a smirk. In the past couple months, I have accrued enough income to necessitate an account at the local treasury. Pushing back my chair, I rise, stretching my back after the hours spent at the tables. Cartwright looks my way and tips his hat to me before getting to work alongside Shell, cleaning tables and collecting glassware. I head out inot the cold night to make a deposit, the still-chilled wind biting at my cheeks as I leave the comfortable warmth of the tavern. I can smell the man before I see him, the same rot and powder stink that filled my nostrils from across the Orakulua table. He lurks outside, leaning a shoulder against the western wall of the tavern and smoking a cigar.

I mean to walk past him, but he whispers, "Your time is coming, witch."

Turning on my heel, I face him with an indignant glare. "Excuse me?"

He bares those cracked teeth in a malicious smile. "Your kind is not long for this world. Plenty seek to remove your scourge from Idythia, and I look forward to seeing it."

He grinds his cigar against the wall, letting embers and loose bits of tobacco fall to the floor before flicking the butt in my direction.

With an impassive glance, I look at the wisp of smoke curling about my feet. My eyes narrow and I lift my chin, allowing the smallest hint of a smile to touch my lips as I speak. "You are a sore loser." I walk away without sparing him another glance.

Shell is still behind the bar when I return, my winnings safely deposited, and I inquire about the man. She simply shrugs, nothing to tell, but Cartwright overhears my query and comes over, taking a seat beside me.

"He came in last night," he says in his dusky baritone. "I've never seen him before. He gave a phony lookin' name on the player register. Need I keep an eye out?"

I shake my head. "I can handle bitter men just fine on my own. Though I am curious about his threat. Have you heard anyone else speak of purging the witches from Idythia?"

Cartwright shifts on the barstool, adjusting his collar and looking away. "I've heard plenty from Athydis. Nothing specific, just talk about men needin' to take back their land and such. Seems a bit foolish to me, seeing as Iowain has belonged to the witches since long before men took up residence. Same with Minos'Idyl. Minotaurs have lived on that island all its recorded history. But men are fickle, you well know. See somethin' they want and decide it's theirs to have whether or not they got a true claim."

"Keep me apprised of what you hear if it is not too much trouble, Cartwright," I request with a sigh. "I have only just settled in here, and I am not interested in threats from human men."

He tips his head and heads back to the tables.

Shell slides me a whisky with a twinkle in her eye. "You look like you need a drink."

I press the heels of my hands against my eyes. "I certainly do."

My thoughts circle back to the man as the whisky burns a path down my throat. He spat the word "witch" at me as if it were an accusation rather than a statement of fact. I am indeed a witch, and I do not apologize for that. I have as much right to this continent as anyone.

IT HAS BEEN QUIET HERE LATELY, THOUGH CARTWRIGHT HAS mentioned rising unrest in Athydis. I think on last night's encounter as I walk to the tailor's shop. My footsteps are more cautious, less resolute. I was not expecting to be harassed so close to my home. However, the day is pleasant, and I find it difficult to sulk. The sun warms my shoulders and I am glad to have pulled my hair back. The displeasure of the encounter slips from my mind as I allow myself a small smile. Today I am doing something indulgent, just for me, and it draws a rare bit of excitement from my chest.

I have become rather fond of the tailor in town. I have developed a love of nice clothing after my many years in rags, and I often stroll through her shop admiring new fabrics and patterns.

She is a squat woman of indeterminate "motherly" age, with wiry dark hair and quick fingers. She always seems happy to see me, despite my reticence. Few people in Konidas seek out the tailor's shop for more than the occasional repair or simple garments, and I can see the gleam of creative excitement in her eyes whenever I inquire about more involved designs.

I have always preferred trousers, and have never owned a nice dress, but I have decided I would like at least one. With spring well in bloom and summer coming quickly to the already warm city, I opt for a light silk georgette in a deep green shade to offset my blue eyes. The bodice will be fitted with a pleated skirt that reaches mid-calf and swishes nicely. I am not as gaunt as I was when I arrived here, thanks to regular food and drink at the tavern, but I am still very thin, and the shape of this dress will accentuate my tiny waist and give the illusion of full hips. Though I appreciate my frame, most of the women in Konidas are built like Shell, and a small, vain piece of me wishes for hips like hers. Though, I am glad to avoid the attention of men if I can. I also order a lovely deep plum blouse to wear at the tables. The image of the "dark and mysterious Card Witch" is good for business, and I have no shame in playing up my intrigue.

The tailor's assistant is a pretty young man, tall and lanky but with broad shoulders and a narrow waist. For a human, he is quite lovely. His hair is a rich chestnut brown, and his large eyes are hazel green. He looks to be in his early twenties, and the smooth skin of his hands marks him as a man who has not done hard labor. He does not appear to be the son of the tailor, but certainly has worked for her for many years based on their quiet familiarity and his skill with shears and pins. I catch him stealing appreciative glances in my direction as the tailor takes my measurements and pins dress patterns on me, and I give him what I hope comes across as a kind smile. I feel as though I should make more of an effort to be pleasant to the humans who like me given the current climate, but I am uncomfortable with male attention. I do not know if it is something I will ever desire, or if that part of me is forever damaged. I am woefully inexperienced even in casual social cues and etiquette. A life among minotaurs, thieves, and the vagrants of Iowain did little to prepare me for life in a more civilized place.

I am oddly on edge about the games this evening. It is not as though I have been losing, or need the money, but I have a creeping feeling that the animosity growing in the streets may trickle into the tavern. Shell and her family have truly been kind to me, and the last thing I want to do is cause them distress. Shell's mother has not been herself lately, and I can tell her husband is feeling the stress of his added duties around the tavern. I make a mental note to check in with Shell later this evening to see if there is anything I can do to help. I am a tenant, but I also would like to think I am a friend to Shell and her family. I would not mind helping to ease their burden if I am able.

Cartwright gives me a gruff kiss on the cheek as he welcomes me to my table. I flinch, but quickly recover. Despite me never returning affection towards any of them, everyone here treats me as one of their own—like family. He keeps close throughout the night, and I feel comfort in knowing he has my safety in mind. The man from before has not returned, but there is a tension in the air nonetheless. I am glad to find my unease is unfounded, and the games run smoothly throughout the evening. Other than a small fight breaking out at a nearby table over a tavern girl, no issues arise.

As I pack up my cards, sliding them into their small velvet bag before heading to bed, I notice the tailor's assistant seated at a table in the dining room. For a moment, I wonder if he has come to update me on my order, but he appears simply to be enjoying a meal alone. The stairs to my apartment are just past the dining room, and I walk by his table, trying to look kindly as I pass.

"Maelwen, right?" he calls out as I walk by, and I pause, looking back.

"Yes," I reply. "I am sorry. I do not think I have ever asked your name."

He grins broadly. "Godrick. Nice to meet you, officially. Would you care to join me?"

I hesitate but take a seat across from him, recalling his furtive glances at me earlier in the day. We chat for a while, finding a comfortable rhythm with no awkward silences or stilted speech between us. I surprise myself with a genuine smile as he tells me a story about the tanner's wife and a mishap with some sewing pins. Something about him feels less threatening than other men, and I find that I do not dislike his company. I surprise myself by staying, enjoying a conversation. The witch I have become shares so little with the witchling I was in Iowain, choosing to spend time among people instead of in solitude. The time passes quickly, and before I am aware, I can see the early rays of dawn peeking through the large window that faces the sea.

"I have enjoyed speaking with you, but I really must get to bed."

He glances toward the window, and his eyes widen slightly as he realizes the hour. "Oh, indeed—I had no idea it was already so late. Early? Either way," he laughs as he drags a thin hand over his chin and pushes back his hair with narrow fingers. "Thank you for the conversation, Maelwen. I would love to share a meal with you again, should you find yourself hungry."

I am unsure if he is making a joke, but I reply, "I have been known to experience hunger. I live upstairs and play here nearly every evening. You may inquire about me if you visit again."

He stands as I do, and steps toward me before I can turn to head upstairs. His green-gold eyes slide down to my lips for just a moment, and I feel an odd tingle in my chest. I am worried he may attempt to kiss me. I have never kissed a man willingly, and I am not interested in the prospect. My hands feel instantly hot, and my heartbeat picks up as I mentally prepare to flee. Instead, he bows slightly at the waist before donning his wool hat and heading for the door. Yet the comfort of his company remains as I ready myself for bed and slide beneath my silk sheets.

KONIDAS

CHAPTER NINE
SHELL
YEAR 993

There's been too many creepy fucks in my bar lately. Ma and Pap are too busy with the kitchen and the bookkeepin' to pay much attention to the front of the house. Ma seems tired lately, sittin' in the kitchen more often than standin'. I have a headache. Rumors of witches in the city and the castle keep comin' in from the docks, and I've started jottin' them down in a notebook just to keep track of 'em all. I've inquired about the servants from summer and heard neither hide nor hair about what became of them. I lean my elbows on the bar and loose a long breath. I ain't got the energy to be keepin' up with this much. My back aches and I yearn for a good sit.

Cartwright, ever the trusty cad, has kept true to his word regardin' the talk of a human uprisin' from Athydis. Ale loosens tongues almost as well as a lady on her back, and these fools at my bar spill far more than they intend after a few tankards. There's someone stirrin' up unrest in the city—speakin' out in the palace square, calling men to arms against the witches. No one seems to have a name, but it goes hand in hand with some of the church folk within the city walls. Over here in the devil's land, we don't parse the texts of the church. Nobody here gives two shits about the definition of sin. Sure, we say a little prayer here and there before doin' somethin' foolish, but Konidas is not a town of faith. When the old gods died, so did our concern for their opinions.

Athydis houses a massive chapel for worship, and those frilly nobles sit their fancy asses in seats to praise Idyth before going home to beat their housemaids. But there's always someone who has to go beyond, and in the last few years there's been quite the influx of doomsday preachers and "fathers of faith" wanderin' into my neck of the woods to indoctrinate the masses. They don't drink, so I toss 'em out without a thought, but we've had a few try to set up shop in town, erectin' little wooden platforms to stand and yell about sin and evil. I suspect one of these kooks is behind this tomfoolery, but I haven't yet figured out who or why.

My bar has an odd assemblage of patrons this mornin'. I clean some sticky ale from my fingers and let my eyes wander the room. I've never considered myself special or particularly kind, just realistic about life. But I've never once thought my kind were better than anyone else. I've met all kinds of folks, and there's asses and gems in all of 'em. Who am I to say that a witch or a minotaur is less worthy than a human? This is why I've never chained myself to a man, or limited myself to their affections. Men can be such cunts, and though I am not above cravin' a good fuck now and again, being a bartender gives me a front-row seat to their fuckery.

There's a rather pretty couple in the bar and they keep givin' me the eye. She sits with her legs crossed at the ankle, a bit of skin peekin' from below her skirts. He leans back in his chair with a smirk and an attitude of nonchalance that I can't deny is tempting. I like tips as much as the next girl, so I swish my hips and smile right back.

Ma made some fine meat-filled pasties this mornin', buttery crust folded over a hearty scoop of spiced beef. I place a few of 'em on a plate, plannin' to drop 'em at their table when I overhear the man tell his girl, real quiet so I won't overhear, "We *could* stay late to see the Card Witch. We aren't expected back on board til dawn."

I pour two more cups of ale before loadin' up my tray, keep 'em drinkin' and they'll keep us paid—just like Pap always says. Gods bless that witch for puttin' on such a show. This is the third time this month someone has come solely to watch her play. Talk of her trouncin' all the menfolk has made its way clear up to Athydis, and I'm glad for the extra coin it brings in. I lean over to set down the cold ales, poppin' my hip out as I do. The woman's fingers graze my ass as I straighten, and I slip her a wink. Her fella is a good lookin' bloke, tall and big with a firm-lookin' chest and black hair that swoops down over his eyes. She bites her lip, lookin' at me from behind wavy, auburn hair that just barely grazes her shoulders. I usually like my girls with a bit more meat on their bones, but she's got a sparkle in her eye, and I've been long overdue for some fun.

I see to my other patrons, wipin' up a few tables and refillin' glasses where needed. My knees are smartin' and I take the opportunity to sit, sliding into the empty chair beside the couple. "How are you two on this fine spring mornin'?" I say with a wicked grin.

The girl doesn't miss a beat. "Better now," she says, runnin' her hand across the table slowly to pick up the glass in front of me. It's an obvious bit, but I'm a sucker for a girl who knows what she wants.

Her man shifts in his seat, adjustin' his suddenly tight pants. Gods, men are easy. "When do you get off?" he asks.

"That all depends on you, doesn't it?" I tamp down the urge to laugh as his face reddens. Flirtin' is half my job, of course I ain't shy. "You two just visitin'?"

He pushes back that swath of black hair as he answers, his

voice a low bass that curls my toes, "Yes ma'am, staying at the inn for a night. We sail back to Athydis in the morning, but wanted to *see the sights*."

"And how have the *sights* been?"

Her fingers slip over my thigh, and she replies in a husky voice, "Beautiful."

Martine walks through the door like I summoned her with my fuckin' mind. She shoots me a look, and I raise my eyebrows suggestively. She knows me well enough to roll her eyes as she heads behind the bar.

"Well, you two, my name's Shell, and I'm one proprietor of this fine establishment. It's only right for me to give you a full tour so you can see *all* the sights."

I hear the woman's breath catch, and a low noise of agreement sounds in his throat. "Lead the way," he replies as I stand.

I don't bother being surreptitious. Ma is in the kitchen, and I'm a grown ass woman, so I simply lead them up the stairs to the little supply room in the hall. So much for takin' a break to rest.

MY HAIR A MESS AND MY DRESS ASKEW, I HEAD BACK DOWN the stairs, waving goodbye to the pair as they leave. When the door swishes closed I lean back, hands pressin' into the small of my back. Gods, I am tired. There's not a ton of patrons in the bar this evening, so I take my time tidying up, dusting the counter with lazy strokes, replacing burnt out candles as I go. Someday I'd like to add more decor, give the place a little more pizazz. The golden wood of the walls and tables is pretty, but it could use some more personal touches. Maybe I'll paint a mural. Who the fuck knows?

I jerk, droppin' a candle stub at the sound of a loud crash from the back. I nearly fall as I hightail it through the double doors separatin' the dining room from the kitchen. Ma's on the floor along with the soup pot and about a dozen bowls.

"Ma!" I holler as I rush to help her up. She looks wan, bleary-eyed, and a bit confused. I get her into a chair and bring her a glass of water to sip on. "Ma, what happened?" The blankness in her eyes as she looks back at me makes my heart jump in unease. I crouch down beside her, bringin' my face right up to hers, clutchin' her fingers in mine. "Ma, are you alright?" She takes a long drink and closes her eyes, seeming suddenly much older than her sixty some-odd years.

"I slipped," she says quietly. "Fell on my ass tryin' to get that soup kettle."

"I can help you, Ma." I pat her knee. "Just holler for me next time, and I'll pop right in and grab it for you. No trouble."

She sighs heavily. "I been feeling confused, Shell—tired. Like it's all gone murky in my head."

I sit back on my heels and lay my head in her lap like I did when I was a girl. "Maybe you should take a break, Ma. Plenty of girls in town who can cook just fine. No need for you to be spending your time sweatin' in this kitchen when we've got more than enough to hire someone on."

Her shoulders sag, and it breaks my heart a bit. "Shell, this is our place. I'm not ready to bring on anyone else yet. This kitchen's been mine to tend for close to forty years. It's as much a home as the house. I'm just tired's all."

I lift my head and pull her close. Kissin' her cheek, I tell her, "Well, we're not gonna offer lunch anymore then—if you're too pigheaded to get some help, then I'm too pigheaded to let you work yourself to death for folks. Brunch and supper is more than enough, and I'll get Martine to come in a bit early to help with the bakin'. I ain't kickin' you out, but I'm gonna take some work off your plate."

"You're a good girl, Shell. Always have been," she says with a squeeze to my shoulder.

I struggle up off the floor and stand, taking her glass. I look at her with a sad smile as I head back out to the bar. I feel too grown as I wonder for the first time how I'm going to run this place when she's gone.

KANITOSH WOODS

CHAPTER TEN
CICERINE
YEAR 993

I wonder if the trees feel different with fruit hanging ripe and heavy from their branches. Do they know they had a purpose beyond growing leaves? I thought my life was complete. I never knew I was missing something, but now, with Jynn sharing my bed, I realize I was. We cross from friends to lovers seamlessly. The first few days, we are a tangle of limbs and tongues and teeth, but we settle into an easy calm. We take our time learning one another, and as spring finally falls away into summer, it feels like it has always been this way. Today the air scrapes over my skin like when I retrieve Mamère's bread from the woodstove. My cotton shift feels too heavy, though it is barely more than a nightgown. Heat from the rocks beside the stream leaches into my hooves, and I curse my faun heritage for the tenth time today. I'm pulling the last of the spring fruit from the cold cellar to make a tart, momentarily reveling in the cool air beneath the earth. It's far too hot to continue using the woodstove, but I have ginger cookies to crush into a crust, as well as the last of the small strawberries. Sweating, I make my way back home, my bag slung over my shoulder. I spot Jynn's red head disappearing into the woods and smile. Hopefully she's doing something useful and not something foolish to earn Father Farragen's ire. Fortunately, our cottage is well shaded, and I breathe a sigh of relief as I step into the cool air.

My tart pan is an import from Athydis, made from thin copper and expertly crafted. It was a gift from Mamère a few summers ago, brought in by traveling traders. She must have traded something very fine to get it. We don't have currency in the glade like they do in the city; we simply have no need for it, but it is always a treat when traders come through on their way to or from Konidas. My fingers tamp the crushed cookie crumbs down into the fluted sides. I've done this so many times it takes no thought whatsoever, and I find my mind wandering.

Athydis itself is a great city, I've heard stories of the sprawling cathedral, with stained glass windows that span floor to ceiling, and congregations of thousands coming together each week. I have never been outside of Kanitosh, but Father Farragen came here from the city before I was born. He was on a mission to bring Idyth to these woods, and I am eternally grateful. He has taught us about all of the Idythian peninsula during our schooling, otherwise I would know nothing of the world outside of our wood.

Sometimes I'm amazed by the knowledge of all that exists outside our little glade. As I assemble slices of juicy red strawberries within my small tart, I wonder about the lives of the people who live out there in the world. Do they, too make food like me? How exciting it must be to meet so many strangers, to see mysterious creatures and exotic lands. I would love to taste the many cuisines of the peninsula, learn to cook all their alluring dishes, share my humble pies and stews and maybe even some of my subpar bread.

I chuckle to myself as I place the last layer of honey-soaked strawberries. Nobody here wants to eat my bread. I'm sure nobody out there would want to either. But unlike Mamère, I wonder. I wonder about the world outside our secluded copse, and I wonder if I'll ever get to see it.

I don't see Jynn until suppertime, and we chat idly over plates of asparagus and roasted sweet potatoes. Our knees knock together beneath the table and my cheeks flush from even such small contact. Jynn made a tangy salad with slices of tart tangerine and peppery arugula, and it's delicious. I raise my head to say so and notice Mamère's face, still and slack as she stares ahead toward nothing. Concerned, I ask, "What's wrong, Mama?"

Her eyes seem oddly glassy as she replies, "Oh, nothing love, I've just been remembering lately, and I'm a bit lost in my head."

I consider keeping my questions to myself. I'm often more inquisitive than I should be, but my curiosity wins out as I ask, "What have you been remembering?"

"This summer has been so warm, and I always wonder around this time of year if your father would have liked it." She still stares ahead blankly, and I set down my fork, not hungry anymore.

I'm taken aback. My mother rarely mentions my father. I know the old wound still stings, and the small bits of their story she has shared with me have always been vague.

"You met him in the winter, didn't you?"

"Yes, I did," she says with a dreamy gaze. She goes on, "It was one of the snowiest winters I can recall ever hitting the glade. My hooves were positively frozen. I saw him trudging through the snow, and he just looked so cold, I couldn't help but invite him in."

I wait expectantly, hands clasped beneath my chin, eager for more of this story she so rarely shares with me. "My parents would have been furious," she laughs. "Here I am, a young faun during my first winter alone, and I'm inviting strange, stray humans into my home." I smile. Mamère has always been a generous soul. "He only stayed through the winter. I had hoped he would want to remain, but he left as soon as the thaw began. He told me he lived in Konidas; I bet he would have enjoyed this heat." Her eyes seem to clear and she shakes her head, soft curls rustling in an auburn whisper.

She goes back to her meal, and I'm struck by a sense of longing. Not for me, but for Mamère. Father Farragen arrived later that year, and I've often wondered if her loneliness explains the devotion she shows to Father Farragen. If she is just longing to belong to someone.

Mamère has told us stories about our village before Father Farragen arrived. We had little religious influence then. Sure, our people prayed to the gods for good harvest, celebrated the coming spring and thanked Idyth for his light, but there were no offerings or pennyway. It was after Father Farragen's arrival that they converted the schoolhouse into a worship space and began offerings.

She told us he thought our people were rather quaint, maybe even slightly uncivilized when he first arrived. He taught them how to make mead and to set an altar. Under his tutelage, they learned to revere the pennyway, to atone for sins, and the cost of indiscretions. There had never been a single cause for punishment or penance in our village before. They were ignorant of sin, but with his arrival came a whole new set of rules for living. Corporal punishment and penance of the flesh became a part of life in the glade, and the few families who objected to the change moved to other areas. Mamère said some left without even saying goodbye, their cottages simply empty one day—nothing but a few scattered belongings to indicate anyone had ever lived there. But our village has thrived under Father Farragen's hand. Our harvests are bountiful, and our community is strong in our resolve to live a good life together in the service of Idyth.

We are all quieter than usual after dinner; Mamère kisses me goodnight and heads to bed, her steps seeming heavier than before. Jynn and I tidy up without much conversation. We share a slice of my tart and sip tea, not saying much to one another.

"Do you think Mamère is sad?" I finally ask, breaking the quiet.

"I don't know," Jynn says, setting her cup on the table with a soft clink. "I worry about her sometimes, too. Farragen is hard on her. She seems so worn down."

Nodding, I take a bite of the tart. "I wonder if she would have found someone else if Father Farragen hadn't come," I say after swallowing. "She looks so young, but she *feels* so old."

"Yeah," Jynn murmurs. "Farragen seems to suck the life out of people."

I set down my fork atop my plate a little rougher than I intend to. "What do you mean?"

"Don't you wonder what life would be like without all this fear?" she asks. "Honestly, do you think Idyth cares whether or not we pour mead into a chalice? Don't you think he has better things to do than worry about a patch of flowers and whether or not some fauns in the woods worship him enough?"

I'm taken aback. Jynn has never said anything like this to me before. "I think," I reply quietly, "That he would like us to live a good life."

"And who decides what is good, Ceci? Farragen? That old creep made you stand naked so he could leer at you in the woods. Do you seriously think that's a commandment from a god?"

I don't know what to say. I've never really questioned Father Farragen's intentions. I've never known differently. This has always been my life.

"I don't trust him, Sunbeam, and I don't think you should either."

Tonight when we go to bed, I feel a strange tension between us, like a string pulled too taut. Her soft kiss feels different against my lips, and I wonder what led her to this conversation. Is there something she knows that I don't?

KONIDAS

CHAPTER ELEVEN
SHELL
YEAR 993

I awaken stiffly, rubbin' at the tight muscles in my lower back as I get out of bed and head to our bathin' room. The small mirror above the washbasin reflects deep circles beneath my eyes and a messy straw colored heap of hair. I'm fuckin' exhausted. Ma has continued to have moments of clarity, but the moments where she fails to recognize me or Pap, drops somethin' or forgets what she's doin', have gotten more frequent. Pap is buryin' himself in the tavern, and I know it's out of worry and a need to keep his hands busy to avoid the situation. Martine has been a godsend, pickin' up most of the mornin' bakin' and coverin' extra hours when needed. I offered her a raise last night, and she nearly knocked me over with a hug. The girl is carin' for her younger brothers, and I know money is tight, so a few extra coins a week is a blessin'. I sigh, lookin' at my disheveled reflection. I quickly wash my face and drag a comb through my ratty hair, slippin' into a pair of Pap's old pants and a shirt with buttons that are near to burstin' at the chest. Shit, maybe they will burst by the end of the night, and I'll bag some extra tips.

My walk is short and easy. It's still early, and the streets are pretty empty save for the night crews comin' off the ships headin' out for food and drink. I guess I don't look as shitty as I thought, since I catch a few looks as I walk through the bar. That pretty boy from the tailor's shop is leaned up against the wall of the tavern as I walk up. Goodwin? Gordon? Glenn? Fuck, I'm bad with names. He's been sniffin' around Maelwen, and I'm not sure about him yet. He seems like a nice enough kid, but my little witch doesn't know shit about men or the world, and I'll eat this boy alive if he hurts her.

"Hey there," I greet him as I walk to the door, "Waitin' on someone?"

His cheeks flush, and I can see him contain a giddy little smile, "Yeah, I'm supposed to get breakfast with Maelwen."

I narrow my eyes a bit. "You been spendin' an awful lot of time around her, boy. I better not catch you doin' her any wrong."

He's smart enough to go a bit pale as he replies, "Oh no, ma'am, I have no intention of doing her wrong. She's not like the girls here in Konidas."

"Damn right she's not," a corner of my mouth rises in a bit of a grin. "You do know she's a witch, right?"

He sounds confident as he replies, squarin' his shoulders a bit. "I've seen her hands plenty. But she seems different, you know? Not that I've met many witches or anything, but she doesn't seem scary."

My head leans back in a hearty laugh, and I plant a hand on my wide hip. "Boy, that girl is as scary as they come. She's a good girl and a good friend of mine, but don't make the mistake of thinkin' she's harmless because she's got a pretty face. Those claws ain't just for show." I think I might like this kid. He plunges his hands in his pockets, takin' up a strong-lookin' stance as he looks me straight in the eye.

"She won't need them. I'm not that kind of man."

I give him a nod as I walk in. "Better not be."

Maelwen glides down the staircase with that easy grace she has, wearing fitted leather pants which show off her little ass, and a gauzy shirt in a pretty shade somewhere between red and brown. Her hair is loose, and it shines in the lantern light of the bar as she slides it over one shoulder. She's got on her black gloves, and she looks fearsome and beautiful as she looks my way.

"You're getting breakfast with the tailor boy?" I ask and waggle my eyebrows at her. "Look at you dallyin' with the rabble."

I could swear her cheeks blush a bit as she looks back, stoic as always. "Believe me, it is just as odd to me as it is to you."

I slide her a shot of whiskey with a chuckle and a wink, "For the road." With an almost-smile, she shoots it back and pushes the glass toward me.

"I will stay out of trouble."

I nod. "He seems all right. Just be careful. Even pretty young men are still men."

Twenty years old, and I'm given' advice like Ma. I take a shot myself. Better get to work.

The mornin' crowd is pretty easy, and my shift goes by without incident. I serve some ale, bring some bread and eggs to a table of old men who look like mainlanders, and take inventory as I go. Ma's usually the one who keeps tabs on how much booze we have on hand, but with her current state, I guess it's up to me now. My small ledger is a mess of numbers and notes, but it makes sense enough to me. We have a whiskey supplier who imports from Athydis, a winemaker who lives in town and works out of a building on the docks, and a few different ale suppliers who provide a couple varieties of beer we buy by the keg. Our whiskey man is old as dirt and has the attitude of an ornery seal, but he brings decent bottles, so I put up with his shit. The winemaker is an old friend of Pap's, and he's sweet as pie. If the dock trash knew a winery was right under their noses, they'd likely rob him for all he's got, but we keep our mouths shut, and his people are loyal. We are set for the month, but I'll definitely need to touch base with everyone as we enter into summer. I've got a full crate of plum wine from Athydis I need to push a little harder. It's not actually brewed from plums, but they take fresh fall plums and steep them in some sort of liquor. It's tangy and sweet and absolutely fuckin' delicious. I snag a bottle to take home with me. Might as well. Pap walks through the door as I finish takin' inventory of our kitchen supplies and gives me a big hug, wrappin' me up tight against his warm, wide chest.

My Pap is a big, soft man with a heart of solid gold. There is no man alive who is more lovin' or givin', and he's been my biggest champion my entire life. He's made me into the woman I am, taught me to take no shit, but always start out with a smile. Folks used to call him Papa Bear, long before he and Ma ever had me. It's been breaking me down bit by bit to see him so torn up about Ma. They've always been the perfect image of love. Even now, when they've gone gray and squishy in the middle, they love each other madly. Pap looks at Ma like she's the only girl to have ever walked Idythia. I wish I had a love like theirs, but I never got around to it. I suppose I still have time.

I hug my Pap tightly and feel him buckle in on himself, lettin' loose a sound I've never heard from him before. I've almost never seen him cry, and it hurts to feel his broad shoulders shake as he sobs. "Shell, I don't think Ma can come down here anymore," he chokes out. "She didn't know who I was this mornin'. I had to chase her down; she tried to leave the house all alone."

My heart plummets, and my own eyes stick with the sting of tears. "I can hire someone to stay with her," I say gently. "She shouldn't be by herself."

I see genuine worry and fear in his eyes as he replies, "I think it's best for you to hire on someone to do the bookkeepin' and another server for the tavern. I'm going to stay with her. I ain't gettin' younger neither, and it might be time to hang up my apron. Shell, I think it's time we discuss you takin' charge of the tavern."

For a minute I can't breathe. I knew eventually the tavern would be mine, but I didn't think it would be any time soon. This is all too much. I'm not ready, but I know Ma and Pap can't do it anymore, and nobody knows the ins and outs of this place like I do. I take three deep breaths, counting the seconds as I focus on the air filling and leavin' my lungs. I can do this. I've worked here as long as I've been walkin', and I can do this.

"All right, Pap. Let's talk when I get home. I'll hire on another server, and you can show me how to do the bookkeepin'. I don't want that goin' to someone else."

His eyes are silver and sad as he looks back at me. "I'm proud of you, my girl. And I know your Ma is too."

KONIDAS

CHAPTER TWELVE
MAELWEN
YEAR 993

Godrick asked this morning if he could court me, and I did not have an answer for him. We have been spending time together for a little over a month now, and I have yet to let him kiss me. He has not pressed the issue, and seems content with time spent in the tavern, gently holding my hand across the table. However, I feel as though men expect affection, want physicality. Lying on my bed, I stare at the ceiling, thinking. This is a path I have never walked. The only physical touch I have ever known was by force at the hands of Jarrus. Godrick is good looking and genuine. He is nothing like Jarrus, but the idea of another body on top of mine, of another body inside of me, fills me with dread and turns my stomach.

Standing, I begin to pace as anxiety buzzes in my chest. I have tried to imagine what it would be like, and each time I have ended up here, in a panic, hyperventilating, as images of Jarrus's massive frame fill my mind. I can smell his thick breath and hear his rutting grunts, feel his body violating my own. I retch, sweating and clutching the side of my armoire. I peel my sweat-damp shirt off and toss it on the floor, making my way over to the washbasin to splash cold water over my hot skin. I look at myself in my silver mirror and see a woman, not the weak girl who lay beneath Jarrus night after night. My gaze hardens as I remember the taste of his hot blood on my tongue, his massive chest slowing to a stop as he died on his floor like a common beast. I am not weak. But I do need to feed.

It is dark outside when I don my cloak and slip into the balmy night. The tavern is busy, and no one spares me a glance as I quietly slink by. The salty reek of the dockside air fills my lungs as I take a deep breath. It has been weeks since I last fed, distracted by Godrick and feeling foolishly human. It does not take me long to eye a man with cruel eyes and a tattered coat lurking outside the closed tannery. He flips a dagger in his hands and eyes the street, undoubtedly looking for someone with heavy pockets. I am no vigilante, and while I do not make it my job to rid the streets of wicked men, they are easily found here in Konidas, and I feel no regret for ending them. I make my way toward an alley near the water and begin to sing his song. The notes flow from my mouth so quietly that no one else would be able to hear them on the wind, but he does. His beady eyes go glassy as he pushes off from the wall and trails behind me in a daze. I let him follow nearly the entire length of the alley, standing motionless in the shadows, my deep sapphire cloak hiding me from sight. When I raise my ice-blue eyes to him, I smile in spite of myself. Not for the first time, I say a silent thanks to the blonde witch in Iowain for showing me how to feel alive.

Rather than keep him compelled by witchsong, I ease my song just enough for him to gain some awareness. Instead of fear in his eyes, I see rage and hatred. It is far more satisfying when they are angry. His lips pull back, and his chipped brown teeth catch the moonlight. He makes as if to move, but my song keeps his body just beyond his control, and I see his fury burn like a flame in his glare. My steps are slow and calculated as I stride the last few feet to him. He stinks like tobacco and sour wine. I can smell weeks of sea travel on his clothes, and it would repulse me if not for the solid thrum of his pulse. That pulsing beat matches my own heartbeat, calling to me silently.

My index finger reaches towards his bearded throat, and with a single slow slice, his skin parts like butter beneath a warmed knife. The salty silk smell of his blood hits me, and my mouth waters. I reach a gloved hand up to his open throat and palm handfuls of his thick blood to my mouth, eyes closed in bliss. Delicious, like a rare steak cooked over flame. When I allow my eyes to drift open once again, the alley is bright as day, my senses alight once more. Like removing a blindfold after weeks in the dark, I can see again. I can hear all the way to the tavern, hushed voices and giggles winding their way through the night. My skin sizzles, and my fingers twitch in anticipation. I suck in deep breaths of the warm night air, the smell of wood and wax from the moored ships nearby sweet on my tongue. I do not know how I lived in darkness for so many years with this bright world just waiting for me to grasp it. Life rushes through my veins, and I feel nearly feral. Is this why men fear us? Prey knows a predator. I was not made to be prey. I smile a wicked grin with bloodstained teeth, enjoying my conquest slowly, reverently in this stinking alleyway.

There is a large copper tub in a small room just off the tavern kitchen, but until this evening, I never felt compelled to bathe in it. Tonight, however, I take my time filling it with ewer after ewer of hot water from the kitchen, and I drizzle some sweet lavender oil into the steaming water. Leaving my clothes on a wooden stool sitting against the wall, I sink into the water up to my neck. The scalding water is nearly hot enough to burn my skin, but I like it. My muscles loosen as I soak, and I lean my head back over the rim of the tub, my long hair grazing the stone floor. The soft floral scent of the oil drifts up with the steam, and I inhale deeply as my stress and tension melt away.

A bath is a luxury I never knew until now, and I think I may make a habit of it. The hot water envelops me, rinsing away the dust and dirt of life, cleansing me of any blood remaining on my skin. I allow my head to slip below the water, my hair floating around me in dark tendrils. It is silent beneath the surface of the water. The only sound I hear, the strong rhythmic beating of my own heart. I bring my face back to the surface only to breathe, basking in the steamy solace of the tub. The steady thrum of power in my veins lulls me toward sleep, and I think more about Godrick and his request. I am not certain I desire any more from him, but I enjoy talking with him and do not wish to cause him any pain. It is odd, considering the emotions of a human man only hours after I killed another with my own hands. I lay here until the water has cooled, skin soft and muscles loose.

As I drain the tub, wrapped in a fluffy towel, I decide that tomorrow we can discuss his desire, and I will be forthcoming with my past. I have not told a single soul about my life before Konidas, and the weight of it is heavy to bear alone. But Godrick is a good man, and I trust him to listen. I do not wish to live forever under the shroud of what was done to me. I cannot move forward if I do not let go of the past.

KANITOSH WOODS

CHAPTER THIRTEEN
CICERINE
YEAR 993

Our summer is filled with mundane tasks, peppered by moments of sweetness between Jynn and me. She hasn't shared my bed in a few days, but I don't worry too much about it. We are both busy with the day-to-day, and the heavy heat leaves both of us tired by nightfall. We don't talk again about Father Farragen, but I see something dark and sharp in her eyes when she looks at him. Mamère doesn't bring up the past again, and the time flows by as the grasses yellow and the branches hang heavy. It is evening, and I am well and truly spent from my busy day. I've prepared a simple meal of thinly shaved summer squash, tossed in a light sauce made from garden herbs and butter, and we chat idly around the dinner table, the three of us all leaning on our elbows.

"Cicerine, did you teach at the schoolhouse this morning?" Mama asks.

"I did," I say with a bit of pride. "I showed the children how to choose a ripe melon. We worked a bit on tending the soil, and Jynn stopped by and talked about the life cycle of bees."

Mamère's eyes shine. "I'm happy to hear it! It's so lovely that you share your love of growing things with the little ones. I'm sure they loved tasting the melon they chose."

"They certainly did, especially in this heat," I reply. The summer sun has us all feeling sleepy and spent by day's end. Even now, I'm only picking at my dinner, counting down the moments until bedtime.

Suddenly, a loud shout rips through the glade. We all leap from our chairs, jostling our dishes and knocking over one of the cups. Water drips to the floor with a quiet patter, quick like the heartbeat in my chest.

"What was that?" I ask, already halfway to the door. Another yell sounds, this time close to a scream, then a long wail. Other screams and shouts join the fray, and we run outside to see what has happened.

I cannot believe my eyes as I gaze across the expanse of the glade toward the schoolhouse. The roof is burning, massive flames licking at the sky as they race across the dry straw and reeds that make up the roof. Our neighbors hurl buckets of water toward the flame, but the water doesn't reach the top of the tall building. Jynn springs to action, her human height making her the only person here who could possibly reach the roof and quell the blaze. Mamère and I grab buckets and sprint for the closest bend of the stream, gathering water as quickly as we can and trying our best not to let it slosh onto the forest floor as we run back toward the blaze.

Bucket after bucket is hurled at the fire, but it seems to dance away from each splashing throw. The fire looks alive. It seems to taunt us as it moves to and fro, somehow dodging the water and quickly spreading down the building. Children cry as they are herded indoors, and every able-bodied citizen struggles to save the schoolhouse. My eyes sting from the bitter smoke, an oily taste lingering on my tongue. The flames light up the entire glade, casting an ugly orange glow over our homes. We fight the fire for what feels like hours, but as the flames start to wink out and fade into shadow, I can see it was all in vain. The schoolhouse is a blackened husk, sitting in a cloud of gray-brown smoke. It looks like a corpse. I search the crowd for Father Farragen, but I see only shadows.

We all gather in the center of the clearing—faces streaked with soot and tears, our clothes dusted with ashes that still flurry and fall like winter snow. There are a few injured among us, and I work beside Mamère to apply bandages and poultices to those with burns and scrapes. We mill about in somber silence, stunned—unable to find words. The schoolhouse was one of the oldest buildings in the glade; it has stood since long before Mamère's parents were children. We mourn the loss like the death of a friend. Sitting on the soot-stained grass, I begin to cry, the heels of my palms pressed to my eyes as I hang my head between my knees. None of us knows what to do. I look for Father Farragen once more, and I spot his dark robes as he strides toward us.

"What is this?" he growls in a tone I have never heard him use. "Who did this?"

Nobody answers, none of us know.

He bellows again, "*Who did this?*" and for a moment, I imagine his shadow moves, separately from him. I blink, but his shadow is still.

"We don't know, Father," someone chokes out. "We heard screaming and came running. The schoolhouse was already burning when we got outside."

Father Farragen seethes, "Nobody saw? Nobody knows who has committed this atrocity?"

Heads shake throughout the crowd. It is stiflingly hot this season, there is no reason whatsoever to think this anything more than a tragic act of nature. I'm puzzled by his rage.

Father Farragen's eyes dart to Jynn. "You, *Jynn*, where were you when this happened?" Her voice sounds like a curse on his tongue.

Eyes wide, her face pales. Jynn replies "I was eating dinner."

"Who can confirm this?" Father Farragen barks, a rough accusation in his voice.

I shoot to my feet. "I can, Father. As can Mamère. We were all together when we heard the shouting."

Mamère nods in affirmation.

"Before that," he snaps back. "Before dinner, where were you?"

I am confused by this interrogation. Why Jynn? Why would he assume she had anything to do with this?

"I was teaching the kids this afternoon, ask Ceci."

Father Farragen looks at me, and I confirm.

"She taught them about bees. The children will tell you the same."

"So every moment between lessons and dinner, you were together?" he asks me.

I'm quiet for a moment, remembering Jynn's quick flight from the schoolhouse this afternoon. She did leave before me, but it was only a few minutes. There's no way she could have had anything to do with this. She wouldn't have.

"Yes," I say. "She was with me the entire time."

Father Farragen lets out a low sound. I flinch. I've never seen him show unrestrained rage like this, and it scares me.

"I know you did this, outsider," he spits. "And when I find out how, you *will* meet your end here."

Jynn stands as still as a sculpture, frozen in place by the accusation, worrying her fingers together. Distrustful eyes flick over her, and she looks as though she may cry at any moment. I'm instantly irate. How dare they, after Jynn worked so hard to put the fire out? Her forearms are red and raw from being so close to the flames. I walk to her and take her hand, glaring at our neighbors as I lead her back home. *How dare they?*

My hair stinks of smoke, but as I slump at the edge of my mattress, I can't bring myself to care. I press my fingers to my temples and rub them with slow circles, hoping to ease the tension I feel. I am still so angry. Jynn walks into our room with bowed shoulders. I hate the look I see on her face, lips thin and downturned. I reach for her as she heads to bed, but she shrugs me off with a sigh. For the first time since she has been with us, she goes to sleep without saying goodnight.

The morning is somber. Everyone's eyes stay down as we silently navigate our necessary tasks. Nobody looks toward the wreckage of the schoolhouse. It is a bleeding wound in the heart of our village. Mamère has been gone since before sunrise, somewhere off with Father Farragen as usual. Jynn won't speak to me, and my heart aches at her silence. I watch as she solemnly walks toward the apiary, and I see a group of fauns step into her path. She stops as if halted by invisible reins. The malice in their eyes is palpable. A raging fire fills my veins, and my fingers twitch in barely contained fury. I take a step toward them and Jynn hears my hoof crush a small, charred twig. She turns and meets my eye, giving a slight shake of her head before jogging into the forest. There are tears on her cheeks.

I am rooted to this spot, physically unable to move. My anger is a living thing; it flows through my body like molten lead. My breath quickens, and I lean against a nearby tree and close my eyes, trying to steady myself. My gift leaps, unbidden, to my hand, but it feels different than it ever has before. I feel searing heat rushing from me, and my eyes snap open as the bark beneath my fingers turns hot under my touch. I pull my hand back quickly, and there's a small black handprint marring the tree's smooth surface. *What is happening?*

Branches whip my face as I run through the tightly-packed

trees. My eyes are full to the brim with salty tears, spilling onto my cheeks in rivulets. I scan the woods, searching for Jynn. There, just past a large, gnarled oak, I spot her shock of scarlet hair and begin to cry in earnest. She sits curled around her knees, pressed to the massive tree, and I sink down next to her.

"Jynn," I whisper with a quavering breath.

She doesn't lift her head, and I wrap my arms around her. Her shoulders shake as she begins to cry as well. We sit in silence, and I allow myself a moment to feel this pain. Nothing is as it was yesterday, and I don't know how to fix it. At last she looks at me, and my heart breaks at the sorrow written on her features. My thumb traces her cheek, and she leans into me.

"I didn't do anything Ceci. You know I didn't."

I nod, pressing my forehead to hers gently. "I know."

"He hates me, he's always hated me. I told you before, there's something not right. Why would he blame me? I've done nothing wrong in my entire time here."

"I know."

Her voice cracks. "He wants me gone. He's trying to push me out, turn the village against me."

I kiss her tear-stained cheek. "I will never let that happen."

Nothing else in this Idyth-damned glade matters to me except Jynn and Mamère. I don't need a single person here. My own anger surprises me as a fierce thought crosses my mind. *Fuck them.*

Fire rises in my blood again, and my fingertips pulse and throb. This time I feel more aware of this power, this heat snaking through my veins. I can almost see it, the black tendrils of my anger. I lean back, my palm pressing into the grass and it withers in an instant. I focus on pulling the heat back into myself, spooling it into my chest like thread on a bobbin. I feel like a volcanic chasm ready to burst.

Unaware of my rapidly changing gift, Jynn turns her face to mine, and our lips meet. The fire dies within me in an instant. Her kiss is soft, at first, but then more insistent. Her hands press to either side of my face, and I slide into her lap. Her lips are salty from her tears, and I kiss her fiercely, losing myself in her. Swiveling my body so I'm straddling Jynn's lap, I press myself to her and rock my hips slightly against hers.

If I cannot change the glade, I can at least remind Jynn of what is truly important.

There is nothing between us but bits of cloth, our souls entangled through the years. I want to drive this anger and hurt from my heart, erase the pain from her mind. There are no words that I can say to truly explain how vital she is to me, so I tell her with my body. In a moment I am throbbing, wet heat between my thighs aching for her. With a breathy moan, her hands grip my waist, and I fumble with the buttons on my dress. I shrug the top down, freeing my heavy breasts. I feel her hot, quick breath on my skin, exposing the desire and need we both feel for each other.

The sultry summer air is thick and damp, and I tingle at the touch of her lips. She pulls a nipple into her mouth and sucks gently, and I hum with pleasure. Each pull of her mouth throbbing in kind with the agonizing need between my legs. I grind my hips into her, desperate for more—wanting to give her more. She reaches her hands to her narrow hips and shrugs her pants down slightly. I push forward onto my knees to slide my hand between her legs, finding her wet and hot. She pushes her hips toward me, and I use the same motions she's used on me, slow lazy circles causing her to buck against my hand. My hand is slick, and I press my palm against her, pulling a feral sound of desire from her mouth. The rough linen of her pants rustles against the grass as she moves in rhythm against me. I press harder, giving her the pressure she begs for. She grazes my breast with her teeth, and I suck in a breath, my head falling back as I let out a sigh of pleasure. The slight pain of her teeth pressing against my nipple sends waves of ecstasy down my body, and I moan loudly, too entrenched in this moment to care. Hesitantly, I slide my fingers down further.

She whispers into my ear, "More, give me more."

I let two of my small fingers sink into her wetness, and she shifts her hips down onto me, pushing my fingers deep inside of her. This woman is mine to touch, mine alone. Her hand reaches around from behind me, between my thighs in an instant, her fingers pressing frantic circles against me to match the rock of my hips. I have never felt so powerful. I feel her clench around my hand, and I move in and out, picking up my pace to match her thrusting hips.

My fingers are drenched in her desire, pressing into her body with growing intensity as she tightens around them. My thumb moves quickly against her, and she sucks at my flesh as she rises closer and closer to climax. Small noises escape her, and I'm struck by the sight of this powerful woman coming apart beneath my hand. I push a third finger into her tight body, and she cries out against my heaving chest as her body shudders around my hand. She opens to accommodate me, wet and hot and needy. My name tumbles from her lips in a whispered gasp. She presses her forehead to mine, and my eyes prick with tears. My body is overwhelmed with sensation, my heart spilling over with love.

Her hand still presses against me, and my breath quickens as I feel the pressure building within me, so close to that same peak. The sound that escapes her is primal, a physical reaction unbound by emotion. Her body quakes around me, her moans matching each pulse against my hand. It does me in, and I am over the edge, nearly screaming as I grind into her touch. I am in awe, looking down at her—this gorgeous creature who has spent her life next to me. My fingers slip in and out of her body as though they were made to be inside of her.

I want every first to be with her, to experience everything together like we always have. I would fight this glade and everyone in it if it came to it. I will never let Jynn go. I slow my movements, letting her ride out her pleasure to its end as she does the same for me, pressing against my shaking flesh. She kisses me passionately, moaning into my mouth and tasting of sunshine. Her crimson hair is stuck to her sweat-damp face, and she is soft and pliant with pleasure. Pleasing her is more than I could imagine. I could spend forever tangled up with her like this.

"I love you Ceci," she pants into my ear.

My heart races and tears escape my lashes, rolling down my flushed cheek. "I love you too, Jynn. I think I always have."

She groans as I slowly withdraw my fingers, her body tensing around me as I slide from her. I sit back onto her lap, still shaking and throbbing against her hand. She makes one last circle with her fingers as she pulls her hand from between my thighs and grips my waist again. This moment feels monumental, this bond between us. I would stay against this tree with her forever if I could. We don't need the glade, we don't need anyone but each other. I let my forehead fall forward onto her shoulder, kissing the flushed skin beneath her collarbone. This is all we need.

My breath begins to slow and I begin to button my dress, watching her try to yank her pants up with a mischievous smile. The forest is quiet, and her soft breathing is loud against the silence. I giggle quietly, happy and sated, glad to have stolen this moment. But a shadow falls over my hands as my damp fingers fumble with the buttons.

To my horror, I hear a low voice whisper, "And what is this, I find? Such sin from such an innocent girl."

Father Farragen stands above me, leering down at us.

KONIDAS

CHAPTER FOURTEEN
SHELL
YEAR 993

A local woodworker who is fond of our ale stands before the tavern, hammer in hand. Pap and I spoke long into the night many times over the past month, and the tavern is officially mine. It's a big deal, and I don't take the responsibility lightly. I'm here more often than not, bein' hands-on with every aspect of runnin' this place. By the time I stumble home, ready for sleep, the smell of ale has settled into my very skin. I've hired another server, a girl named Leita, and her mama is working in the kitchen, equipped with Ma's recipes and her own lifetime of experience. Things are actually pretty good here. However, back home, Ma hasn't been lucid in weeks, and Pap spends nearly all of his time readin' to her, bathin' her, trying to make sure she knows she is loved. It hurts my heart to see 'em like this, but I've kept my thoughts occupied with work.

I've been makin' slight changes here and there, not wantin' to lose Ma's touches but wantin' this place to *feel* like it's mine. Today the biggest change I've made is finished, and I feel a weird minglin' of pride and fear. The tavern has never had a name, always just been "The Tavern." And that's all well and good, but with the growin' popularity of our game tables, and all the men who come and go 'round here, I thought it might be time to change that. I stand beside the woodworker with my hands on my hips, neck craned to look up above the front. I feel weird, flutterin' inside from some kind of blend of fear and excitement. I tuck a loose strand of hair back behind my ear and squint in the sun. Well, here it is.

The sign above the door is pretty big, probably close to my own dimensions. It's simple and bright—"Shell's Tavern"—in white, with large scallop shells on either side. The writin' is in a vibrant teal, which cost a pretty fuckin' penny, but the woodworker assured me the pigment would stand up best to the caustic sea air and all the wet that comes from living dockside. I know Ma won't notice or care, but I'm excited for Pap to see. I pay the man and give him a full tankard when I step back behind the bar. *My* bar.

It's hot as a sweaty asscrack today and just as humid. The winds comin' from the east are dry, but they blow the wet ocean air inland, and it feels like walkin' through soup. I've sold twice as much cold beer today as I did this spring; men are thirsty and spent from workin' hard in this heat. Even my little witch is wearin' a sleeveless blouse today as she walks downstairs, her hair in a long ponytail swinging behind her. She looks uncomfortable. I wonder if it's got anythin' to do with that Gordon kid. Garret? Gerard? Whatever. I didn't scare him off her tail with our little talk last month, so maybe he's a decent guy. There sure aren't many around here, so for her sake, I hope he is. I catch her gaze as she strides by the bar, and wave a hand toward the basket on the bar beside me. Steam still rises from the towel nestled within, and anyone within ten paces would be droolin' from the aroma waftin' up.

I reach into the basket and retrieve a warm bun, tossin' it to Maelwen. Her quick fingers dart out to grab it. "It's a new creation from Leita's mama. Made from wheat and sweet molasses, nuts and dried fruit. I've been swipin' 'em fresh from the oven all week, and I ain't ashamed to admit they're the best breakfast we've ever had."

Ma was a wizard with soups and stews, but breakfast has never been much more than bread and eggs, so this is a welcome addition. Maelwen's eyes widen as she takes a bite, which is massive praise coming from her, and then she's out the door with that thick hair swishing behind her.

My own eyes go wide as pies a few moments later as a minotaur steps through the doors. I've never been speechless in my life, but there's a first time for everything. He's massive, ducking through the tall doorway, and even with our high ceilings, he has to dodge the hangin' lanterns. His voice is low and gravel-rough as he asks for a growler of dark beer. He slides me a few coppers, and I pass him the huge jug, which looks like a regular cup in his giant hand. He downs it in a single long swig. In twenty years, I've never yet seen a minotaur. I know they live up north in Minos'Idyl, and we've gotten some stoneware from their quarries, but the creature sittin' in front of me *far* surpasses what I had imagined.

The minotaurs rarely leave their island. Idythia has always been fairly segregated, so it's a rare sight for a minotaur to be in my tavern. I've heard stories about creatures outside of Idythia, but I haven't ever seen one. When I was a kid, Ma told me bedtime tales her mama told her, about another continent to the far northeast; stories of dragons and a tricksy fox with a bunch of tails. She said dragons still live there, flyin' overhead and protectin' folks, but I ain't one to believe old bedtime stories.

My knowledge of the minotaurs is limited, and all I know about this one is he could crush my head like a grape. He was smart enough not to try sitting at any of the barstools, instead taking a seat in a heavy chair to the right of the bar. He's quiet as he drinks another growler of beer—slower this time. He keeps his eyes down, but his expression is hard to read. A sort of snufflin' sound comes from his nose, and he scratches at a thick horn with his free hand. I don't try to make idle chatter. I certainly ain't got a clue what to say to him. But he tipped me well, slidin' a few coppers across the bar as he lumbered to his seat. Over his shoulder, silhouetted in the light comin' through the door, I notice a small figure in the doorway—Maelwen, jaw clenched so hard her lips have gone white, eyes unblinking as she shakes.

The minotaur doesn't even seem to notice her, but she quakes in that spot against the doorjamb, so leached of color that she looks like a godsdamned ghost. I've never seen her scared of nothin'. Tossing my barcloth down, I hurry to her, wrappin' my arms around her shoulders and just tryin' to get her to breathe—calm down, whatever. I know she's not much for touchy-feely stuff, but I don't know how else to get her mind back to the present. The look in her eyes says she ain't here, she's far off somewhere that she clearly don't wanna be. Her hands are shakin' and her claws have slid out, prickin' little grooves in the wood of the door.

I half lead, half pull her toward the kitchen, just hoping to get her out of the dining room. I'm guessin' the minotaur is what set her off. I know she's from Iowain, and they probably have a few minotaurs. Iowain is a cesspool of criminals, worse even than Konidas. They've got a quarry there as well, would be good work for a minotaur. All I can think is she must have had somethin' real traumatic happen, poor thing looks like she's about to be sick. Her teeth are chatterin' and her skin is moist with sweat, but cold as hell.

The kitchen is empty, Leita's mama havin' gone home for the day. There's a bench against the wall, and with my hands on Maelwen's shoulders, I guide her to sit down. Walkin' to the barrel in the corner, I get a glass of water, and manage to get it into her hands before settlin' down beside her. She lifts it to her blanched lips, but her eyelids flutter and her eyes roll back. She starts to fall forward, and the glass slips from her fingers. It shatters against the floor with a loud jangle as the pieces land all over the damn place. I reach out an arm to catch her by the shoulders on her way down, not wantin' her to fall and cut herself up.

"Leita!" I holler, hopin' she's close enough to hear. I ease Maelwen down onto the floor, kickin' away the bigger shards and clearin' a space. She looks so small, so different from the fierce girl she's always seemed.

"Oh, gods Shell!" Leita hurries around the corner, wiping flour-dusted hands on her apron. "What happened?"

"I could not tell ya," I say. "She fainted, can you run upstairs and find a blanket? There should be a few in the room next to Mael's."

"Yeah, of course," she says. "Can I grab anything else?"

"Nah, just toss me a blanket and watch the bar if you don't mind?"

She returns quickly, shaking it to get all the dust off before handing it to me. It smells like camphor and stale air, but I tuck it around Maelwen. I settle down beside her, content to wait until the storm passes. I can hear the minotaur walk across the bar, his heavy hoofbeats rattle the floor beneath me. I hope he's not dentin' the floorboards. I ain't got the time, or coin, to be replacing floorin' this year. But the hoofbeats stop and the bar returns to a quiet hum, interrupted only by Maelwen's soft breathin' beside me.

I hear her breath catch when her eyes open. I try not to shout, but I know my voice is a little shrill, "Maelwen! Are you all right?"

"I, uh...I am not sure what happened. Are we...on the floor?" She pauses briefly before whispering, "Oh."

She starts to breathe like she's goin' to pass out again: short choppy breaths with no rhythm. Her shoulder is shiverin' against me, and I turn to face her, takin' her hands in mine. I want to wrap her up in my arms like a babe. Whatever's causin' this cut her deep, and the gash in her heart is still bleedin' and raw. I squeeze her fingers, hopin' to ground her and keep her conscious. When I was a girl and found myself too full of feelin' and started to panic, Ma always got me to count breaths with her. At the time, it seemed so stupid, but even now it's what I go to when shit gets to be too much. I let my lungs fill with the warm kitchen air, my chest expanding as I take a deep breath. "Hey, whoa, you're okay Mael, just breathe with me. One…Two…Three…"

Her eyes stay open, but they're sad, shinin' with tears below a puckered brow. She stares at her hands, chewin' the inside of her cheek. "I am sorry." Her head drops lower, shoulders bowing, lookin' defeated and wilted.

"What is going on, Mael?"

"I…I have some history I should probably tell you about. I had planned to tell someone at some point in time. I just did not plan for it to be like this."

I put an arm around her, pulling her close to my side. To my surprise, she leans into me, her head coming to rest on my shoulder. Her fingers twist about each other and she keeps her eyes down, but she leans into me like she needs a mama. I don't think this girl has ever needed someone in her whole life. But I'm happy to be here now that she does. This is what friends are for. "I'm here."

KANITOSH WOODS

CHAPTER FIFTEEN
CICERINE
YEAR 993

Time stops. There is no sound, as if a dome of glass has fallen over the three of us. I am too stunned to even move, still as a statue in this shocked silence. Father Farragen's eyes stay locked onto mine, boring into me like burrowing insects. He moves like an adder, hand darting out to grab me in a merciless grip. His bony fingers press so hard that I cry out as he rips me off of Jynn with a violent yank.

Jynn leaps to her feet, clumsily pulling her pants over her hips as she does, and yells, *"Let her go!"*

"No." His slippery voice croons, "I do not think I will."

Shadows swirl around us on the forest floor, seeming to move of their own volition. My eyes cannot work out what they are seeing, whether the shadows are a tangible thing or merely a trick of the mind. They do not maintain the shape of trees, twisting instead into tendrils of black that reach for my feet. The same smell of burn and rot snakes into my nostrils, and I nearly gag. It's so strong. I feel sick. I have to move, run, and I know that Jynn will follow. Without warning, Father Farragen's too-long fingernails grip a chunk of my hair and pull me to my feet. Jynn's eyes are aflame, fury radiating from her in waves. She starts toward me, but he yanks my scalp, making me howl with sudden pain.

"I do not believe it would be in your best interests to take another step, *Jynn*." He says her name as if it was a curse. I squirm against his grasp, but he holds fast. "Cicerine and I have much to discuss. This does not concern you."

"The fuck it does!" Jynn shouts, looking like a stag ready to charge. "Get your slimy fingers off of her."

Father Farragen's answering laugh makes my blood run cold. The surrounding shadows expand, circling us in darkness. His voice lowers and chuckles. "I warned you."

The next few moments happen in slow motion. Father Farragen hurls me to the ground, and I land on the heels of my hands against a protruding tree root. Tiny rocks embed themselves in my palms; feeling like the stings of bees. My head smacks into the earth. I feel my skin split, and hot blood runs down my face into my eyes. I look up, dizzy, and through a red haze. Father Farragen stalks toward Jynn. I try to scream, but nothing comes out. Jynn strikes first, throwing a powerful punch at his sallow-skinned face. His head flies back with a crack to his jaw, but he only laughs, not faltering a single step. Before she can raise her arm again, his thick fingernails grip her throat, and he has her lifted against the tree. The sickly yellow hue of his clawed hands is a stark contrast to the shocking red of Jynn's blood as his nails dig into her skin. A shriek of rage is caught in her chest and silenced immediately as his hands grip her tighter, cutting off her airway. I find my voice and scream, jumping to my feet and running, still dizzy, toward them. One of the shadows throws me back like a gust of wind, and I stumble. *What is happening?* I push forward again, the sight of Jynn's feet kicking as she claws at his hands, spurring me into action. Again, I am pushed back by some unseen force. Rage builds in me, and my blood boils in my veins. That now-familiar heat awakens.

On instinct alone, I drop to the earth and press my palms to the ground, sending my rage hurtling toward Father Farragen. I feel the power release from me like a scream from my soul. The roots and grasses turn black as they burn from the inside out. Tendrils of smoking onyx heat shoot across the forest floor and charred embers sketch a path. Like veins, they branch and flow toward him. When they reach the spot on which he stands, Father Farragen lets out a pained, gurgling scream, and Jynn drops from the tree as he falls to his knees. I do not stop. More and more of my rage pours through the earth, shooting toward him like blackened lightning through the earth. The bottoms of his shoes are smoldering, his feet visible in patches where the leather has burned away. His knees are smoking, his pants melting into cinders as they burn. He screams as his palms begin to blister. With shocking speed, he leaps to his feet and darts toward me. The last vision I have is of his foot kicking towards my head, the crack of my forehead against the ground, surrounded by nothing but oily darkness

MY HEAD THROBS, PULSING AGAINST MY SKULL. I TRY TO REACH up but find that my hands are bound behind me. I open my eyes and shake my head to clear my swimming vision. Although I am somewhere dark, a bit of light filters through a crack above me. It appears to be a cellar? A cave? An abandoned home? I can't tell. The floor is dirt, free of any vegetation, and it smells musky and slightly wet. A muffled groan comes from behind me, and I turn to find Jynn, bound and gagged, in a slumped bundle to my left.

"Jynn," I hiss. "*Jynn.*" But she doesn't stir.

I don't know how I got here. My last recollection was being knocked out in the woods. I'm not sure how long we sit there, an occasional murmur or grunt coming from Jynn, but nothing more. Gods, I pray she is all right. When I saw Father Farragen lift her by her throat my soul screamed for her. I'm disgusted recalling Father Farragen's intrusion into our intimate moment. I have had so few moments of true unabashed joy, and being with Jynn defines all of them. She had been trying to tell me he is not the man I see him as, but I just couldn't listen, and now look where we are. Tears well up in my eyes as I think about my regrets. I hear footsteps approaching and try to curl my body back against the wall. But it is not Father Farragen who approaches.

Mamère looks strange. Her eyes are glassy and distant, and a strange, sweet smell comes from her as she walks toward us.

"Mama," I choke out. "Mama help us."

She doesn't even look down. There's something wrong with her footsteps, they're jerky and disconnected. She shuffles like a poorly handled puppet. I stare at her with pleading eyes, begging her to look at me. Her gaze is unfocused. She stares ahead as if she cannot see. Another set of footsteps echoes behind Mamère, and Father Farragen steps from the darkness.

"Ah, I see you are awake." He looks down at me with a sneer. "I am so glad you are unharmed."

"What?" I growl fiercely, "*You* are the one who hurt me! Where are we? What is this? What is wrong with my Mama!?"

"All in good time," he replies with a sinister smile. "All in good time."

KONIDAS

CHAPTER SIXTEEN
MAELWEN
YEAR 993

I cannot breathe. I am shaking so hard I can barely stand, gripping the doorjamb hard enough that my claws gouge deep scratches in the wood. I am too terrified to blink. The hulking beast at the bar does not even seem to notice me, but the panic coursing through my body glues my feet to the floor. I can smell him. He smells like Jarrus—bull and yeast and beer and barley and stone dust.

I hear a strange huffing noise and wonder where it is coming from before realizing it is my breathing. I am hyperventilating, my chest rising and falling, quick as a mouse. That is what I feel like: a mouse, stuck in a trap conceived of all-consuming fear. Phantom hands grip my body and my face throbs, remembering the pounding of that massive fist. Sharp pain strikes my chest and my knees buckle as my vision starts to darken at the edges. I cannot catch my breath, cannot move. That wet spittle on his bristly mouth, grunting into my face as he splits me open with his grotesquely large body. My chest hurts, a sharp, biting pain as though my heart is trapped in claws of iron.

I do not notice Shell until her arms are wrapped around me,

pulling me upright with a firm hold. She nearly drags me to the kitchen and sets me on a wooden bench just inside the swinging doors. I taste his moist tongue on my face, feel the scratch of his skin against mine. Shell presses a glass of water into my hands and I try to tilt it into my mouth, but I am choking, unable to drink. Drowning, drowning, drowning. Flashes of too-bright light fill my vision as the world tilts and spins. I do not see it fall, but I hear the shattering of glass and the drip, drip, drip of water—or is it blood? Was that a cup or horns through wood? I lose consciousness. My last coherent thought is a hope that someone will catch me before I hit the floor.

I come to, leaned up against the smooth wall in the kitchen. Shell is crouched before me with eyes like an owl, a dusty blanket tucked around my legs.

"Maelwen! Are you all right?" Shell exclaims as she notices my eyes are open.

My mouth feels like it is full of sand, but I reply, "Yes, I…I am not sure what happened." I look down and see the smooth wood of the tavern floor below me. "Are we on the floor?" I remember the intensity of my memories, of Jarrus pawing at my young body. Realizing what happened, I am filled with shame, and manage to whisper only a soft, "Oh."

Then I recall the real minotaur, here, now, at the bar. My heart rate and breathing grow fast and jagged once more.

"Whoa, whoa, whoa," Shell puts a hand on my upper arm. "Breathe with me. Let's count. One…Two…Three…"

I try to match my breaths to hers, and after a minute or two, my breathing is calmer and the iron fist clutching my heart seems to have loosened its grip.

"I am sorry," I let my head fall between my knees.

Shell's eyes narrow. "What is going on, little witch?"

I swallow hard, my throat rising and falling, "I, uh…I have some history I should probably tell you about. I had planned to tell someone eventually. I just did not plan for it to be like this when I did."

Uncertainty clouds my mind, making my thoughts murky and abstract. Shell sits next to me on the floor and puts a reassuring hand around me. Her warm weight presses into me, and I feel a little more safe.

"I'm here," is all she says, and with a deep breath, I begin.

My words break free like a flood shattering a dam. Whatever part of me has kept it all sealed away breaks into sharp fragments as the words begin to stream from my lips. I tell her everything. I tell her of the first man I killed, the cloak, I tell her of my childhood and Jarrus and everything he did to me. I tell her about killing him, my journey here, I even tell her about the people I have killed in Konidas. I lay myself terribly bare. I had not intended to tell anyone about my witchsong or that I continue to kill and consume humans in this city.

By the time the tumble of words begins to slow, I have begun to shake knowing I cannot take them back. I have risked my only genuine friendship, and for what? To explain why seeing a minotaur makes me lose consciousness on the floor of a tavern? My whole body quakes, as if I was naked in the snow, and my mind races with the possibilities of what Shell might say. She might kick me out, she might not want me to play orakulua here anymore, she might not want to be my friend.

She might be afraid of me.

My emotional rambling might have cost me everything I have gained in my new life. I sit in silence, waiting for Shell to reply. She says nothing for a long time, and I finally raise my head, chancing a glance at her face, unsure of what I may find.

But Shell is openly crying, big, fat tears rolling down her round, rosy cheeks. Her eyes glowing like peridot. Her lips wobble a bit as she reaches to take my hand.

"Oh, honey," she says softly and pulls me into a tight hug. "Why didn't you tell us?"

I reply gruffly, "I did not know how."

Shell's arms around me give me feelings I am unfamiliar with—safety, comfort, belonging. I feel lighter, as if just a small part of my burden has been lifted, like I have sailed through a storm and finally found a bay. I am not accustomed to all this touch or these emotions, but it feels good to have told someone my truth—to have someone know me and accept who I am. Shell sits with me for long enough I am no longer as concerned that I have ruined our friendship, though a niggling fear still prods at the edges of my mind. I am glad it was Shell and not Godrick. I do not know if I would have been able to tell him all of it. I do not want him to fear me, do not want him seeing me as a predator, though I am. I make no apologies for who I am or what I do, but I do not want him to be afraid. I feel as if I am living two different lives: the witch I am, and the woman I am pretending to be. I do not know how to reconcile the divide, if there is a way to be both people. If I *want* to be both people.

Shell makes me drink three glasses of water before she will let me get up from the floor. My lower back aches from sitting on the hard ground, and I slump into a chair in the dining area. Martine has begun her shift, and she wordlessly delivers me a plate of roasted fish and potatoes. The meal is simple but good. Leita's mother is generous with the salt and spices, and I begin to feel more steady as I eat. When I have finished and my plate has been whisked away by Martine, Shell slips into the chair across from me. She speaks quietly and calmly, but I can tell from her worried eyes and soft tone she is still shaken.

"Maelwen, we are happy to have you here. Nothin' is goin' to change that. This is my place now, and if I say you belong, then you do. Don't you think for one minute that I give a fuck about who you are or what you do. I know damn well you're not eatin' folks from under my roof, and the scum who walk these streets surely deserve it. I always knew you were a scary bitch, now I just know for sure." She smiles. "So long as you need a roof, you're welcome under mine. I've got your back, witch."

Relief washes over me, and I know it is visible on my face when she clasps my hand in hers.

"If another minotaur shows up—and I'll tell you, it's not likely to be a regular affair—I will come tell you or make sure Martine and Leita know to tell ya. Now that I know, I won't let you be blindsided. Lucky for you, they stick to Minos'Idyl more often than not, and that was the first one who's crossed my doorway in twenty years. I can't keep you safe, and I clearly don't need to, but I'll make sure you're not caught off guard. That sound good?"

My eyes sting with tears of what I suppose is gratitude. I look at my friend, my true friend. "Yes, yes, that sounds good."

KANITOSH WOODS

CHAPTER SEVENTEEN
MAMÈRE
YEAR 973

Mamère looks down into the lovingly carved tiny bed at her sweet little babe. Cicerine's tiny horn buds have started to grow and curl at the ends. Her auburn ringlets are fluffy and soft as dandelion down. She rarely cries and has started to walk, toddling about the cottage on unsteady little hooves. She loves flowers, especially the purple ones that grow at the edge of the glade, and Mamère picks bouquets of them to set around the house to brighten her tiny smile. Autumn has descended across the glade, and the breeze has the first hint of chill. She shrugs a shawl over her shoulders and heads to the kitchen to prepare dinner as Cicerine naps. A soft rapping sound catches her attention, and she wipes her hands on a towel as she heads to see who is at the door.

A thin man stands before her. He is dressed in a charcoal colored cloak and pants, and his eyes are deeply set and ringed with faint purplish circles of fatigue.

"Good evening," he says in greeting. "My name is Father Santoro Farragen." He extends a hand, and she shakes it cautiously. "I have made my way here from Athydis, as a priest of Idyth. I have felt a calling to come to these woods, and to be honest, I am seeking the reason, looking for my duty."

Mamère looks at his clothing of simple but fine make, his high collar and crisp lapels. His gray-black hair is nicely trimmed, his face neatly shaved. There is a faint scent of campfire coming from him, with a strange note of sickly sweetness she cannot place. His fingers are long and bony, and his nails are a bit too long. He doesn't appear to be a vagrant or miscreant. He seems to be what he says.

"Well, Mr. Farragen, welcome to our glade. I would be happy to introduce you to my fellow townspeople tomorrow. Do you have proper lodgings?"

The man looks back toward the wood, shifting his weight from foot to foot. "You are the first person I have encountered. Your kind…might I ask what you are called?"

Mamère laughs gently. "Athydis, the great city, doesn't have fauns? I find that hard to believe."

He gives her a small smile. "None I have had the pleasure to meet."

"Well," Mamère goes on, "The glade is spacious, and we can discuss your plans with the townsfolk tomorrow. For tonight, I can lend you a pallet, and you are welcome to sleep in the schoolhouse. It will be empty tonight, and in the morning I can make introductions."

After Kovic, she has no interest in inviting strange men into her home. The wound is still too fresh, her heart still fragile and aching.

The man sleeps in the schoolhouse on a homespun pallet made from wool and straw. He speaks well, and the glade's residents are responsive to his words. He asks to stay, and they agree. The come together to help him make himself a home, and the come together in newfound faith. It feels nice, Mamère thinks, to belong to something.

Konidas

CHAPTER EIGHTEEN
SHELL
YEAR 993

I'm not surprised our little witch spends the rest of the night in her room. She needs the rest after the day she's had. The boy stops by the bar askin' for her, but I tell him to bugger off for the night. He's got the good sense to listen, and heads on out after havin' a beer. I always knew Maelwen was fearsome, but *fuck*. I can't seem to keep my hands still today, wipin' out glasses and orgazinin' bottles, never givin' myself time to stop, time to overthink.

Few girls can say they got real retribution from their abusers. I've certainly considered it a time or two. Konidas is a rough place, with plenty of folks who think "no" means somethin' else. Even my girls have dealt with heavy-handed men, Martine comin' in a time or two with a shiner and shame. I've never been a gentle woman; thank the stars no man has ever tried to have his way with me against my will. I've had my fair share of ass grabs and lewd remarks, but I've been safe. I always had Pap at my back, and he's a big man that even strangers knew better than to fuck with. But Maelwen, that little bitty girl all alone for *years*. I can't imagine it. It's a gods' damned miracle she made it here at all, and that she's able to even walk down the street with her head held high. She's made of stronger stuff than any girl I've ever met. I understand why she pulls away from touch and keeps her emotions close.

The minotaur doesn't come back, and I'm glad for it. Not that I don't appreciate the sales, but I don't want to see that kind of pain again. It scared the shit out of me.

The games are busy tonight—likely because the men think they can finally take home some coin with Maelwen away. I busy myself keepin' glasses full, checkin' in with Cartwright as I pass. The energy in the bar is boisterous and fun, and the time passes quickly as I slide drinks and clean spills without a moment to sit. An odd light bobs in front of the front windows and I narrow my eyes, peerin' out into the darkness. Cartwright and I both react at the same time, headin' toward the doors on quick feet. A group of about ten men are walkin' down the thoroughfare, the one in front holdin' up a sign that I can't quite make out. They're too far down the way now to see clearly. Somethin' blows by across the dusty ground and Cartwright kneels to pick it up. His mouth settles in a grim line as his heavy hand passes the crinkled paper over to me. It's the front page of a tattler from the capital. In big block letters it says—FIGHT FOR MANKIND, *blessed by Idyth, protected by his grace.* I flip it over, hopin' to see more, but the back is smudged and blurred beyond recognition. I ball it up and toss it back on the ground like the trash it is.

We head back into the tavern without words, not knowin' what to say. I jump when the doors swing open a few moments later, but a brown-haired man with a scruffy beard walks in carrying a lute. I suppose that's the best possible outcome, we ain't had a bard in ages. From time to time, they wander through Konidas, and it's always a fuckin' treat. I love live music. I'm a decent singer, though I can't play an instrument for shit, but music makes my heart soar in a way that not much else does. Ma can play the fiddle, and I spent a lot of time sittin' beside her singin' harmony while she played back when I was a girl. This bard's lute sounds like fallin' stars when he strums to warm up. He's an unremarkable lookin' fella, but his voice is big—high and bright, liltin' and sweet. He sings like I imagine an angel would speak. I find myself swayin' along when he begins, bobbin' my head in time with the beat, smile wide. His first couple songs are traditional bits, ballads popular in Athydis, a song about the King and Queen, a song about flowers in springtime. They're lovely, but nothin' we ain't ever heard before. I always love a bard for their travel songs—things they wrote along the way, people they met, places they've seen. The next song starts in a minor key and catches my attention. He starts with a soft hum and then begins.

~

On feet so weary, long and cold, did tread a humble bard of old
Through glades of green and hills of white, a lonely bard, a warm spring night
She called the wind, she sang my soul, I wandered in, a love-struck fool
A single kiss to lure her prey, a body built to forget my way
O' lovely, O' danger in your fingertips
I cannot find the will to fear, as long as I can hold you near
O' lovely, a wanderer and a witch
A finger tipped in a dagger long, but yet her mercy bore a song
A waist so narrow for these hands, to clutch and worship as a man
Hair like ivory on the wind, the song an invitation in
Cries of carnal fierce delight, piercing through the black of night
Idyth's light has shone upon, this humble head that carries on
To let me leave her bed alive, to let me kiss her flesh of fire
I ne'er again can taste a lass, there's no compare to what has passed

A ruined man, a humble plea, to bring the witch again to me
O' lovely, O' danger in your fingertips
I cannot find the will to fear, as long as I can hold you near
O' lovely, a wanderer and a witch

HE FINISHES ON A LOW CLEAR NOTE THAT SOUNDS LIKE THE golden shine of brandy through a glass. I sigh, elbows propped on the bar. Ain't nobody can tell me that music isn't magic. The heart in my chest aches with it, burns with the emotion that drips from his words. I've never before heard a love story between a man and a witch, and the plaintive plea in his words touches some deep, untapped part of me. Gods, to be loved like that. Even if it's only for a single night, I want to be someone's world, someone's total ruin. I wonder if he ever got to see his witch again, or if the story's even true. So much of what I know about the witches, I'm not sure I believe anymore. Maybe there is a witch out there, pinin' for this man like he's pinin' for her. His shoulders sag a little as wanders over to his table, grabbing his hat for tips. I holler, tossin' him a coin when he approaches. Though his mouth makes the motion of a smile, the soul-deep sadness in his eyes tells the truth of his song.

It's late, and most of the men at the Orakulua tables are absolutely piss drunk. A few of 'em stumble out with pockets heavier than when they came in, and with Cartwright's help, I toss a few more out into the street. A new group wanders in not long after. I haven't seen 'em before, and they look too clean to be ship workers. I wonder if they're the fellas from earlier, but there ain't no way to tell. They sit together at a vacant table in the corner and murmur among themselves. There's somethin' off about 'em that I can't quite put my finger on. Somethin' about the way their eyes shift around the room, and the hunch of their shoulders. They give me a bad vibe and so I sidle up to the table to take their orders myself instead of sending Leita. When they notice me, their conversation stops short, makin' the little hairs on my arms rise.

"Get ya somethin' to drink boys?" I ask in my cheeriest chipper tone.

The man seated closest to me grunts, lookin' up at me from beneath low brows. "Round of ale," he replies in a clipped tone.

I give a little curtsy and slap a smile on my face before walkin' back to the bar. As I head back with a tray of pints, I overhear a few scattered words. "Next week we can…the crates aren't in… alone and we will…fucking witches."

It's that last bit that really puts me on edge. These men don't look like ravin' zealots. They look well dressed, organized. They look like they ain't from here. I've wondered if the rumors about Athydis were true or exaggerated, and I've been wonderin' how much of it was gonna make its way across the sea. The tattler from earlier confirms for me that it ain't just sailor's tales. Just because some folks don't like witches don't mean there's somethin' important goin on, but I've felt a lot of somethin' lately. Maybe its always been like this, and I only started noticin' when I got close to Maelwen. As I slide past Cartwright, I murmur to him to keep an eye on the table, and he tips his chin.

I'm so busy tendin' bar I don't notice the men leave, but when I glance at their table again, it's empty. Cartwright catches my eye and I lift a brow. He gestures me over with a jerk of his head. I maneuver between chairs and patrons, doin' my best not to knock into anyone as I do, but the bar is still fairly packed and we ain't got much in the way of walkways. Cartwright's always been good at his job, subtle and quiet, but big and assertive if we need it. I stand beside him, lookin' out at the dining room floor, hip leanin' against the waist-height wall that separates it from the bar.

Cartwright's voice is a low rumble against my ear as he tells me what he overheard.

"They're the men from earlier. The tall one sailed in last night," he says. "He's come from the capital and met up with the others this morning. They talked about a gatherin' but I can't be sure if they meant here or in Athydis. None of 'em went into any sort of detail, but they were talkin' 'bout the witches. We need to keep an eye on Maelwen." His head turns and his eyes flick to the staircase for a moment before he continues. "One of 'em mentioned a shipment of some sort too, but they didn't seem to like him bringin' it up, and the big one hushed him real quick."

I brace my elbows on the little wall and take a deep breath, leanin' back with my eyes closed. I don't know what none of that means, and I ain't got the time or energy to figure it out. But I know I'd rather be cautious, and this close to the docks, I don't wanna chance any sort of trouble if they're talkin' about shipments. Without Pap here, I'm not big enough on my own to keep my hands in every basket, so I ask Cartwright, "You got any boys who can come on for a week or two and mind the door?"

He replies as solid as stone, "Yes, ma'am, I do."

Walkin' back over to the bar, I rest my ass on a stool and think. Martine and Leita are here alone quite a bit, and with Maelwen livin' upstairs, I feel like there's too much room for trouble. Other than Maelwen's apartment, there's a few small rooms upstairs we use as storage. We used to rent 'em here and there, but haven't since the Orakulua tables took off, and we didn't need the money or the stress anymore. One of the rooms at the front of the building has a small window we cover with a dark curtain to keep the second story from getting too hot. There's a few cases of glassware and extra jars of preserves and jarred produce stacked on the floor, but there's also a small bed. Not that I want to spend *more* time here, but I'd rather be around. Just in case.

Martine comes in for her shift, settin' a small bag on the

counter and tyin' on her apron. I head home to fill up a bag of extra clothes and a blanket. Ma's in a rocker by the fire, lookin' at the flames. I lean down to kiss her hair, and my chest tightens. I don't know if I'm makin' the right call.

Pap gives me a small smile. "What do you got there?" He asks.

"I'm thinkin' of sleepin' at the tavern for a few days," I reply. "There's been some weird stuff goin' on, and I got a bad feelin' about it."

"Shell, if somethin's goin' on, you should be here." His brow wrinkles and I know it worries him.

"I just feel nervous leavin' the girls alone," I reply. "I'd just rather be there in case someone tries to start somethin'."

"Who's startin' somethin'?" he asks. "There somethin' goin' on you're not tellin' me?"

Guilt gnaws at my middle. I know Pap has taken care of all this for decades, but he's home now. He's got enough goin' on with Ma, and I don't want to put any more worries in his head. I reach around his middle and give him a big hug. "No, Pap. I ain't keepin' secrets. I just got a weird feelin' and I'm gonna have a sleepover. Don't you worry 'bout me." I kiss his rough cheek and he takes my hand. The wrinkles by his eyes are deeper than they once were, and there's shadows beneath 'em that I don't recognize.

"Be safe, Shell." He gives my fingers another squeeze and then drops my hand, walkin' back to Ma's chair and settin' his hand atop her shoulder. I leave before he can see the shine of tears in my eyes.

I TRUDGE UP THE STAIRS WHEN I GET BACK TO THE TAVERN, MY knees aren't happy about all the walkin' I've done today. The door sticks a little, and I have to push it open with my hip, coughing as a cloud of dust fills the air. I get to movin' boxes to the larger closet. Some of the crates in the back are *old,* and I feel a pang of nostalgia as I heft and move boxes of jams I made with Ma and crates with doodles on the sides from five-year-old me. This tavern is my home. My history is written on the walls of this place, my parents before me, and Pap's dad before that. Konidas runs through my veins. I don't like this feelin' that somethin' bad is comin'. I can only hope it's all in my head, and there ain't nothin' goin' on but a bit of worry.

There are far more good people in Konidas than bad, and I think we can do somethin' here. The tavern has been my safe place for my entire life. Maybe it's time for me to share that with my city. Crate by crate, I shift the past from this room to make space for myself, grab a duster and get to work cleanin' up. After givin' the floor a quick sweep, it looks fairly liveable, and I make the small bed with my blankets from home. It smells like dust and beer in here, but it's comfortable enough. I slip into sleep, the din of the tavern a familiar lullaby.

Kanitosh Woods

CHAPTER NINETEEN
MAMÈRE
YEAR 974

The winter is brisk, and Mamère bundles little Cicerine in layers of cozy wool before strapping the babe to her back and heading out into the snow. There is enough snow on the ground to reach her ankles as she trudges through the cold on her way to the schoolhouse. She has agreed to bake bread for both Father Farragen and the children at the schoolhouse, and she has a long day ahead. Counting quickly and doing the numbers in her head, Mamère knows she will need most of the day to get the full number baked.

The schoolhouse is warm and cozy, and she sets little Cicerine down to play while she begins her work. Measuring, scooping, proofing, rolling, loaf after loaf is formed and left to rise in the warm kitchen. Cicerine plays quietly, and the repetition is calming, almost meditative. Looking out the window, Mamère sees nothing but white snow and barren trees. Their branches reach toward the sky like fingers yearning for the sun. With a smile and a soft sigh, Mamère prepares to return to her work when a small spot of red in the snow catches her eye. She leans closer to the window and peers out at the glade. There, right at the treeline—a small patch of red. A bird maybe? It moves slightly, and she grabs her coat to go investigate. As she's pulling her arms through the sleeves, she hears it, a plaintive little wail. Her eyes shoot to Cicerine, but she is playing happily with a carved wooden horse. The wail comes again, louder now, and she looks out again at the snow. It is then that she spots it, a tiny hand.

Mamère races out the door, hurtling through the snow in unbridled panic. Her ankles are frozen, but she doesn't feel the sting of cold as she races for that tiny hand in the snow. A rough sob escapes her at what she finds. A baby, barely bigger than Cicerine, naked save for a diaper, sits alone in the snow. She pulls the tiny baby to her chest and wraps it up in her coat. Its freckled skin is so cold. It makes a tiny mewling sound, and Mamère's hands shake as her adrenaline spike begins to fade. She hurries back into the schoolhouse to find Cicerine safe and sound. She unwraps the freezing baby and looks it over. It's a girl, tiny lips blue, and she's trembling.

Mamère takes the basin of warm water she's been using for the bread and sets the babe inside, careful to keep her head above water. She isn't a healer, but she's lived long enough to know that she needs to get her warm. After a few moments, the little arms and legs start to squirm and kick, and Mamère wraps her in a warm blanket, holding the precious bundle to her chest. The baby cries quietly, and Mamère rocks her softly until she finally falls asleep.

KONIDAS

CHAPTER TWENTY
MAELWEN
YEAR 993

I take a full three days to pull myself from my bed and decide to talk to Godrick. I have done a lot of thinking while curled up under my blankets alone. This is all new to me. Who I am was formed on a foundation of pain and abuse, but who I want to be has yet to be revealed.

I cannot see myself settled down in a human life—having children and cooking dinner in a home of my own. The thought turns my stomach. I am a witch, and my heart beats with the blood of men and the whisper of witchsong. Human domesticity is not a reality that I want. I am still learning what it means to be me, but I *am* a witch; I will always be a witch. Now that I have felt the wind's icy caress on my face as I fly and the rich thrum of power in my veins, I will not go back to the dull monotony of the life I led before. But perhaps I want a partner. Maybe I could take a lover.

I meet Godrick at the docks and ask him to walk with me. The seaside breeze ruffles his hair, and he pushes it back with a smile. He really is a beautiful man. I never cease to be taken aback by the ease of being around him. It is easy in a way I never knew to be possible. He reaches out and takes my hand, and we stroll along the sea. The water is a bright aqua under the summer sun, and the assemblage of ships moored at the docks bob in the sparkling water with the flow of the tide. Despite the hustle and bustle of the docks at midday, it is fairly quiet, and we fall in step together quietly, feeling the creak of well-worn wood beneath our feet.

I take a deep breath, the salt of the air sharp on my lips as I try to sort out where to start. "I have some things to tell you, and they likely will not be easy to hear. However, if you are truly interested in pursuing me, I think it best you know who I am and where I came from."

I tell him the condensed version, explaining my childhood, the abuse I suffered at the hands of Jarrus, the moment I killed him. I explain the gift and discovery of my cloak. My first flight, and I do my best to succinctly explain witchsong. I leave things out; I am not quite comfortable telling him how I prowl Konidas to kill and consume his kind in the shadows, but most of my story is there. The bones of what I have lived and who I have become. I feel vulnerable and exposed, too open in a way which makes me uncomfortable. He listens to every word, saying nothing until I reach the end, simply holding my hand lightly and matching me step by step.

"I am so sorry," he says when I finally reach the conclusion. "I am sorry you suffered through any of that. I'm glad you killed him. He should be dead."

Silence stretches out before us, and I waver at its edge. "Are you afraid?" I ask in a voice that comes out thin and fills me with self loathing at its weakness.

He stops walking, taking my other hand in his, "Maelwen, I know what you are." His fingers gently drift to the small exposed tips of my claws. "I know what these are for. I have lived in Konidas my entire life. I have seen witches, and I know what they do. I meant what I said when we met. You are different. So no, I am not afraid of you. I do not mind waiting for you. I enjoy your company, and if you decide to allow me to be your man, I'll be here. Until then, this is enough."

It's the last words that do me in. *"This is enough." I* am enough. And for the first time in my life, I make a choice for myself. I reach my hand up to cup his face, draw him down to mine, and I kiss him.

His lips taste like summer fruit, and he is as gentle as a butterfly's wings as he brings his mouth to mine. I loathe that my hands shake, but he takes my free hand into his and holds it lightly. He allows me to lead. He does not touch my face or put an arm around me like I have seen lovers do. He stands still, letting me control each action. It is a brief and gentle kiss, and when he pulls back to look at me, I am glad I did it. His smile is so bright that I cannot help smiling back at him. I have never smiled like this before. It feels uncomfortable on my face, like a coat that does not quite fit, and it fades quickly, leaving a warmth to my cheeks that I do not dislike.

"Worth the wait," he says and squeezes my hand.

For a moment I wonder if he is going to want to keep kissing me, but instead, he pulls my hand to urge me forward, and we resume our walk. The way back to the tavern feels easy. I do not flinch when he kisses my hand at the door. "I took the liberty of having your purchases delivered from the tailor," he says with a mischievous wink. "I hope you enjoy what you find." Eyebrow raised, I watch him walk back toward the shop, and I head inside to get some lunch. Cartwright is busy setting up the Orakulua tables and a small hum of anticipation buzzes in my chest. Days have passed since I last played, and I crave it. Orakulua has become an emotional outlet in a way, allowing me the means to work through my own feelings while learning to understand those of the surrounding humans. It is nice to have a blueprint of how I *should* feel. Emotions are complicated and I find that they do not come easily to me as they do to the people around me. Perhaps it is my witch's blood, or maybe I am simply damaged. I do not know. However, in addition to the emotional aspect of the games, there is an appeal to competition. I find great satisfaction in dominance.

When I reach my room, I find garment bags draped across my bed, and my breath catches in effusive delight. I slip the hangers from the bags one by one and marvel at the articles of clothing before me, all stunning and perfectly fitted to my measurements. I cannot resist trying them on, the georgette dress is stunning—nipping in at my waist and floating around me gently. I look like a faerie queen in summer, the length perfect for these stifling hot days. The deep plum blouse has bishop sleeves that fit my fine-boned wrists exactly, draping beautifully as my arms move. There is just enough extra space to accommodate my gloves, and the rich color makes my eyes glint like faceted aquamarine.

A third bag sits on my bed, and I eye it quizzically. I only ordered two garments. When I remove the hanger, I gasp. An opulent sapphire dress slides from the bag, crafted from a silk so fine that it pools like water in my hands. It reaches the floor, with tiny delicate straps of the same luxe material draping gently in the front. I slip into it, and the fit is like a second skin. Without a single embellishment, it still looks like the most lavish gown ever made. I spin, and the bottom hem swirls about my ankles.

Looking down at the garment bag, I notice a note scrawled in a somewhat messy hand. "I am not simply a dressmaker's *assistant* —to match your cloak, G." I read the note twice. *'Godrick made this? Godrick?'* I toss my cloak over my shoulders, and it is indeed the *exact* same shade of sapphire blue. How he managed to match the fabric so precisely is beyond me. I have never been given a gift, and I am at a loss as to how to respond. This gown is the most beautiful thing I have ever touched. Perhaps I should give him another kiss.

The tavern is far from fine, and I look wildly out of place, but I cannot bring myself to change out of the gown. Shell stares as I descend the staircase and lets out a low whistle from between her teeth.

"Gods save us," she breathes. "A goddess among mortals."

My eyebrows narrow as she looks me up and down. "It was a gift from Godrick."

"Girl, you had better marry that boy," she huffs out, "If he's givin' gifts like that."

I run my hands down my thighs, feeling the slick silk. "Does it look good?"

Shell laughs, her head tipping back and eyes closing as the bright sound bubbles from her throat. "Nothin' that fancy has ever set foot in this tavern. Truly, Mael, you look like a queen."

I give her a wicked look. "Well then, I had better go rule my kingdom."

I win each and every hand. After days away from the tables, no one expects me to be here, and I trounce every player. My pile of coin grows large enough to necessitate Cartwright collecting the majority of it to move it to a lockbox beneath the bar. I play and play, each hand a different story crafted. Men start to play in a near-desperate fashion, slapping down cards as though their force alone will win the hand. The man seated across from me mutters something under his breath, but I do not catch it.

"Pardon?" I ask as he draws three more cards.

"I said," he growls, "Shouldn't let your kind in here. Swindling honest men out of all their coin."

"Swindling? Sir, you sat down of your own accord. Your lack of skill is your own hindrance, not mine."

The strike happens before I can react, a heavy fist hitting the side of my face, cards flying from my hand. In an instant,

Cartwright has the man pulled against his chest, dagger to his throat. Breathing heavily I look at him, a dirty man in an old tweed jacket, cheeks red with unchecked rage. My claws beg to be freed, pricking my palms as I clench my hands. How many men will strike me in this life? I want to shred this man as I did with Jarrus, but I cannot bring my terror into Shell's tavern.

"Oi, Shell!" Cartwright calls, "What you want done with this one?"

Shell's steps thunder across the floor as she comes over, and to my surprise, spits at the man's feet. "You are no longer welcome, *sir*," she croons. "You can take your business elsewhere."

"You'll be sorry you did that, wench," he declares in a growl. "You'll be sorry."

Cartwright throws the man out on his ass in the dusty street. I breathe deeply, and resist the urge to follow him out. I am not alone anymore, this is not Iowain. I can allow my friends to stand beside me. For tonight, at least, he lives.

His man at the door, a red-haired fellow named Fergus, watches him skulk away. "I've got the door, sir."

"Make sure you do," is Cartwright's short reply. "You're on 'til morning?"

Fergus nods. "Yessir, and Miss Shell promised me a few of those brekkie buns to take home to the missus and the kids."

Cartwright lets a small smile quirk the corners of his mouth. Everyone loves the breakfast buns.

KANITOSH WOODS

CHAPTER TWENTY-ONE
MAMÈRE
YEAR 977

Mamère named her Jynn, after the magic creatures from the Deserts of the Rahkul, creatures who can grant wishes or destroy lives depending on the heart of the wisher. Jynn was a gift, a frail human child who should never have lived—but did. Mamère chose to raise her alongside Cicerine. She had ample space and plenty of love to spare. Father Farragen seemed suspicious; at first he advised her to let him take the babe back to Athydis and find a human home for her, but Mamère was not willing to let such a tiny baby out of the arms of a mother.

Today is Cicerine's birthday; she is 5 years old. Jynn and Cicerine grin like mad as their eyes land on the cake Mamère has baked for them to share. It is three layers, filled with fresh berries, and drizzled with honey and cream. Father Farragen says that moments of indulgence are sinful, but there cannot be sin in the joy of a child. The little girls eat great mouthfuls of cake, spitting crumbs all over the table as they giggle and chat, and Mamère's heart is full. This is the life she has always wanted, the only thing missing from that vision is a husband, but she stopped longing for that the day Kovic left.

The children are snug in their beds, snoring softly, and Mamère hums a song as she tidies up the cottage. A knock sounds on the door, and as she opens it, she finds Father Farragen standing before her.

"Good evening. May I come in?" he asks. She opens the door fully and welcomes him inside. He takes a seat at the table and she offers him tea. "Oh, no—I am well, but thank you for the kindness," he answers her with a smile. "I have come to discuss some village matters."

Father Farragen explains that some of the village residents have expressed a desire to leave the glade. "I worry for their souls, but I will not keep them here against their will," Father Farragen explains. "I would like you to prepare some provisions for their journey, if you could?"

"Of course," Mamère replies, "I am always happy to provide for my neighbors."

"Excellent," Father Farragen nods, "You are such a gracious servant of Idyth."

Mamère says with a kind smile, "I can deliver it to them if you can let me know which homes to visit."

"That is unnecessary," Father Farragen responds a bit sharply, "I will take it. Can you stop by my home when you have finished?"

Mamère agrees and says goodnight as she closes the door behind him.

It is late midday when the parcel of loaves is complete. Mamère made a variety of breads that would withstand travel well, some dotted with nuts and dried berries, some heavy with buckwheat. She carries them in a cloth covered basket across the glade to Father Farragen's small cottage. It is rather dark inside, so she knocks a few times to make sure he is home.

"Ah, Mamère," he greets her at the door. "Do come in."

The cottage has two simple rooms and is sparsely furnished. He beckons her to have a seat at his plain table, and he hands her a cup of steaming purple-hued tea. The tea smells sweet and mildly astringent, an herb she is unfamiliar with alongside lavender and maybe chamomile? She takes a small sip. They chat about the bread she has brought and the soon-to-be vacant cottages. As Mamère glances up from her cup, her vision slows a bit, as if there is a slight delay. Placing a hand on the table, she stands, *preparing to say her goodbyes, but the floor seems to roll beneath her, and she sits again suddenly.*

"Are you well?" Father Farragen asks, concern in his eyes.

"I'm...not sure?" she replies shakily.

He places a cool hand on her shoulder. "Perhaps you should lie down for a moment."

Mamère awakens slowly, groggily. The room she is in smells musty and slightly foul. Her head swims. Looking around, she realizes she has no idea where she is. Snippets of the afternoon dart in and out of her recollection like fireflies, unable to form a cohesive picture. She stands up unsteadily and takes a few steps towards the door. As she pushes the door open, a biting metallic tang hits her nose. Is that blood? The room beyond is a mess of overturned furniture, scattered belongings and a dark liquid spatters the floor.

With a trembling hand, she reaches out to touch it. Red coats her fingers, sticky and viscous. But where is she? She stumbles out the front door into the morning light of the glade. She squints at the sunlight, looking around. The house is one at the edge of the village. The couple who live there are kind, albeit a little spirited. But they are nowhere to be found, their house in chaos. Mamère's confusion shifts to fear. What time is it? Were her babies alone all night? With still quaking hooves, she hurries home and flings open the door to find the girls still asleep in their beds. Thank Idyth. A note sits on the table, written in a scrawling hand — "Meet me at the schoolhouse - Fr. Farragen."

After tending to the children, she walks to the schoolhouse, full of trepidation. Father Farragen sits at the long table, hands steepled before him.

"Mamère," he begins. "What happened last evening?"

Her thoughts are a jumble of images and sounds. She searches for some sort of explanation but finds none.

"Sir, I am not sure. The last thing I clearly recall was meeting you at your cottage."

His eyes darken, and he looks disturbed, "Mamère, there was an incident," he goes on reluctantly, "I changed my mind, and asked you to take the farewell packages to the residents who are relocating. I heard a commotion and came to find you wild, screaming as if in a furious rage. It took all my strength to restrain you, but by then, well," he takes a deep breath, "It was too late."

Mamère's hand rises to cover her open mouth. Faintly, nearly in a whisper, she asks "Too late for what?"

Father Farragen looks grave. "They are dead, Mamère. They are all dead."

She struggles to remain upright, nausea and dizziness rush through her like a churning sea. She turns her head and heaves, spitting bile onto the dusty floor.

"What do you mean? What happened?"

Farragen's eyes are dark. "I believe you killed them." He hands her a cup of tea, and she sips it, clearing the taste of vomit from her mouth.

No, no, no. This cannot be not possible. Mamère begs her mind to pull the memories clear from the hazy fog, but nothing comes. "Father, I have never harmed a single person in my life. Why would I ever do such a thing? It's not possible, it couldn't have been me." she sets down her cup with shaking hands, the porcelain rattling.

"Oh, but it was," Father Farragen says darkly. "You killed them, Mamère. I saw your hands drip with blood. I heard them scream. But I know your heart, dear one. There is nothing impure within you." Mamère shivers uncontrollably, but Father Farragen continues. "Your soul has always been the brightest in this village. Perhaps Idyth guided your hands. They resisted his word, and he chose you as his divine vessel of retribution. This was a gift, Mamère. You have been touched by Idyth himself."

Mamère trembles, unable to find words.

He looks to her and says, "Your secret will never leave these walls. I will tell no one of what transpired here. I washed your hands, and it is taken care of. Now help me, if you will? Be my hand, as you have served Idyth."

Her brain seems to betray her; she wants to fight back. There is no way *she hurt anyone, but her mind is a swirling mess, and she seems to have lost her voice. As though she is a prisoner in her own mind, she nods in acquiescence, and with her eyes locked on the ground, she carries out his requests.*

KONIDAS

CHAPTER TWENTY-TWO
SHELL
YEAR 993

I head up to my temporary quarters an hour or so after dawn. The mornin' light is still gentle, and steam rises, driftin' up from the street like smoke. I'm still pissed as all hell. A man *struck* a woman in my bar. In *my* bar. I'd have cut his hand off if Cartwright hadn't thrown him out. Maelwen's face was better within the hour. But the sheer audacity of that grimy fuck to put his hands on her because he was a shit gambler...I've rarely been this mad.

I was glad when she went up early—seein' her face only fueled my fire. Wasn't the first time a drunk ass threatened me and my bar, and it won't be the last—but it don't sit right nonetheless. I'm glad for Cartwright's men at the doors, even if they're just for show. I don't know jack shit about his life outside my bar, but he's a good fella, and he brought me good boys to help. I told all of 'em they could have breakfast on the house when they finished their shifts. I'm payin' a fair wage, but they've got families at home and mouths to feed, and part of ownin' this place is takin' care of mine.

I've just put on my nightdress and washed my face, ready to

slip into bed when I hear glass shatter, the unmistakable tinkle of shards falling to the floor. As a barkeep, I'm no stranger to broken glass, but each glass has its own sound, and this didn't sound like a beer or a wine glass. I cock my head to listen, maybe a plate knocked off the bar? You can never be too careful. I'm on edge tonight. But the crash is followed by a shout, and another, and another. I race for the stairwell as I hear the beginnin' of a brawl. Gods be damned.

The bar is chaos. The first thing I see is a group of four scraggly men surroundin' a screamin' Martine, and I rush for her. I keep a massive stick near the base of the stairs for precisely this reason, and it's in my hand before my feet hit the bar floor. It's a well-worn branch with a smooth length and the heavy knob of a burl on the end. One swing of the thick-ended wood and one man is on the floor, his teeth scattered all 'round him. I get in another swing before the men even notice and clock another one in the temple, blood pourin' from his ruined eye socket. The other two turn to me, and I grip my makeshift mace in both hands, ready to swing. I get one in the gut and he doubles over, but the remainin' one charges me and knocks me on my ass, right onto the pile of bloody teeth. With a grimace at how fuckin' gross that is, I haul myself back up. My stick sits just out of arm's reach, so I cock my fist back instead and punch the man who knocked me down right in his ruddy face. His hands fly up as blood spurts from his nose, which is most definitely broken.

Martine clambers back over the bar and is safe for the moment, so I quickly take stock of the situation. One of the front windows is broken, and a puddle of fire burns just inside the shattered pane. Someone threw a bottle of flamin' booze through my gods damned window. One of Cartwright's men lies crumpled by the doorway, but Cartwright himself is clobberin' the remaining few men, knockin' them down like dominoes.

Seein' that he's got it under control, I rush over to the man at the doorway and my heart plummets in my chest. It's Fergus, and —he's too still, a dagger stuck hilt-deep in his chest. The front of his shirt is glistening black with blood. Tears well up in my eyes. I'm furious and hurt and all sorts of angry. Standin', I stalk through the bar, rakin' my gaze over the seven men who lay in heaps all over my bar floor. Next to Cartwright, I recognize a ratty tweed jacket, and my rage ignites.

We tie the man to a chair in the kitchen. He's still breathin', much to my annoyance. Four of his buddies are dead in a pile by the back door. The other two bolted the moment they saw Cartwright and me draggin' this cunt into the kitchen. His squinty little eyes flutter as he regains consciousness and pulls at his bindings.

Cartwright's face is a mask of restrained fury, and he crouches down, eye to eye with the man. "Your friends are dead," he growls. "Tell me one reason why you shouldn't join 'em."

The man spits out a mouthful of blood and nearly topples over as Cartwright's fist smashes into his face. The man laughs, quietly at first, but it becomes a loud cackle in a moment.

"I told you, wench." He looks at me. "You'll be sorry."

I wrinkle my nose. "I'm not the one tied to a chair with a pile of dead cronies."

He coughs and lowers his brows. "Something is coming for your ilk. And you won't be stopping it with an old man and a stick. I promise you, bitch. It's coming."

With the word "bitch," Cartwright stands, dense corded muscles tensing in his arms. He grabs the chair and lifts the man clear off the floor. I gape like a fish as he kicks the back door open and walks right out, a whole man tied to a chair in his arms. A few minutes later, I hear a shriek, but it stops abruptly with a splash.

We take a few hours to set the bar right again. Martine won't stop shakin' and cryin', so I send her home, and we board up the broken window. I'm still wearin' my gods damned nightdress.

There's a scorched patch of floor, but no real damage to the planking. We toss the bodies into the sea, and it takes me three buckets of water before my mop comes up clean of blood.

Cartwright has moved Fergus's body to the kitchen and sent one of his other men to collect his wife. I do my best to clean him up while I wait for her, my cheeks wet with tears. She barrels through the door with a choked scream, racin' to the kitchen and fallin' to the floor beside us. Bile rises in my throat at the grief that soaks the air. I don't try to comfort her while she sobs, but I sit with her. Nobody should be alone in loss. Her hair is a wild mane of copper, and her skin is flushed with agony. Her linen dress is simple but lovingly made, and I can tell that Fergus worked hard to keep his family cared for in this shit city. His family didn't deserve this.

After a while, her shoulders still, and she lifts her swollen face. "What happened to him?"

Cartwright's voice is gentler than I've ever heard it. "Well, Agnes, your Fergus was workin' for me here at Shell's place." She looks surprised, but doesn't respond, and he goes on, "Likely he didn't tell you 'cause it had the chance of bein' a dangerous gig. We've had some real bad men in town lately, men who wanna hurt a friend of ours, and I needed men I could trust to help me keep this place safe. I been knowin' Shell for near on a decade now, and she's good people." Cartwright's hands wring in his lap as he searches for the right words.

"Fergus was a man I trust, you know I've known y'all for a long time. Well, I asked him, and he said yes, and he's been standin' watch at the door for a few days. We had an incident, and today the same fella who started some shit last night came back, and he brought his friends. He weren't strong enough to be trouble alone, but there was trouble today. Fergus kept people safe, Agnes. And not a single soul who hurt him left this building alive. My condolences aren't enough, Agnes, but it's all I got."

She nods, big wet eyes bright with tears and terror. "What are we gonna do now?" she asks in a voice so defeated it nearly breaks me. "We ain't got any money, and I've got a babe at home and another on the way." She places a thin hand on her small belly. "My ma is long dead, and Fergus ain't got family in the city. We ain't got a soul to help us, Cartwright."

"I'll take care of you," I say immediately. "He died protecting my bar, and that's on me. He was one of mine, and I take care of my own."

She sobs quietly. "I can work after the baby. I've got a boy, he can watch the littler ones."

I shake my head. "No need, ma'am. You take care of those babies. I can handle things here. Your boy, he can come once weekly to pick up some coin, and y'all are welcome any time for a hot meal and a drink. I'll take care of any cost if you want to bury him, and I'll handle arrangements if you wanna send him to sea." Gratitude shines in her eyes for a moment but is quickly replaced by that same desolate fear, as her face crumples and she lays her head on her husband's still chest. I sit with her until Cartwright brings down a blanket for Fergus. They wrap him up gently, respectfully, and they take him home for the last time. I sit on the floor with my head hung low.

KANITOSH WOODS

CHAPTER TWENTY-THREE
MAMÈRE
YEAR 977

True to his word, Father Farragen has said nothing of the events that occurred in the spring. Mamère assists him with all his needs and says nothing to anyone about what those responsibilities involve. Father Farragen has set up a patch of those purple flowers Cicerine loves so dearly. He says they are holy, and not to be touched, so she no longer picks them to decorate her home. She misses the joy in Cicerine's eyes.

Her happiness fades day by day, replaced by distrust and guilt. Her soul feels heavy and weary. She tends his house, bakes his bread, cleans the schoolhouse, and helps set up for the offering ceremonies which now occur every half and full moon. Father Farragen's commandments have become more restrictive. The glade is a solemn place. There are no more dances around bonfires for midsummer. The glade has stopped making wine. There are no celebrations, and the air itself has begun to feel listless. The deaths of those fauns lay heavily on her shoulders. She still cannot fathom what could have happened. The only thought which remains clear in the chaotic memories of that evening is Father Farragen handing her a glass of tea, chatting about loaves of bread.

This afternoon she takes Cicerine to help tend the flower patch. Her *gifts have blossomed with each passing season, and she now can coax new shoots from the earth with only her hands. Father Farragen calls it "botanurgy" and claims it is a special gift from Idyth sent to a rare few woodborn children. Though she is still so small, he has decreed she should use her gift to help the village by growing fruits and vegetables and encouraging herbs and flowers used for medicine to grow and blossom year-round. They sit together and work with the purple flowers while Jynn works alongside the apiarist to learn his craft. She is fearless and clever—well suited to the job. The faun requested her assistance earlier in the season, and Mamère knows it filled her small chest with happiness to feel included, to feel wanted. It is hard on her, being the only human in the glade other than Father Farragen, and he has never been kind to her.*

Cicerine looks up at Mamère, beaming as a purple blossom opens, her little sunny smile full of precocious pride. Mamère breathes in deeply, enjoying the summer warmth and the comfortable company of her dear, sweet child. These are the moments that make everything worthwhile. She lets some of her burden slide from her back as she looks at her daughter with the full scope of a mother's love. Then, Mamère catches a scent on the breeze. Her ears perk up with recognition. That smell, she knows that smell. Closer, she leans in toward the newly opened blossom and sniffs. There, that astringent scent. She does know it. She can taste it on her tongue, can feel the steam on her face, can imagine the cup between her hands as she remembers.

As she remembers that cup of tea.

KONIDAS

CHAPTER TWENTY-FOUR
MAELWEN
YEAR 993

By the time I hear the commotion downstairs and throw on my clothes, it is nearly over. Dead men litter the bar, and Cartwright and Shell have the man who punched me last night tied up in the kitchen. I steady myself with a hand on the staircase railing as I realize what has happened. This is my fault. These men came here for me, and because of it, the bar is in shambles.

I walk quickly down the stairs, cloak floating out behind me. I rush past a too-still Fergus, and I dart out into the street before Shell can spot me. Air. I need air. I cannot breathe, and I feel my chest start to seize up as my panic spirals into a living thing. I need to leave. I walk toward the docks without realizing I am moving. Flicking out my claws, I look at my hands. Is this what makes me so hated by these men? Being a witch? It is not like I can be anything else—this is what I am. I wish I knew my kin, wish I had others like me to turn to. I know nothing about this life. I did not grow up with anyone who could teach me. I am sure there are countless things I know nothing of, but I have no one to ask. Despite all of this, they still hate me for being something I cannot, nor will not, change. A muffled scream and a loud splash interrupt my self-loathing, and I turn to see Cartwright standing at the edge of the dock as the man who struck me sinks into the sea — still tied to the chair. He sees me and walks over, saying nothing.

I am not sure how to say what I am feeling, but my eyes sting as I turn to him. "I am sorry."

Confusion wrinkles his face, and he narrows his eyes at me. "None of this is your fault. That man was a weak-hearted fool, and he got what he deserved."

"But they came for me. I am why he was mad to begin with."

He shakes his head. "No, little witch. He came to be angry. He was angry when he sat down at that table, and he was angry when we threw him out. Angry men are angry, and it's not got anythin' to do with you."

"I feel like it is getting worse," I say quietly. "The speeches in the streets, the things said in passing. It is getting worse, and you are all further at risk by having me under Shell's roof."

He puts one of his thick arms around my shoulder, knuckles raw and split and his shirt stained with blood. "Good luck tellin' Shell that. You're family now, and she'll slap you silly before she lets you run off because of some barfight."

I cannot think of a reply, so I nod and lean into him a bit. It feels like what I imagine a father would feel like.

"I have something I need to do," I say as he lets me go and turns back toward the tavern. "Please tell Shell I will be back."

I am in the air in an instant. Konidas shrinks beneath me until it looks like a tiny toy city. The air up here is light and cool, and free from the stink of the docks. I feel free. I feel like a witch. I know this is a long shot, but I cannot think of another way. I have seen witches fly over the city before, far enough up to not garner attention, but I always recognize the shape of their cloaks on the wind.

The thin line of stitching where my cloak joins my body pulls slightly as I catch a gust of briny air and raise higher, gliding like a gull. I am not sure what compels me to do so, but I begin to sing quietly. The song rises in my chest and dances across the breeze as the notes reveal themselves. I close my eyes for a moment, feeling the wind on my face and the freedom of flight. When I open them, I catch sight of a crimson cloak emerging from the light cloud cover. The witch who wears it is diminutive, nearly the same color as the scattered clouds beneath us. Her hair is a pale brown, nearly blonde, and it floats out behind her like brass ribbons. She approaches me warily, brows pulled together. Her eyes are so bright, the same blue as my own, and my heart races.

"I heard you, witchkin, let us speak."

I follow the crimson cloak eastward over the inlet which separates Konidas from Kanitosh and Athydis to the north. The terrain below is bare of men—trees and bushes scattered about in small puffs of green. The rocks here are colorful from the sky, shades of rust and blue-gray, giving the little green inlet pops of color. She begins to descend, and we head toward a rocky outcropping by the water. A small copse of trees surrounds a little flat valley nestled between rocky hills. It is in this copse we touch down, my feet meeting the ground just after she has landed. She sits on the sparse grass without speaking, and I sit a few feet away from her, hands in my lap.

"Why did you sing for me?" she asks in a clear, high voice.

"I feel unmoored. I do not know my kin. I am alone in this world, and know none of my kind. I sought only to speak with another witch."

She is quiet for a moment before speaking in that same bright voice, "Most of us are solitary. Some of us grow up among witchkind in the tower in Iowain. Many others are raised by men, and join the tower once grown. If you were seeking community, we have little. What do you wish of me?"

I am not surprised by her words. I knew witches lived outside of human society, but I had hoped to learn that there was something somewhere — some way to learn more about what I am.

"Beyond witchsong and flight, are there skills I have yet to discover?"

She gives me a slight smile; it brightens her entire face. She is as lovely as a child, though I know she is grown. I envy the way she smiles easily. "Our gifts vary between bloodlines. Many of our kin do not discover the full scope of their abilities until far later in life than you have reached, little one."

My cheeks heat in what I imagine is shame. "I do not know my bloodline, nor my true age. I know little."

Her smile falters slightly, no longer reaching her eyes. "I am sorry. If I could tell you more, I would. But I have visited the tower only once. My bloodline is weak, and my only gifts lie in shifting the clouds and witchsong. You will continue to flourish, child. Who you are will develop in time. If you venture to the tower, they may be able to help you more, but I cannot say. The Crone has been quiet for years, and we are all adrift."

"Do we all hear her when she speaks?"

She nods. "Her voice carries on all winds for witch ears alone. If she calls us, you will hear, even from across the world."

She stands without a sound, graceful in every fluid motion. She looks at me with eyes so like my own and inclines her head. "I urge you to the tower. Should you have questions, they may have answers. The knowledge we keep to ourselves lies in the libraries and rooms of the tower. Seek the witches there, and perhaps what you yearn to find will be revealed. May you be well and find your truth." She lifts into the air on a mellow breeze and disappears into the sky.

KANITOSH WOODS

CHAPTER TWENTY-FIVE
CICERINE
YEAR 993

"Mama!" I cry, pleading with Mamère to look at me. Father Farragen smiles darkly from beside her, his eyes onyx in the dim light. *"Mama!"* I scream for her, terror a living thing in my chest.

He laughs, a dark sound—slick and oily. "Oh, Cicerine. You are so naïve. You see so little."

A noise, somewhere between a sob and a shriek, escapes my lips.

"Have you never before questioned why your dear mother spent so much time with me?"

I struggle to contain my tears, and Farragen goes on.

"You are an ignorant, insolent child. All of you are. This entire glade of *primitive creatures*. It was so easy to bend you all to my will. None of you even questioned me. It was child's play to burn down your schoolhouse, turn your neighbors against the human."

He spits at Jynn. He glances at Mamère's unfocused eyes. My heart races in my chest as Farragen's words continue to slither from his lips like black snakes.

"So easy to kill the families who stood in the way. Easy to make your poor, dumb mother believe she was responsible. She has spent more than a decade in my service, you know. All to protect herself from shame, to protect *you* from thinking she was a murderer."

I stare at him wide eyed. "Mamère has never..." I begin.

He interrupts me. "Yes, this is true," Farragen laughs, a gravelly chuckle. "But belief is more powerful than the truth. In faith lies power."

Jynn was right. This entire time, she was right. I should have listened to her.

He goes on, "Have you ever wondered why you grow so many pennyway flowers for me? Ever wondered where they go?" He gives me a mocking glance. "Of course not. Well, allow me to enlighten you. Pennyway is a powerful thing. In fact, it is what brought me here to your woods." He sneers, "It can do many things. A small bit dried in a tea can make you pliant, receptive to suggestion. It can make you forget, to comply. It can make you the perfect servant, quiet, unthinking, responsive only to the commands of another. The flavor is easy to hide"

He caresses Mamère's cheek. She doesn't move.

"More of it? Crushed into a poultice or made into a paste? It can stop a heart, kill in a matter of seconds. But the most valuable application of all is when the flower is in its newly opened form. Those precious, fresh buds you have opened for me all spring. All you need to do is burn them over a flame, and your mind can journey many places. Places far from this mortal plane. I am not a priest of Idyth, dear one. I am his mouthpiece. Thanks to you, I have spoken to him with my own mouth. I have touched him with my own fingers. And soon? I will take him into my own body. I will *be* Idyth. A second coming to cleanse this world of all the filth it contains."

I stare at Mamère, at her purple-hued lips. She stands rooted like a tree, unmoving. Her hair rustles slightly from the breeze filtering in through a crack in the ceiling. Panic hones my thoughts to a sharp edge. I need to get out of here. I need to get us out—all of us. I stare at Father Farragen with burning ferocity. He meets my gaze with one of careful assessment.

"I need you to tend the pennyway, Cicerine. But I do not need your... *lover*." He spits out the word in disgust. "I also do not need your mother. Consider your actions wisely." He turns and strides from the room, Mamère following behind him as if pulled by an invisible tether.

I stay still until I can no longer hear their footsteps, and then I move. Shuffling across the ground, still seated, I scoot to Jynn.

"Jynn, please, please wake up," I plead in a whisper. She cracks her eyes, and I nearly sob at the sight. Turning away from her, I use my bound hands to pull the gag from her bloodied mouth. Her eye is swollen and nearly black. Dried blood crusts her nose and mouth; her hair is matted with it.

"I heard, Ceci. I heard what he said."

"We have to get out," I hiss. "Now."

I squirm and pull at the cloth binding my wrists. Not for the first time, I am grateful for my small hands, and after a few moments of pushing and pulling against the strips of cloth, I manage to free one. Once I am loose, I get to work on Jynn's restraints, untying the rope and cloth silently.

"Can you walk?" I whisper.

She nods at me, and we get to our feet, quiet as wraiths. We sneak along the wall and down the hallway which seems to be the only exit from this place. I see a sliver of light ahead and gesture for Jynn to stay back as I creep towards it. Overgrown brush hides the doorway, but I can see we are in an abandoned cottage at the edge of town. I beckon for Jynn, and we silently flee for the trees.

Jynn and I know these woods. We dart across abandoned

deer trails and under hanging vines as we rush through the trees. After what feels like an hour, but is likely just a few minutes, we emerge into a tiny clearing where a massive oak stands. We have climbed this tree hundreds of times, and muscle memory leads us clambering up its massive trunk to hide in the apex of two large branches hidden by the canopy. I am shaking from terror and adrenaline and rage. Jynn takes my hand, and I allow myself a moment to lay my head on her shoulder for comfort. What are we going to do? How can we possibly save Mamère, save everyone?

In hushed voices, we make a plan. I am not cunning, but I am quick and small, and Jynn is strong, despite her injuries. Over and over, we review our plans, trying to account for any possible scenario. I don't want us to separate, but we have to for this to work. We have to rely on her strength and my innocence. I feel my heart cleave in two as we silently make our way back down the tree and into the anonymity of the woods.

"I'll find you," Jynn whispers as she gives me a quick, but passionate kiss. "I will always find you." She disappears into the green trees.

I head for Farragen's home beside the schoolhouse, slinking through the trees like a mountain cat. I am well hidden in the shadows. For our plan to work, I need to get Farragen away from Mamère. I say a silent prayer that this will work, then I shout his name.

"*Farragen!*" my voice booms through the silence of the glade. "*Come out!*" The door opens, and he steps outside with a sly smile on his thin lips.

"Oh, Cicerine," he croons. "I thought you would be smarter than this."

"Where is my mother?" I ask, none of my terror coming through in my voice, though I am petrified.

"She's resting inside," he replies coolly. "She's had a very long day."

My eyes dart to the door of his cottage. "Just let her go. We will leave here and never say a word." I hope my tone comes across as penitent, pleading. It's nearly impossible to push my rage down.

Farragen laughs, "And why would I do that? Did you know, Cicerine, that I was the first person to ever lay eyes on you?"

My confusion must show on my face, and he goes on.

"I watched these woods for years before I finally approached your mother. I watched her fuck that filthy man, unwed, laughing in the face of Idyth. I watched her shit your little body onto the grass, knowing even in that moment you would be gifted. I smelled it in the air, smelled it in the patch of blood where you landed. I watched her pine for him while his corpse rotted miles away."

This creature spied on Mamère. How long had he watched her? My stomach roils at the thought of his dark eyes seeing her most intimate moments.

"You may be born of sin, but you are woodborn, and I knew you would be just what I needed. So thank you for being so dutiful with my flowers. It is you, after all, who gave me the ability to do all that I have done."

My eyes go back to the door. I need to get her out. I can drag her if I have to, but I need Farragen out of the way. Like before, I feel that furious power build inside me. It is molten, flowing through my soul.

I make as if to kneel. "Father, I beg you. Please let my mama go." I press my forehead and hands to the earth, feeling my palms heat as they touch the brittle summer grass. Not yet.

"No," he says, words icy.

And I let go.

The hot black veins of power shoot from me like lightning and skitter through the grass, burning it all from the core. I have realized in these few days, I do not make fire. I don't even really make heat. I am the sun that seeks the plants. The same way I can use my light to coax flowers to bloom and grow, I can scorch them from the inside, turn them to embers. Farragen is quick, and he darts into his cottage but not before my rivulets of power hit the sides of the mossy straw and mud walls.

The cottage makes crackling noises as my gift skitters across the growing moss. It blackens, and the straw in the walls turns to ash. The thatched roof begins to smoke, and I run inside, palms ablaze with rage. I fling the door open expecting to see Farragen's dark frame, but the room is empty. I race to the back room, mouth dry, and see him standing beside Mamère, who lies prone on his bed. She is nude, and his sinister claws stroke her skin as he stares at me. I prepare to leap at him, to use the power in my hindquarters to propel me further than a human could jump, but then I see his other hand. His hand that holds a shallow bowl of deep purple paste.

I scream at him. Maybe I say "no", maybe it is just sounds, but before I can move, he shoves that bowl into Mamère's beautiful face, grinding it into her mouth. She seems to gain consciousness for a moment as she struggles against the suffocating paste pressing into her mouth. He drops the bowl to the floor and grins as he turns to a small back door I had not noticed, and disappears into shadow.

I am at Mamère's side in an instant, clutching her hand and staring wide-eyed into her face. *'No, no, no, no, no'* repeats in steady staccato in my mind. She looks at me, her eyes clear, and she smiles. Her mouth and face are stained purple; her bright eyes are full of tears.

"You are a sunbeam in winter, Ceci," she says. "You have been the greatest gift of my life."

I search the room frantically for water, for anything. Anything that might help. The room is bare but for the door. "No, no, no, no, no," I pant the word. Terror seizes me as the tears spill from her lovely wide eyes.

"Tell Jynn," she whispers. "Take care of each other." She opens her mouth as if to say more, but it goes slack. The light in her eyes dies.

KONIDAS

CHAPTER TWENTY-SIX
MAELWEN
YEAR 993

Shell is pacing when I return, and as I walk through the doorway she crushes me in a fierce hug.

"Where have you been?!" she exclaims. "I've been worried sick. What the fuck Maelwen?"

I did not realize she would be concerned by my absence, and I do not pull away from the hug despite my unease.

"I am sorry. I needed to seek answers elsewhere. It was not fruitful. But I am here now. What can I do?"

Of course, Shell will not give me any sort of meaningful task, so I busy myself cleaning the games area and dusting the bar. Apparently there was another gathering in the city near the docks, and nobody wishes for me to go outside. I am bent over, stretching to reach the bottles in the far back when Godrick comes in. He grins as he takes in my fitted pants and my current position. I hurriedly stand up straight and wipe my hands off on my thighs, feeling uncomfortable being gawked at. He walks over and presses a quick kiss to the top of my head.

"Did you like the gift?" he asks, excitement clear in his tone.

"Godrick, it is the single most beautiful thing I have ever seen. I do not know how to express my gratitude."

His smile beams like sunshine. "How about dinner? There's a ship coming into port in a few days that happens to house a restaurant—a nice one. I may have asked the captain when they last pulled in if I could reserve a table for two."

My eyes widen. "A restaurant? I think I would enjoy that."

He squeezes my hand and bows at the waist. "Then it is settled, my lady." With a wink and a promise to stop by after work, he heads out, and I am left sitting here at the bar, my mouth nearly smiling.

The days pass by slowly, though I am glad they are uneventful. The tavern is back to normal in less time than I expected, and other than the scorch marks below the window, no lingering sign remains of the night that killed all those men. I see an occasional tinge of sadness in Shell's eyes when Fergus's son stops by to pick up money or food. I have been giving her some of my winnings each evening to send along as well. The boy is a tangle of gangly limbs and bright red hair with a face so similar to his father's that it hurts a bit to see. He seems like a good kid. Next time he visits, I will slip him some extra coin when I can, just for him. Becoming the man of the house has to be hard for a boy that young.

This morning the ship Godrick is taking me to pulled into port, and I am off-kilter. Is this what it feels like to be nervous? I take my time styling my hair, braiding back the front section and pinning it behind my ear, and I apply a small amount of rouge to my lips. There are very few women in Konidas who share my skin tone, so it is difficult to find cosmetics, but my complexion is clear. I think I look beautiful, though perhaps still intimidating. The deep blue of the dress looks like a bottomless lake against my skin, and my eyes have never looked this bright. Godrick arrives to escort me to the ship a little before sunset, and we walk down the docks holding hands as the light fades into a pink and orange glow. The ship is moored at a dock a bit far down from the tavern, but the evening is balmy and warm, and the walk is comfortable. There is a sturdy gangplank leading from the dock to the deck of the ship, and Godrick places his hand on the small of my back as he guides me across the narrow passage. The ship is strangely quiet, and I look around for any crew or staff and see no one.

"Did you reserve the entire ship?" I ask.

Godrick looks confused as he, too, glances around the empty deck. We walk around with trepidation, my enhanced hearing picking up no sound other than the lapping of the waves against the wooden hull.

"Godrick, I do not hear anything," I breathe.

He grips me a little tighter. We locate the stairway leading to the lower deck, and Godrick walks a step ahead of me. His sharp intake of breath sounds like cannon fire in the silent room. Every sailor is in this room, and they are all dead.

Godrick makes as if to rush to the men to check if they are alive, but I hold him back.

"They are not breathing," I tell him plainly. "None of them."

We walk around the room, careful not to touch any of the bodies. Man after man lay in crumpled heaps across the benches, chairs, and floor. I lean down, inspecting them, and notice a strange purple stain around their mouths, every single one. There is an unpleasant smell in the air I cannot quite identify, slightly botanical and astringent. It is almost like the smell of cut flowers, left to rot in a vase. As we walk around the lower deck, the smell becomes overwhelming, and I pull the edge of my cloak over my face.

"What is it?" Godrick asks.

"You cannot smell it?" He shakes his head. "It smells terrible. I cannot place it, but it smells disgusting." He furrows his brow.

We find a small doorway leading down to a lower area of the ship, and Godrick pauses in the doorway and looks to me. I nod and we head below. The lower hull of the ship is packed with hundreds of crates. None of them bear any marking except for a stamp I recognize as a mark from Minos'Idyl. The stench down here is so intense that I gag against my cloak, nearly vomiting. I flick out a claw and use it to pry the lid off the nearest crate. It is filled with flowers, thousands of dark purple flowers. I pluck one from the crate and turn it in my fingers gently, careful not to crush it. It has six petals and defined ochre-colored stamens in the middle coated in bright pollen. They are wilted, but not dried, as if they were packed shortly after picking.

I hold it up to Godrick. "Have you seen anything like this before?"

He shakes his head. "Flowers?" He reaches out his hand, but I pull it back out of his reach.

"All those men, their mouths were stained with this color. Do not touch it; it may be poisonous."

"But why? They're the ones transporting them. Wouldn't they know if they were poisonous?"

I shrug. "I am not sure. I do not know what is happening here, but I do not wish to remain."

He nods in agreement, and we make no sound as we walk up to the deck. When we are back outside, I can breathe again, and I take a few deep gulps of ocean air. The stench of the ship feels sticky and thick in my nostrils. We head back toward the gangplank, but cannot locate it. My eyes narrow. We did not remove it, and I have not heard a soul on this ship. I walk the length of the deck railing, but it is nowhere to be seen. My skin prickles as if someone is watching me, and I look around but see no one.

"We need to leave," I say under my breath.

His face is a picture of concern. "How do we get off this boat without the gangplank?"

"I think I can fly us," I say resolutely. "Do not scream."

The extent of my true strength pleases me as I slide my hands beneath his arms and lift us off the deck, cloak rippling. My cloak seems to extend, a portion of it wrapping about Godrick. The color of my dress fades into the now dark sky, and we vanish as I take flight. It is an odd sensation, carrying someone while flying. I feel ungainly and awkward, but I get us back to the docks and touch down safely on quiet feet. We do not speak as we walk back to the tavern, unsure of who may be listening. For the first time, I direct Godrick up to my apartment, and we sit on my bed. As the adrenaline from the situation ebbs, my irritation returns.

"What was that?" I ask, feeling foolish sitting here in my elegant dress.

"I honestly have no idea," he replies. "I have never seen anything like that."

"Do you think we should ask Cartwright?" I ask.

Godrick replies, "Do you trust him?"

I reply with no hesitation, "Yes."

KANITOSH WOODS

CHAPTER TWENTY-SEVEN
JYNN
YEAR 993

Ceci disappears into the cottage, and I dash through the verdant woods. In our brief moment of planning, we agreed our best bet was to separate so she could draw him out and I could attack from behind. Farragen hates me, but he also underestimates me. Ceci is sweet and soft—traits I've never had; if anyone can lure that wicked man, it is her. Leaving her side tears at something within me. I hate knowing she is alone with him, but I know Ceci needs to save her mother.

Despite everything that has occurred, Mamère is good. She could have left me to die in the snow, but she saved me and brought me up alongside her own child. She sacrificed much to provide for me as well. She taught me to be kind and caring, to be gentle but strong. Mamère has shaped me just as much as the blood in my veins. I may be human, but she has been a mother to me in all ways which count.

I hear muffled sounds coming from Farragen's cottage, but I can't discern the words. Ceci's voice rings out above Farragen's, and I hear the anguish in her tone. I don't need to know what she is saying to know what she feels. I ache to run to her, to fight whatever battle she faces. I promised I would always find her, and I mean that more than anything I have ever said. A sound like lightning rips through the cottage, a strange crackling like nutshells in a fire. I strain to see inside, but they must be further in the building. Smoke filters through the thatched roof, and my heartbeat skips and sputters. I need to get to her.

Racing toward the cottage, I aim for the back door we discussed, praying she is inside and safe, but the door swings open before I get to it. Smoke swirls out from behind a dark figure as Farragen steps from the doorway. There is something wrong with his eyes. His hand is stained a deep purple, and his eyes crease with pain. He limps forward slightly, and I prepare to charge past him, but the shadows shift and somehow he is upon me.

His fingernails clutch at my skin leaving half moons of broken flesh beneath their yellowed grasp. He kicks my knees out from under me, grabbing my hair with snakelike speed, and hurls me upward, smiling grotesquely. My scalp feels like paper, threatening to rip from my skull as he grips me by the hair. My skin crawls from the contact. His disgusting gnarled fingers feel like teeth. I didn't even see him move as he grabbed me by the hair and lifted me off the ground. There's no way such a frail frame could lift me like this. I outweigh him by at least two stone.

"*Murderer!*" His voice booms across the glade, reverberating in my head. "*Sinner!*" Fauns rush from their homes to stare at the spectacle before them. "This *creature*, this abhorrent outsider has corrupted one of your own!" The villagers look around in confusion. "Because of this vile creature, one of your own is dead *at the hands of her own child*!" He pauses for a moment before hissing, "*Where is Mamère?*"

I am drenched in sweat, but I shiver from the emotion that is close to drowning me. *Ceci. Where the fuck is Ceci?* Maybe she went out the other door. She had to. And where is Mamère? I search for Cicerine, struggling to find her cinnamon hair in the teeming crowd. And then I hear her voice. She's shouting toward the crowd, but instead of listening, I see them begin to throw rocks toward her, pelting her with hatred one by one.

My beautiful girl, still lovely to me as stones fly from the hands of the disgusting, zealot fauns. Her eyes are alight with rage and hurt. Another rock hits her, and I see blood trickle down her cheek. I don't care if it kills me; I don't care if I die. I have to get to Ceci. I kick at Farragen, certain my height will give my legs the leverage I need to break free. My fingers scrabble against his, and I can feel my fingernails gouging skin from his hands. He doesn't even flinch, staring ahead with those dead eyes of his, emanating a rage and hatred that tastes putrid in my throat. His oily stink sticks to my nostrils. I'm drowning in sheer repulsion. Again and again I fling my body against Farragen's grip, but he possesses some sort of inhuman strength, and I can't get loose. A feral growl escapes me as I writhe and shake and struggle against him. I will snap his fucking neck. He is going to die. I know he is shouting something to the villagers, but the roaring dread in my brain drowns out all sound. Without warning, he drops me, and I hit the parched earth in a tumble of limbs.

I clamber to my feet, my hands twitching with the need to wrap my hands around his thin bobbing throat, but then I hear the words dripping from his foul lips—"WE MUST CLEANSE THE GLADE!"

I know what this means; I know Ceci's life is forfeit. If I kill him now, she will be dead before I can get to her. He's tricked all these fauns into believing his disgusting fucking lies. Their *faith* is killing my Ceci. My Sunbeam, fuck. If I kill him, it will only confirm what he's told them. They'll murder her in cold blood for their "god." I beg the universe for strength. Please, grant me the strength to get through this.

She looks to me, and I meet her gaze. *Please don't fight, Ceci,* I beg her in my mind as I give her a small shake of my head. *I am coming for you.* My life without Ceci is a pile of leaves in the fall, nothing of worth or value, just the remnants of something once beautiful.

I race for the trees. If I can get through the woods and come out of the trees close to her, I can grab her and run. The woods are thick, dense trees still heavy with summer leaves. The paths between them are narrow, but I know them with an intimacy few share. I've lived in these trees, spent years dodging Farragen and longing for somewhere to belong. I've been an outsider in my own home for as long as I have lived. Without Ceci, I cannot belong here. This will be difficult, but I am quick. My legs are long, and I am taller and stronger than any of the fauns. I stare through the trees toward Ceci. Gauging the distance, I estimate the most effective location from which to burst through the brush, grab her, and get back into the forest without having to stop and lose momentum. I have to be like a fox. I can do this. I cannot live without her. I cannot let her go. I peer through the brush lining the edge of the clearing, spotting her cinnamon curls amidst the chaos. I nearly vomit as I see countless rocks smack into her small frame. There's so much blood. They're killing her. The crowd of fauns seems to delight in this, rocks flying from their hands at a frenzied pace.

Time stops as I see her fall. Her bright eyes roll back in her head, and she collapses. The sound of her soft body hitting the ground tears my soul in two. Her soft pink dress is smeared with blood, like a peony crushed underfoot. Whimpering sounds reach my ears from my hiding place in the trees, and I shake with agonizing fury. How can I get to her? To gather her in my arms and run us out of this fucking disaster; this horror that has befallen the glade.

The teeming, crazed mob surrounds her, continuing to hurl rocks at her slumped form. The villagers closest to her are kicking, punching, beating her. Their screams don't sound like words, but the sounds of beasts. Some sort of pure chaos has infected those who were once our neighbors. We taught their children, baked them bread. I see the apiarist among the throng, and I retch, knowing the countless days I spent beside him, his hands gentle with the small bees, the way he spoke to them with a quiet voice. He was tender; he felt genuine sorrow at the loss of even a single queen bee, but yet there he stands bludgeoning an innocent girl to death. Blood leaks from her mouth. I see it drip to the dirt with fat, wet drops. Hooves batter her as she lies curled on the ground. I try to scream, but nothing comes out except a choked, gasping cry.

One faun grabs her by the hair and drags her sagging body toward a post jutting from the charred remains of the schoolhouse. Others pile straw and branches around it, shoving them into her soft flesh, tearing at her sweet skin. The faun flings her at the post like a parcel of garbage, and she crumples into a bloody pile. I watch her chest, silently beseeching any god who can hear me *to please let her breathe*. Time ticks by. Minutes or seconds, I have no way of knowing. But her chest remains still. She doesn't move at all, a broken, beautiful doll amidst ugly hatred. I vomit into the grass. They've killed her. The only person I have ever loved is dead.

KONIDAS

CHAPTER TWENTY-EIGHT
SHELL
YEAR 993

Maelwen and the terrified lookin' boy walk downstairs, clearly shaken. I know they were seein' each other tonight, but it is far too early for them to be back so soon. I wonder what the fuck could have happened up in her apartment to cause such obvious unease. Maelwen heads across the tavern floor to Cartwright and whispers in his ear. He jerks upright when she's through, standin' at attention so rigidly that I wonder if he's ever been a soldier. Mael catches my eye, and I gesture for them to come over here. She actually allows Godrick to hold her hand, and they walk over with steps too quick to be casual. She sounds nervous as she says, "We need to talk."

Their story is fucking insane. It sounds like a bedtime story to frighten naughty children. A ghost ship filled with nothin' but dead men and crates of purple flowers? What the fuck? Cartwright has connections with some dockworkers, so he pulls one of his men to stand in for him in the cardroom and heads out to see what he can find. The look on his face as he leaves is one of well-controlled fear. He's been in this city for as long as I have, and I know all this recent bullshit weighs heavily on him. I push two shots of whiskey across the bar to the witch and the boy, and they shoot them back immediately. Day by day it seems we find more and more things to be worried about. This city isn't what it was when I was a child. Back then, all you had to worry about was shakeroot junkies and gettin' mugged. Now there's cults and ships of dead folks and gods know what else.

"Let's keep our mouths shut until we can find out what Cartwright hears," I tell them both. "No use gettin' involved in business that ain't ours."

They both nod, and I refill their glasses. It's always somethin' in this damn city.

Cartwright doesn't return for a long time, and when he does, his face is grim.

"There is no ship moored at the end of the dock." He rubs his temples in confused frustration. "Shift turnover was an hour ago, and all my men were gone. I have a bad feelin' about all this, but I don't know how else to look into it. I stopped by Eddard's house, but nobody answered. He's one of my best fellas on day shift. I can't imagine where he'd be if he ain't here or home with the missus. But I seen those flowers in the water. Looks like some of 'em didn't disappear with the ship. Prob'ly twenty or thirty, floatin' in the water at the end of the dock. I don't like it one bit. Where the fuck does a whole damn ship get off to?"

The boy's face is pale. "The captain was at the tailor's shop just this morning. I spoke with him directly. I know he was here in town, but I didn't look closely on the ship. I don't know if he was one of the bodies we saw. I'm sorry. There was so much going on, and I just wanted to get Maelwen someplace safe. Hell of a first date." He looks sad, and I feel for the kid—not the best impression.

Cartwright looks at each of us before sayin', "We need to keep this quiet. Until I can find someone who saw somethin', this doesn't leave this room. I don't know what is goin' on, or how a ship of that size could jus' vanish in such a short time, but I don't feel good about it. I have a real bad feelin' 'bout this whole mess." He holds out a balled handkerchief to Maelwen. "I grabbed a couple of these. I don't know a damn thing about flowers, but maybe your kin might?"

Some unnamed emotion crosses Maelwen's features before she schools them back into a flat expression. "I do not know who could help, but I will do my best."

He nods. "That's all any of us can do."

THIS MORNIN' I CAN FEEL FALL ON THE WIND. I'M UP BEFORE Maelwen, and I really hope she's sleepin'. I slept like shit, kept poppin' up to look out the window. Every sound had me on my feet. When I finally got my ass downstairs, there was a hint of cool in the air, and I made a pot of hot coffee. My head aches from lack of sleep and excess of thought. I haven't been home to see Ma and Pap in a couple days, and I'm honestly a bit glad. I don't want to bring stress into their lives; they have enough to handle. And I'm worn thin as it is. I'm sittin' behind the bar with a hot mug nestled in both hands when Cartwright comes in, pale as death.

"All my men are gone, every man I knew on day shift—none of them made it home last night. None. I thought it was just Eddard, but it's all of 'em. I walked to six houses, all 'round the city: Lucius, Alfred, everyone. The men with women at home? Fuck, they're petrified. They're good men, Shell. I need to know where they went."

I don't say a single word as I snag a bottle of brandy from the top shelf and tip a hearty pour into my cup, then grab a mug of coffee and do the same for him. We don't need to discuss this. We communicate just fine without words. I ain't gettin' myself involved in this shit. It's not knockin' at my door yet, and I have plenty on my plate already, but I know Cartwright will do the right thing and look for those men. Mael and the boy know not to run their mouths, and in the meantime, Cartwright will keep an ear to the sea and shoes to the street. All we can do is wait.

The sun is halfway across the sky by the time Maelwen comes down the stairs and into the tavern. Business is slow but steady this mornin', and I'm glad for it. The routine in this place alive keeps me goin', and I don't have time to get lost in my own head. The witch's eyes are bloodshot, but she has that look of stoic determination on her face. She sits, and I pass her a cup of the now lukewarm coffee and gesture toward the brandy with a shrug. She nods, and I top her off with a glug.

"I think I should go to Iowain," she says. "I think there are witches at the tower who could tell me what this is." She pats her pocket where I'm guessin' she has the flowers.

"You think that's wise?" I'm not sure of the witches. I've spoken to a few here and there, but I've never known one aside from her. And it doesn't take much to know that she's different.

"It will take me a week to go there and be back. I might find out what these are. At best, maybe someone knows what is going on here. There are too many whispers. This place has become my home. I do not want anything else to happen to the tavern due to my presence."

I open my mouth to tell her not to be a fuckin' martyr, but she cuts me off.

"I know you will say the bar fight was not my fault, but I do bear some responsibility, whether you like it or not. I will do what I can to keep you safe."

I hate it, but I know I can't stop her; it's her choice to make and clearly it's been made. "Would you mind sniffin' around town before you go?" I ask her. "Cartwright's friends at the docks are nowhere to be found, and he's nervous. That ship had to have gone somewhere, all that cargo...I doubt it just vanished into thin air. Maybe you'll pick up somethin' we missed."

She nods curtly and dons her cloak, headin' out the door without a word, her lips pressed into a sharp line.

KANITOSH WOODS

CHAPTER TWENTY-NINE
CICERINE
YEAR 993

Bile rises in my throat, bitter and burning, before a sob wracks my body and a scream escapes me. A rough, primal, unbearable scream. Mamère lies before me, still, stained with that purple paste.

I shake her, softly at first, but then violently, screaming, *"Mamère! Mama!"* again and again. She's still in my arms and I unhand her shoulders, loss tearing a void in my chest that I cannot find the bottom of. My body shakes uncontrollably, and I stand, frozen. But the quiet is torn apart by a scream from outside, and I whip my head toward the door. I run, knowing that scream. Jynn's scream.

As I emerge from the doorway, all eyes shoot to me, and I open my mouth to shout, to scream the truth, but the crowd stares back with a virulent gaze clearly filled with hate, though I've done nothing to warrant it. Farragen stands, gripping Jynn by the hair, screaming to the fauns gathered around him. His eyes find me and I can see the words forming on his lips. *"Where is Mamère?"*

I yell as loudly as I can toward my neighbors, "You *know* me! All of you know me! Please, listen to me! My mama is dead." I choke on a sob before regaining my voice. I scream, "It was Farragen! *He* killed her! *He* poisoned her!"

But no one looks at him; their eyes stay fixed on me. Our neighbor bends to the ground and picks up a heavy rock, throwing it and striking me in the face. Blood trickles from my split cheek and I scream at the pain. Another stone strikes me and then another. As if floating underwater, I can hear a distant muffled cry of encouragement from Farragen. I hear the village shout my name as they lob stones toward me. My hand explodes in pain, and I hear a rock strike my horns.

"WE MUST CLEANSE THIS GLADE!" Farragen bellows, and he drops Jynn to the ground. I see her fall through my rapidly swelling eyelids. She hits hard, shakes her head, and runs for the trees. My eyes ache with the pressure of tears that don't fall. The next faun to hurl a stone is one I made soup for last winter when he was ill. Beside him stands a faun whose child I taught to count. My mind reels from the shock of everything happening. My knees buckle as I collapse onto the earth, feeling my skin tear as I hit the ground. My spiraling panic is ended with the impact of another sharp pain to my arm. I curl in on myself, my body going numb to the agony as my thoughts tumble through my mind.

Jynn and I were supposed to stay together. The world moves around me, but for a moment my mind slows, working through the painful realization. I thought the loss of Mamère was the summit of this mountain of agony. I thought that were we to escape this place of horrors, Jynn and I could at least lean on one another and slowly find contentment once again. But my heart is decimated. My soul is reduced to a whisper of smoke as all the love I held burns to ash. Jynn fled. I can't recall a moment without her. She held my hand when I scraped my first knee. We shared cake on every birthday. She was my first kiss, my first touch, my first love. I gave her my whole heart, and she ran. Jynn ran. Is she coming back for me? Why didn't she do as we planned? Why would she leave me here? Rock after rock, stone after stone. I feel feet and fists pound into my limbs and then I hear nothing at all.

Everything hurts. I can barely open my left eye, and a finger on my right hand is clearly broken, splayed at an unnatural angle. I am tied to a post before the remains of the schoolhouse. Tinder surrounds me, piles of straw and wool and small branches. With bleary eyes, I lift my head and see most of the village looking back. Flashes of recollection play through my mind. They stoned me. My own people. They hurled rocks at me and beat me until I lost consciousness, and they dragged me here and tied me to this post. And Jynn—Jynn ran. Where is Jynn? She cannot be gone. Tears sting my cut and swollen cheeks. I look frantically to the treeline, praying to see her there, preparing to save me. She has to save me, she would never leave me. But she isn't there. I am alone. Jynn is gone, and now I am going to die.

My wrists are tied to the post with sisal rope, rough and chafing against my skin. I am seated against the half-sunken log, and my legs, extended before me, are bruised and battered. Blood is smeared across my dress, and I can feel I am missing a back tooth from behind my dry, split lips. They beat me, they stoned me. They want me dead. I gave them so much. I have never raised a hand against them, harmed no one, and spent my life as a kind person. I blindly followed Farragen, gave my heart to Idyth. I taught their children, I grew their food. My mother, oh gods, my mother, she is dead and I will be soon. What has this man done to my village? How has a single man decimated my entire world?

For too long, I have served others and never once questioned why no one did the same for me. I gave and gave, never questioning why I didn't receive in kind. I shared my heart and soul with them all, and it was taken with nothing given in return. I think of the eyes of my neighbors as they stoned me, the beekeeper and parents of the children I taught. I think of the kindnesses I granted them throughout my life. Slowly, I feel my eyes go hot with rage. How dare they? Not today. Not me.

There is no way Farragen bound me himself; maybe he thought I was already dead. The rope is not nearly tight enough. I twist my hands toward the earth and smile as I feel dry, but living grass beneath my palms. I smile as I let the rage build in my core. My heartbeat feels steady and strong, and I use its rhythm to unwrap my power from the pale-green coil I picture resting in my chest. I take a deep breath…and release it all.

In less than a second, the surrounding ground is charred and smoking. My rope bindings fall away as I stand. The tinder surrounding me flashes ablaze, but I step from the flames unscathed. I stride from the fire like a demon of the abyss. Blackness shoots out in bolts of malice, singeing the hooves of the villagers closest to me. They fall to their knees, and the scorching soil bubbles their flesh, chars their hair. They fall, screaming, and the earth burns them alive. I feel no remorse for them. They secured their deaths the moment they turned on me in the name of faith. They chose their path. I can feel each plant and root beneath my feet—a network of death and destruction. I see the thousands of intersecting and branching lines in my mind's eye as clearly as the venation of a maple leaf. I stalk toward Farragen, palms like molten stone, and he catches my stare. The black of his robes seems to absorb the sunlight. His onyx eyes are odious pits. The waxy, sallow skin on his face shifts into a foul smile. I swear he lets out a laugh before, with reptilian grace, he turns toward the forest and vanishes into shadow. I roar, drowning out the dying cries of the villagers. I scream for Mamère, I scream for Jynn, I scream for the vengeance I will have.

I scream his death into the world.

Konidas

CHAPTER THIRTY
MAELWEN
YEAR 993

The bite of fall in the air cuts through the stench of the sea as I head into town. I need my senses sharp, for both tracking the missing men and crates, and the flight I intend to take to Iowain soon. I do not typically hunt during the day but my skin itches with the need to express some of my emotion, and I can feel my cloak's hum flagging. It has been too long. I head away from the main thoroughfare, not wanting to draw any attention to myself, and I end up on a quiet street full of refuse and shoddy homes. I have never been in this area before, and the sight of these shacks makes me mildly uncomfortable. These are not just the poorer citizens of Konidas, these are people who wish to live away from the eyes of the busy docks. Plenty of these houses have something to hide.

I walk silently along the street staying to the side of the lane, attempting to blend in as best I can. A wisp of smoke in the air draws my attention, followed by an acrid and slightly familiar smell. It is not shakeroot; I have smelled that particular smoke enough in back alleys to know it with some familiarity, but still...I follow the odor as it gently slides on the breeze, and before long I am standing before a particularly dilapidated house with planks falling off the sides into piles of overgrown brush. I make no sound as I walk around the side of the house, peering through the fallen slats.

A man sits in the center of the decaying room, leaning over a small brazier. The tendrils of smoke drifting from the coals are thick as they slither up his nose and into his mouth. His eyes are glassy and unseeing, and his hands reach up and grasp for things only he can see. Strange sounds come from him, grunts and moans and growls that do not sound quite human. I sniff the air again and catch another whiff of an odd bitter smell. It is right there in my mind—just beyond my reach. I know that smell. I take one more deep breath and, without warning, darkness claims me.

My eyes open to nothing, black. I turn my head, looking for any sort of light and find only darkness. Have I gone blind? My hands grope below me, and I feel nothing. Just a vast, empty plane, devoid of light or sound. I breathe deeply and smell nothing. I hear nothing but my own heartbeat pounding in my chest. Where had I been? My thoughts are murky and tangled. I sort through the swampy pit of my mind, searching for a single light of memory.

Like the smallest flame sparking, things begin to come into shaking focus slowly. The house, the man, the brazier. Images flit through my mind as I recall the last moments before this endless black. There is an odd thrum to this place as if it has a pulse of its own. A heartbeat in the black. I take a step forward, and to my surprise, my body indeed moves. It is strange, to feel no earth beneath me, but I walk forward regardless. I do not know how long I walk. This place seems out of sync with time, another thing lost to the void. But after a while, a faint glow appears in the distance, and I head toward it.

As I get closer to the light in the distance, a low howl sounds, like the wind over mountains. My skin prickles, and my hair stands on end. My body responds to the sound unbidden, as if it belongs to me. I cock my head to hear it more clearly, and I swear I can almost make out words. Like witchsong, the sound seems to resonate in my chest, building a pressure within me that aches for release, and notes of my own pour from my mouth. The glow ahead pulses with my heartbeat as I sing, my song low and deep. The words leaving my mouth are unknown to me. I have never heard this tongue, but I feel the shape of them on my lips, familiar as a kiss. I close my eyes, listening to the sounds merge, the way the notes lay on top of one another and dance up and down in a strange haunting harmony. The sounds have a color to them: blues and purples and a warm, deep brown. A discordant dip slides the color to a peridot green, but it rises back up, effortlessly, from teal to blue once more. It is beautiful, a painting of sound, dancing in the air of my mind. I have never experienced such a sensation, but it feels like home. The notes drift to a soft end, the colors fading into mist in the dark, but I do not feel its loss; I feel as if it has come to its true end. I nearly cry with the satisfaction I feel in my heart. When I open my eyes, I see her. *The Crone.*

    I am at once in a large room crafted from roughly hewn stone. The floor is worn smooth, the walls made from massive stone blocks stacked up to high, vaulted ceilings. There is a small window behind me with thick velvet curtains covered in a thick layer of dust. The room feels old, empty—it feels like a tomb. She sits before me in a wooden chair, looking with milky eyes. Her hair is long enough to reach the floor, and she wears it loose over her shoulders. Every part of her—her skin, her hair, her clothing—is the color of ash. She closes her lips, and I realize it was *her* song dancing through me. The air here is cold, but the sunlight filtering through the window is clear and bright. Wherever I am, it is late summer, as it is in Konidas. There are rows and rows of books along the far wall and a rug on the floor, which once was finely made, but now looks old and faded with time. The Crone is still, so still that I do not even see her chest rise and fall with breath.

Her eyes do not leave my face as she speaks, "How has this come to pass?" I do not know how to respond. I am speechless. I stand before the most powerful witch in all of existence, dumbstruck. "Do not fear me." Her quiet voice is melodic. "I did not call to you, but I felt you, lost, and so I guided you out of the dark."

"Where am I?" I do not recognize this place; I see a city outside of the window but it is not Iowain. The roofs are crafted from terracotta tile, and the streets appear clean and bright. People stroll the roadways in brightly colored finery and horse-driven carriages roll over cobblestone paths. This is a place of wealth, a place of nobles. I do not belong in such a place. "How did I come to be here?"

Her pale gray eyes narrow slightly as she replies, "You are in the castle. In Athydis."

Confusion and disbelief war in my mind. Athydis? Moments ago I walked the streets of Konidas, and yet by some insanity or magic, I have awoken in Athydis?

"Is this a dream?" I ask the Crone.

"Of sorts," she says in a smooth, dark voice. "You are here, and you are there."

I shake my head, trying to understand. "My body is in Konidas, but my consciousness is here?" She nods. "What brought me here?" I press, feeling emboldened.

"This," she says as she folds her hands in her lap, "I do not know."

There are no other chairs in this room, but I wish for one as my knees quiver. There is much for me to bear—in mind and body alike. The memory of the dancing colored witchsong keeps gliding through my mind. I am overwhelmed. As if sensing my thoughts, the Crone raises her long, clawed fingers and with a flick of her wrist, a chair appears before me. I stand and stare, blinking, and she gestures for me to sit. The chair is solid beneath me, feeling like any other chair. I can feel the wood beneath my fingers and the stone beneath my feet, this all feels completely real.

When the Crone speaks, I listen as if compelled. "Twenty-one years ago, I completed my descent, ceased to be the witch I was, and was born anew. The plains of Iowain, the tower, all lands our kin have laid claim to for millennia—they are all crumbling. We have long lived on the outskirts of great civilizations, long have we been quiet. Our territory is small when this entire world exists beneath the control of weak humans and dense primitive creatures. I am not content to spend my vast existence in this body as the leader of a scattered people. I am not content to watch my people slink quietly through the dark and never live in light. I can only guess you have been brought here to hear my message, to know the truth I work toward, even now. I have spent years here in this castle building the foundations of an empire. The Crone before me fell into madness before my ascension, but she possessed the gift of foresight. She left me tomes, volumes of words, words that even I have not yet begun to decipher. I have only pieces, weaving a basket of knowledge with each new prophecy I uncover. I cannot yet know what this basket is meant to hold; I know only of the events which may come to pass. I see visions through the eyes of the forest, see gifts that have yet to bloom, but I know of three truths spoken to me by the Crone before me. We have waited for them, and I believe that soon they will come to pass."

"What are these truths?"

"A witchling has been born who carries a gift long lost to time. Should that gift be revealed, it will face a darkness made of man. There is a woodborn babe who is tied indelibly to my lifesthread.

I know not how or who, but they cannot be lost. There is a child of the sea who can speak with the waves. The nereids who have long yet slumbered will awaken, though, I have yet to see for what purpose they rise. This is a time of change, a catalyst, and I have taken what I can from the minds of the mortal rulers of this kingdom. I hold much within, the threads unravel more with each passing season. And now, as I ponder the next steps to take toward our future, a witchling appears before me unbidden, carried through darkness and song? I can smell your blood, witchling. I know who you are."

My heartbeat threatens to crack my ribs, and I struggle to keep from shaking. "Who am I?"

The Crone's milky eyes go glassy, and she raises one clawed hand with unnatural slowness as she opens her mouth.

The sound that comes from her lips is a scream that rends my mind in two.

Part 2

ATHYDIS

CHAPTER THIRTY-ONE
THE CRONE
YEAR 981

*S*he knows she once had a name, and if she tries, she can remember it. However, it fades more with each passing day like smoke through her fingers. Since completing her descent, the power at her disposal has become a vast, unending well. She can reach down into the Chaos and pull forth whatever her mind desires. She no longer has need for flight. Her mind is unfettered and can travel on the winds to all corners of this world. She has watched the creatures of the deserts, the spirits of the sea, and her people below as they struggle to survive. Humankind is a virus—insidious and opportunistic. Whereas her people once stood tall and proud, they now live scattered and isolated—weak in power and in ambition. The Crone before her was indolent, content to sit in the tower and ignore the realities of the world outside until her mind became tangled and wild. But she is different.

The witches have what the humans and other beasts do not—Chaos magic. Each witch, her own frequency, tapping into magic that is hers alone. There are shared gifts, but each witch possesses her own skills as well. She can feel each witch, the web of power connecting them all, the vast network of Chaos that flows through their veins.

Chaos magic is infinite, non-corporeal in a way, alive insofar as to react to her coaxing of it. She molds it like summer clay, feels the warm slide of it in her hands. She slips it into the castle. It curls about the feet of the monarchy like manacles. It liquifies and seeps into the mind of the king, the mind of the queen. The castle is hers to command, the first step of her plan enacted. First the castle, then the kingdom. Witchkind will rise again.

She feels a ripple in the web of Chaos, a tiny movement from an unexpected place. Her inner eye opens, gazing through countless trees in search of the source. Oddly, this place is free of her kin, populated by simple creatures in a provincial life—but it is here somewhere, that little ripple in the web.

Suddenly alert, her head snaps up. Even while using her inner eye, while watching a place across the sea, she can feel the dark creature who approaches. It is inky black, oily, and slick. A man, yet not a man. He walks among the placid creatures of this place, and they are unaware of that which slithers around them. She possesses the memories of every Crone before her, and somewhere in that vast record there is a twinge of familiarity. Does she know this man? She will think on it later, will pore through the volumes of memory and life to search for this sensation.

The ripple is of little importance now. Perhaps one day it will matter, a connection to Chaos where none should be. But for now, she will leave it to time. She will wait to see if the ripple becomes something more.

KANITOSH WOODS

CHAPTER THIRTY-TWO
JYNN
YEAR 993

Ibolt. I run and run and run. My face is bloody as branches slap my cheeks. My feet are numb, my legs burning with exertion. I keep heaving, thinking of her body on the ground. Thinking of the feel of her beneath my fingers. The taste of her on my lips. Spit flies from my mouth as I retch. I'm not even sure which direction I'm running, I just run.

The muscles in my thighs start to spasm, and I stumble. My body has reached its limit. I don't know how long or how far I've run, but I fall to the ground in utter despair. My body quakes with great wracking sobs. My face becomes muddy as I lie pressed to the dirt, screaming and crying. My filthy shirt sticks to my sweat soaked skin, and I shiver. The canopy of trees is so dense here that I'm unsure of the time of day. I shake and cry, and my body gives up. My eyes close and I lose myself to grief and sleep.

It is dark when I wake. There's no way to discern how long I spent huddled on the forest floor. I piss before spitting a mouthful of dirt and blood from my dry lips. If I'm going to make it out of these woods, I need to find water, and soon I will need food. I take stock of the surrounding trees, all oak and ash. Nothing with fruit or nuts. I don't hear any water, but I know this forest is crisscrossed with streams, so I take a breath and head further into the woods. After a while, the canopy opens and I am able to see the sky. Ceci taught me to navigate by the stars, and I decide to head north. My grief hits me again like a punch to the gut, and I have to brace myself against a tree as massive bellowing sobs pour from me.

I should just die. What is the point? Where will I go? What the fuck do I have to keep going for? Where do I even fit in this world? I've spent my entire existence not fitting in. The faun girls of the glade never accepted me; I was never one of them. I don't even fit in my own skin. I have only been cared for by two people in my entire wretched life, and they are both dead. But I'm a coward, too weak to die. So I continue northward, heading nowhere, anywhere—just out of these godsforsaken woods. If I get out of Kanitosh, I will never come back. I never want to see another tree.

It takes a full three days to reach the outer edge of the forest. Along the way, I've managed to find some fruit and greens, and though my stomach rumbles and cramps, I have enough energy to keep going. I've been following a stream for the last day, trusting it to lead out of the woods. The edge of the treeline is dotted with bramble bushes, and I scratch myself as I push through them. My eyes sting with tears as I think of our secret bathing spot. I nearly fall to my knees, hit with the pain of the memory. Her sweet, soft lips on mine... the best moment of my life. I spent *years* dreaming of that moment, stolen glances at the dinner table, the smell of her skin that day we laid on the forest floor. I built her that stupid rope swing just to hear her musical laughter. I nearly kissed her then; my hands shook the whole afternoon thinking about it. When I pulled her into me and she put her head on my chest, it was a wonder she didn't balk at the rapid metronome of my heartbeat. I have loved her since I was old enough to love. I remember the first time I noticed we weren't kids anymore. Her soft hips swaying as she chopped vegetables. I always made salad just to be close to her. I fucking hate salad. But I would have done anything just to have her arm brush mine in the small kitchen while we cooked.

She's gone. My Sunbeam is gone. How can I face the world? How can I go on knowing I am alive and she is dead? And Mamère, the only mother I've ever known. Mamère saved me from certain death, gave me a home, loved me like she loved her own child. And he took them from me. That one disgusting man took my whole world from me. I'm so fucking broken. This loss pulls at me like a child at their mother's sleeve. I cannot shake it off. The trees feel like a prison, and I'm suddenly claustrophobic, breathing heavy as my heart screams at me to get out. I just want to keep running until my legs give out and my mind gives up. The sounds of the birds in the forest feel like an assault. The world is too much for me right now. Gods, I tried to warn Ceci that something wasn't right. I saw the look in Mamère's eyes when she came home from his cottage. I knew he wasn't what he claimed to be. I should have fought harder. I could have saved us all. Why didn't I fight?

The shore beyond the trees is sandy, and seashells are scattered along the water's edge. Small waves lap against the coast and seabirds squeal as they fly and dive overhead. I can't see anything but trees and shore in either direction, so I just walk to the west. If nothing else, eventually I'll reach Athydis. I don't care where I go or what I do as long as I never have to see Kanitosh again. I come upon a bird's nest hidden in a pile of sand set back from the water. The little sticks that house the eggs were chosen with care, and I feel like an ass for what I'm about to do. It takes me far too long to make a fire, the branches here are all damp. But eventually I get a small campfire going, and I toss the small, speckled eggs into the smoldering coals. I have no idea how long to leave them in the fire. I don't know a thing about cooking, but after a while their shells are blackened, and I fish them out with a stick. I crack the charred shells and peel the eggs, grateful for some protein after my days of eating nothing but fruit. The eggs are slightly smoky, and the yolks are pleasantly creamy. I feel so fucking guilty for enjoying them.

I rise with the sun and pick my way along the shore. It's oddly soothing to walk in silence. I'm able to shut off the roiling sea of my thoughts for a while and focus on my feet. The sand gives slightly beneath my steps; I leave a path of footprints as I walk, a record of my presence for anyone who might come upon them. My steady focus is precisely why I don't notice the tall, looming ship ahead of me until I'm already within viewing range. I freeze as someone shouts in my direction, "OY! You there! Where the fancy fuck do you think you're headed?" My eyes shoot to the bow of the ship where the strangest looking person I have ever seen stands.

I honestly have no idea what I am looking at. The person is wearing men's trousers and a white loose blouse tied up in a knot at the waist, knee-high leather boots with mismatched massive brass buckles glinting in the sunlight, and a hat that appears to depict a large, feathered bird curled in a circle around their head. Their hair is strawberry blonde and cut choppily around their ears, but still falls onto their forehead in stick-straight strands like hay. Their smile is wide despite their words. I lift my hand in an awkward wave. In a ridiculously dramatic gesture, the figure grabs ahold of a large rope and leaps from the side of the ship, swinging above the shallow water and landing with a loud "Ooomph," right in front of me.

In a now recognizably female voice, she bows and says, "Ello there, name's Ballad Rourke, and you've wandered your way into my keep." I'm sure I look like a fish pulled from the sea as my mouth opens and closes while I search for some sort of reply. Ballad stares back at me with humorous confusion written on her features. "Do. You. Talk. Girl?" she asks me slowly, gesturing at me like I don't speak common tongue.

I stutter, "Yeah, uh, yes. Yes, I talk. I'm sorry, you took me by surprise."

She lets out a hearty laugh. "Same could be said of you, lass! Not often a ginger girl washes ashore."

Eyes still wide, I reply, "I can imagine. I didn't know where I was even headed, this…" I gesture at the ship, "Was the last thing I expected to see." What am I doing, having a casual conversation with a random person on the beach? This feels surreal, and I wonder for a moment if I am hallucinating.

"Well." Ballad nods toward the ship. "This is the Sea Song, and I'm her captain. Pleasure to make your acquiescence."

"Acquaintance," I reply.

"Yes, that's what I said."

I'm back to staring. Ballad seems like a very strange person.

She walks back toward the ship and I follow, momentarily forgetting everything else as she points to things and describes them to me with pride. I can't keep up with every feature of the ship as she rattles off information: telling me about the sail, the rigging, the figurehead. The front of the ship features the carved wooden upper body of a generously curvy woman emerging from a spray of water. We clamber up a ladder tossed down the side, and I step onto the deck. The sails are tall and white, patched occasionally with pieces of patterned cloth. Warm, honey-colored wood gleams in the midday sun, and crewmembers busy themselves cleaning and moving various things along the deck. The ship looks like Ballad, quirky but well kept, and I do not spot a single man amongst the crew. They work together effortlessly, clearly comfortable in their roles and with one another. Many of them smile or sing as they work, and the atmosphere is one of camaraderie. I'm taken aback by the unfettered joy of this ship, so different from the somber glade. Thinking of the glade is a blow to my heart, and I have to reach out a hand and steady myself. All at once my tears begin to flow again, and I swallow a sob as I think about Cicerine. Ballad walks nearly twenty steps before noticing I've stopped, and her eyes widen when she sees my face. She quickly jogs back to me and, without a sound, puts an arm around me. The only people to ever hug me or hold me were Ceci and Mamère, and the thought crumbles the small wall containing my emotion. Huge, wracking sobs hit me, and I can no longer stand. Ballad slips to the ground with me, all the while holding me tightly. We sit on the deck together while I cry, held in the arms of a stranger.

I don't know how long I sit on the deck, but eventually I open my swollen eyes and wipe my face with my forearm. The Captain's hand moves in comforting circles across my upper back, and she looks at me with concern. I don't know where to begin, and words just tumble out of my mouth in an avalanche. Ballad listens without saying a thing, just nodding occasionally. I tell her everything: Father Farragen, the fire, Mamère, Ceci, the words pouring out without pause.

When I finish, she draws her hand from my back and sets her elbows on her knees. "Well then, 'spose you wandered to the right beach. This ship ain't much, we ain't rich, and we oftentimes ain't legal, but we're a family—made up of all sorts of folks with nowhere to go. You say you lost everything? Well, you found us. Welcome to the Sea Song.

KONIDAS

CHAPTER THIRTY-THREE
SHELL
YEAR 993

The boy won't stop pacin', and he's drivin' me fuckin' insane. Maelwen didn't return last night, and it is now late afternoon with no sign of the little witch. I've tried to reassure him by telling him she probably just went to Iowain early, but I don't believe it for a moment. She may not be a mushy-gushy girl, but she wouldn't leave without tellin' us. The tension in the bar is so thick I'm about to choke on it, so I pass the boy a bottle and tell Martine to watch the bar. I'm headin' out.

I don't have a clue where Maelwen went, but I'm assumin' she was lookin' for some lowlife to snack on, so I head toward the docks first. I peek in all the alleyways, but there's no sign of her or anythin' else unsavory. I keep walkin', needin' to do somethin' to stay busy before my mind gets away from me. I head toward the sketchy part of town. These houses are fuckin' nasty, full of shakeroot addicts and drunkards, the dregs of Konidas—which is sayin' a lot in a place like this. The sun hangs low in the sky, but it's still bright out, and the whole place stinks like garbage and rot. A great deal of these folks work at the docks, and I know a lot of these houses will be empty, so I don't mind peekin' in some windows here and there. The people who live here rarely have families, just bottles and ramshackle houses. There's a house to my left that used to be blue, but now with all the peelin' paint and bare wood it looks like moldy cheese. I peer in the window as I walk past and don't see anyone inside, so I dare to walk onto the rottin' porch and look through the main window. The house is disgustin' inside. A full chamber pot sits against one wall and piles of filthy clothes lay scattered around the floor. I can smell it from outside. Gaggin', I head to the next house. The next few houses are more of the same, silence and filth. There is an old man in one of the homes, but he's so lost in shakeroot that he doesn't even notice me lookin' through the slats in the side of his shanty. The house next door is in the same condition as all the others, but there are footsteps in the dust on the porch; someone has been here somewhat recently. Once again I sneak around and look inside, and all I can see is a man slumped in the center of the room alongside an extinguished brazier. His chest isn't movin', and his head lays at an unnatural angle. I'd bet money on him being dead. I press my face to the filthy pane of the window, and my heart drops out of my chest. There is an open bag lying on the floor, and from it spills half-dry purple flowers.

    I cover my face with my shirt as I push the door open with my foot. I'm not goin' to touch a damn thing in this place if I can help it. There is a broken crate just inside the door, and it's exactly like Maelwen described it. The stamp of Minos'Idyl on the side is clearly visible, and inside are the remnants of some very wilted purple flowers, close to rottin'. They smell disgustin', like a compost heap in summer, and I smell old smoke in the air as well. The man in the room with the brazier is indeed dead. His face is burnt as if he fell onto the coals, and there are charred remnants of those same purple petals in the metal tray around the coals. So this is what they were doin', smokin' these fuckin' things. I nudge his head with my shoe, and his head flops over completely. Vomit fills my mouth as I gag at the sight of a man with a backwards head, his neck broken. What the fuck?

I don't want to be in this house another minute. Clearly there's somethin' goin' on, and whoever broke this man's neck could be anywhere. So I decide to take one more sweep of the room just to pick up anythin' I might have missed. The crate, the man, the brazier, the fucking neck. There's nothing else here except for an empty water basin and a pile of dirty rags that might be clothes. My nerves are on fire as I head back toward the door to get back to the tavern, and out of the corner of my eye, I spot a small glimmer of blue. *I know that color.* I rush around the side of the house to a pile of overgrown bushes and find Maelwen, unconscious in a tiny little heap. Thankin' the gods she's so small, I bundle her up in my arms and take off at a full run to the tavern.

I'm a strong woman, and Maelwen can't weigh much more than a child, but it's still exhaustin' to run and carry her at the same time. Sweat pours down my face from nerves and exertion, and I start to holler as I get close to the tavern. Martine rushes out, wide-eyed as a doe, and races to me to help carry the little witch inside. We lay her down on the long table in the dinin' room, and I shout for everyone to get out. The look on my face must say enough because no one balks at the request; they turn tail and get the hell out of my bar. She's breathin', but she's out cold, and I have no idea how long she's been unconscious. Martine brings me a wet rag from the bar, and I mop at her little face, hopin' the cold might wake her. She makes a little noise and her face scrunches up, but she doesn't rise. The boy must've headed back to the tailor shop, so I send Leita to go fetch him and a healer while I sit with her. Her small hand feels cool to the touch, but I hold it anyway and talk to her quietly. "Come on little witch, I can't have you dyin' in my bar. It's bad for business."

The healer and the boy fly through the door like hellcats, and he drops into a chair beside her. I tell him what I know and pass a couple of the flowers to the healer. "You ever seen this before?"

She shakes her head, turning the flower over between her fingers. "No, but I can take it with me and ask the other healers, if that's all right with you?"

I nod, and she starts to look over Maelwen. The boy's eyes are wide and scared shitless, so I put a hand on his shoulder. "She's alive. That's the first and most important thing. She's a tough little creature. Let's let the healer do her job."

The healer isn't too familiar with witches, and tells us so, but she doesn't see any injuries or signs of trauma or poisoning. She tells us to keep an eye on her and come fetch her if anythin' changes. We move her upstairs to her own bed and work out a rotation to sit with her.

The boy stays at her bedside 'til after the dinner rush, and I head up to relieve him as soon as I know Leita has the bar handled. I send him downstairs to eat, and I sidle up next to Maelwen on the bed. Her bed is nice as hell—clearly she's replaced the mattress since she moved in, and her covers are all sorts of fancy. There's a stack of books on her bedside table and I pick one up, thumbin' through the pages as I sit and wait for her to do somethin'. My eyes are startin' to close, the day's exhaustion finally hitting me, when she sits up with a start.

She scares the livin' shit out of me, and I nearly fall off the bed. "The Crone," she nearly shouts. "The Crone."

KANITOSH WOODS

CHAPTER THIRTY-FOUR
CICERINE
YEAR 993

It burns, all of it burns. I watch my home smolder, bodies scattered before me on the scorched ground. There aren't any tears to cry, as if they were boiled to steam in the flame of my rage. The air smells like fire and death, and I stand here breathing slowly for a moment, spooling that power back within me, shoving it down deep in my chest where it can rest and be replenished. The village is a wasteland of ruined homes and blackened earth. The forest has gone quiet, and the only sounds I can hear are the crackle of dying embers and the rasp of my breathing. I don't know if anyone survived, if they ran, but the village is empty of life save for me and the bees. I walk toward the smoking remnants of Farragen's house as if in a trance. Most of the roof is gone or collapsed, but his bedroom remains fairly untouched, and my breath catches as I see Mama's body on the bed. She is beautiful, deep plum smeared across her soft face, still and silent on the bed. I cover her with a blanket as though she is only asleep. I brush the soot and ash from her hair and face, trace the familiar curve of her cheeks and nose with a finger. I lay beside her and breathe in her scent, sullied by the foul bite of the pennyway, but still sweet, smelling faintly of bread. I hold her like she held me as a child while curled in the bed of her murderer, alone in the village I've lived my whole life. I lay with her for a while, stroking her mane of curls and talking to her. I tell her how sorry I am, how angry I am. I tell her how much I love her. I tell her about Jynn running away and all the people I killed. I promise her vengeance, though I know she wouldn't want it. I promise to try to bake better now that she is gone. I hold her cold hand and I weep, tears finding me at last. The claws of sorrow tear at my chest like a wild beast, and my soul bleeds. I sit and cry beside her until the well of my grief runs dry.

It takes me hours to bury her. I dress her in her favorite pale yellow dress and clean the purple smudges from her face. I smooth her hair and wrap her in my favorite childhood blanket. It takes me time to carry her out, but I'm gentle and careful, not wanting to jostle her even in death. The place I choose for her is quiet and still green, beneath a tree where we gathered flowers when I was a child. The earth is heavy, and my muscles ache as I dig and dig until I've made a suitable grave for Mamère. The hole in the earth seems too dark for someone like my mama, someone with such a bright soul. The yawning pit is like a mouth, aching to devour everything I once had, everything I love. I should have loved her better.

When it is done, and her small bundle lies nestled in the earth, I dig up some nearby flowers and plant them above her. She would like knowing that she rests beneath growing things. I will them to bloom, my power gently coursing through me, opening the blossoms wide and full. If only my power could bring her back as well, I would give anything to have that gift. The earth here is rich and loamy, and it takes only minutes for me to coax the grass back over the grave. It's as if she was never here. No one but me will ever know my whole world is buried in this ground. I am numb inside, this final task done. My sadness gives way to an icy numbness. I gather some clothes and the last two loaves of Mamère's bread I will ever eat. I don't take the last jar of honey; I don't want to think about Jynn. I don't want to think about anything ever again.

I head south. Konidas is maybe a week or two from here on foot, and the warm summer will make it easier to sleep outdoors, at least for a few days. I can feel the bite of the approaching fall in the air. I have a blanket and a couple changes of clothing, a waterskin and what food I can carry. Fortunately, I can force the trees to fruit, so food will not be an issue for me. I do not know what I will do when I reach Konidas, but it is the only place near enough to go. I cannot remain here. The sun beats down on my shoulders as I walk, the smell of smoke fading and the steady clop of my hooves on earth keeping time with the beat in my chest. The sounds of the forest surround me as I say goodbye to the only life I have ever known.

My heart is numb; I feel like I am seeing through someone else's eyes. I sleep under the stars and wake up to cheeks wet with tears. During the day, I go through the motions: my legs move me forward, I eat, I drink, I walk. But at night, I can't escape the faces of the people I have lost. Jynn's red hair disappears into the trees, Mamère's eyes fade, Jynn's lips press against mine, I hand Mamère a loaf of bread, over and over again. I cannot bring myself to bathe in the streams I pass despite the layer of soot and grime still coating my skin. My muscles ache, but I move onward, making my way slowly toward Konidas.

I have never left the glade, but I know if I stick to the coast and move due east, I will hit Konidas. There are different birds here than at home, large sea birds with wingspans as wide as I am tall. In the evening, large crabs scuttle ashore and dig in the sand. The plant life is also new to me, but I discover a new facet of my botanurgy—the ability to sense if a fruit or flower is safe. It happens accidentally when I come upon a bush of plump berries and collect a few to eat. They feel wrong in my hand, my magic recoiling away from them as if in fear. In the morning there is a red, raw line where it has touched my skin. Fortunately, I have come across plenty of edible fruits since, including a large green fruit with creamy white flesh. I pack a few of them in my bag and make note of the shape of the tree's leaves so I can identify it when it is no longer fruiting.

There are ships in the distance, massive things with tall white sails and gleaming wooden hulls. I have never seen anything so large. The people aboard the ships look like ants in the distance. Everyone else, living their lives, all unaware that I live too. The ships are far bigger than any of the buildings in the glade—even the schoolhouse. Thinking of the schoolhouse hurts, remembering the sweet eyed children I taught. I hope they escaped my wrath. My soul could never recover from taking the life of a child. I saw the bodies of their parents, but I refuse to feel regret. I will not regret protecting myself.

The Sea

CHAPTER THIRTY-FIVE
JYNN
YEAR 993

The Sea Song stays moored for a week before pulling anchor and heading back to sea. I work alongside the crew, being helpful when I can, and spending my evenings wrapped up in my misery. I spend the first three hours of our journey to the open ocean hurling my guts into a bucket. Who knew being in a boat on the rolling waves would reduce me to a blubbering pile of puke and sweat? Certainly not me. Luckily, Ballad had some candied ginger root, and chewing it eases my roiling stomach enough for me to find my equilibrium and stop projectile vomiting at every wave. The other crew members didn't laugh at me as I expected. Instead, they surprise me by being kind and understanding. One woman, an older lady named Georgette, brings a cool cloth for my forehead and dumps my bucket for me. The small action makes me think of Mamère, but I am able to hide my tears with my retching. The crew of the ship are a well-oiled machine, working together seamlessly. I was correct about there being no men among them, and it's comforting after being in the glade for so long with Farragen. I feel safe here. I know nothing about ships, and I have no skills to add to the crew, but I am strong and tall, so they take turns showing me various tasks to find where I can help best. This morning I hauled rope across the deck, took on a great deal of cleaning, and learned some kitchen skills. I'm not great at any of it, but I was able to heft more rope than any of the others, so at least I know I can be helpful. I feel at peace out here on the water. I still cry myself to sleep most nights, and there is a ragged, gaping hole in my heart where Ceci should be, but I feel like this ship, unlike the glade, is somewhere I could truly belong.

Captain Ballad is an odd captain. I obviously have no experience with any other captains, but I do not think most would operate like her. She swings around the ship's rigging like some sort of tree-dwelling creature, hollering commands and barking jolly orders at the crew. She has a collection of bizarre hats, and I have never seen her bare head. We currently have no set destination. She keeps calling this a "liberty cruise," and I have absolutely no clue what we even do other than sail around and drink excessively. The drinking. So much drinking. As soon as I had recovered from my seasickness, a girl named Ardelle pressed a tin cup into my hand, and I had my first drink of what they all call grog. From what I can tell it's some sort of liquor mixed with sugar, water, and citrus juice. Ballad says it's a "tonic for sea wellness," but I'm pretty sure it's just an excuse to party as often as possible. I learned quickly that I have to stop after a few cups, or I'll spend the entire following day wanting to die in my hammock.

Our sleeping quarters is a large communal space below deck with hanging hammocks. We take turns sleeping, and I think there are roughly twenty-five crewmembers. The ship is outfitted with cannons on both sides. The captain's cabin is to the rear of the ship directly below the upper deck, and below our quarters is the hold. The ship has two masts, and seven sails. I'm learning how to use the sails, and my strong upper body has made me an asset in climbing the rigging to release them. This afternoon I am seated in the crow's nest, staring at the horizon. The view from up here is like nothing I have ever experienced. There is nothing but bright cerulean seas in all directions, birds gliding by, and the occasional leaping dolphin or breaching whale. It is from up here that I hear Ballad's unmistakable voice call for all hands on deck. It takes me no time at all to climb down the mast.

The Captain smiles as I hop down onto the deck. "Truly 'tis a joy to see you findin' a spot on the ship, Jynn."

I blush. "It is an honor to be welcomed, Captain. I hope I can serve you well."

Her grin makes me nervous. I recognize the flash of mischief in her eyes, and I am not surprised in the least when she replies, "Well...here's your chance. We've got ourselves a job."

CAPTAIN BRIEFS US ALL ON THE JOB. THERE IS A SHIP DUE TO be sailing through nearby water, carrying a huge haul of spices and glassware heading out from Athydis. The ship is supposed to be minimally crewed, and they aren't expected in Konidas for another six weeks, so we will have more than enough time to intercept. If we sail west, staying toward Iowain, they won't see us when the ship turns to head south to Konidas. I know nothing of piracy, but Ballad says that she has three rules for her crew— no ducks, no eyes, no dead.

When I stare blankly in response, she laughs heartily and explains, ticking up her fingers one by one, "We don't leave ships stranded. Make sure you leave enough food and water for the crew to get back to shore. No breakin' oars or pokin' holes in the hull. We be pirates, but we're not asses. We don't want witnesses. We are small and quick. We strike at night and stay unseen. There's a reason we ain't notorious, and I plan to keep it that way. And we don't kill no one unless it's absolutely necessary. If someone's got a cannon at your head, they're askin' to die, but no goin' around killin' people who don't need killin'. Got it? No ducks, no eyes, no dead." I nod and grin, caught up in the fun, nervous energy of the crew. "Well then! Get to it lassies!" yells Ballad, and we all scatter.

The older woman who helped me when I was ill, Georgette, always stays with the ship. She isn't as nimble as the rest of us, but she can sail better than anyone. A tiny wraith of a girl named Cenna is our lead scout. She is barely larger than a child, small and thin. She moves like she's made of smoke, winding in and out, disappearing into shadows, even without trying. She doesn't speak much, but the rumor amongst the crew is that she was an assassin before joining the Sea Song. I don't doubt it. I am the tallest person on the ship, but they manage to find me some black pants and a long-sleeved black tunic that almost reaches my wrists.

One of the girls tosses me a black knit hat and laughs, "Better cover up that red head of yours."

I laugh back, but I feel a stab to my heart as I remember Cicerine making fun of my hair in the stream. I wonder how she would feel about this ship. She would like Captain, but I doubt her hooves would make for a very effective pirate. She would probably kick Cook out of the galley and take over, and I wouldn't mind. I miss her food, but not as much as I miss her presence. Wiping my eyes on the sleeve of my shirt, I swallow down the emotion. If I am going to be helpful and learn on this raid, I need a clear head. I have the rest of my life to cry.

WE SET SAIL TOWARD IOWAIN AND GET TO OUR DESTINATION IN five day's time. The cool bite in the air tastes of early fall and reminds me of autumn in Kanitosh. I've found a rhythm here, and the hard labor of sailing keeps my mind occupied until I pass out in my hammock, lulled by the sway of the sea. Ballad briefs us again as the sun sinks below the horizon, and she cuts quite a figure standing on the deck silhouetted against the bright coral sunset. The hat she wears tonight has a massive plumed feather which arcs backward from its large brim. We are ready. Everyone has their responsibilities, and the energy on the ship is electric. Cenna is dressed head to toe in flat black, her dark hair hidden beneath a knit cap, her obsidian eyes rimmed in kohl. Two other girls are with her, twins who I haven't spoken to much—both broad and strong, and they will man the small rowboat Cenna will use to board the ship. We don't have a single lantern lit aboard the Sea Song, and the sails have been tied back to hide the bright white cloth. The only light we have to see by is that of the full moon, hanging low in the sky.

The rowboat slips silently into the water, the oars making no sound as it heads toward the ship in the distance. It is not as large as the Sea Song, but is still a decently sized vessel, and the rowboat looks tiny in comparison. Time ticks by slowly as we wait for Cenna's signal. I stand in the crow's nest, watching intently— scared to blink. But in less time than I expect, I see the flash of a mirror from the deck of the other ship, and I signal down to Ballad. Our second row boat holds a group of five, including Ardelle and a woman named Tuii, who is our weapons master. She carries two long sabers on her back, ready for conflict. It is late and I should be tired, but nervous anticipation keeps me alert as I watch for the next signal. This crew is charged with blindfolding and restraining the crew of the other ship, which is the most dangerous task. When I spot their signal, I call down to Ballad and the crew gets the Sea Song moving. The night is completely silent save for the soft lapping of the sea against the hull. We sidle up next to the other ship, and I climb down the rigging so I can toss the heavy ropes to our crew on the other deck. Once they're secured, we leave five of our crew on our ship, and the other ten clamber over the ropes to the other deck. Ardelle's group has the crew tied up above deck, leaned up against the railing. There are ten men, and though they are all blindfolded and gagged—it's apparent none of them have been harmed. Their shallow breathing is loud in the moonlight, ragged and full of fear. Though we are still a dangerous lot, I wonder if they would be as afraid if they knew we were a ship full of women. In a matter of minutes, we have boarded the vessel, formed an efficient line, and passed the majority of the cargo over to our ship, hand to hand. There are about twenty heavy crates now safely stowed below the deck of the Sea Song, but we have left a good supply of food and potable water aboard the other vessel. The row boats are tied back to the Sea Song, and we have all safely boarded when Cenna tosses a small dagger to one of the men.

"You can cut yourselves free," she says in a falsely lowered voice, "but not until dawn breaks. If we find out you've done so before, you won't live to tell a soul."

The men all nod frantically, and we set sail.

By dawn we are far from view of the plundered ship, and we all grin like alleycats. Ballad inspects our haul and lets out a loud laugh as she holds up a bottle of grog. "Success looks good on ye girls!"

The whole crew erupts in cheers, and cups are passed around as we celebrate. We will sell the crates when we next stop in Konidas, and the profits after we restock and provide any necessary repairs will be split amongst the crew. I have never made a wage, and it's exhilarating to know I actually helped on the job and will be paid in coin for my work.

A strong, small hand claps me on the back. "You did good, Red," Tuii congratulates me.

The camaraderie is infectious, and I hold up my cup in a toast as I reply, "To the spoils and the sea!"

THE RAUCOUS LAUGHTER FROM ABOVE DECK IS A JOYFUL murmur from where I lay in my hammock. After a long night and hard morning of work, I am ready for sleep at last. I've just pulled my wool blanket up and closed my eyes when I hear footsteps approaching.

Ballad stands near the foot of my hammock. "A word?"

I hop up quickly. "Yes, Captain?"

She pulls a small pouch from beneath her coat and holds it out to me. I give her a questioning look, but she nods for me to open it, so I do.

Pennyway. The small bag is full of pennyway blossoms.

I recoil, pulling back my hand as if burned, nearly throwing the bag to the floor.

"I take it you know what this is, then?" Ballad asks. "We found an entire crate of it mixed in with the spices. None of the girls have ever seen it before."

My face is a mask of fear and sorrow. "It's called pennyway, or at least that's what we called it in Konidas. Supposedly it's holy, sacred. That man I told you about, Farragen? He used it to compel Mamère. It can kill people, and somehow it's used for magic, or for visions. I don't know the details, just what he told us, but it *is* dangerous. I don't presume to tell you what to do, Captain—but you should throw it overboard before someone gets hurt."

Ballad is quiet for a moment, thinking. "Aye, I think that would be best. Can you think of why they'd be transporting it?"

I shake my head. "Could be anything. Maybe they want to make poison, or they could be using it for magic. There's no way to know. But if it's anything like it was in Kanitosh, someone is going to be very, very angry it's missing. Ceci got whipped for destroying a single flower, I can only imagine the punishment that would follow losing or destroying that many of them." As I mention her name, my face pinches and my eyes sting. Tears threaten to fall, but I school my face into an expression of determination. We have a job to do.

Ballad puts her heavy hand on my shoulder. "I'm sorry to bring it up, Jynn. But I'll make sure it's disposed of. We have enough trouble without whatever this may be. Get some sleep, you'll be needed at dawn"

I give her a nod and climb back into my hammock as she returns above deck. I lay with my eyes closed for a long time, but a stream of dark memories keeps me awake long into the night.

KONIDAS

CHAPTER THIRTY-SIX
MAELWEN
YEAR 993

I wake with a start, shooting upright with a scream. The Crone's face fills my mind, and the strange sense I've traveled a long distance leaves me queasy. I realize Shell had been lying beside me, and is now half-off the bed, staring at me with wide eyes. She rights herself and calls for Godrick, and I try to steady my breathing.

The instant Godrick arrives in my room, I tell him and Shell the whole story. Shell informs me the man I saw is dead, neck snapped and face charred. She saw one of the crates in the house and confirmed my suspicion that the man must have been smoking the flowers.

"Do you think that's how you ended up in Athydis?" Shell asks.

How the smoke from a flower could send me hundreds of miles across the sea is beyond me, but I cannot think of any other explanation. "I suppose that could be so," I reply. "But the Crone did not know how it occurred, so I do not think she has orchestrated this." I am still shaken by her scream, that sound so unlike anything I have heard before. It felt as though it was tearing me in half, a weapon hidden within a scream. "She knows who I am," I tell them. "Who I really am. I need to know what she knows."

Godrick shakes his head. "If that's how she reacted seeing you, I don't think it's anything good. Leave it be; we don't need to be involved in any of this."

I snap at him, "We are already involved, Godrick. If you are afraid to remain involved, you are free to leave."

Hurt shines in his earnest face, and while I feel a stab of regret at my harsh words, I do not apologize. I may have been unkind, but I am correct. We are already involved in whatever this is, so there is no use pretending that we are not. "I would still like to fly to Iowain, but I need some time to think and to gain some strength," I tell them both. "I will leave in three weeks."

Shell eyes me warily when I tell her I need to feed. "Are you sure you're strong enough to be gettin' into that kinda thing?" she asks carefully.

"I have to." I raise my hands in exasperation. "I am not even strong enough to fly right now. It will likely take me the full span of these three weeks to make up for whatever was done to me. I feel human. It is disgusting."

Shell chuckles. "Yeah, we are pretty wretched, aren't we?"

"That is not what I meant," I begin, but she interrupts me.

"I know, little witch." She laughs. "Someday you'll understand what a joke is."

Godrick has gone home for the night to his apartment over the tailor shop. I feel badly about how I treated him, but I can deal with that tomorrow. I am far too hungry for discussion. I pull on my black gloves, an old black linen shirt and pants, and hook my cloak through my belt in case I need it. When night falls, I make my way out to the darkened streets of Konidas.

Even with my dulled senses, it takes me only moments to find what I am seeking. Tucked into an alley just off the docks, there are two men arguing, both fairly clean but clearly crewmen from a nearby ship. One of the men slides a dagger from his coat and presses it to the other's throat in a swift motion. Laughing, he pushes the blade's edge into flesh, a thin line of blood trickling down into the man's shirt collar. There is malice in his narrowed eyes, and a wicked grin twists his mouth at the pained begging coming from beneath his dagger. He is not a skilled criminal by any means, and he does not hear my soft steps approaching from behind. My claws slide from my fingertips, the sensation nearly brings a moan to my lips. I have missed this.

I grip his throat from behind, all ten fingers pricking the skin of his thick neck, and he freezes in terror. His arms immediately slacken, and the other man looks at me with wide eyes before clapping a hand to the small cut at his throat and racing swiftly into the night. I laugh in a low tone, sounding as malicious as I feel, and pull both hands into fists, tearing his throat out in one smooth motion. I do not bother staying tidy, lowering my face directly to the gaping maw of his throat and gorging myself on the flow of thick blood. The bright metallic smell of him makes my mouth water, and I tear into him like a feral creature. With each gulped mouthful, I feel my strength returning, my senses sharpening. My eyes roll back into my head as I groan into his ruined flesh. I tear at him until the steady flow has ebbed to a weak trickle, dropping his rapidly cooling corpse to the ground with a quiet thud. I slink further into the alley before tearing off my shirt, standing bare chested in the dim moonlight. I catch my reflection in a stagnant puddle, and I cannot help but smile. I have never looked so magnificent.

I wipe my face and hands off on my bloody shirt before tossing it onto the body at my feet. I pull my cloak back over my shoulders to hide my naked chest and sigh in pleasure as it stitches itself back into my skin. I feel whole, strong, new. I am in the air in a single breath, quickly hidden in the clouds above the sea. The cold wind teases my bare flesh and a foreign sensation settles at my core. Heat races through me despite the chill in the air, and for the first time in my life I find myself craving touch. The memory of Godrick's kiss slips into my mind unbidden, and I imagine his hands around my waist, what they might feel like on other parts of my body. I have touched myself plenty of times; I am not unfamiliar with pleasure, but I have never before allowed another to do so. Until recently, the idea wholly repulsed me, and even now parts of it are still unappealing. But in this moment, with my body bared to the sky, it consumes my thoughts. I allow my own fingers to graze the curves of my body as I fly, my skin tingling in the wake of my touch. My senses are so vibrant right now, my mouth falls open slightly as a small sound flutters from my lips. The city below is a smattering of lights on a dark canvas, and I can see the bobbing of ships in the harbor. I have come to know this city well, Shell's Tavern below me to the right, the tailor shop just above. There is a candle lit in the apartment above the tailor's shop, and it glows like a beacon.

    I alight on the flat roof soundlessly, my leather-soled shoes flexing with my feet. I curl my cloak around me, hiding the bare skin beneath. There are a few planter boxes up here with herbs and flowers growing that I know are tended by both the tailor herself and Godrick. I run a finger along a small mint plant, and the cool scent of it clings to my finger as I make my way toward the staircase that leads into the building. The buildings in Konidas are mostly flat. There is rarely any rain here, and sloped roofs are not necessary. Many of the roofs are used as gardens or sitting areas, and it is common in summer to see people having drinks or meals atop their homes or businesses, lanterns hung from the rails. They are quite lovely at night. The tailor's shop is not in a particularly large building, and Godrick lives above the shop. I have not been here before, but I know which door is his. My hand hovers over the wood for a moment as I hesitate. My knock sounds so faint I wonder if he will even hear it, but the door cracks open a moment later. Surprised gold and green eyes peer out at me. "Maelwen?"

Before I lose my resolve, I kiss him. He freezes for just a second, taken aback by both my presence and my brazenness. He has never seen this side of me, and honestly, neither have I. His hand runs up my back, and I feel his breath hitch when he realizes that under my cloak I wear nothing else. "Bed," I murmur against his lips, and without breaking the kiss, he walks me further into the apartment and into his bedroom. The room is sparse, and the bed simple, but it is soft as he gently lays me onto the mattress. He makes as if to climb over me, but I quickly slide out and pull him down instead. A flash of memory sneaks into my thoughts: Jarrus's massive form caging me to the bed with his hulking arms on either side of my head. I swallow the memory down like water. In one fluid motion I bring my body atop his, my knees resting on either side of his narrow hips, one hand on the bed and the other on his chest. Our bodies are not touching save for our lips and my palm pressed against him. His eyes are closed and his chin raised, pushing his head back against the bed.

My cloak is no longer held shut, my chest and stomach exposed. When his eyes open, I feel his body tense beneath me, and his kiss becomes more adamant. He curls a hand around the back of my neck, fingers settling in my thick hair, and a low growl rumbles in his chest beneath my hand. He pulls away slightly, murmuring, "Maelwen, I..." I stop him with my tongue, kissing him deeply, not wanting words. I lower my hips onto him, feeling the hard ridge of him beneath his pants. My hips move ever so slightly, grazing over him and pulling a moan from his mouth into mine. His other hand grips my waist, fingers digging into my skin, and I move my hips with more pressure. Our kisses grow more fervent, and he grinds back into me, wanting. His hand at my waist moves upward slowly, lightly. I do not stop him as his fingers slide up my ribcage and gently cup my breast. My full weight is upon him now, and we move in rhythm against each other, every inch of my skin alight with sensation. My hand on his chest moves, slowly unbuttoning his shirt, and I push the thin fabric to the side as I slide my palm over his bare skin. His hand kneads at my breast, rolling my nipple between his thumb and finger, and I moan in pleasure. I break the kiss as I push off his chest to sit up, breathing heavily, removing my cloak and reaching for the button at the top of my pants.

He raises up onto his elbows, looking at me reverently. We both shrug out of our pants, and I see him, straining against his braies. The linen shorts have a small tie at the waistband, and as he moves to untie it, I replace his hand with my own. He lays back as I remove them, looking at the expanse of skin before me and pausing hesitantly at his rigid length. Again, images I wish to forget slink into my mind's eye, and I shake my head slightly as if that will erase them. But I am drawn back into this moment by his hand in mine, interlacing our fingers as he pulls me back down until our naked bodies are pressed together.

He is gentle and pauses before every moment, silently seeking consent. I give it freely. Despite the warring thoughts in my head, my body responds to him instinctively. I am flushed and damp, my breathing heavy. The persistent throb between my thighs grounds me, and I focus not on thought, but sensation. His hands are soft. Hands that are skilled with luxurious silks caress my skin just as carefully. His palm runs over the slim curve of my hip, stopping at the top and pressing me down onto him. I feel him twitch beneath me as I slide over him. His hips rise, pushing against the slick skin and making me shiver as he rubs against the bundle of nerves there. He reaches a hand between us, and I feel his nimble fingers carefully slide down between my thighs, pausing just before the apex. I let a tiny whimper fall from my lips as he presses two of his fingers against me. He starts slowly, rubbing in a circle, and I move with him, aiming for that peak I have only reached on my own. I move myself up and down over him, and he moans at the touch of my wet heat. Our movements quicken, but release is still just out of my grasp. I pull back slightly and grip him in my hand. He is so much smaller than Jarrus, and I am not afraid of my ability to handle him, though I am still hesitant to allow anyone into my body. But I look down at him as I move my hand up and down his cock, and the look on his face gives me the small bit of courage I need.

His eyes open as I move him to my entrance, and he places a hand on my forearm. "We don't have to."

"I know," I say huskily. "But I would like to try."

There is only the slightest bit of resistance before he slides into me. I let out a little sigh as I lower my body onto him fully. Being in this position, in full control, eases my tension. Nobody is doing anything to me, this is my will and my choice. I control this action. I brace my hands on my thighs and begin to move my body up and down, feeling him inside me. He reaches his hand back between us and circles with his fingers again, pressing slightly and matching the rhythm of my hips. I focus on his fingers and the feeling of my muscles clenching around him. I move faster, and his breaths become ragged. My name is on his lips as I kiss him. It feels good, better than good, but I cannot seem to focus long enough to find true pleasure. Thoughts of Jarrus plague me, though I banish them just as quickly. He pants against my mouth, and I brace my hands on the bed on either side of his head. With the leverage from my hands, I can move faster still, and the sounds of our wet bodies colliding fill the room. Noises tumble from his mouth erratically, and his hips jerk as he grips mine and cries out, spilling his release into me. I like the feeling of him here, hot and hard and pressed fully within me. I ride him as he pulses, until his breathing begins to calm, and I feel him begin to soften. I raise my hips and begin to move off of him, but he stops me with a hand on my ass.

"I want you to finish too," he says in a low voice, near whispering.

I kiss him in response. "It is all right. I should get back to the tavern before Shell worries."

He looks disappointed, but he kisses me back, and as I stand he walks to a pitcher in the corner and wets a cloth. "At least let me clean you up," he says with a mischievous twinkle in his eye.

I huff out a small laugh. "Very well."

He is tender but efficient, sliding the cloth between my legs, pausing between them and pressing against me. I smile, but I do not take the invitation, and reach for my pants at the foot of the bed. He does not dress, just sits on the edge of the bed watching me pull on my pants and look around, realizing that I do not have a shirt.

With a laugh, he hands me his. "A souvenir," he says with a grin.

The corners of my lips tug up in a small smile.

"Are you all right?" He asks, brushing his hair from his face. "I don't want you to leave if things are off between us."

I give him a quick kiss. I do not wish to have this conversation right now, when my body is still feeling his touch and my mind reels with too many thoughts. "I am fine, we will talk tomorrow. Sleep well, Godrick."

His shirt is huge on me, but it does the trick. I don my cloak, hissing as it stitches to me, and head back up to the roof and into the night black sky.

Shell notices the shirt and lifts a brow as I head upstairs. I roll my eyes in reply. My apartment is quiet despite the din of the bar below, and I wash myself quickly before putting on a nightdress. I did not expect to enjoy sex as much as I did, though I did not find release. It was easier than I anticipated, and it felt nice to give Godrick pleasure that I know he has desired for a long time. My own hand is between my thighs as I think over the night, my fingers far more familiar with my body. However, even after a few minutes, I am not any closer than I was with Godrick. With a sigh, I grab a drink of water from my bedside table, and try again —attempting to clear my mind. This time I think less about him and more about the small fingers that slide between my delicately parted flesh. Quicker and quicker, I move against myself, hips bucking as I imagine soft lips on my neck, my breasts. And to my own surprise, the thought of *my* lips arises again and again. My lips against soft flesh, my hands on a soft and curvy body, and long, curling hair falling around my face.

KONIDAS

CHAPTER THIRTY-SEVEN
SHELL
YEAR 993

Cartwright comes in, lookin' darker than I've seen before. He sits at the bar and removes his wool cap, settin' it beside him on an empty barstool. I haven't spoken to him at length since his men at the docks went missin'. "I found my men, Shell," he says in a quiet voice.

"Are they all right?" I ask, already knowin' the answer from the look on his face.

"They found the bodies this mornin'," he responds in a tone laced deeply with sadness. "All my men from early shift and a bunch of others. Dead, dumped in a warehouse past the far dock." He hangs his head in his hands, heavy elbows on the bar. I didn't expect good news, but I also didn't expect this.

"Oh, gods," I say, reachin' out and touchin' his arm. "Did anyone see anythin'?"

"That's the part I can't wrap my head 'round," he mutters from beneath his hands. "Not a single soul saw or heard a godsdamned thing. And the building? The doors were locked from the inside. There wasn't a single broken window neither, just a part of the roof that caved in this winter. There's no attic or ladder that could reach that high. It's a warehouse for fuck's sake." Cartwright shrugs his shoulders. "I don't know what happened."

I have Martine pack up all the day-old bread we have in the kitchen, and I fill a few growlers of ale and send the whole parcel with Cartwright to bring to the families. He knew half a dozen men on that shift, leavin' wives and gods know how many kids without their Pap comin' home. I'm gutted.

The afternoon is busy, and I don't get much of a chance to chat with Maelwen. Word has gotten out about the warehouse, and dock men fill the bar lookin' for a way to numb their woes. Today is the busiest lunchtime so far this fall, and I'm glad of it. Pap found a healer who says they have some experience with folks like Ma. After tonight, I'll have a good amount of money to put toward payin' the healer; maybe she can help Ma get a little more time. Maelwen slides into her regular barstool just as I finish droppin' off a plate to a man at the bar.

"Good night?" I ask as I slide her a beer.

"Always," she replies in that flat voice of hers.

"So...you gonna tell me what happened last night?" I wink, hopin' for a distraction from the somber energy of the bar. She rolls her eyes with a sigh.

"I am sure you already know, Shell. Do we really need to talk about this?"

I can swear I see the tiniest bit of a blush on her cheeks. "I've had a long night, little witch. Give a girl somethin'!" The look in her eyes would kill a lesser woman, but I'm not put off. "Please?" I beg with my sweetest pout, drawin' the word out long.

She makes a huffin' sound that sounds suspiciously like a laugh and closes her eyes in feigned exasperation. "Fine. Only for you." My grin comes easy. "I had a successful evening." She flicks out a claw. "And after I was through, I was in a...mood."

I set my elbows on the bar and rest my chin on my fists. "Tell me more."

"I happened to see a light in Godrick's apartment, and I paid him a visit. He was amenable to my suggestion, and I spent some time with him."

She looks at me like she's through speakin', but no ma'am, I need *details*, and I tell her so. Now I am sure I see her blush and she puts her fingers to her brow, massagin' her forehead.

"Shell, I am not going to tell you any more. Is it not enough that I came home in his clothing? I had an enjoyable evening. Imagine what you will."

Smiling, I pat her hand. "Oh, I will." She flips me off before headin' upstairs to ready herself for tonight's games, and I sigh. "Love you too!"

SOMETHIN' WEIRD IS AFOOT TONIGHT, AND I DO NOT LIKE THE feel of it. The vibe of the bar is all wrong. The quiet sadness has given way to something more tense. Cartwright and Mael see it too, aware and ready for trouble. I've got half a mind to cancel the games tonight, but gods know we need the coin, and the tables are filling up fast. Last thing I need is to piss off men with full pockets. There is a table in the corner with a group of men in dark clothes, and I have an uneasy feeling about them. Their eyes are shifty and they sip at their drinks like men unfamiliar with liquor. Maelwen takes her seat at the Orakulua tables when one of the men stands and walks toward her. He says somethin', but I can't hear over the din of the bar. Cartwright, however, does.

For being such a bulky man Cartwright moves fast, and before anyone has noticed, he has the man pinned against the wall just inside the kitchen. The doors swing back and forth before coming to a close, and I shout out to Martine to watch the bar before hustlin' back to see what the fuck is happenin'. I walk in to the sight of Cartwright holdin' the short man from behind, his arm twisted up behind his back and his face pressed against the kitchen wall. Clutched in the man's hand is a tiny purple...somethin'. I raise an eyebrow at Cartwright, and he nods toward the man's hand.

"This fuck called Maelwen somethin' I ain't gonna repeat. Told her she didn't have long left in this town. Was wavin' somethin' around."

It takes both my hands to pry the man's sweaty fingers apart, but I finally wrench the crumpled wad of purple from his grip. It's a piece of paper, colored deep plum, with a drawin' of a flower inked on it above what looks like a date.

"What the fuck is this?" I ask the man as he struggles against Cartwright's solid form.

"It's...It's nothing!" The man stammers. "It's just an invitation to a religious service!"

"What? What religious service?"

The man's eyes flit to the door and back to me. "It's to praise Idyth, for the New Church. We are bringing back faith to this ungodly place."

"Okay," I say, rolling my eyes. "But *where* is this service?"

"It's invite only," he chokes out. "Women aren't allowed. I thought we could make an exception for a witch." His laugh is low and cruel. "Show her what we think of her kin."

I scoff. Really? Sexism? *Shocking.* "Is that what y'all are talkin' about over there in the corner?"

Cartwright lets go of him with a little push. The man stumbles forward, and when his eyes meet mine, I see a shade of defiance in the set of his jaw.

"We *will* cleanse this city," he says with more confidence than I expected from his weasely little mouth. "We are going to make this land a place Idyth will be proud of."

"Hmmmkay," I say as I roll my eyes yet again. "You do that. In the meantime, leave my bar out of your business. The owner is a woman, and I hear she's a real heathen. You wouldn't wanna sully your good names."

He doesn't respond but leaves the kitchen quickly, and I share a look with Cartwright. He shakes his head and rubs his brow with his meaty fingers. We are both already sick of this "New Church" nonsense and it's only been a couple months. Can't people just say their prayers and keep their kooky shit out of my life? We walk back out onto the bar floor, and I shove the purple paper into my pocket. The date on the invitation is soon, only a couple weeks from now, and it's yet another thing we need to be mindful of. I need a drink.

Thankfully, the little weasel man seems to have told his cronies to kick rocks, and they all slowly filter out of the bar. They pay their tabs and tip decently, so I hate them a little less, but they're creepy and unwelcome all the same. We find another invitation stuck under a chair at their table, and I hand it to Cartwright.

He's formed a sort of security operation both here and in town. Konidas is a lawless place, and we don't have any sort of royal guard like they do in Athydis. We've always been a place for those who aren't too keen on laws and regulations, but it's feeling like a good idea to have some men on the street with open eyes and ears right now. I'm glad they're around and that this is their home base. If we're gonna have a militia, I'd rather they be on my side. I head back to my place at the bar, and Maelwen lifts her chin in question. I hand her the sweat-stained paper, and she wrinkles her nose in disgust.

"This stinks," she says with a grimace. "It smells like the flowers." I didn't expect that. "And death," she says. "It smells like flowers and death."

She looks at the date and time, and I can tell that she's committed it to memory. I know she plans to be in Iowain. "Don't worry about us," I tell her. "We will be fine with you gone. No need to change your plans. Hell, we don't even know where this thing is gonna be. For all we know, it could be in Athydis."

She nods. "I would feel better if we knew more, but I am not concerned about your ability to handle yourselves. It is still best for me see what I can learn about these flowers and this *movement* the humans seem to be involved in." She dips her head as she stands to go to the Orakulua tables, her lips pressed together in determination.

KONIDAS

CHAPTER THIRTY-EIGHT
CICERINE
YEAR 993

I reach Konidas in eleven days. I am filthy and exhausted; my stomach aches from days of only eating foraged fruits. The city is overwhelmingly busy, countless people milling about. I don't see a single non-human, and I garner strange glances as I walk down the thoroughfare. I have never seen this many people, let alone this many people who are unlike me. My skin crawls with shame. I wish I could hide somewhere, but I have nowhere to go. I do not have any coin or goods to trade, and no idea what to do or where to head, but I am here. It is early afternoon, and though I am warm from exertion, I can feel in the air that fall has reached Konidas. I look down at myself and cringe, seeing the filth coating my skin and clothing. I need to find somewhere to sleep, or I'll be on the street for the night.

It's not likely anyone will take me on, but I'll have to try. I step into a few businesses and am quickly dismissed from all of them. The looks on the faces of the humans when they see me are a mixture of disgust and contempt, lips pulled back and noses wrinkling. I feel heavy, pulling my pants down further to help hide my legs. I'm not sure what I expected in coming here, but it wasn't this. Everyone is so unkind. Is this how all humans are?

I spot a rather dingy looking inn and head for its doors, feeling dejected. The woman at the front desk is older, human, and has frizzy black hair that circles her head like a looming storm cloud.

"Good afternoon," I say softly, eyes on the floor. "I'd like to inquire after work." The woman looks me up and down and raises an eyebrow, but I continue. "Please, I have only just arrived here. I have no coin and nothing to barter for keep. But I am a hard worker and a skilled cook. I can clean, I can work in your kitchens, I can do anything you need."

The woman's knobby thumb strokes her chin, and her voice is gravelly as she replies, "I suppose I have a room. It's the old servant's quarters, and it ain't nice, but it has a bed and a basin. I could use a cook."

My eyes widen.

"I don't keep freeloaders, it's hard work here—but you ain't likely to find work anywhere else, so you can't be choosy. Shell might take you on, but there's no tellin' if she'd want you either."

I give her a shallow bow and thank her for the opportunity before asking, "Would it be all right for me to rest a bit?"

The woman's laugh turns into a cough, and she replies, "You can start in the morning. Down the hall on the right, the last door. You'll have to clean it up yourself, but there's a bed in there at least." She hands me an old-looking iron key, and I head down the hallway, trying as hard as I can to walk quietly on the wooden floor.

The room is small and musty. A light coating of dust sits upon every surface, covering the rickety wooden bed and its lumpy mattress, the small table pushed against the peeling wallpaper. A moth-eaten rug tries its hardest to soften the floor, but my hooves still clatter against the uneven wood as I walk, leaving hoofprints across the dusty space. A stubby candle sits on the table, and I light it with a match I find sitting beside it. This place feels like a tomb.

All at once I am sobbing, head in my hands as I sit on the bed. I miss my home. I miss Mamère, Jynn, our house full of light and life and laughter. I struggle to contain the loud, gulping sobs that shake my entire body as I cry. This is a nightmare. For so many years, I dreamed of the world outside the glade, imagined adventures and excitement, sprawling cities beneath spires and battlements. I never pictured this grimy city with its hateful denizens and dusty darkness. I didn't think about a life without people who loved me. I took so many moments for granted. Already the smell of our home has begun to fade from my clothes and my memory, Mamère's eyes shifting color in my mind's eye. I can't recall exactly what pattern Jynn's freckles made across the bridge of her nose in summertime. My sobs quiet, and my tears turn to still silence as I sit pinned by the weight of my grief. I lay on this bed with its poorly stuffed mattress and threadbare blanket, and I sleep.

MY FIRST WEEK IN KONIDAS IS A BLUR OF SWEAT AND TEARS. I work from sunup to sundown, cooking and cleaning and falling into my lumpy bed at the end of the night. I don't dislike the work; in fact, it's almost enjoyable to spend my day cooking. The inn receives regular deliveries of meat, grain and produce, and it's my job to ensure the supplies last until the next. I stretch the meat using lentils and rice. I bulk up vegetables with potatoes and sauces made from canned and tinned tomatoes and other out of season produce. I make pasta from scratch and dry it on a repurposed rack near the ovens. The innkeeper is named Beatrice, and she runs the place alone. There is a small staff, mainly housekeepers and service people, but I don't interact with any of them. The attitude towards me from the humans in Konidas hasn't changed—I get a lot of wary stares and very little kindness. I get a sense that a great deal of the citizens of this town want nothing to do with anyone who isn't human. The only person who is kind to me is a man named Salvatorre. He is an occasional guest at the inn, and a winemaker who supplies both the inn and the tavern in town. He told me upon our first meeting that he spent a summer in Kanitosh when he was young and that the fauns were kind and generous towards him. He is an older man, gray, with shoulders that have begun to bow with his many years. He is far too old to have known Mamère, but I think he takes pity on me. Beatrice allows me one free day a week, provided I prepare food in advance to cover the day's meals. Yesterday, Salvatorre approached me as I was finishing up a large tureen of beef and barley soup and asked when I had some time off. I was hesitant to respond, concerned about the reason for the query, but was absolutely delighted when he told me that he would like to teach me winemaking.

 I woke this morning with genuine excitement, and as I dress in a simple half sleeve frock of rust-colored linen, I cannot help but smile. This is the first day since my arrival in this unwelcoming city that I have felt anticipation. I meet Salvatorre in the inn lobby and follow him to his cellar, located near the outskirts of Konidas. The building is unassuming from the street, but inside it is a jumble of barrels and basins. The rather arid climate of the areas nearby lends itself well to the year-round harvest of grapes, and Salvatorre receives regular deliveries from nearby vineyards. In his youth he also grew the grapes, but as he aged he transitioned to hiring vignerons to grow grapes in his stead. He tells me that the white grapes are crushed and filtered before fermenting, but the red grapes are fermented with their skins, which helps lend complexity to their color and flavor. As we walk around the winery, he shows me barrels of fermenting wine, vats of grapes ready to be crushed, his bottling area and crates of the various types of finished wine he has ready to deliver to customers.

"I would be remiss if I did not tell you that your lovely hooves...how do you say, *encourage* me to approach you about learning wine," he says with a bashful smile. His accent is quite lovely, the ends of his words swooping up in a musical cadence. "You were made for crushing grapes, sweet girl." I chuckle and follow him to an area containing protective garments to wear while crushing the ripe fruit. Another worker passes us and a sneer twists his lips, but Salvatorre gives him a quick shake of the head, and the boy carries on elsewhere. Salvatorre hands me some odd-looking breeches with built-in socks. "These will keep your coat nice and clean." I don them along with a large shirt of heavy fabric with a tight weave and accompany him to a large trough full of juicy looking green grapes. "These are muscat grapes," he explains. "They are most dolcett. Er, I mean, *sweet*." His cheeks redden. "So sorry, sweet girl. At times, my mind...it slips into old habits."

I laugh and smile; he is a kind man. "No problem at all, sir," I say. "Had I not grown up speaking the common tongue, I am certain I would be the same."

He demonstrates the method of crushing the vibrant globes, and I get to work. Once the grapes are crushed, I help him filter the skins and pulp, which he calls the must, from the juice, and we place the liquid in open barrels. He tells me that within a few days, wild yeasts will begin to ferment the juice, and we will cover the barrels to allow it to ferment for two weeks. The process is interesting, and the sweet smell of the winery seems to stick to my hair and follow me out as we leave at the end of the day.

"You will come again?" I nod enthusiastically. "Eccellente!" He claps me on the shoulder with a firm hand. "I am not the man

I once was," he says, gesturing down at himself. "I would be so glad to have you. You will make some deliveries next week?"

"I'm not sure if that would be wise," I say, looking down at my hooves. "The people of this city do not seem friendly toward me."

He scoffs loudly. "Nobody will be unkind to a girl bearing wine, even a girl such as yourself!" He smiles broadly. "You will be the most popular signorinette in Konidas!" He gives me a warm hug, and I nearly tear up. This is more kindness than I have been shown in my entire time here. "I will see you soon!" He hands me a bottle of wine with a wink. "Enjoy!"

KONIDAS

CHAPTER THIRTY-NINE
MAELWEN
YEAR 993

I am avoiding Godrick. I do not know how to act now that we have slept together. I have never experienced a relationship, nor have I ever experienced consensual sex. I worry he will be displeased that I did not find release with him, but I do not know how to approach a conversation about it. I do not know how I feel about it at all. My thoughts from that night are tangled and confusing, and I am not sure how to make sense of them. There is one question in my mind. *Do I want to continue this?* Luckily, he is busy with work, and I have no reason to visit. However, he is not the focus of my thoughts today.

I have begun to feel a new sensation stirring; my magic feels… different. I feel it in the notes of my witchsong, and I sense it when I am linked to my cloak. There is a new, burning ember within me. I sense the small molten pebble of power, but I do not know how to stoke it. It is midday, and the air is brisk on my skin as I step out of the tavern and onto the street. I will need to feed soon, but I still feel the heady buzz of power when my cloak settles across my shoulders. Today I plan to see how long I can remain airborne to prepare for my flight to Iowain. My leather pants and high boots keep me warm as I rise above Konidas, looking down over the city that has become my home. The ember within me flutters, and my fingertips feel icy, colder than they should in the cool fall air. I am able to spend a full four hours in the air before my energy starts to flag, and I make my way back down as the sun sinks low in the sky.

I touch down just outside the inn, and the feeling of my feet hitting earth is electric. I cannot explain it, other than to say I feel as if the ground comes to life beneath my feet. I stand for a moment, analyzing the tingle, wondering what may be developing within me. But in a moment the feeling fades, and I make my way into town.

The streets are busy as I head toward the tannery to pick up a new set of gloves for my journey to Iowain. I leave tomorrow so I plan to spend the morning making sure I have all I need. The gloves I have ordered are made from black leather, much like the pair I usually wear, but these are reinforced with a thin layer of iron mesh. They cost more than some of these people make in a week, but I have a feeling the added layer of protection will be necessary in the coming months. Unrest is at an all-time high, and many of the tavern's patrons linger through the day to avoid the streets. Shell's place is a safe-haven for anyone who needs it, and I am certain Cartwright and his men will continue to preserve that safety even in my absence. I am lost in thought as I head toward the shop to retrieve the daggers I ordered when a strange tingle runs down my spine. That odd pebble of power pulses within me, and I stop, looking around to see if I can identify its cause. Nothing seems amiss, but I catch the eye of a girl in the window of the inn. A faun? Odd. I was not aware there was a faun in the inn's employ. From the immediate scarlet of her cheeks I get a sense she was looking at me before I noticed her, and she clumsily leaves the window, nearly running. My fingertips buzz and that molten power surges, feeling as if my ribcage is full of seething hot magic. Lifting a finger, I flick out my claw and sparks skitter over the tip of it. My nose wrinkles in confusion as I watch the tiny electric charge dance from claw to claw as I extend my full hand. This is a new development.

"Repulsive." I hear from over my shoulder. Turning, I see a man in what I have come to think of as the uniform for the 'New Church.' His robe is dark, and his eyes are full of unrestrained malice. "Filth," he growls at me. "Go back to your tower."

I meet his eyes from underneath lowered lashes, my gaze malicious and cruel. "No."

He spits on the ground before turning and disappearing into the crowd. Sheathing my claws, I look back to the inn once more, but there is no sign of the faun, and the fire in my chest seems to settle back to a dull thrum. I will have to ask Shell if she knows anything about a faun at the inn. With things how they are, I feel somewhat of an obligation to be aware of the non-human residents of the city. It is not witches alone who face danger from these men.

Godrick is waiting at the bar when I arrive back at the tavern, and guilt twists my stomach. That same question plays over and over again in my mind, though I know the answer. I do not feel for Godrick what I once did, or thought I did. He is a friend, a kind man whose company I enjoy and value. I am glad for him, and I know he cares for me, but the depth of affection within me is simply not the same. I do not know if I am even capable of the emotion. I am not being fair to him, and I think it is time I acknowledge this truth.

I go over the script I have written in my mind as I sip my ale and listen to Godrick speak about his day. I hope I have worded this correctly, but the doublespeak of humans confuses me, and I am never sure I am saying things in a kind way. With a resolute breath, I turn to him as he finishes his story. "Godrick, may I speak plainly?"

"Of course," he says with a smile. "Why would you need to ask?" He chuckles. "You'd think you'd have caught on by now, but you don't have to worry about how you speak to me."

"I do not want to be in a relationship with you." He sputters a bit and sets down his ale as I continue, "I enjoy your company and value your friendship. I have tried to determine if I feel the way you feel, and I do not. I am not sure if it is something I can feel, to be candid. As with everything, I know nothing about myself and my kind. I do not even know if witches mate. But I do know I do not wish to continue this courtship, though I hope you will still consider me a friend." I drink deeply from my ale. "I regret if I have made you feel unhappy."

His smile is sad, but he nods. "I won't pretend to be surprised," he says plainly. "You are unlike any woman I've ever known, Maelwen. I am glad you gave me a shot. But I've known since we slept together that you don't want to be with me." I open my mouth to speak, but he continues, "I will still be your friend, Mael. I've gotten rather used to this place, and I don't have the time to make new friends." His chuckle sounds strained. "I may need a few days, but I'm still on your side. Especially now. Who else will listen in on cult creeps at the shop for you?"

My small smile is genuine. "Thank you." He stands and pushes in his barstool as he finishes his ale. Waving to Shell, he nods at me and gives me a small bow.

"I'll be seeing you, little witch."

THE SEA

CHAPTER FORTY
JYNN
YEAR 993

True to her word, Ballad orders the pennyway be destroyed. The twins haul the crate to the main deck and douse the blossoms in some foul smelling liquid. Tuii stands near the deck railing with a bow and a bucket with the shaft of an arrow jutting out of it, red fletching shining in the early morning sun. I have no idea what's going on until the twins hurl the crate overboard, and Tuii lights and looses the arrow in the blink of an eye. The flaming arrow finds its mark effortlessly, and the crate bursts into roaring flames.

"Everyone get back!" I scream as I gesture wildly for everyone to get away from the starboard side of the ship. "The smoke isn't safe!"

The crew all dart to the port side, and we watch until the last hazy dregs of smoke drift up from the surface of the sea. When I walk back to the edge of the deck, nothing remains of the crate except for a few charred boards and the rainbow hued shimmer of an oil slick on top of the water. Ballad barks orders at us, and we quickly get to work. I work alongside Georgette counting coin and taking inventory of the various glassware and crates of salt and spices. The majority of the crates seem to be cinnamon bark. The fragrance, spicy and sweet, fills the hull and reminds me a bit of home. There is a crate filled with bottles of tiny yellow fibers, and I hold one up to Georgette with a quizzical glace. She nearly drops her ledger, eyes like saucers as she takes in the full contents of the crate.

"Holy shit," she breathes quietly. "Saffron. I have never in my life seen so much saffron." I guess that this is something impressive, but I stare back at her with my eyebrows raised. She shakes her head and rolls her eyes with a smile. "I forget you're a woodland creature," she says. "Saffron is a treasure. Each one of these tiny little stamens is hand plucked. It's more valuable than gold."

I unstopper the little bottle and sniff. Honestly, it just smells like hay and leather. "What does it do?" I ask incredulously.

Georgette chuckles as she replies, "It doesn't *do* anything. It's a spice. It tastes good, and it gives food a pretty yellow color. Maybe if we're lucky, Ballad will let Cook keep a bottle. I haven't tasted saffron in years." I shrug and call out the count of bottles; food has never been where my knowledge lies.

By the end of our inventory we have tallied up roughly a hundred pieces of glassware: cups, plates, goblets, some serving dishes and a few tureens. There is a full crate of fine silverware with engravings that indicate it was either headed toward or stolen from the castle. There are eleven crates of spices containing cinnamon, dried peppers, cloves, ginger, and the crate of saffron, along with two crates of fine flaky salt. Cook looks like a cat in cream as Captain gives her the go-ahead to take a portion of each for our galley. The crew must know more about cooking than I do —they look absolutely giddy as they watch Cook fill bags and little boxes with the fragrant powders.

We also apparently came away with a decent stash of weapons, and Captain calls out to Cenna and Ardelle to distribute them accordingly. I watch as they hand rapiers and fine bows to various crew members, but I am shocked when Cenna stops before me. Her dark hair is pulled back from her face, and her eyes glint like glass as she smiles and hands me a blade. The cutlass is about the length of my arm, curving at the tip into a shining, wicked point. The hilt is bronze and has a basket shaped guard that swoops over to cover one's hand while holding it. It is a beautiful blade. "You'll be needing this," she says as I take the weapon. I nod my thanks. Tuii winks at me from across the deck. I feel my cheeks redden and I drop my gaze to my boots. When I look back up she is gone.

This evening nobody misses dinner. Cook has outdone herself. Her ruddy cheeks are as round as apples as she grins at us from beside Captain. Before us on the long galley table is a veritable feast. Whole fish roasted with onions and potatoes and spicy pepper, carrots with cinnamon and honey, a massive pot full of brightly colored yellow rice steaming with that fragrant, grassy aroma of saffron. There are even bowls of baked apples spiced with ginger and clove topped with a crumble of brown sugar and oats. My mouth waters so violently I'm forced to swallow repeatedly to avoid choking. I haven't seen or smelled food this delicious since Ceci cooked for us, and even then, the food was nowhere near this decadent.

Ballad lifts her tankard and yells out a toast, "May this meal fortify ye and fill your hearts with gladness! To the Sea Song! May she prosper and flourish on the tides of tomorrow!"

The cheer that follows is raucous and joyful, and I grin. This crew and this ship is everything I could want from my life. I miss Ceci terribly, but I am so lucky to be here.

~

I MAKE MY WAY BACK TO MY BUNK, SWAYING A BIT ON MY FEET. The evening's grog has left me with a heady buzz just on this side of comfortable. For the first time, I feel a bit of lightness in my soul. The weight of my loss had pulled me down so low that feeling the tension ease is revelatory. The meals we have shared since the raid have been amazing, and the company has felt like family. Everything from Ballad's silly hats to my little haven in the crow's nest has given me a reason to smile since joining this ship. I miss Ceci, but she doesn't consume my every thought like she did when I arrived. I have begun to walk the path toward a future, and though it will be a long journey, I can see the light of a life well-lived shining at the end.

My hammock is swinging to and fro as I reach it, and I shake my head, thinking perhaps the grog has hit me harder than I thought. But it isn't the grog, and it isn't the sea. It's Tuii, comfortably settled in my hammock, reading one of my books with a soft smirk on her angular features.

"Tuii," I begin, "What are you doing here?"

"I thought perhaps we could spend some time together," she says. "You're our newest, and I make it a point to know this crew. Join me? I may have a place you haven't yet found." She waggles a green glass bottle at me with a conspiratorial smile. "I have libations."

Her voice has a melodic lilt to it. I don't know much about Tuii, but her upturned eyes with their thick midnight lashes, and that faint cadence to her voice, allude to an origin outside Idythia. She's often been part of the crowd when the crew gets together in the evenings, but we haven't spent any time together alone. I hold out a hand to help her out of my hammock and she takes it, her slender fingers warm and dry. She keeps ahold of my hand as she weaves her way through the ship, light-footed as a cat. She moves with a grace born of years of training, her skill with a blade unrivaled. Unlike me, she doesn't have the bulk of muscle; she is lithe and slim, coming barely to my shoulder. Her inky black hair is usually pulled back into a tight plait, but tonight it is free, shining in the starlight. She stops before a small ladder I have never noticed near the back of the ship, leading down toward the captain's quarters. At the bottom is a narrow alcove, tucked where two walls meet. The space is small, barely large enough to accommodate the two of us side by side, but this entire area is blocked from view by a wall and the ladder. It's like a secret room in a ship with very few secrets.

"This is where I come when I'd like to be alone," she says in a low voice. "This space is always quiet, and Captain is rarely in her quarters, so it's the closest thing to privacy I have on this ship." There is a thick wool blanket tucked beneath the ladder post against the wall, and she spreads it on the floor before settling herself on it, leaning against the wall and taking a long drink from the bottle. She passes it to me with a wink. "I *may* also have a secret stash of plum wine from a raid awhile back."

The wine is tangy and sweet on my tongue, reminding me of warm summer fruit picked straight from the tree. I take another sip before passing it back to her. Fuck, it's delicious. In this small space, our knees are pressed together, and I can smell a hint of lemon verbena and amber from her skin. Her complexion is flawless, and her hair is like satin. She undoubtedly also has a secret stash of well-made soaps and bath products. "So," I begin, "what would you like to know?"

She asks about the glade and how I came to the Sea Song. I tell her a condensed version, not wanting to ruin this pleasant moment with talk of tragedy. "I lost someone I loved very much, and so I had no reason to remain." Her hand touches my knee, providing comfort without a word. I find myself telling her about the pennyway, though I leave out Mamère and the majority of the details. Her eyes are the color of obsidian in the dim light, and they widen as I talk about the flowers.

"I'm glad I burned them," she says. Her hand squeezes my knee. "I'm sorry for all that you went through."

"What about you?" I ask. "What led you to a life of nautical crime?"

She giggles, and the sound seems out of place coming from someone so reserved and reticent. "I was born very far from Idythia, across the great sea. My parents were common, though my mother was uncommonly beautiful. My father was a woodcarver and weapon maker. He worked crafting dragons and water spirits from flamewood. It is a beautiful and treasured material on my continent. He taught me weaponry from the time I learned to walk. They both died when I was a child."

I lean into her, my broad hand spanning nearly the entire width of her leg as I reach out in sympathy. "I never knew my parents, they also died when I was very young."

She nods, the gesture sympathetic, and continues. "There was a creature who lived in the mountains near our village. He was clever and evil, a spirit of darkness. He often disguised himself as a beautiful woman to capture travelers and feast upon them in his mountain cave. My father loved my mother with all his heart, and he was also a kind and generous man. He came upon an injured young woman one night while journeying back to our home, and he brought her back to our home to help her. He never thought to wonder if she was anything other than a scared young woman. In the middle of the night she transformed back to her true form and killed my mother in her sleep. He took my father back to his cave, and I was left alone. I was fortunate; the creature hadn't seen me as I had already gone to bed in a corner of our verandah. When I woke, I found my mother dead and a trail left behind by the creature. I recognized the large paw prints and knew what had to have happened. I stole a small boat from the shore and left. I was small and so frightened of the creature returning or what I would face as an orphan. I didn't give myself time to grieve." She takes another long drink of the plum wine, and I watch her graceful throat as she swallows. "I was near death when Ballad's parents found me. I had been adrift on the sea for weeks, but had somehow made my way across the great sea to the ocean northwest of Minos'Idyl. They took me in, and I've grown up here. I'm a few years older than Ballad—we grew up together. She became captain almost four years ago, and I've been beside her since."

"Gods, Tuii," I reply.

She smiles. "My dedication to the Sea Song is my life now. This ship is my home, and Ballad is family. Someday I would like to see my continent again, but until then there is no place I belong more than here." She raises the bottle. "To found family."

I take the bottle and take a sip with a smile. "To found family."

KONIDAS

CHAPTER FORTY-ONE
CICERINE
YEAR 993

The stone wall is cold against my skin as I reach out a hand, bracing myself. The body in the chair before me is breathing, barely, and I can see the slightest trickle of blood falling from his ear. The ropes binding him to the chair look like silk curtain tiebacks, and I glance to the window to confirm it. My hand looks so old, I raise it to my face and stare. My fingers are long and knobby with age, blue veins winding through my ashen skin like rivers on a plain. My nails are so long, so black, so sharp. The tips of my fingers are stained, but I can't make out the color. The room spins, and I struggle to stay on my feet. The floor seems to move beneath me; the world shifts, and I'm falling into black.

I jolt upright with a scream. It takes me a moment to realize I am in my bed at the inn. I am drenched in sweat, my blanket fisted in my hands and my hair plastered to my face. My breaths are coming too rapidly, and I count, trying to slow them. *One… Two… Three…* I have never had a nightmare as realistic as this one. What exactly was that? I attempt to recall the images, but they're fuzzy and quickly fading. Was there a man? I rub my temples and take a deep breath. Dreams are not reality, just the product of an overactive mind set free.

It's been three days since I worked with Salvatorre, and I'm already impatient to do so again. My shift at the inn seems to drag like molasses, despite having plenty to do. I bake flaky flatbread, a skill I have finally mastered, though I'm still lousy with the yeast breads Mamère made so effortlessly. A few braces of rabbits were delivered this morning, and I was able to bribe one of the service staff to clean them for me. Though I have gotten over my reservations about cooking meat, it still turns my stomach to handle animals before they're properly broken down. The rabbit meat is currently braising in the ovens alongside mustard greens and fresh fennel. The smell is actually quite enticing—savory and herbaceous with a bite from fresh garlic. Beatrice sticks her head in the kitchen and barks at me that it's time for lunch. I carefully balance trays of flatbread, eggplant dip, and salty brined olives on my arms and carry them out to the dining room. I'm glad no guests have come down for lunch yet, so I don't have to feel self-conscious about my bare legs. I take a moment to gaze out the window onto the busy city street, feeling a little wistful. I wonder what it would be like to belong here like all these humans do. I let out a sigh, shoulders dropping. It does no good to worry about things beyond my control.

As I turn back toward the kitchen, a vibrant blue catches my eye from outside the window. A woman walks by wearing a cloak of the brightest sapphire I think I've ever seen. Great Idyth, she is beautiful. Her hair is past her waist and midnight black, but I swear I can see strands of silver catch the light as she walks past. Her skin is a rich, cool tone, free from any blemishes, so unlike my own freckled face. But her eyes—her eyes are the most stunning color I have ever seen. They look like shards of ice, cold and breathtaking. Deadly. She turns her head as I stare, and our eyes meet. A strange, bright flare flashes through my chest, and all at once my hands feel electric. But in a breath, the sensation is gone, and I'm left staring at the beautiful woman. Flushing beetroot red,

I shove my hands in my apron and turn so quickly I nearly trip and fall. I hope she didn't notice my staring. But gods, I have never seen a more striking woman.

The rest of the evening I try, and fail, to stop thinking about the woman in blue. There is endless variety in the people of Konidas, people from every continent and in every shape and size, but I have never in my life seen someone so striking. I can't help wondering about where she is from. What she is doing in this dingy city? Why would someone wearing such fine clothing even be here among the filthy sailors and fishmongers of this place? I wonder if I will see her another time, or if she will be gone before I leave this inn again.

THE SEA

CHAPTER FORTY-TWO
JYNN
YEAR 993

We drink long into the evening, the bottle growing lighter with each chime of the clock that echoes from the captain's quarters. Tuii's legs are intertwined with mine, and she leans her head on my shoulder as she laughs joyfully at something dumb I said. I look down at her, and my heart races at the sheer beauty of her—her high cheekbones and sparkling eyes, the warm blush of her full lips. Her eyes meet mine as I look up from her perfect mouth, and I tense. I hadn't realized just how close we were until this moment. The heat of her small body warms me more than the wine, and I can feel her chest rise and fall with her quickening breaths. I freeze, my mind a mess of plum wine and unexpected desire. I've never been this close to anyone other than Ceci. I feel like I'm betraying her, it hurts. But then my swimming, wine-drenched thoughts scatter again, and I can't focus on Cicerine. All my thoughts are on Tuii, so close to me I think I can hear her heart beating.

Her hand lifts from my thigh and drifts to the back of my neck, gently caressing the hair at my nape. I can smell the sweetness of the wine on her breath, and before I can consider the decision, she closes the distance between her face and mine. She tastes like moonlight, dark and bright upon my tongue. Her fingers slide up to grip my hair firmly, and I groan into her mouth at the ripple of gentle pain. She bites my lip in response, and I growl as I pull her to me roughly. She is so small compared to me, but I feel no need to be gentle. This woman could kill me in an instant, and we both know it.

She is nearly on my lap in this small space, and I reach beneath her and heft her onto me with one arm. Her kiss becomes fervent, and our mouths collide in a clash of tongues and teeth. My hands are in her hair, and I grip the sleek black silk, pulling her head back and baring her throat. I run my tongue down the side of her neck, tasting her, before nipping and sucking at the soft skin. She moans and presses her body against me with a roll of her hips. I release my grip on her hair, and she uses her palms on my shoulders to lift herself up, placing her knees on either side of my thighs. Tuii pushes me back against the wall with a firm shove and kisses me fiercely, running a hand down the length of my body and tugging at the hem of my shirt. I push her back and sit up just long enough to pull my shirt over my head and toss it only gods know where. Her breath is ragged as she looks down at me, then she follows my lead, pulling her black shift from her body. Her torso is covered in scars—sword slashes and stab wounds, marks from arrows and claws. The topography of her skin is breathtaking, and I pull her down to me, licking a raised red scar above her left breast. Her hand roams across my freckled chest, and lands on my throat—pushing me back down against the floor. She tightens her fingers around my neck, nails biting into my skin, and a heady rush pulls a moan from my lips. With my eyes closed I can hear her panting breaths, and heat builds in my core. My body moves more quickly than my mind, and when it catches up, I stop for the briefest moment. Am I really about to do this? I move to raise up on my elbows, and she pushes me back down with one hand, tugging at my pants with the other. Her small body eases its way down mine, pulling my pants from my hips as it does, and she tosses them aside before kicking my legs apart with her knee. She looks like a dark goddess between my thighs, her long hair wild, falling across her face and bare torso. My hips raise of their own accord as she runs a finger up the center of me, and I groan at the touch. I am drenched with need, lost in this moment, unable to think about a single thing outside of this room.

She kisses me again as she pulls her own black leggings off. With agonizing slowness, she kisses her way down my body, tongue swirling around one nipple and then the other. Her teeth nip at the soft skin of my stomach, and she licks a hip bone as she grips my ass. I nearly cry out at the combination of pleasure and pain. I feel her hot breath on the soft curls between my thighs and look up at her, perched above me with a wicked grin. Her hands press my legs farther apart, baring me to her, and I moan as she slips a finger into me. My eyes roll back as her tongue slides through my sensitive flesh, parting me. For a fleeting moment, I feel uncomfortable. I don't feel quite right like this; these parts of me feel *good*, but they don't feel right. But the sensations she elicits from my nerves silence my thoughts, and I lean into her touch. Working that finger in and out, her tongue laps at my flesh, sending waves of pleasure throughout my core. She teases me, licking up and down but never quite at the center, until I cry out in frustrated ecstasy. In an instant, her mouth closes over me, tongue flicking up and down alongside her fingers. Another finger slides into me, and I feel my body clench around her. She finds a perfect rhythm, working her hand and mouth against me until I feel as if I may lose consciousness. The world goes white as I come, screaming out her name while I buck against her mouth. She licks at me, pulling every last drop of climax from my body, drinking in my pleasure as her fingers move, stretching me around her. I struggle to breathe, chest rising and falling in rough, gasping breaths as she skillfully pulls another orgasm from me. I wasn't even aware that was possible. I look down at her, hair mussed and her face slick with my pleasure. I grab her hair roughly, and pull her lips to mine, tasting myself on her as my tongue pushes into her mouth with a fierce need. She smiles against me.

I take a moment to catch my breath and try to clear my head. I'm drunk; this is clear. But I want this. Tuii's head rests on my naked chest, and I reach down, pulling her face to me with both hands. I kiss her deeply, my hand running down her back to cup her firm ass in my broad palm. I shift her body with mine, until she's back on top of me, her wet heat pressed against my stomach. I'm at least a head taller than her, maybe more, and I feel huge with her in this position. She is so light, yet so deadly. My hands run down her scarred legs and those lean muscles flex at my touch. I move my hand between her thighs, and she gasps as I press into her. I do not ease into her, and she moans loudly at the brunt force of my fingers pushing inside her. Gods, penetrating this woman is divine. Her moan nearly takes me over the edge again, and I grab her ass in both of my hands, pulling her up to my face in a single smooth motion. I turn my head to bite her thigh before slowly running my tongue through her. My hands are still on her backside, and I pull her down onto me, crushing my face against her, tasting her with a wild groan. She grinds into me, rising up just long enough for me to take a breath before my mouth is on her again. I am at her mercy, and she uses my mouth in a delicious way, riding my face with her head thrown back in ecstasy. My tongue darts in and out of her. Her slick, soft flesh, like a ripe peach against my lips. Her hips begin to lose their steady rhythm, and I feel her body spasm as she gets closer and closer. What I wouldn't give to be able to see her right now, the picture of her lithe body rocking over me like this. Her thighs clench and I feel the tension against my cheek, my hands on her ass pull her against my mouth even harder. I suck her clit into my mouth, pulling at her, ripping the climax from her body as she goes pliant in my hands. I slide my hands under her thighs to support her as she rides out this moment. Such small feminine noises of pleasure falling from her fierce mouth undo me, and I nearly reach down to touch myself.

She can barely hold herself up, sliding her hips from my face and letting her body fall atop mine in a graceful whisper of movement. "Fuck," she says, so quietly I barely hear her. My arms slip around her, and I kiss the top of her head. I can't tell if it's the ship and the sea, or the wine, but my head spins.

"Um…I think I might pass out if we stay here much longer," I say with a slightly slurred voice.

Tuii laughs and pushes up from my body, grabbing her shift and slipping it over her head. "Well then, Red, let's get you to your bunk."

My pants and shirt land on my chest and jolt me awake; I didn't realize I had even closed my eyes. I shake my head, trying to clear my mind, and nausea grips me for a moment. All right. No head shaking. Carefully, I get my clothes back on, and Tuii reaches down and takes my hand in hers, pulling me up. I'm asleep before I realize how I've gotten to my bunk.

KONIDAS

CHAPTER FORTY-THREE
MAELWEN
YEAR 993

The night is silent, a murky gray spreading over the horizon, as I walk down a dockside alley shortly before dawn. The man before me is lanky and long, and gods, he smells of unwashed skin and the sea. I am starving, having gone far too long without truly feeding. I begin to sing, witchsong flowing from me effortlessly, the tune somber and deep. From behind, I cannot see his face, but I can sense the moment the man's eyes go glassy, and I slip behind him like a lover in the dark. I flick out a single claw and gracefully run it along the side of his throat, severing the artery in one swift motion. His blood tastes of salt, likely from months of surviving on sea rations, but it immediately sets my mouth watering. My control is weak.

By the time I lower the man's pale corpse into the sea, I feel heavy, so full of blood and power that I'm sluggish with the weight of it all. I fly back to the tavern rather than walk, careful not to be seen in my current blood-covered state. Slipping through the back, I make my way to the tub, and after washing my face quickly, I begin to fill the large copper tub with steaming water. I soak away the blood and gore, dumping the sullied water in the alleyway when I feel clean at last and the water has cooled. My thick hair is heavy with water, but I am refreshed, and ready to travel to Iowain. Wringing out as much as I can from my hair, I plait it into a thick braid and dress in a comfortable blouse and leather leggings. It is early enough that I do not come across anyone, and I leave the tavern in resolute quiet.

THE FLIGHT TAKES ME FAR LESS TIME THAN IT DID ON MY journey to Konidas, and I touch down on the desolate earth in just under two days. I slept only once, but I am so invigorated from my feast that I feel little need for rest. I avoided the town and came directly to the tower, uninterested in reliving the traumas of my past. A few witches mill about the great stone tower, dressed in shades of gray that blend into the terrain. I approach the witch nearest to me and nod in greeting.

"Good evening. I have flown here from Konidas." She doesn't reply, so I go on. "Have you knowledge of the humans? Has word of 'New Church,' as they call themselves, made its way to Iowain?"

The witch lowers her head. "We have heard of violence toward witchkind, but it has not reached our lands as of yet. Come."

I follow her into the tower, surprised at the warmth of the interior. The walls are rough stone, but the floor is worn smooth from eons of witches' feet. I did not expect the large dining hall that I enter, nor did I expect the plentitude of kind-faced witches gathered around the table in the center. Some could pass for human, but others have skin and hair in shades no human possesses. I am greeted by each of them, whether by a wave or a nod, and I greet them back in kind. I recognize one face, framed in silken blonde hair—the witch who gifted me my cloak. She nods to me with a small smile, gladness in her expression at seeing me in a different life. A small, thin witch with hair like starlight stands and beckons me toward an empty seat beside her.

"Greetings," she says. "Welcome to the tower. My name is Caelfry. I assume you have come to discuss the humans."

I sit and nod in agreement. "I dwell in Konidas. There has been talk of threats to our kind, perpetuated by a rising group called the 'New Church'. There is much to attempt to convey succinctly."

"Do your best, witchling," she says with a gentle smile, brushing her long, white hair over her shoulder.

I tell her of the flowers and the rising unrest in Konidas. Witches have begun to congregate in the dining hall, groups of them filling the large room and listening to my tale with rapt attention. "My primary concerns are these," I say. "I believe these men truly intend on driving us from Konidas, and maybe further. I also believe there to be a connection between this so-called 'New Church' and the purple flowers I spoke of. I trust my instincts, and they scream to me of danger." I reach into my pocket and pull out the small packet of long-wilted flora. "These are the flowers of which I speak."

The witches pass the packet around, sniffing it and examining the bruised flowers. Some of them nod. One, a younger redhead, standing near the back wall speaks. "I know of this flower." Heads turn to look at her, surprise clear on many faces. "When I was a child, it grew near our home. My mother cautioned me to avoid it. Animals who ate the flower either died or fell into long periods of sleep from which they never woke. When she taught me tisanes and herb magics, she cautioned me that it could be used for compulsion, but too strong a dose would result in death. She called it 'pennyway.' Is this the flower of which you speak?"

Gravely, I nod. "I did not know its name, but I am sure it is the same. The crate we found in the house bore the mark of Minos'Idyl. Do any of you know why?"

Caelfry turns to me. "Perhaps, at least in part. We have been aware for some time of something going on in the minotaur's lands. Flying overhead feels wrong, like the air is heavy with death. Many of us have experienced the sensation." She pauses, glancing at the other witches. "I wonder if this flower may be what finally allows them access to our chaos magic."

I am following, but a bit confused. "What is chaos magic?" I ask.

"Oh, how I wish you had grown up here. There is so much to explain. To be brief, chaos magic is the source of our power and what differentiates us from the humans. The Crone has endless access to such magic. In short, chaos magic flows through us all and is what connects each of us to the Crone. Humans have long sought to use it for themselves, and I fear this flower may be what finally allows them access to the chaos."

"Why would you come to this conclusion? And for what purpose do they attempt to gain magic? They hate magic."

"We have quietly faced this threat for centuries. Time is a constant ebb and flow of power and supremacy. Humankind has never wanted to be seen as weak, they have tried many ways to gain gifts of their own, alongside their god and against our kind."

I am stunned into silence. These humans *hate* us for our abilities, and yet they aim to take them for themselves? "What do you think they plan to do if they do at last gain access to chaos?"

Caelfry's face is grim as she replies, "They plan to kill us all, as Idyth once attempted."

"Idyth?" I ask, confused. "The old god?"

Caelfry laughs without humor. "God," she spits out in contempt. "Idyth was not a god. He was a man who sought power. A man who sought to raise humankind above all others. This continent bears his name solely because the Crone of The

Golden Age cared little for titles and land. The old gods fled long ago, driven to the sea and sky by the failures and follies of man. The Crone of the Golden Age slew a single god, which is another story entirely. Idyth attempted to overthrow the Crone when she was still weakened from her battle with the old god. His followers drove the minotaurs from the mainland, relegating them to Minos'Idyl, slaughtering those who did not comply. They burned countless witches—nearly half of an entire generation was destroyed due to their hatred. The Crone of the Golden Age was a vast power, moreso than any of her successors. She sang a song of death, and Idyth, along with hundreds of his followers, died as they swarmed the tower. It is then that our affections for men ended. We were not always cruel; once we loved and lived among them, but after the fall of Idyth, we were kind no more." Sadness etches her expression, and I wonder at what she may have lost.

The words seem to echo in the large hall. I knew nothing of this history, and I suspect the world outside the tower does not either. It would seem the cult of Idyth is rising once more. She is right; the humans will likely kill us all if they are somehow able to obtain magic. I am not sure how, but we must stop them. If they need the flowers, perhaps it would be as easy as destroying the flowers completely. However, I do not know the extent of their supply.

"What do we do?" I look at Caelfry, but my question is directed toward everyone. No one speaks for a moment, but then a witch near the back pipes up.

"Why can't we just recall witchkind to Iowain and simply wait? We will outlive the humans. This is a problem for mortals."

I shake my head. "No, it is not. This is a line in the sand. If we allow the humans to force us back into isolation, they win. I am not prepared to surrender to the weak, and neither is the Crone." At that, everyone seems to snap to attention, and I go on. "I have spoken with the Crone, and I can assure you she will also refuse to bow to men. She had much to share. I cannot explain the bulk of it, but we have a part to play in something larger—pieces from all over the continent are slowly moving into place. One of us may be more vital than we thought." The witches titter among themselves, and I hear snippets of agreement as well as voices of opposition. "I am no leader," I speak out above the din, "but I also am no servant. We must stand stalwart against this threat."

Caelfry nods, and standing, addresses the gathered crowd. "The Crone has been absent from the tower for quite some time, and I have not spoken to her. Whatever she is doing, she does it without much communication. I had hoped to speak with her upon her return, but I am no empathate. We cannot rely on her guidance in this matter. Should we reach her, we will consult her wisdom and adjure her to assist in the ways she can, but we must take action. Let us call our brethren, gather our people, and come together to plan our response. Those of you who are empathates, call to your sisters from here. Those who use hydrology, send out your waters. Maelwen, I charge you with gathering what information you can find. It would seem Konidas is at the center of this, and you are the only one of us with true roots in the city."

I nod before asking, "I do not know these terms you mention."

Caelfry gives me a sad smile. "I forget, forgive an old witch for her shortcomings. Empathates communicate through a plane of chaos magic that touches each of us. Much like the Crone, they can reach all of witchkind through mindspeak. Hydrologists are similarly gifted, however, they speak and work magic through the waters of the continent. Any witch who touches any earthbound water will hear them. There are many other gifts among us, some cast fire, others control storms. We have witches who work in shadows and some who connect to plants. A couple of our kin can speak with animals, some know all languages without study. There are many gifts lost to time, some I do not know, others I can find in our records if you desire. I know of only three: those who can create artifacts of intention, those who shift their form, and those who possess the Song of Death. The only living witch who currently possesses the Death Song is the Crone herself. It is a gift passed through bloodlines, though her mother before her did not possess it. It may be that it only presents in the Crone; we have no way of knowing."

"What is an artifact of intention?" I ask.

"There are some ancient artifacts we guard here in the tower. Items imbued with power that do not necessarily require a witch to wield them. We have a sword which always strikes flesh, a compass that finds the item most desired by the holder, and a torch which can always be lit, regardless of the conditions. There are others as well. I know of items which can rescue people from death's clutches and items which can kill with a single touch. They are rare, seldom spoken of, and no new artifacts of intent have been created in over a century." Her face looks tight, pained, as though something she has spoken elicits hurt in her. I do not have time to inquire further.

I was unaware my kin possessed so many varied gifts and am mildly disappointed to not yet know what, if any, gift I may wield. "Thank you, Caelfry," I reply. "I appreciate both your knowledge and leadership. I will return to Konidas, we will do what we can there, and I will journey to Minos'Idyl to see what may be happening on the island." Caelfry nods and reaches out a hand to squeeze mine. The small gesture brings a rush of unexpected emotion over me. I have gone so long without knowing my people, and now I feel as though I could belong here. However, this is not my home, and I have friends of my own who need me. I squeeze her hand in reply and turn to head to the kitchen to gather some food for my journey home, when at once the tower shakes as a scream of agony splits through the air like lightning.

Every witch falls to their knees, myself included. The scream tears into my mind, clawing and shredding my synapses, an agonizing assault to both my thoughts and my body. The pain is indescribable. Some witches vomit, others convulse on the floor. But in an instant, the pain stops and a voice speaks directly to my thoughts. *"A sister is dead. By the hands of men, in the fires of hatred, one of our own has been taken. We shall mourn this loss, but we shall rise anew and avenge a light burned out long before its wick was spent. I take steps to secure our rightful place in this world. We do not belong in the dirt; we will no longer be tread upon. Do not think yourselves abandoned—I hear all, and I have heard your plans and pleas. We shall convene at the solstice, and I will share my plans for our future. Gather, my children, for the end of the age of men approaches. Light your fires and honor your sister; may she be the last loss we suffer. Our ascent is near."*

The room is silent as we all take in the words of the Crone. I recognize her voice from that strange day in Athydis, but I do not understand her message. "A witch is dead?" I ask no one in particular. "What does this mean?"

"It would seem," a dark-haired witch nearby begins, "the time of executions has begun anew. Fly home; you will be needed."

It takes me little time to gather food and a bedroll for my flight back to Konidas. I feel a sort of loss as I make to leave the tower, but I know my found family is back in Konidas, and they are who need me the most. I say my goodbyes quickly; the witches are all shaken by the news. Caelfry embraces me as I don my cloak. "I await your communications. Fly well, young one."

I take to the sky, the darkness enveloping me as I rush toward my home.

KONIDAS

CHAPTER FORTY-FOUR
SHELL
YEAR 993

I'm ripped from my bed by the shrill sound of a scream. Racin' through the tavern, I hit the street in my bedclothes, thoroughly unprepared for what I see. About a hundred yards down the road, in the center of the street, a massive pyre has been erected. Branches and kindling lie stacked into a rough square that is nearly half my height. Those "New Church" fools are all over the place. They seem to have banded together with some shitty ass tailor to put together matchin' robes in a perfect shade of *mold*. The air feels tense, onerous, as though the world itself can feel the nasty gathered here. The screamin' continues, cleaving the air like a blade. The street is empty save for the cultists, gray-robed specters walking the streets. I look frantically around, seeking the source of the gods-awful screaming, and see Cartwright standing near the tavern door.

"I was about to come for you, Shell," he says. "They built that thing in minutes. The whole group of 'em at once, like roaches."

"Who the fuck is screamin'?"

"I don't know, I didn't want to leave the tavern. Folks are

scared in there, nobody knows what's happenin' and the whole lot of 'em are terrified to come out."

"Well then," I say, "let's keep 'em safe."

"Shell," Cartwright begins. "You can't save everyone. Go home, get your Ma and Pap safe. You don't need to be here, please."

I look at him, shocked he would suggest such a thing. "Cartwright, when have I ever backed down from a fuckin' fight?"

"That's exactly what I'm saying Shell! Godsdamnit. Stop puttin' yourself in the middle of shit! You own a tavern, you ain't the town mayor. This is not your responsibility!"

"What the fuck? You think 'cause I'm some sort of *lowly barkeep* I can't take care of the people in this city? Fuck you, Cartwright. I ain't gotta be the mayor to care about the place that raised me. I've lived here my whole life. I sure as shit am not gonna sit idly by as a fucking cult takes over my home. And I ain't gonna let one more person die because of it. You know how shit like this happens? Because people say it's not their business. Well, I'm making it my business."

Cartwright runs his hands through his hair, lips drawn in from tryin' to contain all the things he wants to say. He takes a deep ragged breath and stands up straight once again. "Alright then, Shell. Alright. I'm standin' with you. I just don't want to see you hurt, Shell. Please."

I turn on my heel and walk back into the tavern with determination. This is *my* fuckin' town, and I am not about to let these creepy fucks scare my people. The tavern is full of folks, faces I know well. The people who drink my ale and eat our food. These are good people, workin' people. Ain't a one of 'em dressed in finery, just regular folks in well-worn shoes, spendin' their lives in hard labor to keep their families fed. Martine is in the kitchen, shakin' but fine, and I send her to get Ma and Pap. Cartwright was right about that; I want them where I know they're safe. Fergus's wife, Agnes, and the kids are here as well, tucked into a corner. The oldest boy stands in front of the family with fire in his eyes, standing tall like a man, even with his gangly limbs and knobby knees. "Athros, right?" I ask as I walk over.

"Yes, ma'am," he replies. "Mam says we should be here, so we came. She's got me wee sister wrapped up. I got the rest of the kids with me, and we're ready to help."

I can't help but smile at this fierce little boy, so much like his father. "Well, Athros, I need your brothers and sisters to stay with your Mam to help keep her safe. Do you think they can do that?" He nods, his small mouth set determinedly in a grim line. "You're a lot bigger, and I need your help out here. Can you help me check in with everyone? Let me know if anyone needs help or if anyone is missin' family?" He nods and sets off toward the nearest table, happy to have some responsibility. I clamber up onto the bar top, and call out above the din. "Oy! All of you are stayin' put til I say otherwise, we clear? I'm going to bar the door, and me and my men will be keepin' guard from the outside. I don't know what the fuck is going on here, but it ain't comin' through *my* doors today!" I hear some acknowledgements and see some noddin' heads before hoppin' back down. Godrick comes down the stairs at that moment, clearly havin' run up lookin' for Mael.

"Maelwen?" He asks, uncertainty in his voice.

"She ain't here," I reply, "But I could sure use your help."

We bar the front door with the heavy oak beam I keep for the rare instance when I close my doors. Slinkin' out the back, I assign one of Cartwright's bigger men to keep watch and Cartwright, Godrick and I hustle back toward the front. Another pained scream rips through the mornin' air, and we all turn to see a girl, tied up and strugglin' violently, being dragged toward the pyre. No, not a girl—a witch. We all move in unison, racin' toward the pyre. She can't be more than twenty, and I know what each of us is thinkin'. We are all picturing Mael in her stead. Like flies, the 'New Church' men swarm out from behind nearby buildings and alleyways to block our path. I have my stick, and Cartwright has a pair of daggers, but we stop as five men step in front of us.

"Not today, witch lover," one growls at me.

"What the fuck do you think you're doing?" I scream at the men. "Let that girl go!"

One of the men laughs. "Oh no, we won't be doing that." Cartwright palms his daggers and steps toward the group, and I follow his lead, heftin' my stick to my shoulder. Sure, there's five of 'em, but me and Cartwright are big, and we've got weapons. I don't know about Godrick, but he's tall and that's gotta count for somethin'. I lean into my back foot, distributing my weight in preparation to strike. But the man just laughs and pulls somethin' from his robes. The bottle in his hand is tiny, but I recognize that shade of purple.

Before we can move, both Cartwright and I are seized from behind. His daggers strike out violently, slashin' at his captors. He takes out one man's eye and rakes a large gash across the chest of another, but they hold fast. It takes four men to hold him, and another two men usin' their full weight to hold me down. I scream and thrash, but the man unstoppers the tiny vial and shoves it between my lips and then Cartwright's. A few drops of bitter liquid make it into my mouth before I can spit them out. It tastes like shit, sour and pungent. My tongue goes numb first, becoming a useless slug trapped behind my lips. Everythin' goes hazy, and my limbs fill with sand.

I hear a voice comin' from somewhere, but I can't tell what direction. I'm all topsy turvy. *"Be still,"* it whispers, and my body fails me. I cannot move. Only my eyes have free range of motion and they flash to Cartwright in terror, only to find him on the ground beside me, still as a stone. I can't see Godrick, but that pyre looms before me, and I hear the witch continuin' to scream as they drag her forward. I cannot move at all.

KONIDAS

CHAPTER FORTY-FIVE
CICERINE
YEAR 993

Beatrice rushes into the kitchen and I jump; I've never seen her move quickly before, and she scares me. "Quick! Get to the basement!" she hisses in a low voice.

"What?" I'm confused. I've only ever been down there to fetch jars of preserved fruits and vegetables. I can't imagine what she could need so urgently.

"You need to hide, girl."

She looks afraid, and my heartbeat quickens. I'm anxious enough as it is; I can't handle much more. Her bony fingers grab my wrist, and I follow her through the kitchen to the basement stairwell door. She has her finger to her lips, standing completely still, ear cocked to listen, and I hear a scream from outside the inn.

"What's happening?" I whisper in a panicked voice I barely recognize.

"Those people who have been yelling about the witches and the other non-human folks? They're doing something in the streets, and I don't know what it is, but it's not something good. You ain't safe right now, girl. Get down there, and do not make a sound, all right?" I nod my head, too scared to speak, and she touches my arm before closing and locking the door, leaving me to the dark.

There's a candle and matchbox on a small table near the door. I've used it the few times I've had to come down here past sunset, and I strike a match now, lighting the candle with shaking fingers. The basement is moist and cold, mostly stone-enforced dirt walls, barely a room at all. It was clearly dug after the inn was built, and whoever built it shored the walls with rough stone bricks. They did a poor job, some of them having fallen out and others broken under the weight of the earth they contain. It smells loamy and dank down here, and I shiver. I might be a woodborn faun, but I'm not accustomed to underground spaces. It feels stifling, claustrophobic. I'm so nervous I can't seem to contain my gift, and the roots around me move like worms in the soil as they grow longer, encouraged by the power that leaks from me in waves. I try to staunch the energy flowing from me, but like a deluge, it cannot be stopped once it has begun. My soul calms ever so slightly as I connect with the network of roots trapped within this deep earth. The life in the soil is a comfort, and I lean into its familiarity. There isn't anywhere to sit down here, so I drag over a piece of loose canvas covering a stack of crates and set it on the ground, sitting with crossed legs and placing my flickering candle before me on the damp floor.

My hearing is more acute than that of humans, and my ears perk up as I hear the thundering rumble of feet and sharp sounds of terror from above. I feel so unsafe here. The glade didn't feel like this—even at the end, I knew it was one man at fault, poisoning the minds of everyone until they were too far gone to be saved. They were evil and tainted, but it was a moment in time, not a state of being. Here, I feel like everyone is constantly a threat, as if everyone hates me. I hope that Salvatorre is safe; hopefully he was away on a delivery or visiting his vignerons. I hope Beatrice doesn't end up hurt. She hasn't been warm, but she hasn't been cruel. Clearly she cares for me a little if she took the time to hide me. I have so few people to worry about here, but that makes them feel all the more precious. I'm so alone in this city. My heart aches for Jynn. What I wouldn't give to lay my head on her shoulder, for her to hold me and make me feel safe.

I'm so lost in my thoughts I don't realize what is occurring around me until something brushes my leg. The musty walls of the basement are no longer stone and earth. They're covered in green: grasses, herbs, flowers, even some thick vines bearing heavy, ripe zucchini and yellow squash. Foliage covers the walls in a thick carpet, tumbling onto the floor in a jumble of leaves and stems. I close my eyes and place my hands on the ground, reaching out with my ability to trace the plants from root to stem, flowing through each leaf and vine, feeling each and every inch of life surrounding me. When I open my eyes they widen with genuine surprise and appreciation. I have never grown this many things at one time, nor have I ever grown *anything* without intentionally trying. The sight of it all is remarkable, like a vertical garden. The plants muffle some of the sound from above, and my racing heartbeat starts to slow. I'm soothed by the familiar scent of green, growing things. The air feels fresher and far more clean. My claustrophobia begins to wane. It smells like home.

There is a scuffing noise from the door at the top of the stairs, and I flinch, listening intently to hear if it's Beatrice or someone else. I hear a voice that sounds like hers but can't quite make out the words as she speaks to what sounds like a man on the other side of the door. Her voice gets louder, and I hear her shout an instant before the door crashes inward.

"I *told* you! It's a *basement*, you fucking dolt," she yells. "There is nothing down there but *food.*"

I scramble against the wall and pull the canvas over me, silently praying to any god who can hear me to keep me safe.

Heavy footsteps clatter down the stairs, and someone steps onto the dirt floor. I am mostly hidden, but I can see the slightest sliver of a gray robe, the same color as the robes Father Farragen wore. My mind lurches, tightening my chest and flooding me with panic and adrenaline. I act on instinct, not thinking, my body taking charge. From where my palms are pressed to the earth, hot rivulets of energy splinter out, following the vast network of tiny roots through the tight soil. It whips toward the boots of the man who now stands in the basement. He barely has time to cry out before he hits the floor, seizing and jerking, smoke rising from his bulk. Spittle foams from his mouth before turning pink with blood as he spasms violently before going still, his body a gray pile. I hear Beatrice yelp, and she dashes down the stairs, eyes ablaze with worry. She stops at the foot of the stairs, dumbfounded, and stares at the walls of the basement for a moment before noticing the collapsed form of the man. I hear her sharp intake of breath as she takes in the scene before her.

"Cicerine?" she whispers. "Where are you, girl?"

I shuffle out from beneath the canvas and vegetation, my legs shaking as I stand. I don't feel weak or spent like I did before, but the adrenaline wearing down chills me, and I shiver uncontrollably. Beatrice looks at me from beneath furrowed brows and does the absolute last thing I expect. She yanks me to her, arms wrapping around my shoulders, and hugs me. I stand perfectly still for a moment before I soften and return the embrace, tears spilling from my eyes. "I'm sorry, I didn't mean to do any of this." A sob forces its way up my throat, and I try to gulp it back down. "I have a way with plants. They grow. I was nervous, and I don't know how this happened. I didn't mean to hurt him." My words catch. "His robe, it's what the man who killed my mother wore. I...I...I don't know what happened."

Beatrice kicks the gray pile. "Good for you," she says in her usual flat tone. "He was one of the people making trouble. Something real bad happened up there. I'm not sure what exactly, but it was real bad. The hubbub is done now, but there's dead folks all around."

"What do we do?" I look at the body, my gorge rising as I realize I've killed someone again. Who am I becoming?

"Well, we leave him here until nightfall." Her voice is no nonsense. "Then we drag him out. Leave him in an alley or something. I have a feeling he won't be the only body abandoned on the streets tonight. Come on, let's get you cleaned up. I think they're all gone now. I need to have a talk with Shell."

"About me?"

"About this city."

KONIDAS

CHAPTER FORTY-SIX
SHELL
YEAR 993

I'm trapped, locked in a prison within my mind. I can move my eyes just far enough to see Cartwright is even more fucked than me, face down with his nose bleedin' into the dirt. I knew what they had in that vial the instant I saw that fuckin' purple, but I didn't know until I went down just what it was gonna do. That godsdamn flower is the cause of all my problems, apparently. From the edge of my vision I see Godrick run and dart into an alley. I need to remind myself to thank whatever god decided to keep him safe. At least one of us can get away and find help. But that isn't what he does. Of course not.

The boy is scrawny, but he's fuckin' pissed, and suddenly he looks like a man as he runs toward the pyre. The 'New Church' asses are not fighters, clearly, and he manages to take a few down. I'm so low to the ground I can't see a damn thing over the scattered crowd, but I spot Godrick's head a few times, still headin' away from us and toward the girl. He catches my eye as I see another gray robe crumple, and the look in his gaze is feral. I know what he's thinkin', what we're all thinkin'. He can't let that girl die—she's too much like Maelwen.

I can hear them lightin' torches, and even through my likely broken nose, I can smell the stink of burnin' liquor and wood. They must be about to light the pyre. From here all I can see is the top, a ragged column of sticks and branches like a gnarled hand reachin' for the sky. The girl is still screamin', but I hear Godrick screamin' too. My eyes hurt from strainin' as I struggle to see. All that's in my line of sight is gray fabric and feet. My fingers tingle, but I'm still completely unable to move my limbs. I've never felt so useless in my life. Guilt floods my thoughts; we shouldn't have come out here. I should've barred the doors and stayed inside. This is all my fault.

One of the 'New Church' fucks moves just enough for me to have a clear view of the pyre. But I don't see Godrick. Wait, there. He's got the witch by the dress, screamin' and trying to pull her free. His voice rises up above the din, and I hear him shout "No." I feel sick; he's so close but there are so many men holdin' him back. This isn't how this was supposed to go. Their fingers claw at him, tearin' his clothes and rippin' at his hair but he keeps going. I hear the nauseatin' crunch of bone as one of them snaps Godrick's arm. It falls limply to his side, useless. But he doesn't slow, just keeps grabbin' at her with the hand he's still got. He's not a fighter, probably never hit another man in his life, but he's the only one of us left standin', and he fights with all he's got. He knows he's her only chance.

I don't want to keep watchin' this; I know how it's going to go. My eyes sting, tears prickin' the corners as I watch the boy struggle against the hateful sea of gray. My chest feels wrong, like my heart is beating outside my ribs and can't remember what it's supposed to be doin'. And then it happens. I don't think the robed men even brought any weapons, content with their pyre and their tied up little girl. But *we* did, and one of the men picks up a discarded sword from the ground. I try to scream, but I can't. I'm helpless, watching in slow motion as the man stands up with the sword in both hands. He draws it back and strikes Godrick straight through.

The blade goes in to the hilt with a sticking sound, jutting from just beneath his collarbone like a boutonniere. Godrick stumbles for just a moment as the man in gray pulls the sword back out in one slick motion. His chest blooms with blood, a bright red flower on the front of his shirt. He looks like a little boy, wide eyed and full of shock. His eyes find mine and I blink furiously, prayin' he knows I'm tryin' to tell him *I'm here, you're not alone, I'm with you.* I don't even know what my fucking face looks like, I can't tell if I look comforting, if my face is twisted with grief or sorrow. I want so badly to be here for him, but I can't move, I can't get to him. I'd give anything to just be able to move my godsdamned limbs. A sharp bolt of pain shoots through my head as I strain against my invisible bonds with everything I have. It's not enough. Godrick turns back toward the witch, his movements slow. I don't want him to die alone, gods I don't want him to die alone. My tears at last spill over.

They come up from behind and light the pyre. It catches far too quickly. The witch is burnin' the moment the flames touch her skin. She doesn't scream, just stares ahead with a strength I can't imagine. I know Godrick is starin' right back at her. I'm screamin' so loud inside my head I'm sure my skull is bound to crack. I can't see his face, and it's killin' me. I want to roar like a beast, to rip these men limb from limb. I want to hold that boy, that sweet kid who I gave such a hard time for so long. He's a good man, and I am so proud of him. I hope the witch can see him, really *see* him. I hope she knows he tried. He tried so fucking hard.

My body won't move, but I can't stop the tears from pouring down my face as I'm stuck here, watchin'. He goes down but manages to stay up on his knees. There's blood spreadin' around him too quickly; I know there's nothin' can be done. Gods, I feel so helpless. The ground is black with it. The witch's body is a mangled flaming corpse, flesh fallin' from bone as the fire rages around her. Her face is long gone, bones beginnin' to separate as the fire consumes her. I know she's dead now, and I'm glad of it. But Godrick is still up. I hope he isn't seein' her like this. I hope this isn't the last thing he sees. It hurts me like nothin' ever has before. I asked for his help. *I* did this. He followed me right into this mess, and I'm still breathin', trapped here in my own limbs, watchin' him die. I keep my eyes on him, knowin' it won't be long.

I see the moment he leaves us. His shoulders sink, and he falls, slumped forward before the towerin' flame. His back rises once, and then he is still.

My fingertips move, just slightly, and I manage to swallow. Vomit rises to my mouth in a rush, but I choke it back down. All that's left of the pyre is blackened bones in a dying fire. Soot falls all around us like black snow. I hear the scrape of sand and see Cartwright's head is movin'. He looks at me and blinks, and I blink rapidly in reply, hopin' he understands my frantic eyes as "stay still." He does. The 'New Church' group doesn't bother to take their dead; they don't even bother to check if we are alive. They just leave, as if none of this even fuckin' matters, the pyre still smoking in the street. I hear a horse whinny and realize too late that this group must have ridden in and met the men who were already here—likely those same men who sat in my bar. They must have brought the girl with them, or picked her up along the way. Movement comes back to me slowly, but I'm able to move my arms enough to reach for Cartwright, placin' my hand on his broad back, feelin' his jagged breaths. When he looks up and sees my face I know that he knows.

People timidly begin to filter back into the street. One of Cartwright's men comes straight to us and helps turn him over. He's able to move his hands and feet, and speak, but he can't get up. I try to push myself upright but the strain is too much, and I fall back down. I let out a long, low sound that's made of grief and rage and desperation. Someone's arms come up under me and help me back to my feet, tossin' my arm around their shoulders to keep me upright. I turn to see who it is, and my breath catches in my throat—it's Pap. My Pap. My legs falter, and I nearly collapse as I fold into him, sobbin'. He holds me up with one arm, but puts the other around me, pullin' my head to his chest as I cry. I'm not ashamed to be a girl in my daddy's arms, not today. Wrapped in the warmth of my home, I let go. All the wild emotion surgin' through me pours out in gaspin', messy sobs. I'd have given everything to be there for that boy, to hold him and let him know he wasn't gonna go alone. My hands shake uncontrollably. My hands that didn't do a godsdamned thing. What the fuck was all of this for? Two dead kids and a heap of smokin' wood. Guilt settles on my shoulders like a suffocating cloak. This never should have happened. I don't know how long I stand there, but my tears begin to run dry just around the time I steady myself enough to stand without support.

"Ma is in the tavern," he whispers into my hair. "Your men kept everyone safe. There's a boy with her, talkin' to her. We're safe, love."

I just nod against him. I don't have words right now. I turn and look around. There are probably ten bodies in the street, a couple might yet be alive, but most of them are clearly dead. The pyre is just a pile of smolderin' embers, the witch's skeleton hard to see among the charred branches. Godrick's body looks so small, a little bundle before the fire. He looks like a kid who's fallen asleep at the hearth, and my heart shatters knowing he isn't going to get up. Pap lets me go as I step forward, hesitating, not sure what to do, where to go. But my feet walk forward with shaky steps, and I follow, knowin' where they lead. I don't mind the blood, and I sit right down beside him. His eyes are still open, and I close them with a tremblin' hand. There's a soft smile on his lips, though his face is battered and bruised. He withstood so much, fought so hard, but in death he looks like a boy. There was a hero's heart in that chest of his, and someone ripped it apart. This kid had a life ahead of him; he would've been one of the best of us, someone who did good for this place. He died tryin' to do the right thing, tryin' to protect someone. But I couldn't protect him. I pull him towards me, layin' his head on my lap and strokin' his hair. He deserved so much better than this. I kiss his head, and in the quietest whisper I can manage, I make him a promise.

"I won't let this mean nothin'. I promise you, I won't."

Cartwright helps me carry Godrick to the tavern. We are both still weak, but I can't bear the thought of someone else touchin' him right now. Guilt tears at my insides. We clean him up, and I send Athros to find the tailor. I don't even know if he had family, but I know she knew him well. I gently undress him. His narrow body is marred with bruises and blood, but I wipe his skin clean with soft, shakin' hands. I carefully dress him in some of the spare clothes I have upstairs. They aren't his, and they're ill-fitting on his long limbs and broad shoulders, but at least he's decent until we can get him somethin' of his own. I'm no healer, but I do my best to cover his wounds. I just want him to look like himself; I just want him to wake up. Athros leads the tailor into the back, and I put out an arm to catch her as she stumbles and nearly falls.

"Oh," she chokes out, the sound raw and keening. "Oh gods, my boy." She shakes, trembling as she reaches for him, opening and closing her hand as though she's afraid to touch him. She cries as she smooths and adjusts his hair the way he always kept it. "Oh, Godrick, what happened to you?" she says so quietly I barely hear her.

"Was he your son?" I ask her, suddenly furious with myself for knowin' so little about this person who has spent so much time with us.

"No, my nephew. His mother was my sister. I took him when he was a boy. He's lived with me for nearly his whole life."

"He is your son," I say, reachin' for her. "I'm so sorry. He was a good man." I sit next to her. "I'm ashamed to not recall your name, but I'm Shell, in case you didn't know mine."

"Helen, my name is Helen. I've known your parents for near on thirty years, but it's been a long time since I left the shop. Godrick kept me company, and my garden."

She sobs quietly for a long time. I don't have words to help ease her hurt, but I place my hand atop hers so she knows she ain't alone. When her tears slow down a bit she pulls her hand from beneath mine and wipes her eyes before asking, "Was he your friend?"

"Yes," I say with no hesitation. "Though I'm realizin' I was a shit friend. Will you tell me about him? I'd like to know about who he was. And I'd like to tell you what he did today. You raised a good boy Helen, and you should be so proud of him."

THE SEA

CHAPTER FORTY-SEVEN
JYNN
YEAR 993

The throbbing in my head is loud enough to wake me, and I barely manage to grab a bucket before hurling up the contents of my stomach. Fucking gods, why did I drink so much? I should never drink that much. The ship is spinning like we've been sucked into a whirlpool, but thankfully it's only the consequences of my own stupid actions. Georgette walks in, carrying water from the galley and sees me struggling to get back into my bunk. She laughs at me heartily before handing me the carafe of fresh water. "Long night?" she asks with a wink. I can't even nod a reply, so I just crawl back into my hammock and pray for death.

Hours later, I wake feeling slightly better and make my way to the deck, exhausted but eager to wash up and change into something clean. My body aches, and I stink—I feel like the picture of a real pirate for the first time. Tuii crosses my path when I reach the deck, and we both freeze. "Uh, hi," I say, so fucking awkwardly that I wish I had chosen to fling myself overboard instead.

Tuii laughs. "Hey, Red." She nods toward my bundle of clean clothes. "Headed to the shower?"

"Gods, yes." I rub my temple with my free hand. "Did you beat me over the head with a club last night?" I'm annoyed at her grin.

"If that's what you'd like to call it." She winks at me.

Fuck. Fucking fuckity fuck.

Honestly, I had forgotten most of last night. I was shitcan drunk, and my only waking thoughts were about puking and showering, but it all rushes back to me at once. I'm sure my face matches my hair as I aggressively look at my feet. Idyth save me. I cannot believe I did that. "Oh gods, Tuii…" I begin. "I…uh…"

She pats my shoulder with a chuckle. "I wondered how drunk you were. Now I know."

"I don't do…uh…that often," I stammer. "I've actually only ever…uh…done that a couple times before. It's never been casual." I feel so embarrassed. Gods. I must look like a buffoon.

"You're fine," Tuii replies, still grinning broadly. "I'm not as wild as you may think, but it's not like casual sex doesn't happen here."

I can't even look at her. "I know, I just didn't think that was something I did. Apparently, that was not the case."

"Maybe I'm just *very* persuasive."

"No, no. I was definitely an enthusiastic participant." My face burns. "I'm sorry if I made an ass out of myself."

She kisses my cheek and whispers in my ear as she walks away, "Not at all."

Gods above.

The shower feels like heaven. Ballad has a genius setup for washing; an area of the upper deck has been fitted with barrels cut in half, secured to a beam. A pipe runs between them, and there are stoppers blocking mesh-lined holes along the pipe. The water in the barrels warms in the sun throughout the day, and when you pull out one of the stoppers, water runs through the mesh into a fine spray. The water just runs back into the sea. We all refill the barrels throughout the day, so the whole crew is able to shower when they wish, and the barrels are scrubbed out each night so that they're clean and ready for the following day. It's a fairly brisk fall day, the water is lukewarm at best, but it still feels amazing to scrub my skin and slip back into clean breeches and a fresh blouse. I don't look at Tuii, a few feet down from me, also showering. I'm sure I'm still crimson. Guilt and shame battle in my chest, and I'm not sure which will claim victory.

We are sailing toward Minos'Idyl this afternoon, scouting out supply ships carrying stoneware to Athydis. We don't fuck with the minotaurs, but they don't sail, so the ships themselves are manned by humans. Captain got word of a large cargo convoy heading out in a few days' time, and we hope to gather info on the schedule and what to expect. The sea is choppy here, rough. We are still a day or two out from the island, and other than my pounding head and muddled brain, I'm enjoying the day of simple sailing. Captain has on a hat that looks like a fruit basket, and she's swinging across the rigging and singing loudly—and poorly—as the ship bites into the waves. Now that I'm clean and fed, I make my way up to my little perch in the crow's nest. My favorite part about sailing is watching the ocean, its vast blue-green surface alive under the midday sun. Spotting a distant swath of land from afar is always awe-inspiring for me after living my entire life land-bound. I've seen more in a season than I feel like I did in my entire existence in Kanitosh.

Thinking of Kanitosh does something to me, and I feel as though I may be sick. I'm so full of shame about last night. I can't believe I was so flippant with my affection, that I fell into another woman's arms so soon. I'm such a piece of shit. I couldn't manage to save Ceci, have done jack shit to avenge her, and I don't even possess the restraint to not fuck another woman mere months after losing her. Gods above, what am I doing? Tuii is a gorgeous woman, clever and brilliant, and more experienced than me in literally every facet of life. She's been a pirate for twenty-something years and has probably killed more men than I've met. Why the hell does she even want to talk to me? I'm a useless bumbling idiot who doesn't know how to do anything except pick up heavy shit and take care of bees. What a great skill for a pirate, tons of bees out here. My head falls into my hands. What the fuck, Jynn?

I'm so lost in my self pity that I don't notice the shapes bobbing in the water until one smacks into the hull. I hear a muffled thud and hop to my feet and grab my spyglass. It takes me a minute to make sense of what I'm seeing, but when I do, I nearly collapse as I grab a bucket and vomit again. Bodies, dozens of bloated floating bodies surround the ship. As if it couldn't get worse, every single decaying corpse is that of a faun.

I call out to Captain and shimmy down the mast as quickly as I'm able. She's already at the railing when my boots hit the deck. "Captain…" I don't even know what to say, so I shut up. What am I going to add to this conversation?

"Jynn," Ballad begins, "do you know of any faun settlements outside Kanitosh?"

"No, Captain. I know some left the glade when Farragen moved in and started the church, but I don't know where they went or anything." She says nothing, just stares at the sea and the bodies bobbing like driftwood in the water. She reaches out a hand for my spyglass, and I hand it to her, not wanting to look anymore anyway.

"Can't see shit," she mutters. "Ardelle! Can you take a boat out and get a closer look? Bring someone with you, and cover your faces. I want to know if this is from illness or execution or, gods help us, something else." Ardelle nods and heads to the rowboats, snagging the twins as she goes. They all wrap their faces in cloth, and Ardelle pulls on long gloves and grabs a long hooked gaff. The twins lower the rowboat, and I watch as the trio boards and rows out toward one of the corpses. I turn away when Ardelle pulls it over with the gaff, the sight of the hook pulling a dead body through the water turns my stomach, and I take deep breaths to avoid getting sick again. I turn as a hand pats my shoulder gently. It's Tuii, eyebrows drawn together, her head tilted to me in question. I give her a weak smile, and she squeezes my shoulder before continuing down the deck. Everyone is silent, the energy of the ship somber as we wait for Ardelle to report back to the Captain.

It isn't long before the party returns, tying off the rowboat and climbing back up to the deck. Ardelle removes her gloves and unties her makeshift mask before addressing Ballad. "I can't be sure, Captain. No sign of injury, no sign of illness. They just look dead."

"Fuck," Captain sighs. She looks at our flag flying from the main mast. "Wind's comin' from the north. Seems likely they're driftin' down from Minos'Idyl. I'm guessin' that fauns ain't sailin' out here, so likely they're from the mainland. But I haven't heard of any fauns from minotaur's land. Keep an eye out, girls. Post a port and starboard watch round the clock. I don't like surprises."

A shout of "Aye!" sounds out from across the deck as the crew scatter to their duties. Cenna and a woman named Briar take the first watch, and I climb back up top to keep a lookout further ahead. I feel a sense of dread in the pit of my stomach, and I hope it's just my memories of the glade.

KONIDAS

CHAPTER FORTY-EIGHT
MAELWEN
YEAR 993

The air is thick with smoke and death as I fly over Konidas. A smolder of charred wood sits in the street, and it's eerily still. No one walks in the thoroughfare; everyone must be locked in their homes. I have never seen Konidas this quiet. It's a graveyard of a city. I touch down near the tavern and head inside, feeling a comfort within which I am unaccustomed to. This place feels like *home*. Despite everything that has occurred, I am glad to be back. Walking into the tavern, I see an odd assemblage of people in the dining room. Shell sits at a table with a vaguely familiar looking human and that faun girl I saw in the inn. Everyone looks somber—aside from the faun, who looks petrified—and I've never seen Shell's face look so hard. She stands abruptly as I head toward them, her chair knocking back onto the floor with a loud clatter. My blood fills with unease.

"Maelwen," she says, looking as though she may begin to cry at any moment. "Something happened while you were away."

My fingers shake as she leads me through the tavern, heading for the small back room just off the kitchen. She has said nothing else since my arrival, but the way she holds my gloved hand fills me with dread. What could have happened to make Shell act this way? As we step into the small room, lit in warm light from the sconces on the walls, I see a figure on a table, draped in a white cloth. My throat closes as I recognize the shoes peeking out from below the shroud. I reach out a hand for the doorway, bracing myself and trying to breathe despite the heavy panic clawing at my chest like a wild animal. Those brown leather shoes—their soles worn smooth from years of walking across the tailor shop floor, pinning patterns and fetching bolts of fabric. Those same shoes sitting beside a bed in a small apartment on the upper floor of the building. Those same shoes walking beside me near the docks. My legs feel like someone else's as I step closer to the table. My hand moves independently of my body, pulling down the shroud slowly, uncovering a pale face that looks handsome even in complete stillness. A face whose planes I have come to know so well. The only lips I have ever kissed. Godrick.

I do not see or hear Shell grabbing a chair, but she eases me into one without a word before leaving me in silence with his body. The rigid wood is cold against my back as I sink down onto it, feeling weak and lost. How can Godrick be dead? He was just here, sitting beside me at the bar, still showering me with kindness despite my choice to end our relationship. I have never cried, but I feel as though I may. In my entire life, I have only had these few friends, this small circle of support. I had never even considered losing them. Is this what it feels like to be human? To live with the fear of losing those you love? I hate it. I hate feeling vulnerable. I have not felt this raw since Jarrus. I want to reach out and hold Godrick's hand, but I do not want my last memory of him to be his cold fingers.

I am furious. After sitting with Godrick for a while, I finally stand and make my way back to the dining room. Shell still sits with the two others, eyes wide as they all move with impassioned gestures. When she notices my return, she waves me over. She embraces me for a long time, saying no words, but I know she support me when it truly settles, when we are alone. "What happened?" I ask, anger sharpening my words to a knife's edge. "What happened here while I was away?" It takes over an hour to hear the entirety of what occurred in Konidas. My claws extend of their own volition when Shell recounts the murder of the young witch. It easily could have been me. She also shares that the faun visited with Beatrice, confirming that the flowers are indeed called pennyway, and at the crux of this dissent. It all fits together like bits of shattered glass: the ultimate goal of the 'New Church' to eliminate non-humans from Idythia and to seize control of chaos magic for themselves. I have no doubt the "priest" who took over the faun's glade was using the girl for pennyway production, but there is no way that crates upon crates of product came out of a small garden in the middle of the woods. "Do your kind all possess the ability to grow plants?" I ask the girl.

"No," she says in a timid voice, her accent soft with a voice like honey. "I am the only one I know of. Mamère told me there had been others, but I never knew of any."

This is a gift known to witchkind as well, though I am unsure if I met anyone possessing it while at the tower. The humans *could* be growing the flowers by traditional means, but they would need a vast space in which to do so. This faun, Cicerine, is fortunate she escaped. He undoubtedly had plans to use her indefinitely. I have yet to see any indication of a leader in their group, but someone must be at the helm, a new Idyth. This is bigger than I originally thought. What I assumed to be only a few street proselytizers seems to be an actual movement. I wonder if this has taken solid root in Athydis. Is this the movement of the entire church? If so, we have little chance of success. We have nowhere near enough manpower. But with their repeated use of 'New Church,' I have a feeling they're an offshoot of zealots, at least I can hope.

"I have been with my kin in Iowain," I begin. "I have learned a great deal about my kind, as well as the plans of the Crone. The things she spoke to me when I somehow visited Athydis, they also fit into this." The group is quiet, watching expectantly. I take a deep breath, centering myself. "The humans seek our annihilation. They plan to use the pennyway flowers to somehow acquire chaos magic, and claim all of Idythia for themselves in the name of their god."

The faun startles in her seat and looks up at me. "The man who lived in my glade told me he *was* Idyth," her voice falters, "or that he was going to be."

"Witchkind tells a different story of Idyth. You all know of him as a god, but he was not a god. He was a man, a power-hungry man who sought to commit genocide, killing any and all non-humans in his wake. Idyth was a weak human who possessed only the power of persuasion. But if the pennyway can give his followers access to chaos magic, this second coming may be more destructive than before." Nobody speaks, stunned into silence. "The Crone spoke of events that will come to pass. Something is coming, and witchkind stands against it. We will gather at the solstice. Already my kind reaches out for the witches scattered to the winds. We will be an army against this new force. I came back both to help protect my home here, and to learn what I can. You are not witches, but will you stand with us against this threat?"

Shell nods and stands. "I don't know when the fuck it happened officially, but my tavern is a safe place for everyone in Konidas. When the Idyth cult, Idythians? Whatever. When they showed up, my bar was full of folks needin' safety. I never thought I'd be much of anythin', but to these people, I was safe, and I won't go back on that now." She lowers her voice to a whisper, meeting my eyes with sorrow etched into her features. "I'm with you, Maelwen. I promised Godrick I wouldn't let this be for nothin'."

The faun says something quietly, and I do not hear her clearly. "What?"

She clears her throat and speaks a little louder. "I have no one and nothing, but I can help." The faun looks at the ground. She reminds me of an infant mouse, so timid and small that I cannot imagine her causing harm to anyone.

"I killed my entire village," she says, eyes not leaving the floor. "But Fa—Farragen got away. I know he's part of this. He killed my mama, and I plan to make him suffer for that. I can help, if you'll have me."

My eyes widen imperceptibly, but I do not allow my surprise to show. Perhaps the little mouse possesses more than fear and sugar. "I have a feeling we will all be needed before this is through. First, I think I need to look into where they are growing the pennyway. One of the tower witches mentioned Minos'Idyl, and the crates we found bore their mark. I plan to fly there and see what I can discover." The faun's gaze meets mine, and a strange thing happens in my chest. That little ember of power flares, just for a moment, and I see her eyes widen as it does. We stare at each other for a beat too long, not speaking, but both recognizing what just occurred. She breaks my stare and lets out a small gasp as she moves her hand off of the table to find a tiny charred handprint where her palm had been.

"Whoa there—Cicerine?" Shell asks. The faun looks as if she is about to cry or bolt, maybe both, but Shell quickly reaches over and touches her arm. "Are you all right, love? Don't worry, these tables have seen far worse than a little burn. I was just surprised, that's all."

"I don't know what happened," Cicerine says. She does not meet my eyes again.

That ember once again kindles from within my ribs, and I cannot help but find this timid little creature intriguing in more ways than one. I watch her from over the lip of my tankard, holding on to this curiosity for later.

The front door opens, and Cartwright walks into the tavern. Emotions cross his face in quick succession, bright eyes widening in excitement at seeing me, brows pulling together as his smile turns to sadness and dismay. He crosses the room quickly and pulls me into his big arms. I am not accustomed to this much touch, but Cartwright's embrace feels like a warm mug in winter, and I lean into him. "I am glad you are all right," I tell him quietly.

He whispers into my hair, and I almost miss it. "I'm glad you're back."

The group of us sit and talk long into the night. Leita comes back just before sunrise and heats up food for all of us, despite Shell's assertion that she does not need to be here. We all eat in companionable silence, taking a momentary respite from the weight of our conversation. We decide I will fly to Minos'Idyl to look into the sensation the other witches mentioned feeling, and to see if I can find anything relating to pennyway or the cult of Idyth. Cartwright and Shell plan to meet with other humans to put together some sort of organized militia. I tell them about the Crone's control of the castle, and we decide that someone needs to go to Athydis to find out what is happening in the capital. Cartwright plans to ask around in the coming days if any of his people are planning to head to the city anytime soon.

"I also feel that I need to be straight about some things with all of you," he says. "My men, you know I've got a good group of folks who I trust. We've been sorta workin' on something like this for a long time." Shell raises an eyebrow. Cartwright looks uncomfortable. He takes a deep breath and rests his forearms on his knees. The fabric of his jacket scrapes against the rough tweed of his pants, and there's a long silence as we wait for him to continue. "Well, to be truthful, there's lots of folks in this town who ain't fully human. A while back, maybe ten years ago, we had some trouble at the docks with some of the workers. People were scared, and at the time I was workin' as a dockhand, runnin' the split shift. Sailors ain't always fond of folks who are different. A lot of them end up cast off of crews when they're found out. Fergus was one of the first I met, and Agnes, his wife. His father grew up just outside Kanitosh, one of the wood folk, and he inherited some of his father's abilities. Fergus weren't all man; he could speak with all sorts of critters. He got me information no one else could, talkin' to dock rats. And from what Agnes tells me, Athros has it too."

"There are other non-humans here?" I ask incredulously. "Why have you not told us this?"

"It weren't my tale to tell. But now, I guess it is." He looks sheepish. "Can I show ya something?" We all watch as Cartwright walks toward the bar. The bar is large, probably twenty feet long, with solid shelving underneath full of glassware and bottles. He places his thick fingers between the bottom of the bar and the floor and lifts. The entire bar lifts off the ground.

Shell's jaw falls open, and for the first time since I have known her, appears to be speechless. "Wha…" Her mouth opens and closes, and we all stare toward Cartwright as he sets down the bar, the glasses clinking as it settles back onto the floor.

"West of Iowain there's a range of mountains. Hills, I guess would be more like it. My parents left them and traveled here to Konidas when I was not yet born. Those hills we call the Troqons, and that's where my people live. My daddy was human, but my ma was a troll. I look near enough to a man for no one to ever ask, but my ma could never pass for a woman, and she lived in our house until she died."

Shell just stares. "Cartwright, I've known you for *years*. What the fuck?"

He blushes, and it looks silly on his stern face. "I apologize,

Shell. It's not like it ever came up in conversation. Most folks don't even know trolls exist, let alone that we're livin' in the city."

"What else do we not know about?" Shell asks.

"We got trolls, dryads, other woodfolk, one of the seafolk, a couple half fauns, a jynn, and a couple shifters. But we keep to ourselves. The world is a lot bigger than Idythia, but Idythia don't know much outside its borders. That's half of why we all ended up here. Ain't nobody crossin' the Troqons, or the deserts of the Rahkul. This place is far enough from everything that it makes a good hiding spot for anyone lookin' to leave. So that's what I do. Me and my men help folks find a new place to be. We call ourselves the Brick Union."

KONIDAS

CHAPTER FORTY-NINE
CICERINE
YEAR 993

There is so much happening right now that it's hard for me to focus on any one thing. I can't stop staring at the charred handprint on the table before me. I don't understand what happened. I recall when I saw Maelwen through the inn window, the same odd feeling in my chest. I didn't know she was a witch then, but the moment she walked through the doors of the tavern I recognized her as the same woman in blue from before. Something happened when we looked at one another, but I don't understand what it means. My hands still tingle, that same feeling of electricity sparking through my skin, but I keep them folded in my lap. The last thing I want to do is damage anything else in this tavern. All the information I've learned today is overwhelming. I came here thinking I was getting away from this darkness, but I've come to find out that the darkness is everywhere. I'm glad Beatrice brought me with her today. Cartwright seems like a kind man, and Shell feels like a good person. This table of people makes me feel somewhat safe for the first time since I arrived in Konidas—even with the chaos that brought us to this place. I want to help them. I want to do something meaningful. I want to stand against the men like Farragen.

Hearing there are more people like me in the city brings up a lot of emotions. I'm terrified to meet more fauns after what happened in the glade. Logically, I know that there is no correlation, but the image of the rage-contorted faces of my friends and neighbors is lodged firmly in my mind. As angry as I am, I am also petrified. I hate feeling like this; I hate being afraid. I feel like a whisper of who I once was, like I've lost some integral part of who I am. I don't know how to find my confidence again, but I want to. I need to.

The food brought from the kitchen is the first thing I have eaten since I arrived in Konidas that I haven't cooked for myself. It's delicious, a rich spiced stew with a tomato base, filled with chickpeas and potatoes. I turn to Shell and ask, "Did you know that I am vegetarian?"

Beatrice looks surprised. "What? Girl, I've had you cookin' meat for weeks!"

I blush, realizing I may have made her feel bad. "It doesn't bother me so much to cook with it anymore, but I still don't eat it. Our entire glade never ate meat, so it isn't something I've ever really wanted to try."

"Well, shit. Now I feel like an ass."

"Please don't," I say. "It really doesn't bother me. I am happy for the work, and I truly don't mind."

Shell has a wry smile on her face as she interjects, "I didn't know for sure or anything, but Martine said we were serving goat today, and I felt like that was fucking weird to serve you. But now I know."

The air at the table lightens a bit as we all chuckle. Maelwen doesn't really eat, just picks at her bread and drinks her ale. Cartwright is done eating before I have taken three bites, and Shell and Beatrice are so engrossed in conversation that their bowls go mostly untouched. I notice the server who came with the meal also brought a bottle of wine, so I pour myself a glass and notice with delight that the bottle is one of Salvatorre's. "Oh!" I exclaim. "You know Salvatorre!"

Shell looks up from her conversation with Beatrice. "I've known Sal for years! How do you know that old coot?"

"He's teaching me winemaking! Up until today, he's been the only person I've really spoken to. He said my hooves are great for crushing grapes." I laugh. "I'm glad to meet one of his customers. I was supposed to help with deliveries soon. Now, having met you, I'm at least slightly less nervous."

Beatrice huffs out a laugh. "Tryin' to hire you out from under me, eh? Wouldn't surprise me. Sal's more clever than y'all give him credit for"

I wonder what she means by that, but quickly realize she may be offended, and my heart races with worry. "No! No, I was just going to help him on my day off. Please don't think I'm not grateful for work, or that I'm going to make the inn less of a priority."

"Ha! Girl, you work yourself to the bone. You don't need to. Before you, my guests ate day old bread and cold soup half the week. Hell, I'm thinkin' of upping rates since you came on, seein' as now they get a *luxury experience*." I laugh at the idea that my provincial fare is luxurious in this place. "I'd be happy to see you take more time for yourself. If you feel safe enough leaving, you're welcome to it Cicerine. You more than earn your keep."

My heart feels warm. Just a couple days ago I thought Beatrice was a cold woman who didn't particularly like me. Seeing this side of her is nice. I think maybe she needed this, too. It has to be lonely running the inn alone, and I've never seen her spend time with anyone. She seems to enjoy talking with Shell. Maybe this is a good thing for all of us.

Cartwright wipes his mouth with a cloth napkin, cleaning his bristly mustache of any lingering stew. "Well then, now all our cards are on the table, I suppose. I meet with the rest of the Brick Union in a couple o' days. I can tell them all what we know about the cult of Idyth and see who is able or willin' to help out. What do we need from my folks? Other than keepin' the bar safe and keepin' an ear to the wind, is there anything any of yeh can think of that might help in the meantime? At least till Maelwen gets back from scopin' out Minos'Idyl?"

Shell seems to think for a moment. "Bea, do you need more help at the inn? I'd feel better knowin' you've got someone to keep an eye on things."

Beatrice nods and looks over at Cartwright. "I wouldn't say no to some muscle. I can pay a decent wage for a doorman, if any of your men are looking for a steady job."

"I think I have just the man," Cartwright replies. "Cicerine would you like to meet one of my fauns?"

My pulse quickens and my hands get sweaty. I wring them in my lap, not wanting to offend, and knowing it would be safer to have someone strong around. Maelwen meets my gaze from across the table and some indescribable emotion crosses her features, tightening her eyes and pulling her lip between her teeth ever so slightly. I feel as if she's studying me, like I'm being analyzed. It doesn't bother me, but somehow being under scrutiny gives me a small boost of confidence, and I nod to Cartwright. "Sure."

"All right then, I'll have him stop by as soon as I see him. You may not know him for a faun right away; he's ground down his horns and wears a cap, and he wears pants and boots that hide his legs pretty well. His name is Tag."

Beatrice nods and takes a deep drink of her wine, draining the glass. "I been away long enough. I'm sure someone needs something, so I'll head back. Send word or stop by if you need anything, Cartwright. I look forward to meeting your fella." She looks at me with an eyebrow raised. "You want to come back now or stay for a bit?"

I glance to Maelwen who is still watching me from across the table, her flat expression lacking warmth, but not unkind. "I think I'll stay a little longer? I'd like to have another glass of wine, if that's all right." Beatrice smiles and pats my shoulder on her way out, and I realize that this is my first social interaction in a long while. Thank the gods for wine.

Cartwright heads out and Shell goes back to the bar, leaving Maelwen and I alone at the long table. That strange electric feeling simmers underneath my skin, buzzy and light. I'm rather intimidated by her icy stare, so I drink my wine in silence, not uncomfortable but quiet. She is just as striking up close as she was from afar, and now that we are alone, I'm able to truly look at her. The blouse she wears is ivory silk, and it makes her skin look rich, its cool tone highlighted by the glow of the lanterns. Her hair looks like midnight, solid silky black struck through with single strands of silver. Her lips are full, and I can't help but notice them each time she takes a drink of her ale. She is quiet as well, and I can tell we are both observing, wondering about what happened earlier.

"So," she begins in her low voice, "you have magic."

"I suppose, if you call it that. I never knew it as magic. I was always told it was an ability."

"Do you know of anyone else in your lineage who had a similar ability?"

"I do not. I only ever knew my mother, and she had no gifts. My father was human, and I never met him."

"Interesting." She takes another drink. "I would like you to meet a witch at the tower, eventually. I am curious if the magic you possess is the same as ours."

"What do you mean?" I know nothing about witch magic, and I'm intrigued.

"We have varying abilities, but they are all the result of chaos magic. The Crone connects to each of us through it. Think of it like a web, connecting each witch by a thread. The Crone can follow that web and communicate with all of us."

"She is your leader?"

"Yes," she says, steepling her fingers on the table.

"And you think I may have this chaos magic?"

"I do not know. However, there is something unique about you, and I would be interested to know more."

I'm not certain how to respond, so I sip my wine and stare at my handprint on the table. I guess that means she felt it too. The bar has started to get quite busy. Cartwright has returned and seems to be setting up some sort of game at tables in the back. Maelwen notices as well and stands, pushing in her chair as she does. "The games will begin shortly. Feel free to stay if you would like, but I will be occupied. Shell and Leita will take care of you if you need anything, and if you need an escort home, let Cartwright know and he will have it arranged. It was nice to meet you, Cicerine."

"It was nice to meet you as well, Maelwen," I say, reaching out my hand. She takes it and our fingers spark. I jerk back in surprise, but she grips me tightly before I can. She stares at my palm and then meets my gaze. Something hot and fierce flares within me, and I draw in a quick breath. Without looking away she releases my hand gently, turns, and walks toward the game tables. I watch her go, lithe and graceful, and wonder where this all will end.

THE SEA

CHAPTER FIFTY
JYNN
YEAR 993

I spot Minos'Idyl not long after dawn, the massive volcanic peak jutting from the sea and catching the early rays of sun on its sheer rock faces. I call out to the crew and swing down the rigging to join them on the deck. The sea here is a deep slate blue, with rough, jagged waves and cold winds. We prepare to drop anchor for Captain's briefing, and I help unfasten the massive iron weight and lower it over the cathead beam. Cenna and Briar loop the cable along the deck while Georgette and one of the twins pass the thick end through the hawser hole so Ardelle can crawl over and fasten the cable to the anchor. We all help; it weighs nearly three hundred stone and takes the full crew's effort. Sweat-slicked and warm from exertion even in the brisk early morning air, we line up as Ballad makes her way above deck. She steps from below, holding a stack of papers in one hand and wearing a purple hat with what looks like a cat curled on top.

"Oy!" She calls out across the deck. "What a fuckin' mornin' to be on the sea!" We all cheer, her energy infectious as usual. "I been plottin' all night, and I do believe we are going to have quite a fun time out here in bull country." She shuffles through the papers before continuing. "There's a wee little island chain due east, not much more than a couple'a sandbars, but they've got some trees on 'em, and they're far enough out from the trade route that unless they're lookin' outright, we ain't likely to be seen. We'll sail that way midday, and with fair winds, reach them within a day. Jynn, you be up top; signal if you see anything at all. I'd rather be over-cautious than fucked and sunk, we clear?" I nod in acknowledgement. "Tuii, Cenna, Dagmar, and Elke, prepare weaponry. Georgette and Abeni, prepare the hold. Hana, Tala, you and the others work out watches. When we spot the first ship, we'll wait 'til it's out of shore range, and board at the darkest point of night. These ships will be well-manned, Be prepared for combat but you know the rules!"

The deck explodes in chanting "NO DUCKS, NO EYES, NO DEAD! NO DUCKS, NO EYES, NO DEAD!" and Ballad grins like a madwoman.

"That's right girls! We'll be in the money before ye know it! Now be off!" The crew scatters to their various duties. I see Tuii duck below deck following the twins, Dagmar and Elke, but she glances around before disappearing. My stomach does a weird little flip wondering if she was looking for me. After grabbing a hunk of bread from Cook, I clamber back up the rigging to my post, dropping down into the crow's nest with a familiarity that has become a comfort in my time on the Sea Song.

The day is bright, and I shield my eyes as I stare out over the rough surface of the vast ocean. The morning goes by quickly, and before I know it, we are pulling anchor and setting off for the small chain of islands to the east. I can just barely see the shore of Minos'Idyl through my spyglass, and I watch the distant shore as the Sea Song cuts through the water. We haven't seen any more bodies in a couple days, but we are still on edge, and I see the crew glancing at the water far more than usual. I nearly lose my footing as a strong swell rocks the ship, and I look around in confusion. The winds are steady, and the sea is choppy but calm. Another large wave crashes against us, seeming to come out of nowhere. I hear a couple cries of surprise from the deck as the icy water crashes over the railing. Wedging my feet against the barrel of the crow's nest, I look at the sea around us for a sandbar or some other explanation for these isolated waves, and I see what looks like a line of people on the shore. I call down for Captain and spot her purple hat as she lopes over, steady even in the rocking sea.

"Men ashore Captain! A whole line of them, maybe a dozen?"

"Well, what the fuck are they doin'? The sea is rockin' like a storm swept summer, but the wind is flat as a boy's ass."

"I don't know, Captain. I can't see much other than them standing there. It's strange, I'm not su..." A massive swell hits the side of the Sea Song tipping her nearly ninety degrees. I grip the barrel of the crow's nest as I get within arm's reach of the sea. Shouts come from below me, and I hear Ballad scream as someone goes over. The ship rocks back upright, and I nearly fly from my perch, hurled like a trebuchet through the air. I try to look to the shore once again, but the ship is too unstable, and all I see is movement: land and sky, rising and sinking in my sight. Below, the crew clambers to retrieve whoever's gone over, and I'm struck with icy fear, wondering who was hurled into the frigid water. Time slows as the ship tips, and I see the dark surface of the water rising to meet me as she lurches. Screams echo from beneath me, and my hands slip from the edge of the barrel, splinters tearing into my palms as I dangle over the roiling sea. And then I fall.

The water is like liquid ice, and I'm immediately unable to feel my skin. I struggle to stay above the rough sea's surface, continuously sucked under by waves and the force of the unstable ship. I can't hear anything over the roaring water, and I can't scream for help either as I barely manage to suck in a shallow breath before being pulled back under. Kicking my legs and using my long arms to push through the water, I try to swim in any direction that leads me out of this violent tempest. My muscles scream, as I use all my strength to propel myself forward. My body lifts with the water as another massive swell begins, but the surface smooths as I reach the crest of the wave, and suddenly I'm over it, swimming in a choppy but manageable stretch of ocean. My limbs are exhausted, and I roll over onto my back for a moment to try and catch my breath. What the fuck just happened? After a few minutes, my breathing levels out and I roll back over, treading water and trying to determine where I am and what is happening with the Sea Song. I'm flabbergasted to see I'm maybe a hundred yards from the shore of the island. Thankfully, not the sandy beach where the figures stood, but instead, a rocky outcropping that looks to be made of limestone. I turn and search for the Sea Song among the waves, but she must have been pushed too far out, and I'm sure my spyglass now rests at the bottom of the sea. I can't breathe; my chest is seized with panic. For a moment, I remain frozen, bobbing in the water. Not seeing any other alternative, I strike out for the shore, unsure what the fuck I'm going to do when I get there.

    The stone cuts my already raw palms, and I slip and fall over and over as I scramble for purchase on the mossy rocks. By the time I heave myself up onto the shore, I'm panting and aching. I can't find the energy to do anything but flop over onto my back and breathe, letting the warm sun chase some of the cold from my bones. I'm so tired that my eyes are fluttering closed, but I hear a shout and sit up, looking around for whoever's voice it was. I nearly cry with relief as I see Tuii and Cenna picking their way across the rocks toward me.

    "Jynn! Thank the fucking gods!" Cenna says, in a tone I have never heard from the normally reserved girl. "Have you seen anyone else?"

"No, just me. I didn't even see who all fell in. What the fuck happened?"

"The ship nearly capsized," Tuii says, breathing heavily. "I saw Captain go over as well, and Hana. I don't know what happened to them. I grabbed hold of Cenna, and we swam as fast as we could."

I cross my arms across my chest, rubbing my arms through my sopping shirt. "Well, now what?"

Cenna sits down across from me, her dark hair a tangled mess over her shoulders. She absentmindedly runs her fingers through it, pulling the strands free of knots and smoothing it as best she can. "I suppose we make our way inland. See if we can find a way off this island. We know they have ships, so they're likely to have dinghies as well. We need to stay clear of the minotaurs. They'll be able to smell us if we get too close, but we can probably find something in the trees to help cover our scent."

Tuii bends down and removes two daggers from each boot, and slides a blade the length of my arm from a sheath on her back. Her leather pants have lots of pockets and snaps, and from within them she also pulls out a folding knife, a compass, and a length of thin wire with wooden pegs on the ends. Seeing my confused look, she smiles and says, "It's a garrote. Easy weapon if we're in close contact or come upon someone from behind. Cenna, take it. You're the quietest and smallest. Each of you take a dagger—Jynn take this knife as well. I'll keep my blade." She slides the thin sword back behind her as she hands us daggers.

We head into the thick brush, and the air heats immediately. The plants here aren't the same as the forest in Kanitosh; there are no evergreens, just tall, branching trees covered in thick vines and climbing plants with big, broad leaves. The air is dense and heavy with moisture, and the jungle is alive with sound. The chatter of birds and other unseen creatures peppers the air with keening cries and calls. Cenna kneels down beside a plant with wide yellow-green leaves and snaps one off. Breaking the leaf in half, she smears greasy transparent goo on her hands and rubs us both down with it. Its smell is pungent and herbaceous, but honestly I don't hate it. It smells green, familiar. Cenna moves like a predator, gracefully ducking under and gliding over roots and trees. Tuii follows her step for step, and I just do my best to try and not sound like a beast stomping through the leaves. Before long, we hear voices, and Cenna gestures for us to get down as she creeps closer to the clearing before us. Sunlight peeks through the treetops, dappling the ground in a smattering of light. She seems to vanish into the foliage; *I* can barely see her and I *know* she's there. Gods, she's good at this. We wait wordlessly, observing the jungle around us. The air is so thick here that it is difficult to catch a full breath. I feel like I'm drowning, yet it is only air. When Cenna makes her way back over to us, we follow her further back into the trees where we can whisper without being heard. Her face is serious, and she takes a deep breath before saying, "This is where the bodies came from. The fauns have a farm. They are growing pennyway."

Part 3

CHAPTER FIFTY-ONE
THE CRONE
YEAR 993

S leep rarely finds her in this place, the cracked stone room leaks pain and the stench of humans. It came suddenly, this slumber, and without precedent. Her ashen lashes flutter as her head comes to rest atop the great oak table, her cheek pressing into the stacked parchment covering its surface. When her heavy lids have fallen fully, the gray disappears. At once, the world is green, dense, filled with shafts of filtered sunlight shining from between lush boughs of the great trees surrounding her. She looks around, taking stock of her surroundings. The Crone knows how to walk in dreams, knows this is a place of importance. But for what, she is not certain. The heavy breaths and sweet whispers of a female voice carry on the gentle breeze, and she follows them on featherlight feet. Drops of dew brush her bare ankles as her steps carry her across plush grass, the stalks thin and soft—so much thinner than the grasses of Iowain. This place feels tender, new, like it has been birthed this season and still glistens with the glow of youth. It is still brisk, just on this side of spring, snow still peppering the shady areas in glittering patches. The energy here is vibrant in a way she hasn't felt in many, many years.

She watches the pair from afar, a faun and a tall human man. They have a sweet, homespun quilt laid down upon the grass, and his hips roll *against her in a gentle rhythm as small noises of pleasure run from her lips like warm honey. The man is unremarkable: large and dark-haired. But the faun is lovely, all curve and grace. Her skin seems to glow with goodness. The Crone can taste her on the air, pure and sweet and untainted. A treasure. As the man's head bows to press a kiss to her temple, a temporal wave rolls through the space. The thin spears of grass blow forward, the leaves rustle in the trees. Inexplicably, the Crone stumbles, and the man lets out a quiet grunt. His narrow hips jerk slightly before coming to rest against her as they pant and hold one another close. The Crone looks about, curious. The pair did not see the wave and had not felt it. But it had certainly occurred. Closing her eyes, she reaches out across the vast web connecting her to the world. The silken strands vibrate, humming as if strummed by great, unseen fingers. Odd.*

She wakes with a start and sits up, opening the inner eye to look across the web of lives. The strands are quiet, the hum absent. However, dreams for the Crone are never just dreams. She rises and walks to the window, pulling aside the thick velvet curtain that blocks her view. The city before her is unchanged, still bland and unappealing. She can sense the corruption as it strolls through the throngs of people, knows that many of these humans conspire against her kin. Replacing the curtain, she stands still, head cocked and eyes lightly shut, as she riffles through the eons of memory there. She tastes that same black taste as before, the greasy smear of it unpleasant on her tongue. Following it she locates the source.

Idyth.

'Of course,' she thinks. 'Of course it is his stink that felt so familiar.' Thinking again of that ripple in the trees, she seeks a map, a location, the place she saw before in her mind's eye when that ripple caught her notice. There. The corners of her shriveled lips tip upward as she begins to place the pieces all together. The image is nearly complete, and with it will come the fall of Idyth — the fall of man.

KONIDAS

CHAPTER FIFTY-TWO
MAELWEN
YEAR 993

The air has a bite to it this morning, the first nipping hint of the winter to come and a reminder that the solstice approaches. I feel no closer to a solution, like I am spinning my wheels just trying to keep things safe here in Konidas without actually addressing the looming threat before us. Inaction makes me feel stagnant, and I dislike it. I feel antsy and uneasy. Cartwright told me last night that in the morning he would be meeting with the Brick Union, and I am planning to join him. I will fly to Minos'Idyl after to see what I can find. Tonight? I feed.

The streets are still sparsely occupied, the residents of Konidas still shaken by recent events. But despite the discomfort in the air, commerce continues. A ship is moored on the far side of the docks, and a line of men work in tandem, unloading crates of cargo and stacking them atop the creaking planks. A trio of men slink away into the shadow, and I scent shakeroot on the wind, scrunching my nose at the biting smell. I follow silently, hoping they will not continue as a trio. I would rather not deal with three men when I only require one. As I round the corner, I see two of the men smoking their shakeroot, the smoke curling into the air in wispy tendrils. The third man is no longer with them, but I hear the sound of piss on stone and follow it to find him with his trousers down, cock in hand, and an unconscious woman on the ground before him. She appears to have been knocked out, her eye already going black. Disgusting. Not wanting to attract the attention of his cohorts, I begin to sing quietly. Soft, low notes reach his ears, and I see his eyes go hazy as he is entranced by my song.

    I walk further down the street, and he follows like a puppy on a string. Passing shuttered businesses and piles of rubbish, I slink between two buildings—the inn and a shop I have yet to visit. Listening for his following footsteps, I stop when I am far enough into the small space to be out of sight from the street. There are no windows on this side of the inn, and the narrow alleyway is dark. The man shambles forward, and I take in his haggard coat and the dribble of piss on his trousers. He is young and cleanly shaven, smelling of stale shakeroot and grog. A man who thought himself powerful for harming a woman in an alley. I do not want to make a mess; rather than slitting his throat, I grasp his wrist with my own and slide a claw down its center. He does not flinch, so well restrained by my witchsong that he feels nothing. I bring my mouth to the cut and let his blood flow freely into my mouth. I can taste the shakeroot on him, unpleasant and slightly disorienting. Can I become intoxicated secondhand? This is something I have never considered. I ponder the idea as I swallow mouthful after mouthful, but a yelp and a loud scuffle breaks me from my wonderings. Three other men stand in the opening to the alley, watching me. One of them speaks in a raspy voice, "Oi! What are ye doin' to him?" I drop the man to the ground, and he does not stir. The man eyes me up and down, his gaze lingering on my figure for far too long. "Nice treat to find in an alley, eh? Hush now, sweetheart, it won't hurt if you don't fight. You might even like it."

I see the moonlight glint off the dagger as the man pulls it from his belt. His companion balls his fists, confident in his ability to force himself upon an unarmed woman. Silly man. I step over the fallen man's body and flick out all ten of my claws. I must cut a formidable sight, long hair blowing in the breeze, cloak rippling behind me, my claws extended like the predator I am. One of the men runs, and I do not follow. The man with the dagger charges toward me, blade held out to slash at my middle. I could sing them to sleep with little effort, but I relish the combat in my recently fed bliss. My blood is hot with power and my senses are sharp and strong. The men are clumsy from the shakeroot, and the slashing man nearly trips as he strikes out. I sidestep him and twirl, reaching out with my right hand and raking it down his arm. The dagger clatters to the ground, and he clutches his arm to his chest with a howl. "Fucking whore," he spits. I smile.

This dance is one I know well, darting between the two men as they scramble to land a hit. My hands are graceful as they rend cloth and flesh. I have just turned to the man who dropped his dagger when an impact from behind knocks me forward a step. Blinking, I turn to see another man, tall and hulking, with a club in his massive hands. He swings it and I duck, head still reeling from his initial strike. Were I human, the hit may have knocked me out. One of the other men kicks out as I crouch, striking me in the knee and pushing me off balance. I stumble and feel a twinge of fear. I have yet to be in this position, and I quickly map out my steps, plotting a way between the men and back to the street. I begin to sing, hoping to lull the men into slow movement, but the man with the club clips me in the cheek right as my song begins to flow, and my voice sputters out at the impact. I begin again, but my mouth swells slightly, and I struggle to compensate for the shape of my lips. I see one of the men cock an arm back to punch me, when a strange sensation flutters in my chest, and I suck in a surprised breath. In the span of a single blink the men are both screaming, the soles of their shoes smoking. I am unsure of how this is occurring. I have manifested no power that would cause this, but I see a small figure, bent to press their palms to the ground at the entrance of the alley. Silhouetted against the moonlight, I see curling horns and a cascade of ringlets, as the faun stands and steps into the alley.

My skin buzzes, the ember in my chest flaring into a small white-hot flame. My palms feel electric, and I open and close them as I breathe in the strange power flowing through me. Cicerine reaches down once again, splaying her fingers against the stone, and the men jerk as they fall to the ground, skin and clothing charred. She looks wild, gazing up at me as she kneels on the stone. My eyes meet hers, and my heart feels too quick and too slow simultaneously. Her mouth is open slightly, and I see her draw in a breath from between lush lips. Time feels as if it has slipped off its path — this moment frozen in an odd space between minutes. She stands and walks toward me, the sound of her hooves on the ground centering me in this reality as my mind reels. We stand, looking at one another in silence, and I reach out my hand. She places her small palm beneath mine and turns it over, looking at my long claws, slightly transparent like quartz and smeared with a hint of blood. I pull my hand back slightly to flick them back in before grasping her hand once again. The pattern of our breathing aligns, and that flame in my chest blazes as sparks flash between our intertwined fingers. Her honey-colored eyes are wide, and I can see the bright flashes of light reflected in them as I watch her. The curve of her cheek shifts slightly as she smiles, and she looks up from our hands to meet my gaze. I let go, and we both pull back but stop as the sparks continue to illuminate the space between our hands. Tiny veins of shattered light connect us, violet and white-blue in the dark of the alleyway.

"Your eyes look like lightning," she says quietly, her soft voice warm and sweet.

My gaze dips to her lips again before meeting her eyes. "And yours like honey."

"Do you understand this?" she asks, looking inquisitive but not afraid. Her simple shift dress sways slightly as a sea breeze flows through the alley.

"No," I reply. "But something is happening. My magic responds to you. I feel this…flame within my chest. I feel magic in me, new magic, and it burns for you."

"I felt that too. Like a flare in my ribs. I've never felt anything like it." She looks at the bodies on the ground. "Should we clean this up?"

I shake my head. "Do not bother. No one will mourn their loss, they will be found and disposed of soon enough." I see her skin prickle, and a small shiver shakes her shoulders. "Come with me."

KONIDAS

CHAPTER FIFTY-THREE
CICERINE
YEAR 993

Maelwen heads into the dim gray night, walking briskly along the docks. I follow, keeping pace but nervous about the sound of my hoofsteps. My heart is racing, though I try to look calm. I have never done anything so brash, nor have I ever gone out of my way to step into someone else's battle. But seeing Maelwen and those men in the alley drove me to action before I was even aware of it. I had just been walking out of the inn for the night, headed for the tavern, when I heard a tussle in the small space between the buildings. I don't even know why I looked, but I did, and my hand was pressed to the stone in an instant—my power snaking through the earth and into the bodies of her attackers. My body felt alight with power. Whatever this is between us, it sets my very soul aflame.

We walk into the din and warmth of the tavern, and I shake off the near-winter cold. Shell, at the bar, nods to Maelwen as we walk through the dining area and head toward a staircase near the back wall. Just when my heart had begun to slow, it picks back up. Is she taking me to her apartment? Oh, gods. I'm not sure why I'm so nervous, but the idea of Maelwen bringing me into her private quarters makes my stomach flip. I follow, down a short hallway and through a locked door into a surprisingly opulent apartment. The walls are wood, much like the tavern below, but they are adorned with a well-chosen selection of art. A framed watercolor of the tower in Iowain hangs on the wall near the entryway along with lovely floral paintings hung further into the room. The table is well made and looks expensive, as do the coordinating chairs. Even through my hooves I can feel how plush the rug is, and as I peek into her bedroom, I see a bed made with gorgeous velvets and silks in rich jewel tones. This apartment is just as beautiful as she is.

"Come, sit," she says, taking a seat on a small couch against the wall. I sit beside her, still anxious about being this close. "Give me your hand."

I reach out to her, gasping as I feel my power flare and mesh with hers. Sparks shower down like stars as our fingers touch. I see her eyes widen, almost imperceptibly, and I know she felt it too. "This feels so strange," I say, staring at the slight glow that lights our barely touching fingers.

"Give me a moment." She closes her eyes and softly moves her fingers until the tips are intertwined with my own. "I am trying to see if I can 'see' this. I know the Crone can see the threads of chaos, and I am not the Crone, but perhaps it is possible with focus." Her cheekbones are highlighted by the glow of our fingertips; she looks like a goddess. She is so angular compared to my common, round face. Her lips fall apart and she sucks in a breath before opening her ice-blue eyes. "I can see your magic."

"What does it look like?" I am curious if her vision of it matches the one in my mind's eye, the faintly green strands that lead things to grow and to die. "Can you see your own as well?"

"My magic is sharp, white. It looks cold. It moves in straight lines, sometimes breaking into fractals like lightning. Yours is, well, it is soft. It flows and curls and curves. It wraps around mine, like a strand of thread. It is green-hued, golden and warm; it feels like life. Our magic…weaves together—into something else."

I'm speechless. That is exactly how I've always envisioned my gift, long before I thought of it as magic. "What can you do? I make things grow, and I suppose I can make them die as well, apparently. But what about you?"

Her brows pinch together. "I do not know. My gifts have yet to reveal themselves, if I even have any. As of now, I only possess witchsong, which is nothing special. I am young, and many times witch gifts do not develop until later in life, but I have no inkling of what my gifts may be."

"Have you tried to figure it out?" The words are out of my mouth before I consider them. I'm an idiot. Of course she's tried. "I mean, have you used the magic you see now?"

"I have never seen this," she says quietly. "This is new to me." Her face tightens, eyes pinching at the corners as she looks to her lap.

I tighten my fingers around hers in comfort. This is by far the most emotion I have seen from the witch. It's clear she feels discomfort over her magic—or lack thereof. "Maybe we can try together? See what," I gesture between us, "this can do?" I look around her room for something living and find nothing. There is a flower in a vase, but without roots, I'm unsure if my gift can reach it. I close my eyes and reach out anyway, seeing if perhaps I am capable of touching something no longer connected to soil. I cannot see the flower, but I feel something else: the steady thrum of Maelwen's heartbeat. I know she senses my intrusion when it speeds up, beating more rapidly as my consciousness brushes up against it. "Do you feel me?" I ask, wondering what exactly she feels in this moment.

"I do," she replies in a near breathless voice. "It feels like you are a bellows, stoking this flame within me." She lets out a small gasp. "That is remarkable, this heat, it…can you stay there for a moment?"

I concentrate on the pulse of her heartbeat, not moving. And then I feel something in my own chest, like a bird fluttering inside my rib cage. "Oh," a soft sound tumbles from my mouth.

"I followed the threads of our magic, they led me here. I need something, I…want more. Your gift, it works with the earth? Would you go somewhere with me?"

"Of course."

When she lets go of my hand, I feel suddenly alone, and it is a new sensation. In those connected moments I felt balanced, but now I feel off-kilter. She rises from the small couch, and I watch her for a moment before standing. She moves in such an otherworldly way, fluidity in each movement. Even the turn of her wrist as she reaches for her cloak feels intentional and artistic. She moves like a dancer. The cloak she wears is a such a deep blue, it reflects in her pale eyes, making them look more like bottomless oceans than shards of glacial ice. We stop at the bar on our way out, and Shell slides us each a small glass. Realizing I am thirsty, I take a sip and splutter at the burning liquid. "Oh gods!"

Shell laughs at me, her warm eyes crinkling at the corners. "Shoot it back, girl. That ain't a sippin' drink."

I think I see a slight smile at the edge of Maelwen's mouth, but I do as I am told and knock back the flaming liquor. My stomach warms immediately. Through a screwed up mouth I manage to gasp out, "Thanks, Shell."

It is near dawn now, the sky just beginning to lighten at the horizon, though still cloaked in darkness. The chill in the air grazes my skin, but the liquor in my belly keeps me feeling warm. "Would you like to fly?" Maelwen asks, breaking the silence.

I'm nervous. I'm a creature of the soil, not the sky. I don't think a faun has likely ever left the ground, but something about the witch makes me feel intrepid. "All right." I hope my nerves don't show in my voice. "How do we do this?"

Maelwen steps behind me, and my skin heats at her nearness. "I have only done it once," she says as she slides her hands beneath my arms. "But he was much heavier than you. My cloak will help." Her voice catches slightly on "he," and I know she's talking about the man who died in the witch burning. I say nothing, but as I squeeze her arm, she tenses as if shocked by the action—as if comfort is foreign to her. Her arms wrap around me, and I can feel our magic intertwined once again. It feels good, grounding. I almost feel whole, like a piece of something larger instead of an individual. "Try not to be afraid," she says close to my ear. "I can feel your nerves in my own chest." We lift off the ground, her sapphire cloak wrapped around me and floating behind us, rippling like water.

I close my eyes as we gain altitude, not wanting my fear to reach Maelwen. Instead, I focus on our connection, feeling the points where our magic is joined. And there, just as I trace a line between us, I can see the air. It's remarkable; I can see the way it moves, the currents that flow all around us. "Gods, it's beautiful," I say.

Maelwen's voice holds a note of incredulity. "Konidas?"

My lips lift at the corners, amused by her disgust. "No, the air. It is like a river."

"Ah, you must see it as I do, then." She doesn't move us out of this flow of air, just lets us float atop it, the warm wind heading east below us. "I would like to try something." We touch down on a small beach, the docks still visible in the distance, but far enough that I'm surprised at how quickly we flew. Maelwen releases me as my hooves settle in the sand, taking my hand as she does and maintaining the connection between us. I feel her then.

Lightly caressing the power within me, she reaches out with *my* magic instead of her own. It is strange, like someone walking with my legs, but I don't protest, interested in what she can do. All around us, small plants emerge from the sand, pushing out their new, green shoots and unfurling tender new leaves. "Gods," she breathes. "That is remarkable."

"Try this," I offer. "See if you can take it the other way, into the darkness." I kneel, still holding her hand, and press my other palm to the shifting sand. I reach out with that hot power, the ruinous power, and the plants nearest to me shrivel and smoke. She closes her eyes, but doesn't touch the ground. Nothing happens. "Try making contact the sand," I tell her. "Visualize my power shooting out through the earth and running up the roots to the plant. Heating the core of them." She doesn't move, but her eyes drift closed. Her mouth opens and a strange melody begins to come from her lips. I'm mesmerized by the sound, captivated by the movement of her mouth. All at once, the plants dissolve into ash.

"Oh." I say with a husky voice, breathing out. "Open your eyes."

Her long lashes lift and her chilled eyes regard the haze of drifting ash that surrounds us. Her lips part in surprise, and I feel her body tense beside mine. "I killed them," she says. "How?" I shrug, not knowing how the magic works, either. I hear a rustling in the brush further up from the shore and see her eyes dart to it. Her head cocks to the side, the look of a predator, and the same haunting song drifts on the air. The rustling stops. Maelwen drops my hand and strides toward the brush, a determined force to her steps. Crouching down, she parts the dry growth, claws flicked out, and retrieves something from the sticks. It's a hare, lanky and long-eared, and dead as dust.

"Did you kill it?" I ask, my voice reedy, feeling pity for the sweet creature who hangs lifelessly in her hands.

Maelwen looks stricken, her face going rigid as she stares at the small body. She replies quietly, shifting uncomfortably as she does, "We spoke of my gifts…I think this may be the Song of Death."

THE SEA

CHAPTER FIFTY-FOUR
JYNN
YEAR 993

The jungle seems to go silent. The hot air is heavy on my skin as I stare at Cenna, and my blood runs cold as her words sink in. Pennyway. The fauns have a farm, and they are growing pennyway. This must be where the crate we found aboard the ship came from. I can't imagine why anyone would need pennyway in such large quantities, but the fact that they have a whole farm of the stuff? It can't be good. I don't want to be involved, and I certainly don't want the crew to get mixed up in this shit. "We need to get out of here," I whisper. "There's no telling who is in charge, and anyone growing this shit in this amount is not someone I want to fuck with."

"I agree," Tuii chimes in, voice low. "After all those bodies, I want nothing to do with this." Cenna nods but looks back toward the fauns, clearly enslaved and suffering. Her expression is pained.

"What?" I ask. "We can leave. We haven't been seen, we have no ties to this, and we should keep it that way."

"They're in chains, Jynn," Cenna says in a halting voice, thick with pain. "They're captives. Are we really going to abandon them to this?"

"Yes!" I whisper forcefully. "This isn't our fight. What are we going to do? We are three small humans, against what? We don't know who is in charge here, but if they have a full farm, someone is keeping these fauns captive. Do you want to fuck with whoever that is?"

"Of course not." Cenna's head whips toward me, incensed. "But I don't want to ignore a fucking slave operation, either. Do you know how many of us avoided slavery? Do you know where Ballad found half of us? You think we all came from happy families? No. They're someone's children, someone's spouses. *Someone* cares about them. What kind of people are we to just walk away?"

I scrub at my face with my hand. "What do you want us to do, Cenna? We have a couple daggers and a garotte."

"I don't know, Jynn. But I don't know how I can live with myself if we just leave. Maybe you can get back to the ship and figure something out. I'll go in alone. I'm perfectly capable. You two can stay here; it's fine."

Tuii shakes her head, her damp braid heavy. "I'll go with you. You need backup, and I'm quiet. Jynn can stay."

I want to scream at them both. They don't understand how dangerous this is. They haven't seen what that damn flower can do. It didn't destroy their lives or kill the people they loved most. But I can't scream, and I'm outnumbered. So I nod and crouch beside a tree with low branches, hiding myself in the foliage. "I'll be here. Is there a signal we can use? In case it goes south?" Cenna whistles, a strange warble that sounds like a bird, and I commit the sound to memory. It takes me a couple tries, but I imitate the sound well enough to earn a nod of approval from Cenna.

"We will be back. If you hear me whistle once, come find us. If I whistle twice, run."

The wait is hell. This jungle is full of bugs and things that rustle through the undergrowth and swing through the trees. My skin crawls from all the insects I've slapped from my arms and legs, and my face is damp with sweat from the oppressive heat and humidity of this place. Time crawls by, and I feel like they have been gone for half the day, when in all likelihood it hasn't been much more than an hour. I flick yet another stinging ant from my ankle and curse right as something shakes the trees in front of me. I've got my blade drawn, and I'm crouched in a defensive posture—ready to strike, when Tuii's head pokes through the leaves. "Oh thank fuck," I breathe out. "It's you."

Cenna follows after, seeming to appear out of nowhere. "It's… not good," she whispers. "There are dozens of fauns, all in chains. There are minotaurs with whips and clubs, overseers it looks like. The fauns all seem dazed, like they're drugged. But there are so many plants—thousands of them. There were a couple fauns who weren't chained, but they had metal collars on. They were walking along the rows of plants and touching the ground; it looked like they were doing some sort of magic? Making the plants grow more quickly?"

My heart plummets in my chest. "Botanurgy." I say in a low voice. Both Cenna and Tuii look at me, waiting for me to continue, and I sigh. "Ceci had that gift, it's why Farragen made her tend his garden. She could make plants grow. Any plant."

Cenna's mouth settles in a grim line, and she nods. "That would make sense. Well, they have a few fauns with that ability, but not many. Maybe five or six?" Tuii nods in agreement.

"Well, what do you want to do?" I ask them both, looking between them.

"We can't take on that many minotaurs alone." Cenna says. "I could maybe take out a few, but the rest would notice and then we'd be caught. We have to get back to the ship, talk to Captain, if she made it."

"Was there any sign of men? In robes?" I ask. "Before the ship capsized, I saw men on the beach, I think they were casting a spell or some sort of magic. Someone clearly didn't want anyone to discover this place."

Tuii shakes her head. "I only saw the minotaurs. But they're not known to be cunning, not enough to be doing this. Someone else has to be in charge."

I nod, turning to Cenna. "How are we going to get back to the ship? We don't have a boat, and I couldn't even spot the ship, so we certainly can't swim back out."

"We might be able to build a raft," Tuii offers. "There are plenty of plants here, maybe there's something we can use."

"I don't think I'd trust a homemade raft in an ocean that took down the Sea Song," I reply. "But there has to be a boat somewhere, right? They can't all be stuck here with no way on or off. Even just to load up the pennyway, like you said, they've got to have a dinghy."

"Let's see what we can find."

WE HIKE BACK THROUGH THE JUNGLE AND MAKE OUR WAY TO the coastline. We stay hidden in the trees but travel parallel to the water, looking for anything that could help us off this island. It's cooler near the water, but still so godsdamned humid that my eyes sting from the sweat that drips down my lashes. The trees curve inland, and there's a wide beach with faint footprints in the sand. I recognize it as the beach where the robed figures stood. Cenna and Tuii notice as well, and we all draw our weapons. We've traveled far past where we washed up when we hear the unmistakable knock of a boat against a dock. I smile at the sound, and we all share a glance, Cenna pressing her finger to her lips in a command of silence. Just around this row of trees, we find what we are searching for. The dock is big enough for a ship the size of the Sea Song to moor, and a pier runs a fair distance along the waterline. There is a small dinghy with a broken mast tied to the far side of the pier. I cannot see if there are oars in the small boat, and it doesn't look particularly seaworthy. I point toward it, and both women nod as we creep closer to the dock. I don't hear anything to indicate there are people here. Fortune seems to be on our side for once, and we reach the trees directly opposite the dinghy. Cenna puts up a hand to stop us, and darts out from the jungle to the dock adjacent to the vessel—nearly invisible, even on the white sand. I see her dark head disappear into the small craft, and in a few moments, she returns.

"There are oars, but only two, and they've been baking in the sun for a long time," she says. "They're splintery as hell, and probably pretty brittle. But they'll have to do. Jynn, do you think you can row us out past the wave break?" I nod. "All right. The rope tying it to the dock is nearly broken already, so I can easily cut it once we are aboard. Tuii, you sit at the stern, keep an eye on the shore; I'll watch for the Sea Song, and Jynn—row like hell."

We run from the trees to the dock, and I try my best to be quiet as I race over the planks to the boat. It barely moves as Cenna drops in, and Tuii slides into the back gracefully. I half hop, half fall into the center of the small craft, and grab the sun-warped oars, pushing us off the dock with a strong heave. I'm thankful for small blessings when the oar doesn't immediately snap, but in a few minutes we are away from the dock, and I put all my strength and concentration into rowing into the open sea. The water is fairly calm, however it is still not easy to row through the waves. My chest and shoulders burn with the exertion, but this is how I can contribute best. I'm strong, and I've never before felt more needed. So I row. The farther we go, the more the temperature drops, and the breeze over the water is brisk on my sweat-damp skin. My shirt sticks, and my hands begin to bleed from the splintered oars, but I push harder with every mild inconvenience I note. Cenna's voice sounds like a fucking song when she calls out, "I think I see her! *Row!*" I strain and push and pull, heaving our small craft through the water. Before long, Cenna confirms, grinning "It's her, but she's far off."

I pause for a moment, trying to catch my breath, and ask Tuii to hold the oars. She slides into my seat, and I cringe at the sweaty ass print I leave behind. The water here is deep and dark, but I am so hot from rowing that I lean over and dunk my head in the sea. It is freezing, and my chest tightens as the cold water laps around my head. Just as I begin to raise my head from the water, I hear something, like a voice from beneath the waves. With a start, I pull my head from the water and suck in a breath. "Did you hear that?" I ask Tuii and Cenna.

"I didn't hear anything," Cenna replies as Tuii shakes her head. Perplexed, I take another deep breath and hold it, gripping the side of the boat as I dip my head back into the water. Again, I hear it. A voice. It seems to be singing in a language I do not understand, but something about it compels me, making me want to dive into the water. I'm mesmerized listening to the strange high melody, when I start to feel my lungs burn from lack of air. Coming back up, I turn.

"There is something down there. I heard a voice, like a song, maybe?"

Tuii's eyes narrow. "There are nereids in the water, Jynn. I've heard stories about them. They've been asleep for many years, but it doesn't mean they are dead."

I don't know why I do it, but I breathe in and out, emptying my lungs and pulling in the deepest breath I can manage, and then I jump over.

KONIDAS

CHAPTER FIFTY-FIVE
SHELL
YEAR 993

It doesn't feel right for things to be normal, but here we are. In the days since the cult uprising, we have spent most of our time tryin' to fix up the shit that got wrecked, and to get people's lives back to a place where they feel all right. It hasn't been easy. Beatrice and I have also forged a tentative friendship. Cartwright's group of non-human buddies declined my invitation to meet here at the tavern, choosin' to continue to meet in the location they have always used, and I get it. They want to continue to be secret, and with all this shit, that is a very fucking valid desire. Fergus's kid Athros has been sniffing around the tavern a lot lately, and yesterday I let slip that I know about his secret gift. He looked scared as hell, but today he showed up bright 'n early and asked if he could help around the tavern. So I'm guessin' he feels glad to have his secret shared. I'm gonna hire the kid on. He's small, but he's smart and quick, and bein' able to talk to critters is a useful skill. Plus, his mam could certainly use the coin. Just as I start plannin' how to bring it up, the kid walks out of the back with a hefty orange cat in his arms. "What the fuck is that, kid?"

"His name is Losh," the kid begins. "He's a cat."

"Uh, yeah. I can see that. Why the fuck is he in my bar?"

"Well, I seen a rat in here a few days past." I cringe. "And I thought it might be good to have a wee set o' ears around, you know, for listenin'."

His eyes beg me to say yes, and gods be damned, I can't break his little heart. "He's yours to care for," I start. "I ain't cleanin' up after a cat, and I'll tell ye now, he can't be in my kitchen. Some folks aren't keen on cats, so you'll need to have a good talkin' to with him about stayin' unseen. Can you do that?"

His red head bobs up and down like a kid's toy, grinning from ear to ear. "Yes'm I can! He won't be no trouble at all."

Rubbin' my forehead with the heel of my hand, I concede. "Alright then. And there's another thing while you're here," the cat meows and it's a weird low sound like a man groanin', "I'm gonna pay you to help around here. There's lots of tasks that Leita and Martine would be glad to have off their backs. Moppin', taking out the garbage, dishes…plenty that needs doin'. I'll pay you weekly, and you can take it home to your mam. You think she will be all right with that?"

The boy's eyes are wide. "You're gonna pay me?"

"Yessir, I am. Now get that big beast out of my dining room, and go check in with Leita. She will tell you what needs doin', and I'll be here if you need me."

He nods and runs off toward the kitchen, and I breathe out a long sigh. I need a drink.

THE BAR IS BUSY THIS EVENIN', AND I CATCH SIGHT OF AN orange tail a few times as I hurry around the place fillin' tankards and droppin' off plates. Maelwen heads out late tonight, and the look on her face lets me know all I need to about what she's gettin' into. Cartwright is having her join the meeting of the Brick Union in the mornin', and I know she plans to head out to Minos'Idyl tomorrow as well. I don't like that she's headin' off into trouble, but I'm more than certain she can take care of herself. Cartwright approaches the bar at a break in the games, and I hand him a glass of ale. Our fingers brush against each other as I hand it to him, and he goes beet-red causing me to chuckle. Ever since finding out he's a troll, I think he's embarrassed about everythin' he does around me. He's been quieter than usual, and he ain't a talkative fellow to begin with. I gesture for him to take a seat and he does, still blushin'. "How's the games tonight?"

"Nothing much to speak of; nobody's sweepin' the tables, game's fairly balanced this evening." He sips the ale and smiles. "This that new batch that came in last week?"

"Sure is," I reply. "Brewed with oranges. I'm callin' it 'Scurvy Sour'. You like it?"

He nods. "It's somethin' different. I like different." He blushes again, and I have no idea why. Men are weird as hell, troll or not.

"I like different, too." I head back out on the floor, leavin' him to his drink, though I feel his eyes on me as I go. I ain't got time to try and decipher that man. I have a tavern to run.

It's near midnight when Maelwen and Cicerine walk through the door. I nod at the pair as they walk in, and the blood on Mael's pants doesn't escape my attention. What the fuck has that girl been into tonight? They head up the stairs to the witch's apartment, the faun glancin' around nervously as they do. Hmm. Not exactly what I would have expected from a girl as private as Mael, but who am I to judge? Athros carries a big tub full of dirty glasses past me and into the kitchen. I hang my towel on the bar and follow him back, leavin' Martine to handle the floor for a bit.

"How goes it?" I ask as he sets to unloading the dishes.

"Miss Leita and Miss Martine have been real kind," he says.

"I've been doin' dishes, cleanin' up, and carryin' coin for Mr. Cartwright."

"Good, good. Has your little kitty heard anythin' interestin' this evenin'?"

He laughs, a light sound that makes me sad thinkin' about all he's gone through. "Losh ain't little, ma'am," he replies. "But he's been listenin'. Nothin' too important. Some smugglin', a man selling shakeroot, and there's a girl askin' around after coin fer her company. She seems real nice. Maybe I can help her out and keep her com—"

"Ach!" I interject. "She ain't lookin' for that kind of company, sweetheart." I can't contain the giggle that tumbles from my mouth. "She's a workin' lady. You let her alone, you hear?"

He looks shocked as hell and stares at his feet. "Yes, ma'am, Miss Shell."

I clap him on the shoulder before headin' back out to the main hall. Guess I'm in the business of givin life lessons now too.

Maelwen and Cicerine head down the stairs just as I reach the bar. They're holdin' hands, but I am not about to start askin' questions. I slide 'em a couple shots of whisky, the strong stuff I keep for personal use. Cicerine, bless her heart, takes a sip and looks damn near ready to burst into flames. With a laugh, I tell her to shoot it down, and she does. The way her eyes water tells me plenty about her experience with drink, but she thanks me as they head into the night. It's gotta be near dawn now, and I'm glad. I could use some sleep. Tomorrow I'll say goodbye to the witch for a bit, and Cartwright and I need to have a chat about our role in this mess. I've got some ideas rattlin' around in my brain, and he's just the fella to help me out.

KONIDAS

CHAPTER FIFTY-SIX
CICERINE
YEAR 993

"The Song of Death?" I've never heard of this, but the look on Maelwen's face frightens me. "What is that?"

"It is a witch gift," she begins, "that has apparently been long lost. From what I know, it ended with the Crone." She rests her chin atop her knee, brow furrowed. "It passes by blood, and the Crone bears no living children. I do not understand."

"Maybe she had a sibling?" I offer. "Could it have passed to you through another family member?"

She stares downward, not meeting my eyes. "I do not know. I know nothing about my lineage; I am an orphan. I do not even know if this is the true Death Song. It may be something else entirely."

"How will you know for sure?" I want to hold her hand again, that feeling of emptiness grating on my soul.

"I am not certain," she says and turns away.

My heart falls a bit, feeling even this small distance between us acutely. She looks around, the streets around the tavern empty, and sighs.

"It is morning. I have to meet with Cartwright and the Brick

Union." I nod. I have not yet met the faun Cartwright said would be coming to the inn. Truth be told, I have avoided the lobby entirely, not wanting to interact with another faun just yet. I'm still nervous, and though I know he is there to help, it doesn't ease my anxiety. "Come with me."

"What?" I'm taken aback. The idea of a whole meeting of non-humans scares me. I know it shouldn't, but it does.

"Come with me. They exist to help people like you. I need to speak with them about the threat of the Idyth cult, and you need to know your own."

"I don't have people." I respond in a much colder voice than I intended. "My people died, and now I have myself and myself alone. I refuse to place my trust in anyone else."

Maelwen pauses, considering my words. "You do not have to trust them, and you do not have to join them. I understand how you feel; I am also alone in the world. But you should know them, regardless. With the humans gathering to unite against us all, we need allies. You do not need to make them your people, but you should be known to them so they are more able to protect you."

"Do I look so weak?" I ask, regretting the words as they leave my mouth. "I killed an entire village. I can protect myself."

"I know this, but you are one girl among many who would harm you. Clearly there is more to you and I than we yet know. If I go to Minos'Idyl and you die, what then? You want to help, then help. Come with me. You will not be alone; I will be with you." Her hand tightens in mine and my heartbeat quickens, the flame within me flaring brightly.

"All right."

∽

THE HOUSE LOOKS NONDESCRIPT FROM THE STREET, A SMALL brown home in a nicer area of Kanitosh. Yellow candlelight shines through the curtains, and there are a couple low bushes out front. It is warm inside. A fire in the hearth bathes the living room in orange light, and an assortment of people sit on chairs and a couch before the fire. At first glance, everyone appears to be human, but a closer look shows slight differences. One man has a bit of moss growing on his skin, and it appears he may be covered in a thin layer of bark. I see hooves peeking from the pant legs of another. The person nearest the fire seems to flicker slightly if I look at them directly, but they're solid if I look at them from the corner of my vision. Cartwright enters the room from what I assume is the kitchen, carrying a large tray of steaming cups. He hands one to each of us, and I smile at the warm scent of spiced tea. Maelwen takes a cup but doesn't drink it, choosing to hold it in her delicate hands instead, glad for the heat on her fingers.

"Ah, 'ello all," he begins. "I'd like to start by introducing someone close to me, as well as a new friend." Maelwen looks nearly bashful, a rather surprising blush spreading across her normally dispassionate face. "This here is Maelwen and Cicerine. Maelwen is a witch, clearly, and Cicerine is a faun recently come to us from Kanitosh woods."

The man with the hooves flinches slightly.

Cartwright continues, "Today we meet to speak about the 'New Church' cult. Maelwen knows a lot, and she will take over for all that. But I want to know if any of ye know any more, and what you might be willing to do if it comes to fightin'." He turns to Maelwen and gives her a small bow. "You've got the floor, love."

Maelwen speaks calmly and directly, telling the group everything she learned while at the tower. She explains the pennyway flowers, the cult of Idyth and their belief that their god will be reborn. She tells them of the witches' plan to assemble at the solstice, and her suspicions about the minotaur island. The group is quiet throughout, nodding occasionally but saying nothing in reply. When she has finished, the gravity of the situation seems to sink into all of us. The reality that a group of men seeks to annihilate us all.

The person with the flickering body rises. "I will help. I am not bound to this form, and can be very useful when I need to remain unseen. I have some ability with fire, though not enough to conjure it on my own, but I can manipulate flame." They see my wide eyes, and their face softens a bit. "I am a jynn, child. My name is not one made for your tongue, but you may call me Asha."

One of the woodfolk also rises. "We will join with you. Should the battle enter the woods, we can help. I am of cedar, and he is of pine," he says, gesturing to the man beside him. "We can call upon the spirits of the trees. Those who still live will help how they can."

The faun shakes his head. "I have a family, and I just can't. I am sorry. My life belongs to my wife and children now—it is no longer mine to risk." I feel sympathy for him, for the family he has the fortune to love, and I understand. I do not begrudge him his choice.

The rest of the group speak, one by one. Most agree to help in whatever way they can. However, one, a nereid with long white hair, remains quiet. I am intrigued by them. I cannot tell if they are male or female, and I don't even know for certain if nereids are gendered. The dark violet of their eyes is otherworldly, and I cannot see how they could possibly pretend to be human. Their limbs are too long, too thin, and their hair moves in a way much like it would beneath the surface of the sea. They seem to feel my eyes upon them and catch my gaze. "Yes, I am…different." They smile kindly. "I am alone here, my kind sleep," they say in a melodic voice. "Centuries ago, they went to rest, and those of us who were land-bound were trapped ashore. I cannot reach them, and I know not how to wake them."

Maelwen's eyes shoot to them. "What did you say?"

They raise an eyebrow but repeat themselves.

Maelwen's forehead tightens in concentration. "The Crone spoke to me of a child of the sea, one who would awaken the nereids who sleep. How would this happen?"

The nereid's eyes widen, becoming impossibly round. "I do not know. I have tried," they sigh, shoulders dropping in clear sorrow. "How I have tried. I have remained on the floor of the sea for as long as my landlocked lungs would allow, begging to hear their song. I have sung my own, praying they would reply. Only silence has met me." They look so sad. Such isolation must be heart wrenching.

"Are there not more of your kind, ashore, like you?" I ask them gently.

"Maybe a dozen of us were trapped on land when our kind went to rest. We have been spread apart since. I know some left for the woods to live among the rivers, but I remained here, hoping for the sea to awaken." The pain in their eyes is deep, a well I cannot dream the depths of. But I think I understand a bit of it. I, too, have lost everything I once loved.

Seeing the jynn reminds me of her—of my Jynn. Of Mamère's stories of how she chose her name after the wild creatures of the desert. How her red hair had reminded Mama of flame. I bottle those emotions, shoving them deep, deep down into the furthest part of my heart. Sealing them behind and impenetrable wall. I remind myself once again, Jynn left. She *chose* to leave me, and I cannot hold on to someone who so callously ran when I needed her more than ever before. I realize, belatedly, that the nereid has been speaking. Blushing, I ask them to repeat what they were saying.

"Only that my kind are spread thin, and I know not if any bore children. I am uncertain if we are able to breed outside the sea, or with those who are not of the water. We do not share the human's idea of 'man' and 'woman,' and I do not know if we are even compatible. Sailors tell tales of sirens luring men to their beds, but they are falsehoods, tales meant to turn man away from our waters. Sometimes our songs can breach the blanket of the ocean's surface and be heard above, but we do not meddle in human affairs. Our lives were peaceful and private. I miss my home. I miss the sea."

"I truly hope your people awaken, and that you can go home," I tell them. "I wish joy for your future."

They smile gently. "I, as well. My name is Galena. I am pleased to meet you, woodborn."

KONIDAS

CHAPTER FIFTY-SEVEN
MAELWEN
YEAR 993

The sun sits high in the sky as we file out of the home where the Brick Union gathers. We have good allies among them and gifts that may be important in the coming conflict. I am ready to travel to Minos'Idyl, though I dread the lengthy flight. It should take me close to three days to reach the island, only if the winds are on my side. I will be able to stop and sleep near Athydis, but I need to be cautious entering such a populated area. My hope is to touch down near the southern coast, which is far less busy. However, there is another niggling feeling that scratches at my mind: Cicerine. I do not pretend to understand what is happening between us, but the fibers of my soul stretch toward her at all moments. The ember within me sputters as if begging for more fuel to burn. Thinking about being away from her for a week makes my heart ache in a way I have never experienced. I do not know how to put the emotion to name, but it is heavy, all-consuming.

She walks beside me, her fingers occasionally brushing my own. I know she feels the same need, the pull to touch me, so I do not move away. Tiny glittering sparks flash between us occasionally, and their crackle pulls my mind from its swirling thoughts. My chest feels fluttery, uncomfortable. Is this what it is to be nervous? I dislike it greatly. I take a deep breath and turn to her, meeting bright, golden eyes already trained on mine. "Accompany me to the island." My voice comes out harsh, a statement rather than a request. Fuck. I had not intended it to come out as a command, but my words tangled in my mind as I attempted to craft the question.

Her eyes widen and her plush lips part gently. Heat snakes through me as I take in the miniscule motion. "You want me to fly with you? That far?"

"It is no great feat," I reply. "I feel...compelled to bring you with me. It will take near to a week, will Beatrice excuse you for that length of time?"

She nods. "She told me I am free to take time as needed. I have already done all the ordering for this month; it would be fine. Are you certain? You want me to come all that way?"

"I do." My voice comes out curtly. I am not doing well with this. I focus on softening my speech, attempting to convey the longing I feel. "I would like you to, if you care to join me." I look out toward the coast, somehow unable to meet her eyes. This sense of vulnerability is unnerving. I feel her fingers lace with mine, and somehow that sense of dread begins to abate. I wrap them more tightly with my own and gently pull her closer. I cannot say why, but it happens all the same.

"I would like to," she says, looking up at me. Her focus flickers to my mouth for such a small moment, I wonder if I have imagined it, but I simply squeeze her hand in response, and we head toward the tavern to gather what we need.

"We need not bring much food," Cicerine says as I gather a change of clothing for my small pack. "I can grow things for us if we need."

"I have fed recently enough that I do not *need* food. I feel better when I eat, but it is not strictly necessary anymore." I try not to stare at her as she folds a dress into a compact square. "You would be better served by bringing tops and breeches, if you have them. Dresses are not exactly made for flight."

Her cheeks go crimson. "Gods. Let me stop by the inn. I can grab a few things there."

"I will finish here and meet you there. Limit your choices, we can wash if we need, but we cannot pack heavily for flight."

"And you're sure you're certain?" Her voice is small, I wonder if she also feels anxious in my presence. Her cheeks pink and a shy smile brightens her face. "Last chance to change your mind."

"I am." I reach across the small table in my bedroom and graze the side of her hand with a finger.

Her answering smile is dazzling, and I return it. It still feels odd on my face, this expression. She seems to cause all sorts of these odd feelings.

We take to the sky in the late morning just as the sun approaches midday. Winter is in the air, and Cicerine, bundled in a wool sweater and a thin coat, is pressed to my body, sharing my warmth. My cloak hugs her to me, as if it, too, wants her near. The scent of the spiced tea has settled in her hair, and I breathe her in. Our bare skin is not touching, but I feel her with me all the same. This close proximity to her is intoxicating, and I cannot quite seem to catch my breath. I think back on what the Crone said about the woodborn child—could it be Cicerine? Did she mean a literal child? The Crone speaks in riddles, and it is infuriating.

Cicerine's soft voice drifts to my ear, a soft sound on the wind. "Where are we now? Are we close to the city?"

Below us lies the sea, the water still and blue from this elevation. The peninsula upon which the great city was built is not much farther to the north. "Yes," I reply. "We will reach the peninsula in a couple of hours, and will rest on the southern shore for the night. If we stick to the coast, we should be safe." I feel her nod against my chest. "If you are tired now, you may rest while we fly." She nuzzles into me, and it feels so comfortable that I nearly sigh; the cinnamon scent of her hair is intoxicating.

"I can wait until we reach land," she responds. She is quiet for a long moment, a pregnant silence in which I know she desires to speak. When she at last does, the words tumble out quickly, pushed forward by an endearing bit of embarrassed curiosity. "Have you ever seen a sea monster?"

I cannot help my smile. "No, I have not. I am not certain if they even exist."

"I'd like to believe they are real. There is so much sea; I cannot imagine it holds only fish and whales and sleeping nereids."

"This is true. There is a vast world beneath the waves. Perhaps you are correct, and there are things we have not yet encountered, I'd like to believe there is more tho this world than what we know."

THE LIGHT HAS FADED TO A DUSKY GRAY WHEN WE TOUCH down on the rocky shore of the peninsula. A soft whisper of waves against the sand is the only sound in the uninhabited area I have chosen. Cicerine looks exhausted. I hand her our pack, and she sets herself to laying out a small blanket behind a ridge of sand that buffers the breeze. She positions my own blanket beside hers and takes out a little packet with two breakfast buns inside.

She offers me one, but I refuse. I have no need for them, and she very well may before this journey is through. I do not dare start a fire for fear of attracting attention, so we huddle next to one another beneath my cloak.

"How does this work?" she asks, running a finger along the edge of the thick fabric. "Your cloak, I mean. Is it…connected?"

"It is," I say, moving my braid to the side to expose the line of flesh where it stitches to my skin. "I do not know the exact mechanics of it—it was gifted to me by another witch, and when I put it on for the first time, it did this. The little scars do not heal, unlike most of my other wounds."

She nods her head and takes another bite of the soft bread. "Do you think it is safe to sleep? Do we need to take turns?"

"I am not concerned. I did not see any other campfires as we approached, and I see no sign of humans. I am quick to wake and will hear anyone who may approach."

She bundles her clothes and lays her head upon them with a yawn, and I follow suit, pulling my cloak over the two of us. It takes only minutes for her breathing to slow and settle, and I watch her a moment before closing my own eyes. I have never slept beside someone, and it is a strangely comforting sensation.

Cicerine's sharp intake of breath rouses me. I cannot be sure how long I slept, but the crescent moon is high in the ink black sky. She is still asleep, but her eyes track back and forth rapidly, her breath labored. I push myself up onto my elbow and face her. It is most likely a nightmare, but I would rather not sleep while she is in distress. When her eyes shoot open, I flinch; the milky-white pupils not her own. Gone is the warm honey glow, only an eerie white remaining. I do not move, unsure of what is happening and not wanting to do anything that may have a bad outcome for either of us. Her lips form words, but she does not speak. I cannot decipher what she says. Her mouth moves quickly, making shapes and expressions I have never seen on her face. She does not blink, simply stares ahead, speaking silently. And suddenly it is over; she falls back against the blanket, eyes drifting closed, her breath slowing once more.

    I do not sleep again.

ATHYDIS

CHAPTER FIFTY-EIGHT
THE CRONE
YEAR 993

She watches the men in the streets, hears their fervent chanting. Her lip curls in disgust, repulsed by the message of these humans who think themselves worthy of gods. They have multiplied in recent days, forming groups in the square and gaining the attention of more and more commonfolk. She pulls the curtain and walks into the bedchamber. The man and woman who sleep within are still. They will not wake without her command, her control absolute. With a sigh, she sits down in the large chair beside the bed. The magic takes little effort for her, but she must replenish it from time to time. She speaks the words and braids the threads of chaos, tying herself firmly to both their minds and bodies. They are hers, their own minds so buried in the tapestry she has woven that they may never be free of it again. While the well of her power is near-infinite, she feels the strain of the day. Too many threads to gather, too many witches to watch. Her eyes close as her head rests against the plush chair, and she sleeps.

She wakes to sand. White sand beneath a moonlit night, the stars flickering across a velvet sea of night. She does not know this place, nor the body she inhabits. There is an ocean; not Iowain then. Her gaze turns, and she starts. She looks upon the witchling. She expected to see the girl soon, as she has called for her kin to meet at the solstice, but there is time yet before that conclave. This is an interesting vision indeed. The girl's eyes are so much like her own, pale and cold, and utterly unflinching. The witchling is so young, so unaware of the many players in this game which stretches through time. The Crone opens her mouth to speak, but her voice is silent. She tries again, but no sound will come forth; the vessel she inhabits, just strong enough to maintain that small bit of control. Yet she speaks all the same; these silent words belong to the witchling. They beg to be freed—no matter that she cannot hear them.

"I could have given you all the pieces, however they were not mine to give. The truth of this moment is far more than my one life can contain. All the Crones, for all of time, have each held but a shard of it. These shards cannot be reassembled, lost to the ether with each passing of the Crone. But within you lies the crucible in which they all will land. You are the flame and the fire, child. The one who should not be. You carry within you the best and worst of this world. I knew not who was to be your sire, but the line of Idyth is long and ever branching. It takes but a single drop of blood, my child. A single drop of blood. Hold fast, fly true, and know that in time it will all be made clear. A shattered mirror is but a thousand new mirrors, and they all reflect a different truth."

She feels the threads slipping, her tensile grasp weakening. The body breathes and exhales her consciousness, pushing her back into the cold stone room. The humans in the bed have not moved, not that they would. Their chests rise and fall of their own accord; any other action is hers alone to orchestrate. Dawn will not return for hours more, but with the sun she will begin again, to dance the dance of human men. To rule the people set to be her ruin.

THE SEA

CHAPTER FIFTY-NINE
JYNN
YEAR 993

The water wraps around my head, muffling the sounds of the world above. There is a murmur that may be Tuii or Cenna calling my name, but it isn't important right now. The song is so loud, I feel it vibrate the marrow of my bones. The melody seems familiar, like a lullaby or a children's rhyme, but I can't quite identify the tune. Oddly, I don't feel that strangling burn in my lungs. I feel calm, relaxed, as if I'm lounging in my hammock on the ship, the sway of the sea now deeply familiar. The light from above seems farther away than it was moments before, and I realize I haven't been treading water; I've been sinking. I kick, heading back toward the surface when I see it: floating in the water, swaying back and forth—long, white hair.

The figure that swims to meet me is lithe and finely boned. Their eyes are round and wide, fringed by curling white lashes. I can't be certain if their skin is pale aqua, or if I'm seeing the color of the sea, but they look otherworldly, ethereal. Their shoulders are broad, well-muscled, built to propel them through the ocean currents. I don't know if they're male or female, and it's somehow more comfortable this way. Their mouth is wide and full, sitting below speckled cheeks, smiling warmly at me as they sing. I watch and wonder how this can be, how song can travel through water, how I am not wanting for breath. I am at peace here, even my softly rustling clothing feels like a bit of the sea. The song continues, a melody that feels known to me but also so very alien. They reach out their hand, long fingers with slightly pointed nails, and cup my cheek. They are so very gentle that their caress is almost indistinguishable from the flow of the sea around me. And just like that, they swim away. I watch their swirling white hair vanish into the darkness of the deep like a wisp of smoke in the night. For a brief moment, I simply float, my feet softly moving back and forth to maintain my position in the water. Then my mind catches up, and I wonder *how long has it been since I took a breath?*

Scissoring my feet back and forth, I propel myself upward toward the flicker of light at the surface. I can see the shallow bottom of the dinghy, and I come up beside it with a small splash. Tuii and Cenna are both leaning over opposite sides of the small vessel, shouting my name. When my head breaks the surface, their eyes shoot to me, and Tuii exclaims "Jynn! *What. The. Fuck?*"

Sputtering, I cough out a mouthful of water and croak, "I'm sorry! Gods, I'm so sorry! I have no idea what came over me. I heard this song, and I just…jumped?" I heave myself back over the side of the dinghy, rocking it to and fro as my sopping wet clothes slap onto the sun-bleached bench in the vessel.

"Yeah, we fucking know that." Cenna sounds absolutely livid. "But *we* didn't hear a godsdamned thing, and the next thing we know, you're fucking gone. We thought you were dead, Jynn! You've been underwater for entirely too long."

"How long?" My curiosity outweighs my need to apologize. I rake my fingers through my wet hair, massaging my scalp.

"Ten minutes? Maybe more?" Tuii sounds incredulous. "How, Jynn? How did you do that?"

I wring what water I can from my shirt and run my hands down the legs of my breeches to squeeze more from the fabric. "I don't know. I had no idea it had been that long." Fuck, the air above the sea is freezing compared to the depths of the water. "There was someone down there. Something. I don't know. I saw a person? They weren't human. I can't explain what I saw, but it saw me too." My heartbeat rattles like a bird in a cage. A strange exhilaration fills me, and I feel as if I am on the precipice of something vital. Who was that figure below the waves? And why did they feel so...right?

They both shake their heads, and Cenna pushes the oars back toward me. "Well, now that you're finished with your lovely swim, can you please get us back to the Sea Song? Some of us would like to check on our *real* friends and not waste our time with magical sea people."

I resist the urge to snap back with something snide. She's right. We do have friends out there on the ship, and who knows what condition they're in? The last time we were aboard, the damn thing tipped into the sea. For all we know, half the crew could have drowned. I feel like a proper ass, and so I set to rowing. The slap of oars on water is the only sound for hours. My thoughts are a tangled mess. I am torn between my desire to return to the ship and my longing to return to the ocean. Shame fills me as I remind myself that the Sea Song may have lost people. There may be sorrow and grief to greet us, and I'm busy daydreaming about mysterious sea people. I steel myself, my friends *are* real, and they *are* waiting. I have a duty to my crew that outweighs my curiosity. The shape of the Sea Song grows steadily on the horizon, but a single rower in the open ocean simply does not have the capacity to get anywhere quickly. I am so thirsty that I feel close to passing out, but there is no alternative but to keep going. Cenna and Tuii both offer to take a turn and to give me a brief break, but guilt pushes me onward. By the time we are close enough to be spotted, my vision has begun to blur at the corners, and my mouth hangs open as I pant with exertion. Georgette's voice sounds like the peal of a church bell as she calls out to Captain, and in a few moments, Briar and Ardelle are headed straight toward us in a rowboat. If I had a single drop of water left in my body, I would cry, but my sweat has bled me dry. I nearly collapse into the other boat as they cast over and pull up next to us. Ardelle hugs Cenna tightly, and I'm surprised to see so much emotion cross Cenna's typically stoic features. Briar grasps my upper arm with a strong, thick hand and hauls me upright.

I hear Ballad before I see her. I can barely lift my head, but the unmistakable sound of her boots hitting the deck sounds from above, and I hear a ladder slap against the hull as it's thrown down. Everything happens in a jumbled series of events, my mind too foggy to focus on any one thing. Once I'm on the deck I collapse, and the already darkening skies go black.

THE CUP PRESSING AGAINST MY CRACKED LIPS IS COLD AS HELL, and I will my heavy eyelids to open. Captain sits on a stool beside my hammock, and Georgette tips the tin vessel forward, pouring fresh water into my mouth, which I immediately cough back up directly into her face. Captain laughs heartily though Georgette's narrowed eyes seem less than amused. She wipes the splattered water from her cheek and hands me the cup before heading back up toward the deck. "Oy! Jynn! Drink up, girl," Ballad says with a grin. "Sooner you get some fresh water in ye, the faster I'll be fillin' yer cup with grog."

The idea of drinking liquor right now turns my stomach, but I sip the water anyway, knowing the pounding in my head won't abate until I'm properly hydrated again. "Captain," I begin, "what happened? Did we lose anyone? Is the ship damaged?"

She pats my knee like a mother would do to quiet an annoying child. "All's well with the Sea Song. She's sturdier than you give her credit for." Emotion tightens her features, sadness crossing her face in a way I've never seen. "We lost Hana and Tala. Nearly lost me too, but the sea was on my side."

I didn't know either Hana or Tala well, but it's a punch to the gut anyway. We aren't a large crew, and every member matters. I only hope I can help fill the spaces they leave behind. "I'm sorry, Captain," I say, staring at my hands. Gods, I feel like an ass. Every moment I spent dawdling beneath the sea, my crew spent mourning their losses. I should have been here helping.

"Weren't yer fault," she says gently. "You went over too. We're feelin' blessed to have not lost you three. I spoke with Tuii and Cenna, and they told me what they could. But now, girl—what did you see in the water?"

I'm surprised by the question. I'm not sure why—of course Tuii and Cenna would have told Ballad about my leap into the water—but the look on the captain's face has an odd hint of desperation to it, as if she knows something of her own. "It's hard to explain, Captain," I begin. "I guess I'd call it a person? But they weren't human. They weren't built for land. They sang the strangest song, but it sounded almost familiar? They were pale as a ghost. I'd guess they didn't spend much time in the sun."

She's quiet, her elbows resting on her knees and her chin set atop one closed fist. She nods slightly before saying, "Jynn, I think whatever you saw? They're what kept me from a long sleep at the bottom o'the sea. *Something* pulled me out of the water, pushed my head back into the air. I thought for sure I was havin' some sort'a hallucination. But I remember arms. Long ones. Long, pale arms, and they wrapped me up like a babe and pushed me back out of the sea."

"Did you hear anything?" Excitement vibrates my bones.

"Nope. Just the water in my head and a scream in my chest.

When the Sea Song righted herself she pulled a whole lot o'water back. It sucked me down in a whirlpool, and I was sure I was gonna die. But then that set o'arms grabbed me tight and got me out. I ain't never been so thankful in my life."

"Do you have any idea what it could be?" If anyone would know what they are, it's a ship's captain.

"Well, I been on the water since I came out me ma's womb. Pa told me many a'tale as a babe, but I only know of two stories with singin' sea folk—the sirens and the nereids. Sirens sing men under and drown 'em, eat 'em too if the tales are true. The nereids, though, they've been known to lend a helping hand here and there. They're called all sorts of things: merfolk, nymphs, sea gods. Old books tell of vengeful sea rulers and beautiful women beneath the waves, gods of storms and sweet seal folk who play in ship's wake. But the tales of the nereids are all old, long before me or my ma and pa were born. Ain't no way of knowin' truth from tale nowadays."

"Damn," I reply. "Well, I guess that doesn't really clear anything up then."

Ballad barks out a laugh. "Nope! But we live to see another day." She slaps my shoulder as she rises. "Get some rest, drink up, and get somethin' in yer gut when you can. We'll be needin' you more than ever now that we've lost two sets o'hands."

I nod and take another drink. "Aye, Captain. I won't let you down." As she walks away I relax back into my familiar hammock and let my eyes close again. I've never felt so tired in my life. Sleep comes quickly, loosening my grip on the tin cup and weighing down my limbs. As I drift off, I swear I hear that tune again, low and melodic, calling my name.

ATHYDIS

CHAPTER SIXTY
CICERINE
YEAR 993

I open my eyes to the sight of high cheekbones and sharply angled eyes, the most remarkably beautiful face I have ever seen. Maelwen lies beside me, our bodies barely touching beneath the cloak, but the slight contact sets my skin aflame. My clothing seems to brush against every single hair on my body, making me feel an excess of sensation. Everything about her makes my thoughts tumultuous, my mind crashing from images to emotion like rough ocean waves. Her glacial eyes stare at me with an odd, suspicious expression, and I rise up onto my elbows. The fuzzy remnants of a fleeting dream buzz about my memory, and I try to grasp them and fail. I manage to snatch a single phrase from the ether —

A shattered mirror is but a thousand new mirrors, and they all reflect a different truth.

I have absolutely no idea what the words mean, but they feel important. Shaking my head, I attempt to clear my thoughts. "How long was I asleep?"

Maelwen narrows her eyes as she replies, "A few hours. You

needed the rest, and we were able to spare the time, so I did not wake you."

My mouth feels sandy and dry, so I reach for our waterskin and swish a mouthful before rising and spitting it into the brush. The air is cold, and I pull my sweater tighter around my shoulders. The coast here looks different than it does in Konidas. The rocks are a mottled gray and black with little bits that shimmer in the morning light. They are rough, large chunks that appear to have broken off from one massive stone eons ago. The sand also has a gray shimmer to it, looking nearly silver beneath my feet. I like the soft sparkle; it brightens the monochrome shore. From our position down at the water, I cannot see much beyond this area, but the brush at the top of the hill is mostly sharp-looking sticks and branches with very few leaves. The lack of green feels wrong to me, so different from the vibrant saturation of color in the glade. I'm so focused on the crashing of the waves against the sand that I do not hear Maelwen's approach, but her hand brushes mine as she joins me.

"Something rather...unsettling happened while you slept." Her eyebrows draw together, and her voice holds a wavering note of concern.

I turn to her quickly. "What do you mean? Is everything all right?" A ragged fear shoots through me. Did I do something? I cannot imagine what could make *Maelwen* feel unsettled.

"I believe so. Have you ever known yourself to sleepwalk? Have nightmares?" I shake my head. "There was an odd moment last night when you appeared to wake but were not yourself. I thought you were going to speak, but your lips only moved. You said nothing. There was something...wrong with your eyes"

I think of the disorienting, fuzzy feeling. The unsurety of her words sets me on edge. "I had a strange dream. I wish I could recall what happened. All I can remember is a phrase—*'a shattered mirror is but a thousand new mirrors, and they all reflect a different truth.'*

Does that make any sense to you?" Maelwen is silent as she stares out over the expanse of water before us. My breath feels difficult to regulate, anxiety pushing against my lungs. I cannot help but lean into her, and even through the thick wool of my homespun sweater, I feel the electric energy of her skin. My fingers itch to touch her. It feels like a need, a physical pull like a magnet to ore. This constant need to be in contact with her, will it ever go away? I want to feel our magic weave together again. It made me feel whole in a way I cannot recall ever feeling before.

"I do not know," she replies at last. "It does not sound like something that came from your mind, but I am unsure what, or who, would be using you as a vessel, or if it was simply an odd dream. Regardless, we must continue. Gather your things and eat."

As she turns to leave, her hand reaches out and her fingers graze mine, littering the silver sand below with sparks that sizzle where they land.

FROM ABOVE, ATHYDIS LOOKS LIKE A CITY OF DOLLHOUSES. The red roofs and tiny bustling bodies remind me of children's toys, bright and busy. Maelwen keeps us above the clouds for the most part, not wanting to risk being seen, but even from this distance I can see the sprawling cathedral, the gray stone of the looming castle, the city districts and their many walls. "Have you ever been there?" I ask her quietly as we pass overhead.

"In a way," she replies, not elaborating.

After a moment of silence, nothing but the whistle of the wind, I ask, "What does that mean?" I want to know her, to know her thoughts and emotions, but I know she is not like me. She contains her emotions, while mine leak from me like water from a sieve.

"I traveled there once, but not in a physical sense. It was a strange situation, which I believe to be the result of the pennyway. I spoke with the Crone. I suppose it could be said it was the true beginning of my involvement with—" She nods toward the city. "All of this. Apparently, it was the first time anyone had spoken with the Crone in a long time. The other witches thought her silent."

"But she chose to speak with you?"

"I do not think she necessarily had a choice. She seemed just as surprised as I was. It was an uncomfortable meeting."

I know she can't see me, so I squeeze her arm in what I hope is a reassuring way. What a strange turn my life has taken. I've gone from living in the glade with Mamère to flying across the continent with a witch. It is like reading a book, a story I could never have imagined on my own. We continue in companionable silence. I think more on the feeling of our intertwining magic. If combining our power led to Maelwen discovering the Song of Death, might there be abilities lying hidden within me as well? I have not even fully delved into the limits of the darker part of my magic. Perhaps the witches in the tower will be able to help.

The great island of Minos'Idyl first appears as a speck on the horizon. It slowly grows, the massive volcanic peak stretching toward the sky and becoming lost in the clouds. The closer we get to the island, the more tension I feel in Maelwen's lithe body. She says nothing, but I feel the shift in her muscles, hear it in the pattern of her breathing. It is nearly nightfall when we are finally close enough to see the island in detail. A thick jungle carpets the base of the rocky summit, surrounding it in a rich green. Despite the lack of light, we see an area tucked into the trees which appears to contain a large building of some sort. We detect no movement on this unpopulated side of the island, the city of Pe'Taur lies to the east.

We land silently on the beach, and Maelwen grips my hand

immediately. "The energy here is off," she whispers. "It feels wrong."

I attempt to reach out with my power, wondering if I can sense something within the island that might be the source of Maelwen's unease. The tendrils of my green-hued magic snake through the earth, searching and reaching. I feel the life beneath the jungle, vast root systems of the giant trees and endless leafy plants. I sense the tiny lattice of grass roots and plants surrounding a nearby estuary. I brush up against the sea grasses and vines, the flowers and the scrub at the shore—and then I feel it. Like a living memory, the acrid taste flows down my magic, filling my mouth with its bitter bite and my eyes with tears. "Pennyway," I choke out. "This island is full of pennyway."

Maelwen keeps hold of my arm as I begin to sink down to the sand. I feel the tips of her claws prick my skin through my sweater and wonder if she, too, is losing control. The damp sand seeps through my pants and up the bottom my coat, chilling the skin beneath, but the shiver running through my body has nothing to do with the cold. I close my eyes to contain the tears that threaten to fall. All I can see is Mamère, her warm face and soft eyes and the way her cheeks crinkled at the corners when she smiled. But those bright eyes dim, twisting into a glassy, blank stare as Father Farragen controlled her, the dark plum stain of her mouth as her breath stopped; her dim, lifeless gaze as she lay dead on Farrgaen's bed, the dirt hitting her cheeks as I buried her. My heart aches, pushing bile into my throat as I try my hardest to swallow down the sorrow. I fight against the darkness that threatens to overcome me. I think of the smell of warm bread baking in our woodstove, and the smooth silk of her headscarf as she readied herself for bed. I hear her laugh as I baked something awful, her grin when I brought her flowers. I try to hold on to the joy. I cannot control the gasp that breaks free from my lips as my breath struggles to catch up to my heartbeat, but the feel of Maelwen's hand on my elbow, her knee pressed against mine, grounds me, and I feel when she stills. I open my eyes.

All around us, the sand is filled with the color of hundreds of flowers, surrounding the small patch of bare coast on which we sit. The explosion of my gift is bright and warm. I can only guess that by trying so hard to escape my sorrow, I pushed out all the good I found within myself. The flowers bob gently in the ocean breeze, and the air fills with their perfume. Maelwen looks around, wide-eyed. I take her hand in mine, wanting to share this moment fully. Her palm is cool and dry against my sweaty fingers, and all at once I feel our magic weave together. I can see it truly, for the first time, as it happens. What once felt like threads wrapping around each other is, in fact, so much more complex. Our magic weaves together like fabric, all the many pieces of each of us knitting and layering to create something more. The dark threads of hers seem to absorb the green-hued light of my own magic. I can sense the rippling green and black fabric connecting us. Tracing the darkness of her essence feels intimate, touching the spaces between us that belong to her. I do not think when it happens, just feel, but in the span of a single breath, every flower dies. They wilt and droop, bright petals going gray and brown. My connection to her black threads drops suddenly. I feel my own magic course back through my body like a warm caress, but the damage is done. Stems and leaves shrivel, cracking and falling to the sand. It takes seconds, but I watch it occur as if time has slowed. We sit in silence, surrounded by a shadow of dark ash.

Maelwen's voice startles me when she speaks. "You used my magic."

My head turns toward her quickly. "I didn't intend to. I was just tracing the bond between us, touching the parts that felt like you. The flowers were so lovely; it's horrible that I destroyed them." For the first time, I am frightened of her abilities, of how quickly I was able to wield death itself.

She doesn't look at me, focused intently on twirling a dead stem between her fingers. "Flowers die; do not mourn the loss of something with such a fleeting existence. I felt you within me. I felt the song in my chest. Somehow you pulled it from me. I heard it even though you did not sing. It was a song of endings, the Song of Death." She fidgets, looking smaller than I have seen before.

"How can it be a song if I did not sing?"

There is a weighted pause, she breathes deeply, dropping the dead flower and running her fingers through the sand in swirling lines. When she raises her eyes to mine, they are full of fire. "I do not know the answer to that question, but I felt it in my lungs. I feel you now, still. Like the remnants of the sun on stone. I feel the life within you, all the light and warmth where I am all darkness and cold. I have never felt like there was room for light within me, like there was room for joy. This feels like laughter, like life. You feel like what I imagine happiness to feel like." Her eyes only leave mine for a fraction of a second, landing on my lips and then flashing back to meet my gaze.

Then her mouth is upon mine, and the world erupts in song.

MINOS'IDYL

CHAPTER SIXTY-ONE
MAELWEN
YEAR 993

She tastes like wildflowers, like warm honey in early spring. I am consumed by her. The air whips around us and the ashes of the fallen flowers fly away on a warm wind of magic and emotion. My hair rises on the breeze and dances around her face. My fingers bury themselves in her curls. I cup her face to mine, wanting to pull her closer, to eliminate any space that lies between us. This emotion overwhelms me; it is so much more than I have ever imagined myself capable of. My heart aches for her, desire gripping my soul with unyielding tension. This pull is instinct, destiny. My fingers shake, uncertain of my own resolve in the face of such powerful want. The waves crash, buffeting the coast and bathing us in sea spray. She shifts her ample hips, sliding into my lap with ease, her hands on my neck. A tiny noise escapes her, sighed into my mouth as we lose ourselves in one another, and my answering growl is primal. I am lost to thought, to reason, to logic. My body acts of its own accord, straining against her, pressing into her soft body and nestling itself into her curves. The walls around my heart, mortared by pain, begin to crack. I *want* to be touched, to touch, and it terrifies me. I am blind to everything else in the world except for her, and when the booming crack of lightning strikes, it tears me from my consumption. I pull her to my chest protectively.

The beach in front of us is streaked and fractured with steaming black veins. In the center, a hole appears to lead straight to the planet's core. I am baffled by what I see before me, and curiosity replaces the lust that had previously flooded my mind. Softly setting Cicerine on the shore, I rise and walk to the strange tunnel. Kneeling before it, I dig my claws into the warm, wet grains of sand and unearth a strange glass vessel. I have heard of this, the phenomenon of pure energy striking sand, and now I hold it in my own hands. It is lightning given form. A hollow center is surrounded by branching arms and figures of nearly opaque gray glass. It is heavy and hot, but I balance the object on my claws as it cools in the ocean air. I walk to the sea and dip the vessel beneath the water, watching as the waves lap at it and fill the center with brine. When I pull it from the shallows, the surface glints in the sunlight like a smoky crystal. It is shaped like an inverted tree, a hollow trunk with a round, branching base. The vessel feels alive, full of vibrant energy. It feels like Cicerine. I remember her sitting just a few steps away, likely very confused. I nearly smile. Making my way back across the sand, I sit beside her once more and pass the vessel into her outstretched palms. She examines it closely, watching the way the light plays off its many surfaces and hefting its weight in her small hands. "What is this?" she asks, face still flushed, and looks into its hollow center.

"Lightning glass. It happens sometimes when lightning hits sand. I have read about it, but this is the first time I have seen it in person." I feel strangely warm, enjoying this feeling of sharing knowledge with her.

She looks at the sky, clear save for a few scattered wisps of cloud. "But what in the gods' names happened? Where did the lightning come from? Did we do that? It scared me."

"I know nothing more than you do," I say with a slight smile. "I feel...*different*, though." I settle in beside her, pressing my thigh against hers, longing to taste her mouth once again.

"I feel it too." She lays her head on my shoulder, and I breathe in the scent of her. Contentment settles over me like an ill-fitting coat—a feeling I am not accustomed to.

I place my hand on the shore, trying to isolate her magic within me. I can still feel the glowing strands, and I reach out with them, sensing the roots and the life buried within the earth. I urge them upward, trying to do as she does. When I open my eyes, however, nothing is changed. "I do not appear to be able to use your magic, but I still feel connected to it somehow."

Cicerine places her hand atop mine, and I feel her warmth flowing through my fingers. Slowly, a small green sprout emerges from the sand, growing and reaching until it blooms into a single deep-blue flower. The shade is an exact match for my cloak. She looks at me with a smile in her eyes, and I cannot resist the pull of her. Cicerine is the light I have sought throughout my entire life of darkness. My dim existence, lacking the sun, feels lighter with her beside me. This cold heart in my chest aches for her radiant warmth. My lips find hers once more, and her fingers curl around mine, lacing our hands together amidst the sound of the sea. This kiss holds something deeper than the passion of the last. It is not fueled by raw need, but by a honey-sweet desire to have her in my arms. Whatever this feeling is, it makes me think of a home I have never had..

We wrap the lightning glass vessel in my spare shirt, nestling it against the base of a tree. I do not want to leave it behind; it feels like her and I want to keep it. It is a moment made solid, her kiss manifested into a tangible thing. We will return for it before we leave the island. First, we need to head inland and find the pennyway. I cannot use magic to feel plants in the detailed way Cicerine can, but she is certain there are a large amount of the flowers growing on the island. Rather than flying, we opt to walk. The jungle is dense, however, my claws easily slice through some of the more restrictive vines. Hooves are not especially well suited to the terrain, though Cicerine manages, and we slowly creep toward the center of the island.

I can smell the stink of the pennyway before we are close enough to hear anything. As the scent grows stronger, so does the jungle grow more quiet. The birds in the trees stop their song, the furred creatures in the underbrush halt their chatter. The air here is thick and hot, feeling like a sheet of wool. The smell of the pennyway sticks to the air and overwhelms me; I feel like gagging. As we snake around a large tree with a broad base, I can hear muffled voices. The speaker sounds aggressive and angry, shouting in a commanding tone, sharp and clipped. I can just barely pick up what sounds like the clinking of metal. Cicerine's hand tightens in mine, and I know she hears it as well. I hate the feeling that fingers at the edge of my mind, telling me I have brought her into danger. I want to tell her to stay here, to stay safe, but I know she will not listen. Reluctantly dropping her hand, I flick out one of my claws and press it to my lips, and she nods in reply, her sweat-damp curls sticking to her forehead with the motion.

There is a small clearing across from us and directly past is what appears to be a farm. Rows upon rows of plants run along the length of the space. It has canvas walls on two sides, but the rest is open to the jungle air. Around the perimeter is a wooden deck and upon it stands a group of minotaurs. My heart races the second I spot them, my claws extending of their own volition. I cannot quell this overwhelming fear. My body instinctively lowers into a defensive posture, weight distributed on both feet evenly, shoulders down slightly. While my mind thrashes about, my body prepares to be hurt, trained by years of abuse. Cicerine reaches toward me, but I shake my head sharply, not sure I can be trusted right now. My mind is like an animal's, struggling between fighting and fleeing. Hurt flashes across her face momentarily, but she does not press the matter and instead moves beside me. I hear her breath catch when she sees the others who occupy the farm: chained fauns tending the plants, gathering flowers, some with hands pressed to the earth just as hers do. I see her begin to shake, whether from anger or fear, I do not know. I wish I could comfort her, but we each have our own memories to endure.

One of the minotaurs grasps a long leather whip in his thick fingers, and with a resounding *crack,* brings it down upon the back of an older female faun. Her shirt and skin split, blood welling up to fill the open space as she falls to her knees between the plants. "*Do not harm the flowers!*" the minotaur bellows, more concerned with the welfare of the plants than that of the faun.

Cicerine lurches forward, but I extend a hand to hold her back. Rather than argue, she takes my hand and clutches it tightly in her own. I focus on the fabric of our connection; the woven magic that exists between us giving me strength. Her fingers squeeze mine, and when I meet her gaze, I know her fire burns as fiercely as mine.

We are a force of nature.

WE DO NOT ENTER THE CLEARING, INSTEAD OPTING TO SKIRT the edge of the forest, obscured by the trees. It takes longer, but when we reach the farm, we are mere feet from the minotaur overseers. Our combined magic pulses, calescent, begging for retribution. I will not deny it its desire. Beyond, there is a small thatched shack set back from the main area of the farm. From the stench, I determine it is likely living quarters and latrines. I count eleven minotaurs on the deck and twenty-four fauns of varying ages currently working the farm. Their clothing is filthy and tattered, stained with sweat and blood. Heavy chains hang from their wrists and ankles, the hair worn away from the constant rubbing of the cuffs. Those who appear to share Cicerine's gift are not shackled together like the rest, but instead, have thick iron collars around their necks. The weight hobbles them, hunching their shoulders and leaving them slumped, walking with pained, shuffling steps. I want to rip the minotaurs limb from limb. My mind plays tricks on me, showing me Cicerine's face on every faun before me. No breeze flows this far inland, and the fauns' skin is drenched in sweat, streaked with dirt from where rivulets of moisture have washed away the filth. Their suffering is agonizing to see. The smell of pennyway permeates the air. I can taste it in the back of my throat with each breath, astringent and bitter.

I am silent on my feet, but Cicerine does not have the same light steps as a witch. Her small hooves are delicate, but they are still hooves, and when she trips over a root and clips a rock with the very tip of one, a minotaur turns toward the sound. We freeze, still hidden enough in the trees. I know the eyesight of a minotaur is shit, but they do have a decent sense of smell. I can only hope the wretched stink of the pennyway muffles our own scents. After a moment, the minotaur turns back to his charges, apparently satisfied that the jungle is free of any impending threat. He kicks out with his massive hoof and sends a chain of four fauns toppling to the loamy soil. Another minotaur stalks over and claps him on the back, his chuffing laughter filling the air as the fauns feebly attempt to untangle their chains and right themselves. I can sense Cicerine's rage emanating from her in waves, feeling like static. She is not alone in her hatred. The fauns finally manage to get back on their feet and continue to tend the plants, cowed. The minotaurs speak amongst themselves, their attention temporarily diverted. The simmering anger within me boils and bubbles to the surface as I watch them laugh amongst themselves after having just caused such pain and emotional turmoil.

The hatred and disgust within me is a cognizant thing. I lose control, sinking in the depths of my own hate. It takes on a life of its own and suddenly pours from my lips in a song I did not intend to call. I embrace the magic, closing my eyes. I envision each of the minotaurs at their posts, see their faces and clothing clearly in my mind. This is my song, after all; I possess the ability to shape it. A smile twists my lips as I allow my rage to envelop me in power. The song crafts itself, layer upon layer of dark melody; a slow-building crescendo toward an ultimate end.

The first minotaur, the one who kicked the faun, begins to wobble unsteadily on his hooves. I think of Jarrus as I feel death approaching. It pushes me further into this raging storm of destruction. His companion stares, unable to lift a hand in assistance. His own black death whips around him in a bitter wind. As one towering body falls, the other is already beginning to slump over. The hair on their hulking forms waves slightly as my magic flows between them like a gale of darkness. One by one, the minotaur foremen stumble and collapse. The sound of horns against wood momentarily fills my chest with panic—unearths that scared girl in Iowain, watching Jarrus's blood pool across the shack floor. I am that girl no longer. I breathe in deeply, tasting the stolen life in the dense jungle air. The sensation of looming death lingers around me, and I revel in the black soul of my magic.

I return to the present, breathing deeply as I remember where I am and what my purpose is. The song still flows from my lips, now but a dull hum. I take Cicerine's hand once again and we emerge from the trees together, stepping into the open clearing. The minotaurs are all still breathing. The first to fall foams at the mouth, gurgling and choking on his own spittle. He begins to seize, his tree-thick thighs jerking, kicking at invisible foes as I continue to sing his death. I reach the black fingers of my mind into the air and snatch his breath like a spider would a fly. I trap his life in the black web of my magic. It does not take long at all for them to die. One at a time, they thrash and spit, vomit and bleed, shake and still. Each life is mine to grasp, I pull them from the air with my song, wrapping them in low harmonies that resonate with finality. I am so absorbed in the creation of this death madrigal that I do not feel as Cicerine drops my hand. I am oblivious to her entirely until I see her kneeling beside the fauns. They tremble in terror. Some are crying quietly, and she reaches out her gentle touch to them attempting to bring them a semblance of comfort. I know she speaks, but I cannot hear her words above the Song of Death I continue to sing. We are darkness and light embodied.

I can feel when the minotaurs are all truly dead. The pit inside of me where the song originates, a yawning black chasm of magic, rumbles like a purring cat and curls back into itself. My magic is sated with its feast of stolen lives. The song ends on a long, clear note. My voice is low, but it sounds like the deep tone of a bell, the note maintaining until my breath runs out at last.

Cicerine's eyes hold a shade of concern. Kneeling in the soil amidst the frightened fauns and the rich plum purple of the pennyway flowers, she looks like a painting, like grace. Her glance is a question I know without words: *"Are you all right?"* I nod, look at the scene of death surrounding us and smile. A cold, wicked pleasure whips through me, and I feel at once powerful and divine. I rise fully, standing tall and looking down at the death I have wrought. I feel like a deity, prevailing, a well of endless death. I am the bearer of a lost gift of witchkind, and *I shall be feared*.

As quickly as it came, the sensation fades, and I am returned to feeling like myself. I have never before felt consumed by my power, and I shake my head, pushing aside questions that beg for answers. I step over the heft of a dead minotaur and walk to Cicerine. She is speaking with the still-shackled fauns, and I hear her assurances that we will free them and dispense of any captors who still remain. A thick brass keyring hangs from the belt of a felled minotaur, and I unhook and toss it to Cicerine. She goes through the keys, trying each one until she finds the key that unlocks the shackles from the fauns' ankles. The skin beneath is raw and red, looking more like meat than living flesh. They have endured great abuse at the hands of those who control this place. One of the fauns looks to me with watery, fearful eyes. "Another guards the bunkhouse."

While Cicerine continues to free the fauns, I head toward the reeking shack and hear the snorting breaths of the remaining minotaur. His song leaps to my lips, a sharp halting melody that strikes hard and fast. In less than a minute, he is dead on the ground, blood seeping from his eyes. The fauns in the bunkhouse scream, but I lift my arms in supplication and gesture toward the farm. "Your kin are being freed as we speak, join them so that we may get you off of this island." They shuffle out tentatively, shackles and chains clinking against the ground as they drag behind. They must wear the chains, even in rest.

I only wish I could kill the minotaurs one more time, to savor their deaths like sweet summer wine.

KONIDAS

CHAPTER SIXTY-TWO
SHELL
YEAR 993

Losh lounges on a barstool, watchin' me with his big saucer eyes. I've told Athros about forty times that I don't want him in my damn bar—the thing gives me the creeps—but here he is. Athros was right about him, though. Since adopting the fuzzball, we've learned plenty about the Idyth cult, and twice now have been able to intervene before someone got hurt.

In the last week, Athros has proven himself to be a good employee. He's prompt, works real hard, isn't chatty, and he pays attention. Cartwright has taken the boy under his wing, inviting him to a Brick Union meeting and helping his mama pay her rent. Her new babe doesn't seem to have a lick o' magic, thankfully. It's cold out, and I've started offerin' mulled cider in the evenings. Tonight, the bar isn't too busy, and I'm actually able to sit and eat a meal instead of snaggin' bites every time I walk by the kitchen. Martine has cooked up some sort of meat, mashed potatoes, and a hearty olive-studded bread. My eyes have closed for just a second, savoring my hot cider, when I hear the creak of someone settlin' onto the stool right in front of me. It's Cartwright, and I don't like the look in his eyes one bit.

"Evenin' Miss Shell," he starts, placing his hat on the bar beside him. He takes a deep breath, and I tense. "I know you ain't gonna like this, but I were hopin' you'd hear me out anyway." My eyes narrow, suspicion pinching my face. "Athros is just a kid, and I know he's got a lot of learnin' to do. But he's clever and quick, and I want him to go to Athydis with one of my men."

"Athros? You want to send a gangly little kid to the city, where gods know what can happen to him? You've lost your damn mind. Have you even talked to his mama?" I snap at him without thinkin' on it first.

"Yes'm," he says, lowering his eyes to the ground before peeking back up at me. "She said I needed to be talkin' to you, as you're his employer."

Cartwright, as always, is the picture of respectfulness. It's endearin', but right now all this damned respectfulness is doin' is pissin' me off. "His *mother* said she don't mind him goin' to the city? I take it back, you've *all* lost your minds. Absolutely not."

"Shell," he starts.

"No! I don't wanna hear whatever cockamamie story you're cookin' up to make me say yes. He's a baby, Cartwright. A baby whose daddy is dead, with a gaggle of siblings and a mama at home who needs him."

"*We* need him, Shell." His voice is low and quiet, the somber sound stopping my arguing for a moment. "Our eyes in the castle say things are gettin' real strange over there. The King and Queen ain't right. We already knew the Crone's been spotted in the castle more than once, but with everything else goin' on, it can't be coincidence anymore."

"What do you expect *a child* to do about it, Cartwright?"

"Listen. Alls I expect him to do is listen, I swear. There's critters in every neck of the woods, Shell. Rats and mice and all sorts of creepy crawlies. That boy has a gift, and we need eyes on the inside. I can set him up with a job in the castle, nothin' dangerous, and he can keep an ear out. You know the witches are plannin' to get together on the solstice. That's less than a month from now. If the royals are actin' odd, and the Crone is still around, who's to say what they're up to? We know we gotta keep eyes on the New Church, but you're bein' foolish if you don't think we should be keepin' eyes on e'ryone else too."

I rub my temples and stare at my mug. "What of it, though? What are you plannin' to *do* with anything you hear?"

"I ain't lettin' you get hurt. None of you. So if I need to get y'all on a boat and ship you off to safety, that's what I'm gonna do."

My foot stomps against the floorboards so hard the cups on the bar rattle. This *man* thinks he can tell me where to go? What to do? Absofuckinglutely not. "Cartwright, I know you mean well, I do." I struggle to keep my voice from soundin' strained. "But this is *my* bar. You ain't keepin' me safe by sendin' me off. Ain't gonna happen. This is where I'm set, and this is where I'll stay. Now, you wanna talk about what we can do to help the city stay safe? That, I'll entertain, but any thoughts you got about sendin' me off somewhere, you'd better shake out of that thick skull of yours right now."

Cartwright's face hardens to somethin' I'm not familiar with — his expression one of determination, firm where he's usually soft. "Where you go, I go. If you won't leave, I can't make you, but I won't be goin' anywhere neither."

"Fine!"

"Fine."

I take a long swig of my cider, enjoyin' the sensation of heat settling into my belly. The damn cat looks at me, and I swear it nods. My eyes narrow. Can cats nod? Who the fuck knows. "If Athros *was* to go, would you be sendin' anyone with him? Would he be safe?"

"I have plenty of contacts at the castle. I got a family lined up for him to stay with, nice folks with a couple'a kids so he wouldn't feel lonely. He would be just as safe as he is here, Shell. I swear it."

Losh stretches, his big paws splayin' out to expose long, sharp claws. His mouth is so damn big when he yawns. He stands, hops off the barstool, pads over to me and headbutts my shin. I refuse to pet him, but as I look down at his big fuzzy body, he lets out a small *mowww*.

I breathe in deeply, my chest pushin' against the laces of my top. Before I can be sensible, I reply to Cartwright. "Fine. Talk to the boy. See what he thinks, and if he agrees, let's do it."

His hand is heavy and dry as it closes around mine, resting on the bar top. "He'll be safe," he says, squeezing my fingers. "And I'll keep you safe too."

My heartbeat goes haywire for a minute, but I shake it off. It's just nerves about the kid, after all.

I FEEL LIKE A BIG SOFTIE, AND I ABSOLUTELY HATE IT. MY EYES are blurry and my hands tremble as I help Athros pack up his meager belongings. "I'll take care of the cat," I assure him when I see his bright eyes land on the furry beast. "He'll get all the fish he could want, and I'll let him sleep in my room."

"Thank you, Miss Shell," he says, sounding like a little baby, which I suppose he is.

"Now, Cartwright tells me this family you'll be stayin' with is real nice, and they're goin' to treat you like one of their own, all right? But if anythin' don't feel right, you just send word, and we will bring you back home. Once a week or so there will be a ship headin' from Athydis back here, and they can bring any correspondence you may have, all right?" His gangly little arms wrap around my middle, and my tears run over. He doesn't say another word before he follows Cartwright out the tavern doors; silence has never seemed so loud.

The bar is nearly empty, so I take advantage of the reprieve and sink into a chair. A furry head butts up against my knee, and I reach down absentmindedly to scratch between his ears. His coat is dense and warm, and I feel the rumble of his purr beneath my fingers. "He'll be back," I tell the cat. At least, I tell myself I'm talkin' to the cat. Right now, Cartwright is taking the kid to a ship carryin' a load of goods to Athydis, and I hope he will come back by when he's done. An achin' sense of loneliness begins to settle in my soul. I've been independent as long as I've been alive, but someone's always been around. With Ma and Pap stayin' at the house full-time, Athros headed to Athydis, and Maelwen off to the minotaur island, I feel the weight of their absence. For awhile we had a nice little thing goin'—Maelwen and Godrick hangin' out at the bar and playin' Orakulua, Cartwright runnin' the tables and stayin' for dinner, Athros pokin' his head in. It felt like a right little family. Now it's me and a big loaf of a cat.

By the time Cartwright returns, the noise of the tavern is loud enough to smother the volume of my thoughts. He looks penitent, and I know he feels awful for makin' me sad. He sits in Maelwen's seat, still empty even though she's been gone for over a week. I slide him a beer, the frothy foam spilling over the side of the tankard as it sits before him, but I can't bring myself to look him in the eye. I bustle around the bar, tendin' to patrons and pickin' up dishes, when a rough hand brushes my hip, and I stop, surprised. Cartwright's eyes are a deep, dark, brown, and they burn into mine as I finally meet his gaze. His calloused fingers wrap around mine and squeeze. I don't have the right words—I wouldn't even know where to begin—so I intertwine my fingers with his, bring his large hand up to my heart before droppin' it and walkin' away. I feel him watch me as I go, but I don't turn around. There are far too many things already weighing on my mind to add Cartwright to the pile.

The Sea

CHAPTER SIXTY-THREE
JYNN
YEAR 993

The screech of seabirds is a welcome sound as I groggily open my eyes. My hammock feels overwhelmingly cozy, but I drag myself from its embrace and pull on my breeches, keeping my fitted nightshirt on. I glance at the mirror before making my way towards the ladder. My hair has grown longer, and I rake a hand through it. I wonder if someone could cut it for me; the length makes me feel uncomfortable. There's something off about the person I see reflected back at me. Grabbing a looser blouse from my bunk, I change. The freely draping fabric obscures my torso, and I feel more at ease. Heading above deck, I see Captain first, standing at the prow, and I head her way. I pass Tuii as she mends a portion of the foresail, long hair whipping in the wind. It's brisk out, and the sky is wide and blue, smeared with faint smudges of white where the strong currents of air have pushed aside the clouds. I can't help but linger on Tuii for a moment too long, her arms stretched high as she stitches the canvas, narrow waist accentuated by her low-slung dagger belt. Ballad sees me and beckons me over. "Red! You ever been to Konidas?"

"No, Captain," I reply.

"Well, lucky for us, our cargo weren't all lost to the sea, so we'll be needin' to stop off and unload. Figured it might be a good respite, take a day or two to lay in a proper bed."

"Is there much to do in the city?"

"Ha! It ain't much of a city, but they got a tavern with plenty o' wine, so 'tis good enough for me. I'd call it a trade hub if anything, but there's lots of men who don't ask questions and who are happy enough to relieve us of our ill-gotten spoils." She grins with genuine mirth. "Plenty o' men who'll be happy to relieve us of a lot of things, if you catch me drift." My nose wrinkles, and she laughs at me outright. "Or not! I ain't one to be judgin'. They ain't my flavor neither, but I never know!"

"How long until we get there?"

"If the wind is on our side, shouldn't take much more than a week. You'll be pickin' up some of Hana's duties. Georgette will be fillin' you in on that. Go find her, and get to work. We ain't got the time to dawdle now that we are short-crewed."

"Aye, Captain," I reply.

"Oh! By the way." She reaches out her hand. "I figured you'd be wantin' this."

My spyglass rests in her outstretched palm. "How?" I ask, shocked that it found its way to Ballad.

"Strangest thing, that. When the Sea Song righted herself, it was just sittin' on the deck. Damn near everything fell in the deep, no tellin' how it managed to stay aboard."

I take it with a smile, tucking it into my pocket. "Guess the sea is on my side." I give Ballad a small bow as I head down to find Georgette.

The energy below is solemn, the crew still reeling from their losses. I feel disjointed and awkward, like I don't belong, yet again. I've been with the Sea Song for only a few months. The camaraderie between the crew existed long before me, and they now struggle to deal with the absence of two friends—two family members. Selfishly, I envy their sorrow; I have lost people, the only people I ever loved, but I've never *belonged* anywhere. I've never felt like I was a part of a family before, not like this. I feel like an ass. Nobody should be envious of grief, but emotions are not rational. Georgette is in the galley working beside Cook to make hardtack. The dense biscuits taste like shit, but they hold well, and once they're dipped in grog, they're almost tolerable. Flour coats every surface of the galley, looking like a fine dusting of snow. Georgette gives me a rueful smile as I enter and drops her rolling pin to the counter with a *clunk*.

"Ah, Jynn. Good to see you, dear. Ballad told me you'll be taking up some of Hana's duties?"

"Aye, ma'am."

"Well, first things firstly, the armory. Blades need cleanin', and we need an inventory of all we lost. Tuii should be there already. When you're done there, head above deck. There's lots to be done—mendin' sails, mopping and re-oiling the deck, and plenty o' repair. Lots of things were damaged. You can hold a hammer, eh?"

I smile. "Yes, ma'am, I can hold a hammer."

"Then get to it!" She hands me a square of the dense bread. "Here, while it's still edible. Might as well eat up."

I bite off the corner and make my way to the armory to find Tuii. Despite our time on Minos'Idyl, I feel like Tuii and I haven't had time to really talk. I don't know if we even need to, but I feel awkward about what happened; there is a tension between us that I'm unable to interpret. I'm not accustomed to this type of discomfort—this tenuous space between us feels vast and difficult to navigate. My hand rises to my neck, and I pull at the overgrown hair there. I flush at the memory of her skin beneath my fingertips. *Stop it, Jynn.* Blinking, I try to clear my head and duck under the doorway to the armory.

The armory is a small room tucked beneath a hatch, and can only comfortably hold a single crew member at once. Tuii is small, but I'm tall as hell, so I feel her proximity like the heat from a flame. I blush when our eyes meet, feeling like an absolute idiot. She laughs, and my blush deepens, my freckles a constellation of shame. The room has a comforting smell—oil, metal, and well-worn leather. Wordlessly, I step beside her and take a blade down from the rack, grabbing an oilcloth from the small table just outside the entry. Each swipe of the cloth across the blade makes a faint whispering sound, and I settle into a steady rhythm beside Tuii.

The ship's armory contains a wide assortment of pilfered weapons: swords, daggers, rapiers, an axe, and some things I can't identify. The salt of the seawater is corrosive and cleaning the blades is vital. While I've not had much experience with this task, I've found that it doesn't take much skill to do a decent job. My mind wanders as I clean, and as I catch glimpses of Tuii's downcast eyes and shining black plait. My skin heats with the memory of her face between my thighs. Tuii, ever-observant, must notice a change in my breath, because she smirks and turns to me. "What is on your mind, Red?"

Gods, my cheeks betray me once again. "Uh, nothing? Just cleaning. Um, this sword." I wish I could sink into the planks. If only I was less of a fool and could improvise.

Tuii chuckles. "That sword is from Athydis. We intercepted a royal vessel a few years past. They carried a full retinue, but Cenna and I snuck aboard while they slept. We managed to come away with close to eighty gold pieces and a set of ceremonial swords. I believe the one with an emerald in the pommel belonged to the captain of the guard. I brought it to Ballad, but she told me to stick it in the armory." Her smile makes my chest flutter. The memory is one she clearly remembers fondly.

"Captain doesn't seem like one to be carrying ceremonial

swords." I grin back at her. "Hard to swing from the sails with the heft of a longsword at your side." The image is a funny one, and we share a moment of mirth. Reaching for another blade, my fingers brush her arm, and I still. My breath catches in my lungs, and I stand frozen for a beat too long before resuming my cleaning. I feel her gaze from beside me, and I try my damnedest to focus on oiling the rapier before me, but my fickle heart fails me; I look up. Her eyes are bright, lips parted as if she is about to speak, but instead of words, she exhales a shaky breath.

We move at the same time, the dagger in her hands clattering to the floor, her fingers finding purchase in the loose fabric of my blouse. I step towards her, lowering my chin to rest against her forehead. Her warm breath caresses my neck like a bit of silk, and her hand slides up the small of my back. It is an embrace of sorts, one that holds a thick ribbon of desire. We are both holding back the same fire, desire pulling us against one another even as we attempt to keep the moment chaste, but the brush of her lips against the hollow of my throat is my undoing, and I lift her face to mine with a trembling hand.

Her hand fists my shirt as she presses into me. I waste no time slipping my tongue between her lips, tangling with hers in a dance of salt and need. She breathes a sigh into me, and my core goes molten, hips pressing toward her instinctively. Her fingertips slide beneath the rough linen, and her nails graze my stomach. I nip at her mouth, my hand beneath her chin shifting to span the width of her neck. Gods, this woman is such a dichotomy: small and thin as glass, but vicious and deadly as an adder. I can feel the strength in her nimble hands as she reaches up to grip my hair. I hiss at the small bite of pain, and she scratches across my broad back towards my chest. My hands drop down to cup her ass, scooping her up and turning to set her on the small table holding the pile of oilcloth. I pay no heed to the oil staining her pants—they're black anyway. She reaches for my waistband, fumbling with the button, hands desperate. I reach down to help her when a loud cough stops me abruptly. Tuii's eyes are wide as she hops down from the table.

"Captain," she says with a wicked smile, standing rigid as a board.

Ballad smirks. "At ease, Tuii. Red? I don't believe this was one of Hana's duties."

My cheeks burn furiously. "No, ma'am," I reply.

"I don't be carin' what ye get up to in your own time. But now you're on my time, and I'd prefer you to be spendin' it at work, eh?"

Tuii and I reply in unison. "Yes, Captain."

Minos'Idyl

CHAPTER SIXTY-FOUR
CICERINE
YEAR 993

The fauns all gather in the clearing, shaking and silent. I try to be gentle as I free them. Their flesh is ragged and inflamed from the shackles, and I can feel infection heating a few of the wounds. Some of the fauns are barely more than children, with horns not yet fully grown. My heart is gripped with rage and anguish seeing their young faces already so shadowed. I am glad Maelwen made sure the minotaurs suffered. They deserved far more agony, but I appreciate their deaths not being quick or painless. When all the fauns are freed, I set about bandaging their wounds the best I can. There are large, broad leaves all around the clearing, and my gift helps me choose some that will not be harmful or cause further irritation to their skin. While I bind them up with strips of cloth torn from a minotaur's jacket, I reassure them that we will help them to freedom. One of the older fauns, a male with graying hair and copper eyes, approaches me.

"We thank you for your kindness."

"It is no hardship," I say, rubbing his shoulder with my outstretched hand. "We will find a way to get you to safety."

"Some of us can sail," he begins. "Not that it's a common faun occupation, but a few of us were picked up in Konidas. I worked as a boatswain for a smuggler. That's where they took me from. If we can find a ship, I can get us off this island."

"Do you have somewhere to go?" I ask, hoping there is a home waiting for some of them at least.

"Most of us do not," he says with a solemn glance downward. "The priest chose us carefully, folks who wouldn't be missed."

Terror rips the breath from my chest, and I clutch at my throat. *No, no, no.* "The priest? What priest?"

"This farm is operated by a group of them. It's not always the same one who comes, however they do have a leader. We don't know their names. They show up when the crates are filled."

"Are they due to come soon?" I ask, hands shaking, too frightened to voice my fears.

"Yes," he says. "Likely today or tomorrow. We sealed up the last few crates today, and they'll be coming to take them."

"So they come and pick up the crates—with a ship?" I ask, a plan taking shape in my mind.

"Yes, miss." He seems to share my thoughts. "A ship big enough for all of us."

A grim smile lifts my lips. "Well, then."

Maelwen and I speak in muted tones, hiding amidst the dense growth of the jungle. "I think it's Farragen," I whisper. "It has to be." My pulse races, and my breaths come too quickly.

"I will kill him," Maelwen replies. "Unless, of course, you would prefer that honor."

I am silent for a moment, contemplating how I feel. I have never craved someone's death before, but Father Farragen took everything from me; he killed Mamère, drove Jynn from the glade. He destroyed my life, and because of him, I killed my entire village. "I think I would," I reply, feeling truly malicious for the first time in my twenty-one years. "I want to burn him alive."

"Good." Maelwen raises her chin, her eyes narrowing as she emanates satisfaction. "I will be beside you."

The aching sense of yearning between us seems to grow as she speaks, and I can't help but close the distance between us. I place my hand against the small of her sweat-slick back, and she steps closer, pressing into me. She looks down with her arctic-blue eyes, and I lift my chin, begging for her kiss. She obliges with a gentle brush of her lips, feather-light across my mouth. Something within me screams for more, and I thread my fingers into her hair before pulling her toward me with a rough hand. We crash into one another with a passionate impact, her teeth glancing off of my lip as we struggle against each other fervently. The weave of our magic flashes alight as we connect once more, the fabric of our combined gifts stretching taut between us. I groan as her tongue finds mine, darting between my parted lips. Her hands skate across the curves of my body, raking claw-tips over my skin when they find the hem of my shirt.

Gods, I want her. I want to tear her clothes from her body and lay her bare in this jungle. I want to taste her, run my tongue along her skin, lose myself to the rich scent of her. I want my fingers to explore every inch of her, to find out what makes her lose her breath, what makes her cry out in ecstasy. I want to drench myself in her pleasure. Just thinking about it makes me moan, my thighs quaking as I press them together to quell my body's shuddering desire. I can tell she feels it too—the link between us carrying the ebb of lust that crashes into us in waves. Maelwen, always the picture of control, purrs against me, her sharp hip bones pressing against me as her body begs to claim mine. A rustle in the foliage and a small voice tears my mind from the throes of this all-consuming want. A faun stands at the edge of the clearing, peering into the jungle towards us.

"They're coming."

Though my body still tingles with sensation from my stolen moment with Maelwen, my mind is sharp as we prepare for the priests' arrival. The faun told us there is a bell mounted at the small harbor, and it is rung when the ship arrives to notify the minotaurs of the impending arrival. The walk from the harbor to the farm takes nearly half an hour according to the fauns, so we hurry to hide the bodies and disguise the evidence of their deaths. Maelwen is deceptively strong and drags the hulking bodies to the building with haste, depositing them inside and closing the door. The fauns are terrified, and she instructs them to flee into the jungle, in the opposite direction of the harbor. They are to hide there until we come for them. They hobble away with fear bright in their eyes.

Maelwen and I are prepared. She has her claws and her song, and in this jungle, my gift will be stronger than ever before. I can feel the life in the soil for miles and miles, and I am fairly certain I can cast my power as far as I can feel life. We have planned for Maelwen to ensnare the priests with witchsong, and once we have determined if Farragen is among them, we will question and then dispose of them. Farragen's death is mine to deal in any way I see fit. With her witchsong, he can be incapacitated but still able to feel, should I choose. I can make sure he experiences every second of pain leading up to his death. We hear the priests before we see them, their trek through the jungle clumsy and loud. It sounds like one of them wields a machete and is hacking away at the plants to make their path less arduous. The first priest emerges from the jungle into the clearing. He wears the same gray robes Father Farragen wore, though his skin is less pale. His eyes are deep-set and he has a face marred by pockmarked scarring. A second priest appears beside him, and they speak quietly. I cannot hear what they say, but I see their eyes shift to the farm and narrow suspiciously. They likely expected to be greeted by the minotaurs and are on edge from the silence. One priest walks toward the farm while the other remains, eyes on the jungle.

Then, Farragen steps into the clearing, and I freeze.

He looks exactly the same as he did the last time I saw him. He seems to be flanked by too much shadow to be natural, his dark eyes and sickly, sallow looking skin making him look monochromatic against the green backdrop of the jungle. He moves fluidly, like a thin snake, and his lips are pressed together in a grim line. From below his collar peeks a thin, red bit of flesh which I have never noticed before. Maelwen's fingers intertwine with mine, and she lends me her strength—our combined magic working to bolster me against my discomfort. Her darkness holds my light, keeping me level and calm. I take a deep breath and squeeze her fingers. It is time.

I'm unsure of how long she is singing before I hear her. The notes are oddly quiet and in harmony with the sounds of the surrounding jungle. I start to hear a low hum and realize it is Maelwen's song. The priest in the clearing and Farragen both still, their eyes going glassy, gazes vacant. She speaks and they walk toward us on jerky, puppeted legs. Once they stand before us, ensnared by her witchsong, I step up to the first priest. I want Father Farragen to see me for who I am, to know that I am no longer the weak girl he once knew. His eyes clear slightly, and I know Maelwen has loosened her hold. "What is your name?" I demand, surprised by the steady resolve in my voice.

His mouth quivers, struggling to speak, but he manages to croak out, "Father…Impego."

"Well, Father Impego, would you like to answer my questions, or would you like to die?"

His eyes dart left and right in terror, the look of a captive creature. He tries in vain to look to Farragen, but the angle at which they are positioned prevents them from making eye contact. "I… will talk."

"What are you trying to accomplish here? Why are you growing these flowers, and why have you enslaved these fauns?"

"Idyth has…commanded it." He chokes on the words, sputtering. "We…will have a great…power."

"You are using the pennyway to gain power."

Nodding, he continues, "We prepare for His resurrection. He…will be reincarnated."

"Who leads you?" Maelwen cuts in.

"Fa…fa…" He tries to form the word, but his mouth seems to be unable to shape the syllables.

"The man beside you?" I ask.

He nods, tears trickling from the corners of his eyes. Maelwen's hum begins anew, and his eyes go glassy once again. She looks at me and raises an eyebrow, and I dip my chin. Her gloved hands rise, her claws extending to their full length. She steps toward him and looks at him hungrily, releasing her hold just enough that I can tell he is conscious, aware of what is happening. She steps against his back, reaching around his neck from behind. She wraps her hands around his throat, claws pricking into his flesh from both sides, in the shape of an exposed ribcage. In a single fluid motion, she brings her fingers together, rending skin and muscle, tearing his throat open. Blood pours from the shredded meat of his neck, and he chokes on it, gurgling and spitting, splattering the nearby leaves with a shower of blood. Maelwen looks at me and smirks before dipping her head to the gaping mess, devouring his blood directly from a severed artery. My stomach turns, but my heart flutters at the same time. I am simultaneously repulsed and excited by the sight. I can still feel her magic within me; it pulses and glows with the vibrant power she drinks from him. My hands open and close at my sides, and I blink, trying to focus my breathing and settle my wildly vacillating emotions. In just minutes, she drops him to the jungle floor, his remaining blood seeping into the earth. I feel its sticky warmth coating the roots below the surface like viscous rain.

Farragen is still rigid, standing entirely unmoving as though he is nothing more than a hideous statue, I hope he is able to understand what happens around him, to see the corpse of his compatriot, to see *me* and know who I am.

Maelwen wipes her blood-stained lips on his robe as she walks around him to return to my side. Her claws retract, and her hand brushes mine, tacky with drying blood. The brief contact sends sparks out in a halo of light, falling to the ground with tiny pops and sizzles. It would seem her newly replenished power and mine react with even more force. I wonder momentarily if I would be able to use her song right now, if our connection is stronger when she is newly fed. Farragen's face brings me back to the present, and I take a step forward, readying myself to speak to him for the first time since my mother died.

The gust of wind comes upon us so quickly I have no time to react. In an instant, Maelwen and I are thrown across the clearing, slamming into the trunk of a massive tree and falling to the ground in a tangle of limbs. I leap to my hooves, staring in the direction of the wind, and see two more priests standing in the trees near the farm. One is the priest who initially arrived with Farragen, the other is a man I have not seen. Their hands are raised, crossing over one another to form an X. Their skin glows faintly, and shadow seems to grow around them, darkening a space of the jungle floor far larger than it should. I hear a soft murmuring moan and look down to see Maelwen getting to her feet shakily, dark blood trickling from a gash on her forehead.

The priests make a strange sound, like a low howl, and their hands shift, straightening before them and coming together. They pull their hands back towards their chests, and the howling noise deepens beyond the register a human voice can make, sounding like an earthquake's rumble. On instinct, I throw my arm over Maelwen's shoulder and pull her down to the ground right as their hands shoot out, pushing another gale-force wind at us. Sticks and leaves slice my cheeks as they hurl through the air. The second the wind has stilled, I slam my hands into the earth, sending out my power in a rampage. The black ropes of my darkest magic tear through the soil, shooting towards the priests in branching veins of scorching rage. They both shriek in pain as their bodies are set alight from the inside, their flesh smoking and splitting as they fall to the ground. They are dead in seconds, their charred flesh blackened where visible beneath burned-away fabric. I whip around to face Farragen, but he is not there. My head swivels desperately, searching for him. I hear the sound of a branch snapping underfoot and look back just in time to see his gray robes, his smiling, sallow-skinned face, and the mass of shadows that swallow him whole.

The Sea

CHAPTER SIXTY-FIVE
JYNN
YEAR 993

The world is a kaleidoscope of colors: blue, green, purple, pink — all crystalline shades that dance across my vision. My body is warm, though I can feel that the water is cold. I sway slightly with the tide, my long legs moving back and forth below me like a pair of tailor's shears. Not a single piece of clothing adorns my body, my skin dappled in the many-colored light, freckles looking like nebulae in the soft rays of sun that have reached down to this depth. Kelp waves in the soft current around me, and small, bright fish swim in and out of its broad blades. I feel weightless. A flicker of fear dances through my mind as I notice I cannot draw breath, but I realize my lungs aren't burning from lack of air. Instead, I feel the oxygen settling into my skin. Tiny creatures float around my face, glinting like glitter in the deep. I have never felt more at peace; this is home.

My hammock swings wildly, and I nearly topple out. My stomach flips — I feel queasy for a moment before my mind settles and I acclimate to the roiling sea. A loud whistle sounds from above deck, and I jump to the floor with a thump, throwing on my boots and pulling on a sweater over my undershirt.

Captain stands on the deck with her legs spread, hands on her narrow hips. "'Ello me crew!" she hollers with a broad smile. "Are ye all ready for some drink and some dick?"

Laughter rings out across the ship. Even in this time of loss, Ballad has a gift for bringing levity to the crew. Someone shouts from behind me, "I'll take some drink, but y'all can keep your dick!"

Captain chuckles and continues, "We'll be makin' landfall in five days or so. Get the Sea Song in tip-top shape so none of ye will have to stay and work. I want the decks clean enough to see yer ass in!"

The crew yells out together *"Aye aye Captain!"* and everyone gets to work in an excited rush of activity. We bustle about, mopping, cleaning, packing, and reorganizing. By the time the sun begins to hang low above the sea, my arm muscles are sore from use, and my undershirt is drenched in sweat despite the brisk winter air. Cook rings the bell and we all file below to the galley, ready for a hearty meal and cup of grog. I haven't spent much time with the crew socially; I'm awkward, and other than Tuii and Cenna, I haven't put much effort into making friends. However, when I walk into the galley, Ardelle waves me over.

"Red! Sit with us!"

Briar, Ardelle, and Tuii sit across from one another at the long table, the spot next to Tuii vacant. I slide onto the bench beside her, my cheeks heating slightly. "Hey!" I say in greeting, looking at Ardelle and hoping I don't sound as antsy as I feel.

Briar laughs as she takes a bite of her soup and pushes a cup of grog across the table towards me. She's taller than even me, with broad, strong shoulders and a kind smile on her large, full lips. I nod in thanks and take the cup, enjoying the sharp bite of liquor. "'Bout time you spend a meal with your shipmates," she says.

"Oh! I didn't mean, I...uh..."

All three of them laugh at me, and I go beet-red. Tuii reaches beneath the table and sets a hand on my knee. "They're playing with you, Jynn."

"Oh." I look into my cup as if it's the most interesting thing at the table.

"We usually eat together when we can," Ardelle says in her soft voice. "We aren't always off duty at the same time, but it's nice when we are."

"Have you three been on the Sea Song for a long time?" I ask.

Briar and Ardelle both nod, and Briar answers. "I've been with this crew for nine years, Ardelle has been here, what, seven years?"

Ardelle smiles and nods. "Yessir!" She looks at me, gesturing toward Briar. "They've been beside me for the last six years."

"Briar and Tuii?"

Ardelle replies warmly, "No, just Briar. Tuii didn't decide to hang out with us until about a year ago."

"Oh, I thought you said, uh…nevermind."

Briar must spot the confusion flitting across my face at the reply and laughs. "Ah, yes. The 'they' threw you. Well, I don't like 'miss' or 'ma'am.' In fact, I don't like 'she' or 'her' either."

"Oh!" I exclaim, a bit confused, but mainly worried that I've caused offense. "I didn't know!"

They chuckle. "Of course you didn't. You can just call me Briar, and if you ever need to, just use 'they'."

"Of course!" I repeat it in my head silently. I never knew this was an option. All the times someone called me "miss" and it made my skin crawl suddenly make a bit of sense. "How did you decide to use…a neutral term?"

They laugh again, and I'm beginning to feel more at ease, like I'm *included* in the laughter rather than the cause. "I've never felt like the feminine title I wore was right. I grew up in a small town to the east of Athydis where everyone—and everything—was very traditional. My parents were not pleased when I hit my teens and got caught with a girl in town. I've never liked men like *that*. I always felt like I myself was somewhere in-between, while also neither? All my friends growing up were boys, and I've always been better in spaces where my gender didn't matter. It's why I became a pirate, honestly. I met Ballad when I was twenty, just before she took over as Captain. She told me she ran a crew with no men, and I asked how she felt about people who don't fall into either camp. She shook my hand and welcomed me aboard."

I try to think of the "right" reply but decide just to be honest. "That's fucking great, Briar, and I'm glad you're aboard."

Ardelle's voice is like cherry blossoms, soft and gentle-sounding even in the noise of the galley. "I was picked up in Konidas. Had a boyfriend who hit me but he taught me to sail—only decent thing I got out of him. I met Captain at the tavern in town, and she took one look at my bruises and offered me a job."

"Gods, I'm sorry," I reply.

"No need," she says with a bit of a wicked smile. "He got what was comin' to him."

We all eat our soup and bread and share a really nice conversation. The three of them tell me all sorts of stories of life on the Sea Song and about the city we are headed to. It sounds like a shithole, but they apparently have a great tavern with card games and music. I've never in my life been to such a place. I'm excited, my first real taste of the world, but also nervous. I don't know how to navigate a city, where to go or how to act. Hopefully, I can stick with the rest of the crew. Ardelle pulls out a deck of cards and a pouch of dice, and she and Briar begin to play a game I'm unfamiliar with. I've had just enough grog to ensure there's no way I could follow along. Instead of trying, I swing a leg over so I'm straddling the bench and facing Tuii.

"You play any games?" I ask her, curious about her hobbies.

"I play Orakulua pretty well," she replies. "I think Cenna has a deck, if you'd ever like to learn. It's kind of tricky but fun. It's popular in Konidas."

"What kind of game is it?"

"Hmm..." She rests her chin on her fist, thinking. "Imagine a game where you try to tell stories with pictures, and then make it much harder than whatever you're thinking."

I chuckle. "I guess I'll have to find out first-hand."

Her eyes glint with a flicker of something heated. "I guess so. Want to find Cenna and see if we can borrow her deck?"

I glance around the galley. It's cleared out mostly, except for a few stragglers. Briar and Ardelle are playing whatever they're playing, and Dagmar and Elke sit off to the side, engaged in what looks like an argument—though, you can never be sure with siblings. I don't see Cenna, but she rarely socializes with the crew, so I am far from surprised. Tuii's hand tugs at mine, and I rise, deciding that whatever she wants to do is precisely where I'd like to be.

WE FIND CENNA ABOVE DECK, SITTING ON THE RAILING AND peering out into the indigo night. She's happy to lend us her deck, so Tuii and I follow her to her bunk and snag the small velvet pouch. The cards are much more intricate than I would have guessed, brightly colored and gilded with gold accents, though areas of them have worn away with use. Tuii leads me to her spot near the captain's quarters and teaches me the basics. Not surprisingly, I'm terrible at this game. Before long, we are both laughing so hard tears stream down our faces and my cheeks hurt. Tuii shifts her body closer to mine, our legs pressing against one another as we sit on the floor beneath the ladder. Without meaning to, I rest my hand on her thigh, and she looks up from the cards, laughter still gleaming in her eyes. She moves slowly, and I get the sense that she is preparing for me to stop her, but her hand reaches up to brush my hair behind my ear, and I lean into her touch. With careful restraint, she leans toward me, tipping her chin up, and presses her lips to my jaw, just beneath my ear. Even in this tender moment, a fist of pain grips my heart in its icy grasp. I don't know how to accept affection like this. I don't know how to be soft anymore, not since Ceci. I know in my soul I cannot live my life tied to the love that died in the glade, but I don't know *how* to move beyond it. Tuii is not Cicerine and never will be. She is another experience entirely: sharp in all the places that Ceci was soft, quick in all the ways that Ceci was careful. She intrigues me in a way I can't quite name. Wordlessly, I reach for her and trace the line of her cheek with my finger. She turns into it, kissing my fingertip gently. I close my eyes for a moment and when I open them, she is close enough I feel her warm breath on my lips. She is giving me this choice — I choose her.

Her kiss tastes of sugared citrus, a hint of grog still on the tip of her tongue. Her strong, delicate hands run up and down my back, her nails against the fabric of my sweater making me shiver. She kisses me greedily, nibbling at my lip and making sweet sounds that set my skin on fire. I reach for her long plait, tugging the cord that binds it free. Her thick, black hair cascades free, soft waves settling on her shoulders. She smells of leather and lavender, and I breathe her in as I pull her to my chest. I kiss the top of her head and realize in this moment that whatever *this* is between us, I think I want it. The energy between us shifts, and when I kiss her again, it feels like a plea. I don't want to hurt anymore. I want to give myself over to something good.

Her black tunic is rough beneath my hands. I pull it over her head in a single motion, seeming far more suave than I actually am. The cloth binding her breasts is trickier, and she reaches up to meet my fumbling fingers. It falls to the floor with a whisper, and my hands are on her body. She has a way of moving that I have never witnessed before her, and I doubt I will ever encounter again. Whatever gift Cenna, with her shifting shadows, possesses, this is far more mysterious. Her limbs move like liquid, her body curving and arching into me with a fluid balance of form and function. Her hands move across my torso as if seeking an answer to a question she cannot voice. I lift her slightly from the floor and set her in my lap, my tongue running along her neck, tasting the salt of the sea from her skin. She groans and grinds her hips into my lap, and I push against her with a sigh. I pull off my sweater, and as she pulls at my undershirt, I still her hands, keeping the thin fabric still in place. She doesn't protest, and instead nips at my freckled shoulder. She swings a knee over my thighs, facing me fully and takes my face in her hands. She kisses me reverently, breathing deeply as her tongue finds mine once again. I reach for her waistband, but she shakes her head slightly, lips not leaving my mouth. Quietly she speaks against my mouth, her lips still touching mine as she forms the words, "Not yet. If you want this, we can take all the time in the world."

Minos'Idyl

CHAPTER SIXTY-SIX
MAELWEN
YEAR 993

My mouth goes dry as I watch the priest disappear. The taste of his foul magic fills my mouth and burns my eyes as I pull myself to my feet. Save for the small scratches and scrapes covering my body, I am unharmed. Cicerine appears to be in a similar condition physically, but I feel the violent tearing agony of her rage and grief, our link screams with the shock of it. I stumble back as the force of her emotions hit me and reach out a hand to steady myself against a nearby tree. Beneath my fingers, the tree explodes into heat, and I stare wide-eyed as the foliage around us dies instantaneously. I do not think Cicerine is aware of the chaos she has wrought; birds and small creatures fall to the earth, dead and smoking, as the wave of death she has cast ebbs from the surrounding jungle.

I walk to her in six paces, reaching for her on instinct, wanting to soothe the flame within her, but she shakes off my hand with an anguished howl and falls to her knees. I do not try to touch her again, however I sit on the ground beside her in the hopes my proximity can provide some calm. She bellows at the sky, hands raking down the sides of her face and grabbing fistfuls of her own hair. The sheer hate and torment emanating from her seems to silence the jungle around us. Tension ripples through my body. She is more powerful than she knows, and while I could be in danger, I feel certain I am safe beside her, so I remain. As quickly as it began, her breakdown ends, and she stands shakily, reaching out a hand to help me up. I take it, sucking in a sharp breath as our magic collides, and I truly feel the depth of her emotions. When she looks at me, her gaze is flat, completely devoid of any feeling beyond anger.

"He got away."

"I know," I reply, gripping her hand more tightly. "We *will* find him."

She does not respond but walks back towards the farm with me in tow. We reach the rows of pennyway, passing the bodies of the other priests. She drops my hand and kneels, pressing her splayed fingers to the soil and the earth shakes with the brunt of her power. I squint and shield my eyes with my hand as the farm erupts in a flash of blinding light. Every pennyway plant is extirpated, combusting into black ash that swirls through the air and blocks out the scattered rays of sunlight. The jungle grows dark, turning into a hellscape of seething fury. Cicerine stands—a fearsome and beautiful thing, silhouetted against the darkness like death given form. Her eyes flash the color of flame for the span of a single blink before returning to their natural gold. She sheds the darkness like an old coat and takes a step toward me, looking like the Cicerine I have come to know in recent weeks, and collapses.

CICERINE REGAINS CONSCIOUSNESS WITHIN AN HOUR. I HAVE wandered into the jungle and retrieved the scattered fauns. They sit in a tight circle, speaking in hushed voices and looking around the trees with anxiety pinching their expressions. One of the fauns finds a cup in their meager belongings, and I bring Cicerine a glass of water when I notice her stirring.

"What happened?" She asks as she sips the lukewarm water I retrieved from a cistern near the bunkhouse.

"You destroyed the farm—every plant was incinerated—and then you lost consciousness," I reply. "The priest you sought escaped, but the other three are dead."

She swallows thickly. "I remember that part. It would seem he has done what he set out to do. He has Chaos magic."

"Yes," I agree. "He does."

"What do we do now?"

I glance at the huddle of fauns. "We get them out of here, then we return to Konidas. Shell and the Brick Union need to know what we have found. The solstice is in three weeks. I have very little time before our convocation."

"What are the witches going to do?" she asks in a timid voice.

"Wage war."

"Are you going to go alone?"

I know what she is asking, and I am uncertain how to reply. "It will not be safe. There is a very real possibility the witches will be defeated. I do not want to watch you fall."

"If the witches fall, we may all die anyway. Am I permitted to join you? Are non-witches allowed?"

"We did not discuss it. I did not anticipate…you. Us…this. However, I would assume we need the power of any magic wielders. This conflict goes beyond witchkind."

"And we are stronger together," she says as she takes my hand.

"Yes," I agree. "We are."

I look at our intertwined fingers and wonder if this is enough. Will we make it out of this alive? There is no way of knowing how this will end, and I can only hope we both will survive. I incline my head towards her, and we rise together. We approach the fauns with cautious steps, not wanting to frighten them. "Come." I gesture toward the coast. "Let us find the ship."

It takes us more time than I would have liked to locate the small dock and the ship moored there. The ship is large enough for perhaps fifteen adults to fit comfortably. The fauns are less than comfortable with their twenty-four passenger roster. Those who know how to sail take charge, crewing the boat with ease, and after providing adequate directions to reach Kanitosh, we watch them disappear into the sea. Cicerine warned them about the demolished village, as well as the probability of finding remnants of the dead, but they did not mind. Having a safe place to start a new life means as much to them as my apartment at the tavern meant to me. A place to call their own, where they are beholden to no one.

It is late in the day, and we decide to spend one more night on the island, leaving with the light of dawn. We return to our original beachside camp, and I retrieve the lightning glass vessel. It tingles in my fingers and when I pass it to Cicerine she says the same. It feels like a living thing, as if it carries small remnants of the lightning which forged it. Now that the priests and minotaurs have been eliminated, we build a fire to warm the chilled early winter air. Cicerine sits beside me, and I wrap us in my cloak, the coastal wind blowing against our backs and the fire crackling before us. Cicerine dug up some sort of root vegetable earlier in the evening, and we roast it on sticks over the flame. It smells nutty, and though I would not typically choose to eat such a thing, I try it because she likes it. I pull a wine skin from our pack and pass it to Cicerine.

"Is this some of Salvatorre's?" she asks.

"I believe so. I do not think Shell sources wine from elsewhere."

She sighs as she takes a drink and rests her head on my shoulder. "I hope he is all right. He was kind to me when nobody else was, and I haven't seen him in some time."

"We can ask after him when we get back to Konidas if that would please you."

I feel her cheek rise against me as she smiles. "I would like that very much."

After eating the starchy vegetable, which I decidedly will not consume again, we finish off the wine and watch the fire fade to embers. The orange glow casts warmth and shadow across Cicerine's face, and I cannot help but stare. Her features are so unique to me, having never before been close to a faun. Fur-rimmed ears peek out from her hair and occasionally perk up at the sounds of the island. Her cheeks are so very round and spotted with freckles that span the bridge of a wide, upturned nose. Her impossibly large eyes are the color of brass in the sunlight. Being here, pressed together, my magic seems wild and feral. We are so tangled up in one another that I can sense each facet of her magic as if it were my own. It is almost as if the pale green light of her gift has begun to bleed into my darkness, giving it a luminescent glow. I am alive in a way I struggle to understand. It is like waking after a lengthy sleep and opening my eyes to a place I have never been, yet know intimately. The softness of her beneath my fingers feels like belonging.

Cicerine catches me staring as we sit beside the dying fire, but I do not look away. Instead, I let her see the heat in my eyes; a blaze she ignites without even trying. She moves carefully, turning toward me and lifting her face to mine. Her eyes land on my lips, and I sense her magic tugging at me, trying to pull me closer. I flick out a single claw and delicately run it along her jawline. She stifles a gasp, her breath quickening and pupils dilating. I cannot hide my answering smirk as I revel in the enjoyment of her arousal. I run that claw down over her shoulder, pushing her top to the side and exposing her skin to the moonlight.

Keeping my eyes locked on hers, I bend to kiss the space between her neck and shoulder, pressing my lips into her freckles. I want to possess her body, to lay her beneath me and worship her until she can no longer think, until her body is no more than a languid waterfall. She touches me gently, her hand running up my side and along the slight curve of my breast. Shrugging the cloak from my shoulders, I let it fall to the sand behind us. The dark blue fabric looks like a depthless pool, and I ache to pull her into it with me. She seems to feel the same as she lies down and looks at me with the most delicious longing I could ever dream possible.

Not wanting to bother with pretense, I pull my blouse over my head and drop it beside me. I wear nothing beneath it. My skin is bare, tingling with the cold wind coming off the sea. Cicerine makes no move to follow my lead. Instead she stares at me raptly, eyes unblinking as she takes in my body. Emboldened, I bend to remove my boots as well, slowly untying the laces, moving from knee to ankle without dropping her gaze. Making her wait. Her chest rises and falls with quickening breaths, but she remains still. After removing my boots, I slide my leather leggings down my thighs along with my undergarments, placing them atop my blouse in the sand. I am inches from Cicerine, yet the distance feels like miles. I wait, exposed and heated, for her to be bold—for her to touch me.

A shiver skates across my flesh as she rises up on her elbow and turns toward me, still fully clothed. Her small hand reaches for my face, and her fingers dance over my ear as she ever so slowly traces the length of my hair. Reaching my shoulder, she pauses briefly before continuing down my chest where my hair lies over my breast. It is nearly impossible to hold back, to not throw her to the sand and ravage her with my mouth. Her soft fingertip barely grazes my nipple, and I suck in a ragged breath. She draws a line of pure flame down my body; her agile fingers slowly moving from my breast, down my abdomen, then along my hip and down my thigh. I am still as stone, not daring to move lest my fragile control shatter. She spreads her fingers and grips my thigh before raking her nails back up to my hip. I cannot stifle the small sound that rumbles in my chest as her hand moves around behind me and down my ass. I fight the urge to arch my back and press into her touch, enjoying this slow torture entirely too much. Wordlessly she places that hand on the cloak behind me, rising and swiveling her body so she is perched above me, looking down upon every naked inch of my form. When she at last lowers herself to kiss me, I groan against her mouth and taste the sweet wine on her tongue. She straddles me gracefully, the weight of her settling. My body responds on instinct, and I press my hips against her, eliciting a faint moan from her lips as our kiss deepens. I close my eyes and lose myself in swirling power, our magic crashing together like the whipping waves of a stormy sea.

Our bodies move together seamlessly. Our mouths fit against one another like they were crafted to be one. This feeling of completeness is new and somehow known to my furthest depths. We lick and bite at each other, unable to stop the need between us from lashing us together in a near-frenzied passion. Her teeth draw a drop of blood from my lip, and she pulls away in concern, but I grab her by the hair and roughly pull her back against my mouth, not caring in the slightest, tasting the salty tang of my blood against her tongue. Heat burns deep within me, soaking my thighs. Her shirt buttons down the front, and I deftly maneuver my fingers along each one, tugging them from their holes as I go. She wears stays beneath her blouse, and I unlace them one-handed, pulling the silk laces free. She shimmies the garment down so it sits around her soft stomach, and her breasts fall free. Gods, I am nearly undone by the sight of her alone. Her full breasts press against my chest as her mouth returns to mine, and I break the kiss to suck her nipple between my lips. She lifts her head and moans to the sky, her hair falling down her back in a cascade of curls. I move both hands up to her breasts, and I am not gentle, squeezing her soft skin in my palms. She cries out, her hips grinding into me as she reaches up and plunges her own fingers into her hair. I grab her waist and pull her back down to me forcefully as my mouth finds hers once more. Her hands smack against the ground on either side of my head, and she reaches one arm back to pull off her pants. Time trickles by as she pulls them from one knee and then the other, tossing them aside and lowering herself back to me. The soft hair of her thighs against my hips is like velvet, and I grab her ass, pulling her even closer against me. She grinds against me for a moment, her slick center rubbing against my own with delicious friction. She tips her hips to better press her pubic bone against me, the pressure of her body against my clit nearly unbearable. This is torture, and my fingers long to touch her, but before I can reach my hand between her thighs, she moves down my body. Using a knee to push my legs apart, she kisses her way along my skin until her hair tickles the slope of my hip. I grasp her thick curls and wind her hair around my fist as she kneels before me.

Her tongue runs down my stomach, lightly swirling over my skin. I am panting as her head moves down, her hands sliding beneath me to raise my hips to her mouth. I have not been touched like this, I have never been worshiped in this way. It is transcendent, this moment like the first dawn of day. She runs her tongue through the molten center of me, and I whisper her name roughly, gripping her hair tightly enough to smart. Her fingers tighten on my ass, and she presses her face against me, slowly teasing with her tongue. I am drenched with desire, and she lifts her eyes to mine as she slowly drives two fingers into me. I clench around her, aching for more. The muscles of my thighs tighten as I press my heels into the sand. The hair tangled in my fingers is like ribbons of cinnamon silk. With my eyes closed, I can almost see our magic dancing, forming a glittering cord that binds us together. I cannot keep my eyes closed, however, needing to watch the beauty of her poised before me. The swell of her hips curving into her waist is divine, her bright eyes looking up to mine from beneath long lashes. Her mouth moves against me, licking and sucking at my flesh as I roll my hips in time with her hand. She moans with her mouth still pressed between my thighs; the buzz of her voice is my undoing, sending me over the edge. I scream her name, the sound wrenching from my chest to shatter the silence of the beach.

I only allow myself a moment to quiver on the sand before I grip her throat and spin her down to the sand, my other hand still tightly wound with her thick hair. This is not how it was with Godrick. A primal force shoots through my veins, and I am lost to near bloodlust with my need to own her body. I realize I have been rather forceful with her, but a positively wicked smile pulls at the corners of her full mouth as she draws her plush lip between her teeth and bites down. I apply the slightest pressure against her throat, testing her limits, and she moans breathlessly, arching towards me as her eyes flutter closed. This sweet creature continues to surprise me.

I have not laid with a woman, yet I feel no hesitation. This body before me is built like mine, and I know precisely how to please it. I let loose my grip on her hair and run my hand down her ample curves. Every part of her is soft and luscious, her plush stomach folding slightly at the waist. I lean down to nip at it, pulling a sound from her that is somewhere between a squeal and a sigh. My hand is still against her throat, and I tighten my fingers more, causing her to quake beneath me. I am forced to remove my hand from her neck as I descend further down, and she gasps when I release her, taking a deep, shuddering breath. Letting the tips of my claws extend, I run them across her bare skin with just enough force to leave little red marks in their wake. Seeing my mark upon her flesh sends fiery heat racing down my body, pooling deep within me like melted iron ore.

When I at last reach the soft patch of curls between her thighs, I sheathe my claws and use both hands to roughly force her thighs apart, baring her to me. She is sweet and pink, glistening in the moonlight like a freshly bitten strawberry, and I lower my mouth to her slowly. The heady taste of her sends my thoughts into a scattered whirlwind, the only focus I am able to maintain is the slow press of my tongue into her honeyed center. I plunge into her, moving my lips against her flesh simultaneously. The friction makes her fist the cloak beside her, and a whimper that sounds like a prayer leaves her on a husky breath. My hands dig into her thick thighs, the soft hair beneath my fingers standing on end as her skin pebbles. She shivers, and I withdraw my tongue slowly, swirling it around the sensitive spot that makes her cry out and arch her back. I can feel her approaching climax, and I stop completely, pulling my mouth from her with a slow, tantalizing lick. I blow cool air over her, and she shakes and reaches for me, trying to push my head back down. I swat her hand away and slap her thigh with a crack. She moans at the sting of pain, biting her lip and closing her eyes. At the forceful contact, my magic bleeds from my fingers, tiny bolts of electricity glittering in the dim dark of the evening. Curious, I run a sparking finger over her hip, and she tenses and quakes, clearly responsive to the sensation. I drag my fingers down her thigh, thin veins of power skittering across her skin, and without pausing, press them slowly into her, knuckle by knuckle, filling her with electric magic.

She spasms and clenches around my hand, squeezing my fingers as her hips rock towards me. A nearly indecipherable "more" reaches my ears on the wind, and I withdraw before pressing back into her roughly until my thumb reaches that spot. I move my thumb in circles, grinding against her as I pound my fingers in and out of her, gripping her ankle with my other hand.

She tries to arch away from me, overwhelmed by the intensity, but I pull her closer and swivel my hand, replacing my thumb with my mouth. My tongue flicks against her rapidly, and I groan as I let my tongue move down to where my fingers still press in and out of her. She is so wet that my entire hand is slick with her, and I taste her on my skin before returning to the apex of her pleasure, continuing to lap at her flesh. I curl my fingers up towards me, adding pressure to that small spot that always sends me over the edge. She comes with a breathy scream, hands flying up to paw at her breasts as she rocks her hips against me and shakes.

I do not stop, sucking at her to the point where I know it must be near pain, knowing the sharp point between too much sensation and taking her right to the limit of pleasure. As her body begins to still, and she lays against my cloak, sweat-drenched and physically exhausted, I withdraw my fingers from her, locking eyes with her as I slowly suck them into my mouth. Her answering sound is closer to a growl than a moan, and she grabs my other wrist, nearly pulling me off balance as she drags me toward her. The salty sweetness of her fills our kiss with fire as our mouths collide. I shove my fingers into her hair and pull her face from mine, gripping her tightly, and in a near whisper, I say the only words I know at this moment.

"Now you are mine."

ATHYDIS

CHAPTER SIXTY-SEVEN
THE CRONE
YEAR 993

It takes a great deal of her concentration to keep hold of their minds. It is one thing to ensnare, to entrance, but it is another thing entirely to maintain complete control. She stands in darkness, the stone curling its looming shadow around her like a cloak. The two humans walk toward the edge of the rampart, their steps smooth, if a little hesitant. They are dressed in finery, long brocade cloaks trimmed with glittering embroidery. Her hair curls down her back in a shine of burnished brown. They give off an air of opulence, of power. The citizens of Idythia gaze upon their monarchs in awe. With his eyes, she looks out onto the teeming masses before her. These children of men, weak and frail, believe themselves superior to witchkind? She stifles a scoff. She has laid this groundwork and soon will reap her reward. When the male begins to speak, it takes her a moment to perfect his cadence. His throat utters her words, and the sea of humans before them listens with rapt attention. Her hold on the woman falters for a fraction of a second, but she feels a flutter of awareness for only an instant before tightening her iron fist around the malleable mind it holds.

"As your King, it is my duty to protect this city and its peoples. As civil unrest has grown, I have come to believe that perhaps we have strayed too far from our faith. This great city was founded upon the principles of Idyth, and as such, we should be united in our praise to him. Henceforth, all citizens shall join us in the Cathedral district for services, weekly. Should anyone be unable to attend due to illness or physical limitations, a notice must be filed with the regent. No one shall be exempt from this decree; we shall worship together and bask in the light of Idyth."

The crowd roars. The people are glad to see their king is well, that the whispered rumors are false. The King and Queen are healthy and committed to the united faith of the continent—the stories they heard are simply falsehoods concocted by idle and mischievous minds. They will stand alongside royalty as they sing their praises to Idyth and make their offerings. Humanity is truly blessed in Idythia.

She guides them back to their beds with her mind, the Chaos stretching to their limbs like the strings of marionettes. She needs rest; this day has taken much of her energy. She reaches out for the threads that bind the King and Queen, retying them, wrapping them around the anchor posts within her chest. She settles into the large chair, plush against her bowed back, and allows her eyes to close.

However, rest is not hers to find this evening. Instead, her inner eye snaps open to a new landscape. The jungle foliage is dense and only the faintest shards of moonlight spear the canopy above. These shadows, though, house more darkness than night alone. From the velvet black, a form emerges. A man, but not a man, the moonlight casting deep shadow across his face. The dark slithers about him like eels, ringing his limbs in monochrome, a sallow tinge to his skin that speaks of rot and wrong. Again, that niggling sensation of familiarity brushes the edges of her mind. His identity does not come to her quickly, perhaps a man she encountered in her youth—a face worthy of recognition but not memory. It matters not; he is unimportant in her current course of action. There will be time again to ponder frivolous mysteries when the humans have been suppressed. The solstice approaches and the hammer of her power will fall.

KONIDAS

CHAPTER SIXTY-EIGHT
SHELL
YEAR 993

I feel like I'm at a costume party, but none of these masks come off. Cartwright convinced some of the Brick Union to meet him at the tavern this evenin' and all around the bar I keep catchin' glimpses of horns and scales and weird-colored eyes. I certainly don't mind—I ain't one to judge no one on their appearance, but it is a bit jarrin' to have *so much* of it all at once. It'd be hard to see if you didn't know what to look for, but I know where the Brick Union guys are seated, so their little differences are easy to spot. A nereid named Galena and the jynn, Asha, are the most noticeable, so I've seated them back behind the Orakulua tables since there's no games tonight. Asha is intriguing as all hell. I'd never known jynn were truly real, let alone met one, until this evenin'. Their body seems to fade away sometimes, like a shadow when someone walks in front of the light that casts it. Galena is a sweetheart. They were full of gratitude when I came to ask what they might like to eat, thinkin' maybe roast fish wasn't gonna be their first choice. I offered to have the kitchens fix 'em up something special, but they said they were fine with a cup of hot tea and not to worry about the fish. *Phew.* The woodfolk like to drink, from what I've seen, though they don't seem worse for wear, considerin' the amount of whisky they've knocked back. And the fauns are shifty lookin', to the point where even I'm glancing at the door and 'round the corner like they are. Cartwright gave me a bit of a warning about them, so I've been careful to not sneak up to their table and to be very fucking welcoming, if I do say so myself.

They're meetin' here tonight—a witch is in town, and she got in touch with Cartwright somehow, wantin' to meet with them. She's a bitty little thing, thin as a reed, with long, dark hair pulled over her shoulder. She keeps messin' with it, and I get the feelin' she's nervous around this many men, even though none of 'em are human. Now I get it. Cartwright picked up most of these fellas at the docks, so it makes sense that they're overwhelmingly male, but it still seems off to me that there apparently aren't any females in the Brick Union other than the wives of these folks. I'm guessing there's a lot more of them than Cartwright knows of, but like most men, women's welfare ain't on his mind much. Maybe I can get the few wives we know of together and see about tryin'g to be sneaky to suss out more.

The witch introduces herself to me when I drop off a basket of bread to her table. "Thank you. I am Ophelie; it is nice to meet you. I am glad for your gracious welcome despite the reason for my visit," she says in a quiet but bright voice. "It is not often I feel welcomed."

"Well, Ophelie, we're welcomin' folks. You've always got a safe place to land here. And if you find yourself needin' anythin', you just let me know."

Her cheeks redden slightly, and I'm struck by how different this little thing is from our witch. Maelwen is a much harder breed; I sure do miss her somethin' fierce right now. I know she and Ceci are doin' important things, but I'd much rather have her closer to home. Shouldn't be much longer, though. I was expectin' them to be gone not much more than a week, and it's been about that already. I pour some more wine for the fauns, and Cartwright reaches for my wrist.

"Shell," he begins, voice low and gruff. "How are you handlin' the boy bein' away?"

I pull my arm from his grasp with more force than I intend. "I'm fine, Cartwright. Just focus on these folks for now."

His face falls and his hands busy themselves with straightenin' his vest. He doesn't look up when he replies. "I'm sorry."

THEY MEET LONG INTO THE NIGHT. ONCE THE BAR HAS MOSTLY cleared out, save for a few lone stragglers, I sit down beside Ophelie and try my best to catch up. It ain't good. The witches want us out of the way. They want to tend their own and don't want us interferin' in their plans. But they also won't tell us their plans, so we're in the dark. I'm nervous 'bout the whole thing. Athros is in the city, and from the scattered bits I've tied together from Ophelie, somethin' is going to be happenin' in there soon. I know he's just one kid, and I know he ain't mine, but I don't like thinkin' he might be in danger.

When the young witch leaves, I approach Cartwright. There's a tension in the air between us, like a rope pulled too tight, frayed at the center and ready to snap. "How quick can you have a letter to Athros?"

He looks up from his tankard with heavy eyes. "Maybe two weeks? You wanna pull him out, don't ya?"

I nod. "It ain't safe, just like I told you. You got any idea what the witches are up to?"

His fingers are too busy; he's nervous, and he knows I can see it. "I don't know anything for certain, but you're right, Shell. I was careless." He doesn't meet my eyes when he says it, just stares into the dregs of ale swirling in his tankard.

My mouth opens, but I close it back up without sayin' a word. Instead, I sit down next to him. The last time I heard this tone in his voice was when he found out about his men dying. He's a big man, but he's just as squishy as I am on the inside, and I know that fear is eatin' him up. Am I angry? Absolutely. But I'm also his friend. My fingers close around his, stillin' their fitful movement, and he looks up at me slowly. I've never paid much mind to his eyes, but they have little flecks of gold scattered through the brown that shine like stars. The lines creasing his face are like a diagram of his joys and his sorrows. I know his expressions well enough that I can pick out the lines that crinkle when he smiles, the spots where his brow furrows, the creases around his lips when he's tryin' to look tough at the Orakulua tables. I don't think I've ever noticed, though, that the right side of his mouth goes higher when he smiles. Noticin' the slight change in his face, my gaze snaps up from his lips back to his eyes—I know he's caught me starin'. I'm about to tell him to shut up, that I was just lookin' at the beer froth on his upper lip. But I don't tell him a damn thing because the godsdamned man leans over and kisses me.

I am never shocked. This life of mine is too full of chaos to let little things surprise me anymore, but this...I am stunned silent. It occurs to me that his mouth is still touching mine and I haven't moved. I'm not a blushing maiden, but damned if I don't suddenly forget how to kiss. Thank fuck for muscle memory because my mouth moves without my brain's input, and I kiss him back. Our hands are still touchin' on the table, and he turns his fingers over from beneath mine so our palms are pressed together. My idiot brain catches up and it hits me: *Cartwright* is kissing me, in my own bar. I shift forward in my seat, making it easier for his hand to curl around me. It's no secret I'm a big girl, but his fingers span nearly the whole width of my lower back, covering the laces of my corset completely. I lean into him, breathin' in the familiar scent of my beer and my bar mingling with the rich earthy smell that is Cartwright.

He drops his hand from my back and pulls away, lookin' a bit nervous, and stutters, "I....I'm sorry miss Shell, I...I shouldn't have done…"

I shut him up with my mouth, and I swear I feel the relief flow out of him like a gust of wind. This isn't a rushed, shallow kiss in a broom closet. No, it's deep and slow, as if he wants to make it last. I test the waters, letting my mouth fall open, grazing his lower lip with my tongue, and the stubble on his cheek scapes against me as he presses into me. He tastes like ale and comfort, and I wonder if this is how a kiss is supposed to feel.

Someone behind me clears their throat, and I spin around to find Martine standing a few paces away, looking sheepish. "Sorry to interrupt, Shell, but I thought you might want to know, the cat is actin' strange."

"What do you mean, strange?" I reply, not out of worry for the fuzzball or anything, just curious, ya know.

"He won't let me near one of the cases of wine. Every time I try to grab a bottle from it, he hisses and swats at me."

My eyes narrow. "Show me."

Cartwright has already scooted back, red as an apple in the fall, and he doesn't make eye contact as he mutters, "I best be gettin' home. Shell. Martine." He stands and bows awkwardly before hurrying out of the bar. Oi. Men.

She ain't lyin'—the cat is being weird as hell. He's pacing around the case of wine with his thick orange tail flickin' back and forth like he's about to attack. I squat down beside him and hold out a hand. He puts his heavy ass head in my palm, and I give his furry chin a few skritches. "What's goin' on, Losh?" I ask. Apparently, I've lost my mind talkin' to a damn cat. But he seems to understand, turnin' and scratchin' at the side of the case while making a low growlin' noise in his chest. The case is marked with Salvatorre's emblem, which doesn't surprise me since I only buy wine from Sal. I lift the lid, pulling out a bottle and Losh hisses, puffin' up like a big orange melon, looking more foolish than fierce. "I ain't gonna drink it, cat," I mutter, still talkin' to a fuckin' animal. I grab a glass from the bar, pop the cork from the bottle, and pour a bit into the cup. It *looks* fine. It's a deep red, probably the blend Sal makes from the leftover varieties of red and black grapes at the end of the season. The bottle isn't labeled, which is weird for Sal; he's meticulous in his bottlin', always markin' each bottle with the type and the date. This bottle has his label and a date, but not the varietal. I sniff it, and it smells like wine, but when I go to take a sip the damn cat swats my ankle and yowls at me. Grumblin' about how tasty a cat stew would be, I take another whiff. I smell it then, just the slightest hint of somethin' off. I stick my nose right up in the cup, swirlin' the dark liquid as I do, and I catch it. The last time I smelled that acrid tang, it was being poured into my mouth from a tiny bottle. My suspicion is confirmed as I hold the glass up closer to the light. The dark red color leaves a thin film of purple on the glass where I swirled it seconds before.

This wine is laced with pennyway.

The Sea

CHAPTER SIXTY-NINE
JYNN
YEAR 993

I wake to the brush of her lips on mine. This feels like the first morning of a life that is completely my own. The last few days have flown by in a tumble of hard work and sweet affection, with Tuii becoming a near-constant fixture in my evenings. In less than a week, we will sail into Konidas, and the nervous flutters in my chest have dulled to a faint buzz of anticipation. Tuii says I'm adept enough at Orakulua to maybe sit in on a game at the tavern, but it's the idea of her sitting beside me that fills me with excitement. Today, however, is a day of hard labor, and as I pull my aching body from my hammock, I cringe at the burning muscles of my thighs. Yesterday I worked from dawn 'til dusk, and even my fingers feel sore. Tuii must catch my grimace as she takes my hand, because she pulls my palm toward her and kneads her fingers into the flesh below my thumb.

"You going soft on me, Red?" she asks with a smirk.

I sigh and scratch at my newly-cut hair with my other hand. "If I say yes, will I be allowed to sleep today instead of work?"

Her answering laugh is like the trilling of bells, and I cannot help but smile. "Of course not. You're a pirate, not a prince."

Warmth spreads through me at her words. "Why prince?" I ask. "Do I not conjure images of a dainty princess?"

She chuckles and replies, "No, Jynn. You do not and will never appear to be a 'princess.' If anything, I'd say you're a lazy king. You'd certainly rather be laying in a comfortable bed and drinking fine wine."

I snort, but through my amusement, I rally a bit of boldness. "I've actually been meaning to talk to you about that. Ever since Briar told me they don't feel comfortable with 'she,' I've been thinking—do you think that's something I could do as well?"

Tuii laughs loudly, and my face heats with shame. I had hoped to broach the subject with her first, but if she thinks it's ridiculous, I guess I won't.

"Jynn, you can do whatever it is you want here. Everyone on this ship will respect any choice you make. Of course you can. You can go by whatever you'd like. I'm surprised it took you this long!"

"Truly?"

"Of course, you dolt." She leans forward and kisses the hollow of my throat.

My smile could rival the sun.

Sweat pours from my face in heated rivulets. It's brisk above deck with a strong headwind that tousles my hair as I heave rope into heavy coils, but my skin burns from the effort. I've been up here for hours, and my arms feel like jelly. I have a few meters left of this rope before I have to move to my next task, and I plan on popping into the galley for a bowl of whatever Cook has going before I continue the day's labors. The surface of the sea looks like a flat, gray mirror, reflecting the sun that lies hidden behind a bank of white clouds. Petrels cry out as they dip below the waves to snatch silver fish that catch the light as they flop to and fro. I breathe in the salty air, feeling at peace in a way I didn't know would ever find me. As I exhale, a sound filters through the crashing waves and squealing seabirds. It begins as a hum, but builds in volume until it reveals a melody of harmonious layers. That same urge to leap into the vast ocean washes over me, and I grip the rope with white knuckles. Looking around, it is obvious nobody else can hear it. Everyone tends to their duties, chatting and whistling to themselves, but the rising volume of the song becomes nearly overwhelming, and I drop the rope to the deck with a loud *thunk*.

The feet that walk to the deck railing feel as though they belong to someone else. It is almost like watching a stranger—this disconnected sensation of my body moving independently from my mind. Before I can stop it, my hands are on the rail, and I am swinging my body over the polished wood, slicing into the sea like a heated knife into butter.

All at once, the world stills. The soft roar of the waves smooths over the sounds of the crew shouting, and the melody wraps around me like a mother's gentle arms. I scissor my legs languidly, not trying to stay afloat, but to guide my descent as I allow myself to sink into the depths. Tiny bubbles escape my nostrils and I watch them dance before my eyes as they race for the surface. Below the sea, time is merely a suggestion.

The colors reflecting onto my skin are bright and ever-changing. A rainbow of light is refracted through the ocean, landing on my arms and hands and painting me in a soft pattern of pastel hues. The song grows louder, seeming to vibrate through my skin. My eyes widen as an extraordinary sight appears before me— dozens of ethereal figures, pale hair waving in the ocean currents. One figure floats toward me with their long fingers outstretched. Their mouth doesn't move, but I hear them speaking to me, regardless. Their dreamy voice swirls around my head and feels like satin in my mind.

"Seaborn," they whisper. "How has this come to be?"

I open my mouth to reply, large bubbles emerging instead. They shake their head, and my brows narrow. I don't know how to speak like them. They tap their temple with a pale finger before gesturing to me as if to say "Now, you," and I try. I focus on the way their voice felt in my chest, trying to emulate the same sensation, and their face lights up as I succeed. "Who are you?"

"The real question is who are *you*?"

I don't know how to reply, and they smile softly.

"The landborn call us the Nereids. We have been at rest for many years," their graceful voice continues. "Several suns ago, our eyes opened and the sea called us from our sleep." They gesture to the crowd, and one of them swims forward. "Saera found you, and then, found me."

My heart warms at seeing the familiar face of the figure who approached me in the sea outside Minos'Idyl. "It is so nice to know your name, Saera."

Their face settles into a satisfied smile, and they speak. Their voice feeling oddly familiar despite never having heard it before. "I will always rise to meet my kin."

The words take a moment to settle, and as I comprehend the implication, my mouth drifts open. I taste the briny sea on my tongue for a moment before I expel the salty water and close my lips once more. *Kin?* It is difficult to focus enough to reply, but I manage to respond, my voice that is not a voice sounding thin and reedy even to my own mind. "Kin?"

"Have you not felt the pull of the sea? Do you not feel a tug towards our home?"

"I grew up far from the ocean," I reply. "I have only been on this ship for a season."

Saera and the other figure look to one another, shoulders

dropping and smiles fading. The first figure speaks, "Your parent must have suffered through great hardship. We cannot live far from the sea, even when land-bound. One of your parents is human, which perhaps is how you were able to exist so far from the water. This brings sadness to our souls. You have missed so much."

"Who were my parents?" I ask quickly, desperate to know the answer to a question that has followed me my entire life.

Saera pauses. "We have slept a long, long time. The world above was chaotic, and it bled into the sea. We chose to rest, hoping to wake to a better world. Some of us did not make it back to the water in time, and they have been unable to rejoin us."

"One of my parents is…like you? But trapped on land?"

"So it may be," their voice responds, tinged with sorrow.

"Is it my mother or my father?" I ask, longing for some small bit of knowledge to tie myself to my past, my heritage.

They look contemplative, confused, before seeming to understand my question. "We do not have differences such as humans do. We do not have different identities in that way. We are the sea, and that is enough. There are many creatures in the sea who share this quality, able to become what is needed. I do not know in your case. I am sorry."

I wish I knew more, that they had the answers to my questions, but I can still be grateful for what knowledge I *do* have. Realizing I likely have little time left to speak with them, I ask, "What is your name?" looking toward the individual who has yet to introduce themself.

They smile and reach out to take my hand. "I am Lafeine, and I am the sovereign of the nereids. It is a blessing indeed to make your acquaintance."

I am stunned silent, and I float without words. Should I bow? Can you kneel while swimming?

"Your people must worry," Lafeine says, hand caressing my

shoulder. "We will have time to speak again. For now, return to your ship. Know that you have kin beneath the waves. Be full of joy. We will speak again soon."

I want to reach for them, to hug them, but it feels awkward and probably just my human side aching for contact. So instead, I fold slightly at the waist in a clumsy bow and kick my legs to propel myself back to the surface. Their gently waving hair disappears slowly beneath me, and I am struck by an odd feeling. *I have a family.*

My head breaks the surface, and I am met with the shouting of the crew. A rowboat that has been dispatched floats a few lengths from me. Tuii is at the oars, worry twisting her face. "JYNN!" She frantically screams my name, and I flinch. She begins to row toward me, and I swim to meet her, hauling my body aboard the small boat with a wet slap. Before I can speak, she grabs my face in both hands and kisses me deeply before pulling away and smacking the living shit out of me. My hand flies to my stinging cheek, and I let loose a hearty laugh.

"I'm sorry!" I can't help the grin that spreads all the way to my eyes. "You shouldn't have worried!"

She moves to hit me again, but I catch her fine-boned wrist in my hand. Her voice isn't angry when she replies, "Jynn, I'm a pirate. 'Man Overboard' is my primary worry."

I raise her hand to my lips, kissing her knuckles gently. "I have a lot to tell you, to tell all of you."

"Fine," she says in comic petulance. "But I'm still mad."

I help the crew tie off the rowboat and heave it back aboard. Ballad stands on the deck when I at last pull myself up, but instead of anger on her face, she wears a wide grin. "I'm guessin' you met the nereids."

MINOS'IDYL

CHAPTER SEVENTY
CICERINE
YEAR 993

My body is deliciously sore. Fine grains of sand linger on my skin and in my hair. I probably look a mess, but I can't bring myself to feel self-conscious. Maelwen woke far before me and has packed up our bags in preparation for our fight back to Konidas. The lightning glass vessel is wrapped snugly in my spare clothing and tucked inside my pack, but I swear I can feel it humming even from across the beach. The water is calm, softly lapping at the shore in easy little waves. Maelwen stands on the sand, her feet bare, long hair flying about her face in the breeze. It is cold this morning, but she wears only a thin blouse and leather leggings, her cloak set atop our packs and her gloves dangling from her pocket. The sight of her leaves me breathless; her narrow shape silhouetted against the sky exudes power. The woven magic between us feels different this morning, no longer like two separate energies, but one. Her dark power thrums in my fingers, skittering across my skin and filling me with a sense of strength. When she turns to face me, the hard angles of her face soften and I rise, striding across the soft sand to meet her.

"I do not know if it will be necessary to stop in Athydis this time," she says as I reach her side. "I feel strong, stronger than I have felt before."

"From the blood?"

"I do not think so," she replies. "I believe it is you."

"Me?"

"After last night, I felt our power meld in a different way. It feels as though it has become one magic. You have far more power than you recognize, and I can feel it within me as well. It may deplete us both, but I am fairly certain I can fly us home without rest. I took to the sky before you woke, and I feel…enhanced."

Home.

She looks to me for a reply, and I realize I haven't spoken yet. "Well," I begin, "if you think we can, I trust you."

The lightning glass pulses against my chest like a heartbeat, the steady rhythm centering my mind as we take to the sky, the sapphire cloak wrapping around my middle in a comfortable embrace. Maelwen's hold on me is firm, but the gentle way her fingers run across my skin makes my breath catch. The ocean below us is a deep cerulean, painted with brush strokes of gray from the frothy waves. I see very few ships, but there are countless seabirds of every size. She did not exaggerate—the speed with which we fly is easily double what it was when we left Konidas. As we pass over Athydis, the city is a blur beneath me. I can't focus on any particular detail, just the red-tiled roofs whipping past at shocking speed. The sky is so vast, so blue, and I feel painfully inconsequential as I realize just how much there is in the world. Even in my wildest youthful imaginings, my worldview was small. I dreamed of leaving the glade, but I had no concept of the sheer magnitude of the world outside that speck of forest. I wonder, in my existential daydream, if any of this even matters at all.

We touch down in Konidas a few hours before dawn. I am starving and dehydrated from the long flight, but Maelwen seems to be fine. Stretching my legs, I curse this body of mine, if only I had her stamina. My hair is an absolute disaster, curls twisted into a veritable bird's nest, and I desperately need a bath. I follow Maelwen toward the tavern to say hello to Shell, but I need to get to the inn as soon as possible to set myself right again. My hooves kick up dust along the cobbled ground as we walk and I do my best to fix my hair with my fingers, but I can tell it's a lost cause. I carry the lightning glass, but Maelwen has shouldered both of our packs. My skin already misses her touch, and I yearn to grab her hand but choose not to, lest she think me foolish.

The tavern is busy; people huddle around tables and bustle around the place playing cards and grabbing ale from the bar. Shell looks up as the bell jangles on the door, and her eyes light with unrestrained joy. "Maelwen! Ceci!" She tosses her bar towel down and hurries to us, wiping her hands on her apron. She grabs Maelwen in a fierce hug, and I giggle at the expression of discomfort that momentarily furrows her brows.

"Shell," she says with a small smile. "It is good to be back."

Shell reaches for me as well, an awkward moment where we both move in different directions, not knowing if the other one wants to hug or not. Her head tips back and she lets out a hearty cackle, grabbing both my hands in hers and pulling me to her chest. "Ah, little faun. I do hope our witch treated you kindly? Not too rough with you, I hope."

I blush furiously, and Shell's raised eyebrow guarantees that there will be questions later. Gods, I wish I was better at subtlety, but the image of Maelwen's hand at my throat is far too much to ignore and the heat in my cheeks is overtaken by warmth settling between my thighs. I manage to blurt out, "It was good!" before shutting my mouth and silently vowing to never speak to another person ever again in my life.

We walk behind Shell, heading to the bar, and Maelwen's fingers brush mine. I don't bother to look down; I can feel the sparks as they fall to the floor, and I smile. The slightest touch of her hand is reassuring, and I muster up some confidence, even if it is a ruse. I'm grateful Shell's barstools are backless. My larger hindquarters aren't unwieldy as I settle onto my seat, swinging my hooves beneath the lip of the bar to rest on the brass railing running along the bottom. Maelwen smiles at the little *clink* they make, and I lean my shoulder into her, wishing we could be alone instead of among all these loud strangers.

"Gods," I say to Shell. "I could drink an entire bottle tonight. Can I have a glass of wine as well as some water?"

Shell's face goes grim. I'm not sure what I said to merit such a response, and I'm about to ask when she says in a low voice, "We need to talk about Salvatorre."

My heart plummets in my chest. I've been so worried about him. He's old, and it's very likely he could have been hurt in the mess with the Idyth cult. "Oh no. Please tell me he's all right?"

The bitter sound Shell growls in reply shocks me. She spits on the floor of the bar and the disgust in her eyes could sour milk. "I'm sorry to be the one tellin' ya this, kid. But it seems as though your buddy Sal ain't what he's led us all to believe. He may be working with the cultists. Hell, he may have been working with them all along."

No. It's not possible. His sweet face and genuine smile when he called me "sweet girl" flashes through my mind. I cannot reconcile the idea of the kind man I know and the pure repulsion I feel towards Farragen and his ilk. "What?" I ask, breathless with emotion. "How can you know? What happened?"

"Opened a new crate of wine a couple days back. The damn cat was actin' a fool, not lettin' me near it, makin' a whole mess of noise—oh yeah, I got a cat now. Well, I almost drank a damn glass but thankfully the orange beast tried to claw my ankle off, and I took a second look. The whole crate was laced with pennyway."

"But how do you know it was him? Anyone could have done it, right? Other people work for him."

"Sal initials the corks of each bottle when they're sealed, and he labels each bottle by hand. These bottles were corked with his signature but only labeled 'Shell's'. In all the years he's sent me wine, not a single bottle has been without a regular label. I have to believe he knew what was in those bottles and wanted to make sure they didn't get mixed up and sent to someone else. They were meant for my tavern, kid. I can't be sure why, but I'd venture a guess that he's workin' for someone who don't like what we been doin' here."

Tears prick at the corners of my eyes, blurring my vision. I look at my hands in my lap, twisting my fingers together to keep myself from crying outright. I can't believe someone I called my friend would try to hurt Shell, try to hurt *me*. He had to know I spent time here. What reason could he have for doing such a thing if he wasn't trying to harm the non-humans in the city? I feel sick, my empty stomach suddenly feeling as though it could not possibly hold down food or drink. Maelwen's hand rests on my knee, and she gently moves her thumb back and forth, a tiny motion that somehow feels more reassuring than anything else ever could. I blink away my tears, anger replacing the hurt. "What are we going to do about it?"

Shell looks contemplative for a moment before replying, "I don't have another shipment coming for around a month. So for now? Nothing. But, it looks like I'm gonna have to take wine off the menu 'til I can get this sorted."

Maelwen groans, and I allow a smile to soften my pain. "Sorry," I say to her warmly, "looks like we're on beer for awhile."

"Shell's ale is fine," she says glumly. "I just prefer to travel with wine, and with the solstice approaching, now I have to bring water? This seems rather unfair—to me in particular."

"Was that a joke?" Shell gasps with a chuckle. "Did Maelwen finally make a joke?!"

Maelwen's expression is flat as she replies, "I am uncertain what you find humorous about that."

We all burst out in laughter.

KONIDAS

CHAPTER SEVENTY-ONE
MAELWEN
YEAR 993

I wake to an empty room, struck by the feeling that my bed is too large. The space beside me feels vast and cold, and my hand smooths the sheets, wishing Cicerine was beside me. I stretch like a cat, my feet pressing to the cold wooden floor as I raise my arms toward the sky. There is too much quiet here now that I have become accustomed to her voice. Perhaps this is what loneliness feels like. *Would she stay with me if I asked?* Tossing on a satin blouse over my undershirt and pulling on doeskin leggings, I twist my long hair up before shrugging a cropped jacket over my shoulders. It is cold; winter has fallen fully upon the city, and even I am not immune to the sharp bite of the air. A quiet buzz emanates from my desk, and I turn to see the lightning glass set upon the smooth wood. In a few strides, I reach the desk and lift the odd vessel into my hands. It does not feel like any item I have ever touched; the life within it thrumming beneath my fingers like a pulse. The words Caelfry spoke to me at the tower return to my mind as I recall her mention of artifacts of intention. Could this vessel hold some sort of magic? Curious, and moving on instinct alone, I pour a small measure of water into the hollow center of the vessel, lift it to my lips, and drink.

My veins burn with the heat of summer lightning. My bones resonate with a booming pulse of energy. I feel as though my blood itself sizzles with the power that shoots through me. I cannot see for a moment, blinded by a light so bright it heats my skin. Life itself pours through me, water transformed into liquid vitality. I stumble, catching my hand on the bed and sinking down into my mattress with shaking hands. I am unable to hold the glass upright anymore, and the small amount of liquid remaining in the vessel dribbles out. No longer water, the liquid spreads across my floor in a tiny pool of shimmering gold. After a few steadying breaths, I kneel beside it and dip my fingers into the shining puddle. My fingertips drip with thick, viscous gold, and a word in a story from long ago forms on my lips: *Ichor.*

Nearly frantic, I rise and stumble to my bookcase, fingers running across the spines of my books on the shelf. My fingers find the battered tome, and I pull the small book from its place and return to my bed, sitting on the edge with one foot tucked beneath me. I cannot read the title clearly from the cover, but it is the same book of poetry I bought from the vendor when I still lived with Jarrus. Opening it to the title page, I find the author's name written in looping script, and nearly drop the book. Caelfry Aestiere. Determined to find the poem I recall, I flip through the pages until I recognize the illustration.

Godsblood

    The golden flow of Ichor goes, through veins of mortal man
    One taste so sweet, the Gods entreat, that life begins again
    Though death is near, he hath no fear, for in the night it shines
    A single sip through mortal lips, a gift from the divine
    A tale so old, of blood made gold, she cannot abide his death
    She lets him live, this gift she gives, eternity on his breath

Did the Caelfry I know write this? I have never felt so confused. Why must poetry be so nebulous and abstract? I can ask her at the solstice, but that does little for me currently. What gives this vessel the ability to turn water into gold liquid? Is this poem saying she made a man immortal with some sort of magic? What has drinking it done to me? I rub my temples with my thumbs. Every day I seem to have more questions and fewer answers. However, none of them will ever be answered by sitting in my apartment alone, so I rise and head downstairs.

Shell is busy drying glasses with a towel when I reach the bar, and my chaotic thoughts must be clearly written on my face. She greets me with a raised eyebrow, "Oh, gods. What now?"

"Have I become that transparent?"

"Well," she says with a smirk, "you look like you're about to punch someone in the mouth, so I'd say so."

I drag my hand down my face before replying. "It is not that. I am not angry at anyone in particular. I am angry at the seemingly constant stream of events which complicate my life. I wish things were simple."

"I'll drink to that!" She raises a still dripping, empty glass to the sky.

CICERINE WILL BE WORKING UNTIL WELL AFTER SUNDOWN, SO I decide to spend my day seeking answers about Salvatorre for her. His winery is located at the city's edge in the warehouse district. The scent of grape must is easy to follow, and I find his building with little effort. I do not hear anyone inside. I quietly try opening a door located toward the back but find it locked. I slink around the building's exterior, locating three entrances and two high windows. Even though each of the doors is secured, one of the windows appears to be ajar. The neighboring buildings are quiet, most likely used for storage or otherwise unoccupied for the winter. Finding no other possible point of entry, I look around a final time before pulling my cloak over my shoulders and rising up toward the open window.

The window creaks slightly but lifts easily, and I slide through the narrow space between the lifted pane and the sill. I drop to the warehouse floor and a soft puff of dust rises from the ground. This building has not been in use for quite some time. By the accumulation of dust, I would guess that Ceci's visit was likely one of the last days it was occupied. There are large empty vats and a long table which holds rows of empty bottles, all covered in a thin layer of disuse. The air still smells strongly of ferment, the floors stained a deep red from years of spilled grape juice. There are empty crates bearing Salvatorre's seal and boxes of cork, but no sign of any humans. Across the large space, there is a door, and I navigate the abandoned equipment silently, heading toward it. My feet leave small prints as I walk. The door is unlocked, and within I find what appears to have been an office. A large sturdy desk sits in the center of the room, two bookcases along the back wall. This room also carries a familiar smell, cutting through the stale dust and old soured grapes. Pennyway.

I look beneath the desk but find it empty. Atop it sits a pile of books and scattered papers. The bookcases are the same, devoid of anything but dusty books. The stink seems stronger along the wall where the bookcases stand, so I lean my back against one and push it to the side. It scrapes against the floor as it shifts, making a ragged screech that echoes throughout the warehouse. I freeze, waiting to ensure the noise draws no attention. When nothing but silence follows, I peer behind the heavy furniture and see a narrow door. Even with my strength, it takes some effort to pull the bookcase aside completely, but when I do, I open the small door. It appears to be a closet stacked full of crates, all marked with the symbol of Minos'Idyl. I do not bother opening the crates, knowing I will find them full of pennyway. Instead, I return my attention to the desk.

I lift the stack of books and shuffle through them, finding two agricultural references, a book on glassware, and a book of scrawled numbers and notes which I assume is a ledger. The last book I examine looks to be a well-worn journal. The handwriting inside is narrow and sharply angled to the right, neat and orderly, though shakily written. I scan the pages, and nothing seems to be nefarious, just the goings-on of a lonely old man and his feelings. The most recent entry is from close to a year ago, which tells me nothing of the current plans of the cult. The journal is thick, and I flip through the pages, noting the dates. He has written sporadically, sometimes daily and other times monthly. There are often large gaps of time between entries, years going by in a matter of pages. It is in the year 970 that I spot something which stills my hand: *Farragen.*

The handwriting on this page is less shaky, the hand of a much younger man having put these words to paper. Twenty years of bleeding ink blurs the writing slightly, but I can mostly decipher the passage.

Third Month of Spring, 970

The bishop spoke with me again this morning as I dropped off the sacramental wine. Again, he noted my presence in services and asked if I had any desire to join the priesthood. I know what he wants from me, but he can continue to pay for his wine. A charity I am not. Santoro Farragen was there as well, and we had lunch once again outside the cathedral. He shared with me some thoughts I worry border on heresy, but I cannot deny the fire that burns in his eyes. Few men carry such fervent belief in their hearts. He has written a holy book of his own and gifted me a copy. I told him I would indeed like to know more, and he was glad to hear it. We spoke of the Bishop's offer that I had declined. I know not how these men so easily forgo the pleasures of the flesh. We discussed my journeys across the peninsula, and I spoke at length about the forest of fauns I visited in my youth—how it led to my career as a winemaker. He was oddly intrigued by the fauns, asking many questions about the location of their village and knowledge of agriculture. I believe he may be looking to spread the word of his newly burgeoning faith, and he would be smart to begin outside the Cathedral City. He could easily be cast out of the clergy for such claims. I hope to see him again; his message speaks to me in a way the Church does not.

The next passage is from nearly a year later and makes no reference to Farragen. I scan the journal, hoping for more information connected to him, but find nothing other than a single short entry from the year 989 that says *I received the crate of books today from Santoro and plan to distribute them with my deliveries. Another man in the city was murdered by a witch last night. Something must be done to protect our people. It may be that he is the key to finding what we need. I will speak with him the next time he visits the city.*

I close the journal and slide it into my pocket. Salvatorre led Farragen to the glade; he is the cause of all the hardships Cicerine has been forced to endure. I could tear him limb from limb. My hands clench with my rage, but I resolve to remain rational. This journal may hold more information. I will have more time to look it over later, but for now, I need to see if I can find any sign of where Salvatorre may have gone, why he would try to poison the tavern. Shell was uncertain of where he lived, but it cannot have been terribly far from this area. I finish searching the warehouse, finding nothing of use. The space is filled with little more than dust and abandoned winery equipment. The old man has disappeared.

KONIDAS

CHAPTER SEVENTY-TWO
SHELL
YEAR 993

Maelwen is clearly pissed when she slinks back into the tavern. We are gettin' ready for dinner service, and the bar is somewhat busy, but I manage to scoot my ass over to her side of the bar for a quick second to ask what the fuck happened.

"Salvatorre seems to have left no indication of his current location," she says in that flat voice of hers. "I did, however, come across a journal which does seem to tie him to Farragen, and suggests he may be directly at fault for Farragen's involvement with the glade in Kanitosh."

I blow out a breath from between my teeth. "You told Ceci yet? That's gonna sting somethin' fierce."

Her eyes narrow into shards of pure ice. "I have not. I am not looking forward to that conversation."

"Understandable." I push a glass of Scurvy Sour her way and get back to work, grabbing a heavy tray full of precariously balanced plates of tonight's meal. The savory aroma of gravy and potatoes sets my stomach to growlin', and my mouth is waterin' by the time I pass the plates out to the patrons. I need to fuckin' eat. I've been on my feet since breakfast, and I'm tired as a pack mule—probably smell just as rank. The door jingles as it opens, and I look up to find the bard, lute in hand, and a sad smile on his face. I greet him with a wave and gesture over to the corner with a nod, but he knows where to head. Fatigue seems to roll off me, tension easin' down my back as he begins to warm up, the clear starshine sound of his instrument awakenin' somethin' in me. Gods, I love music. I wish Cartwright was here to dance with me.

Mael wasn't here the last time he came through—she spent the night sleepin' off the stress of the minotaur—so I'm happy she will get to hear him sing. She watches him from behind her ale, and when he spots her, he goes still as a statue. Oh! I forgot about his song about the witch, and I say a silent prayer he's not scared off by havin' a witch in attendance, but he rolls his shoulders and goes back to his warmup. He plays a quick foot-stomper most of the bar is familiar with, and we all sing along to the bawdy song with raucous laughter and terrible harmony. Once there's some coin in his palm, he strums a hauntin' chord that quiets the place near immediately. He plucks out a melody that raises the hair on my forearms and sends a chill down my spine. Somethin' in this sound is hauntin' and forebodin'. I can tell even before he sings, that it's gonna be a sad song. His voice starts out quiet, almost too low to hear, but as the song continues, it builds and builds.

Alone, alone, I walk alone, a ghost where once was a man
My heart, it beats, but does not warm, as it did before this began
Alone, alone, I sleep alone, my bed which once was ours
My heart, it aches, but does not bleed, though it bears such scars
A river of gold, I sail, I sail
This river of gold, I tell the tale
Of love so pure it defeated time itself

A river of gold, I sail, I sail
This river of gold, I tell the tale
Of a love so pure, I sold my soul to have
Alone, alone, I cry alone, though not a tear does fall
My heart, it pleads but does not receive, an answer to its call
Alone, alone, I am alone, a one where once was two
My heart, it breaks, and does not mend, its days of love are through
A river of gold, I sail, I sail
This river of gold, I tell the tale
Of love so pure it defeated time itself
A river of gold, I sail, I sail
This river of gold, I tell the tale
Of a love so pure, I sold my soul to have

~

I feel tears spatter onto my cheeks as I blink away the weight of his song. My skin prickles and my heart aches, his words seeming to still hang in the air like a loomin' storm. Despite the packed chairs, the bar is near silent. Everyone seems equally affected by the bard's tale. As he walks around to collect his coin, life creeps back into the audience, and by the time he's back onstage, everyone is smilin' and ready for another tune. But I can't help feelin' like there was some sort of magic in that song, something old and sad.

I keep busy while the bard plays the rest of his set. He doesn't sing any more eerie numbers, just classic bar songs and familiar ballads. Nobody in the place seems shaken, but I still can't get the tingle out of my chest, and I feel uneasy. Maelwen is even more silent than usual, sittin' in a shadow and starin' at the bard from beneath her furrowed brows. When he finishes, I wave him over and push a plate of food at him. "I'm guessin' you could use a meal!" I say with a smile I hope he takes as jolly.

"Thank you, miss," he says in a quiet, bright voice. "You're the owner here?"

"Yes, indeed! Name's Shell, like on the sign." I laugh at myself and he blushes.

"I always enjoy stopping by your tavern. I've been coming here a long time, since well before you were even born."

I scrunch up my face and peer at him more closely. "You don't look old enough to have been' travelin' before I was born. Unless, of course, you were carried by your mama."

He laughs, but there is no mirth in it. "Appearances can be deceiving, Shell. Thank you for allowing me to play and for the warm meal."

"You got a place to sleep this evenin'?" I ask, realizin' I have no idea if he has a wagon, or where he stays when he travels.

"I'd planned on getting a room at the inn for the night if I brought in enough coin." He pats the bag at his side, jinglin' the coins nestled in the brocade sack. "I certainly did, so I'll likely be heading over there shortly. I need some sleep before I hit the road again in the morning."

"Nonsense." I say, patton' his hand "I've got a small room you can stay in." Only one of the rooms upstairs is currently set up as storage. The one I sleep in and the one across the hall have been cleared out and set up with beds. "I'll get you a key and show you up there whenever you're ready."

"That's quite kind." His smile doesn't reach his eyes, but I chalk it up to bein' tired after a long day of travel and performance. "What do I owe you?"

"Not a single copper needed. You kept my patrons from causin' a ruckus. It's the least I can do." I feel eyes upon me and look around. Maelwen's stare could freeze the breath in my chest. She watches the bard with a focused intensity that makes me nervous. Not for the first time, I wish I knew what she was thinkin'.

After finishin' his meal, the bard yawns and stretches, clearly ready for rest. I lead him upstairs and show him into the small room, lettin' him know he can take care of his needs downstairs. His gratitude is genuine, though his smile is not, and I leave him for the night. Not wastin' any more time thinkin' about his strange song.

THE SKY IS A HAZY GRAY, JUST BEGINNIN' TO LIGHTEN WITH the early, risin' sun. Martine and Leita have the bar handled, though there ain't more than a handful of patrons to tend to. Standin' in the doorway, I take a deep breath. The salty air actually smells fresh for once, cleaner than normal. I decide to take a walk down to the docks, stretch my legs before headin' to bed. My schedule is all topsy-turvy lately, sleepin' in the days and workin' all night. I'm tired, but I feel like I haven't been outside in forever. I pull my coat tighter over my chest. It's so cold I can see my breath form little puffy clouds before my lips. It's going to be a cold winter; I can feel it in my bones.

The docks are quiet, a few ships moored, but nobody topside save for a few lookouts or slow-movin' early risers. The sun peeks over the horizon like a sliver of silver, just the slightest bit of light beginnin' to spread over the surface of the sea. For all her faults, this town has some beauty to it. Konidas is a lot like me: rough around the edges but full of goodness if you look hard enough. My thoughts feel deep and introspective as I stand in the shimmer of dawn. As I stare at the softly illuminated sea, a tall ship comes into view. She's way out there, probably not gonna be pullin' in until tonight, but even from this distance, I can see the broad sails and the twin masts. Well, I'll be damned. Looks like a brigantine, and since I know damn well it ain't the crown, I suppose some pirates are payin' us a visit.

THE SEA

CHAPTER SEVENTY-THREE
JYNN
YEAR 993

I shake my head like a pup, water droplets splattering Captain Ballad as she laughs heartily. "Oy! Givin' me a taste of the sea, are ye?" Her grin spreads through the crowd. Even Tuii is not immune to the shift, smiling despite her annoyance with me.

"Sure am, Captain," I reply. "And about meeting the nereids… well apparently, I'm part nereid myself."

The crew titters, looking around as their concern gives way to confusion. Ballad is shaken by nothing. She pulls her giant, floppy hat from her head and bows deeply, speaking in an exaggerated hoity-toity accent, "I am but your humble servant, oh, ye great sea ruler that leaps into yer kingdom and scares me crew half to death." For a moment I'm nervous at the admonishment, but then she slaps me with her hat and I double over, laughing. "I won't lie to ye, that's a nifty thing," she says, "but it ain't gonna get you out of work, so don't go thinkin' you're special."

Tuii is staring, but I intertwine my fingers with hers and squeeze, hopefully conveying that I'll tell her later. "Aye,

Captain!" I salute awkwardly with my free hand. "No privileges for seafolk!"

"Enough of this tomfoolery!" Captain says as she sets her ridiculous hat back on. "We'll be sailin' into Konidas on the morrow, so back to work, or ye won't be touchin' land nor lads nor lassies tomorrow evenin'! Everyone best be stayin' aboard or I'll be leavin ye to the fishfolk." She walks off with a swish of her coattails, her footsteps a steady beat on the wood of the deck. Everyone scuttles back to work, news of our impending arrival sparking through the crew like static. Everyone is excited to spend some time on land, and I'm certain the crew will be decked out in their finest this evening.

We finish putting up the rowboat, and I resume my duties, Tuii at my side. "So...you're a nereid?" she asks incredulously.

"Apparently." I shrug my shoulders. "Half, to be more precise. I suppose it explains how I've been able to stay underwater so long. No clue if it has any other benefits, but it's pretty nice to know I have family somewhere."

She bumps me with her shoulder. "You've got family here, too, even if I'm mad at you for scaring the shit out of me."

"I know," I say, pressing a kiss to her shoulder. "And I am sorry, but this is blood, which I have never known. I really hope I get the opportunity to know them, to find out more about who I am."

"I know exactly who you are, Jynn." Tuii looks at me from beneath her fan of dark lashes. I suck in a breath, enraptured by her beauty. "You're an idiot." She smacks my ass and laughs as she heads off across the deck.

I chuckle as I lift a crate, setting it atop the pallet I'm loading. This woman will be the death of me.

∼

I can see the city in the distance, even without my spyglass. The shore twinkles with lights like fireflies, and I can make out ships bobbing against the dock, their tall masts reaching up toward the low-hanging moon. Pressing my spyglass to my eye, I can see that the buildings are humble. Most of them are single-story, with a few taller structures poking up here and there. It doesn't look like much, but it's the biggest human settlement I have ever seen, and my pulse races with excitement and anxiety. I still worry I won't fit in, that it will be terribly apparent I grew up far removed from people like me. I suppose that even now I am surrounded by people who aren't quite like me either. Knowing I am not fully human is odd. I *feel* human, but I also feel different. However, I'm beginning to find my footing. I feel settled here, appreciated for my strengths and accepted as I am. Ceci doesn't feature in my thoughts as much as she once did. I will always miss her, but I think that, perhaps, this place is where I was supposed to be.

We sail slowly toward the city, the harbor coming into view more clearly with each passing hour. Day breaks and a warm blush spreads over the sea, lighting the surface of the water in tones of peach and ochre. Briar points out different types of ships, telling me about them and how they differ from the Sea Song. I enjoy learning, soaking up the knowledge like a sponge. I'd like to be a good pirate and to know the things that make Briar and all the other crew such assets to the ship. They're telling me about the specifics of a square-rigged ship and how they're shit for sailing but stellar for hauling cargo, when a ship comes into view that steals the breath from my lungs. It's not a large boat but the symbols painted on the side, and the flag that flies from its mast, send ice down my spine—why would a ship from Minos'Idyl be flying the flag of the crown?

I hear the hitch in Briar's breath before they speak. "Well, that's a puzzle."

"What do you think it means?" I ask, turning to them as the light on the water warms my face.

"I mean, from what y'all found on that island, it would seem the minotaurs are in league with *someone*. It's possible the church is mixed up in it as well. The King is notoriously devout, but I guess I never pegged him for a radical."

"What do you know about the Capital?" I don't know a damn thing about the royals or the church other than what Farragen taught us, and I know none of his words can be trusted.

"The monarchy and the church go hand in hand. The King is the man in charge, but he takes counsel from the church. The castle is near the Cathedral district. It's its own walled-off city almost, but they work in tandem."

"Well, fuck."

They chuckle in reply. "Fuck, indeed."

We're pulled from our chat as the captain's voice calls out from high in the rigging. "Stations! We won't be lookin' like amateurs!" Everyone hurries to their respective spot. I clamber up the rigging to the crow's nest, spyglass firmly in hand. The crew begins to navigate into the harbor, slowing the ship and manning the oars so as to slowly dock without smashing into anything. The harbor is small, and the space we aim for seems far too narrow for the Sea Song, but I have no doubt the crew will maneuver into it without issue. I can't help but to keep glancing at the ship flying the flag of the crown. While it is still too far off to see anything in detail, I'm filled with a sense of foreboding as I watch the crimson flag ripple in the wind.

It takes hours to dock, but Ardelle eventually hops down to tie us off and the crew erupts into a raucous cheer. Captain comes out dressed in a full-length purple coat trimmed with fur and a hat the color of a robin's egg. Her neck is draped with a bizarre assemblage of chains and pendants, and her pants are red leather, clashing wonderfully with her pale orange blouse. She's wearing a thick smear of rouge on her lips, and the small scar that slices through her upper lip stands out against the vibrant color. The rest of the crew scatter like ants, rushing below deck and back up, dressed in fancy attire of their own. Cenna and Tuii, not surprisingly, stay clad in black. I don't have much, so I find a clean blouse and throw it on over my leggings, shrugging on a suede jacket the color of rich clay at the last minute. My palms are clammy as I realize I'm about to meet a whole city of people. My heart rate picks up, and I begin to play through a million possible scenarios in which I make a complete ass out of myself. I'm paying absolutely no attention to anything around me, so I don't notice when Tuii steps beside me and slides her hand across my lower back. She presses a soft kiss to my cheek and takes my hand. "Ready?"

"Not in the slightest."

CAPTAIN LEADS THE PROCESSION DOWN THE GANGPLANK, Georgette and a few other crew members opt to stay aboard for the moment. Someone will relieve them eventually, and we will all have a chance to explore the city should we desire. The moment my feet hit the earth, I nearly fall. As I stumble like a buffoon, Tuii reaches for my elbow and steadies me, laughing. "It looks as though you've lost your land-legs, Red," she quips.

"I didn't know it would be *this* bad!" I say, still swaying as I try to stay still.

Captain looks over her shoulder and laughs loudly. "Ah, ye baby pirate! Just got used to the sea and now we throw you ashore!" Her smile is warm, and she laughs again before making her way toward the city.

The sun sits above the horizon like a great red eye, and the streets are lit in an odd pinkish glow. Tuii's hair reflects the colored light, and I can't help but run my fingers through it. She reaches around me and pulls me close, bumping my hip with hers. The gesture eases my tightly wound nerves, and I exhale a long breath. The city smells like shit. Small alleyways lie between the buildings, full of piles of refuse and gods know what else. Most of the people on the streets are men, their unwashed bodies and overgrown beards stinking of sweat and the sea. "You want to get a room at the inn?" Tuii asks with a glint of mischief in her eyes. "They have real beds…"

I groan aloud, thinking of the comfort of a mattress and plush blankets. "Absolutely."

Our group splits up, some heading for the tavern, some for stores, and a few of us toward the inn. There will be plenty of time to drink and be merry at the tavern. Right now, all I want is a comfortable bed and Tuii in my arms. The woman at the desk is older and gruff, but she gladly takes our coin and hands us a key, directing us to a room upstairs.

"Kitchen's closed for the evenin' and won't be open 'til dinner tomorrow, but I can bring up some bread and cheese for you, bottle o' wine if you're payin'."

Tuii nods and tosses her another coin. "Leave it outside, if you don't mind."

The woman nods. "I'll knock when I drop it off."

We head upstairs quickly, excitement hurrying our steps. The room isn't large, but it's well kept and clean. The bed is fairly large, bigger than the beds Ceci and I slept in back in Kanitosh, and the coverlet looks soft if a bit well-worn. There are pillows, a whole pile of them, and I resist the urge to jump onto them like a child in a heap of leaves. A small table sits in the corner with a washbasin and a ewer of water, and there is a framed notice on the wall telling us where to obtain more water for drinking or washing, and where the privy is located. Tuii sets her satchel beside the bed and sits, sinking onto the mattress with a sigh of pleasure. She lays back, her long hair fanning out behind her, and I wish I could capture the image somehow. A sharp knock sounds on the door as I busy myself unpacking my small bag, and Tuii begrudgingly rises to retrieve our meal.

We eat on the bed, laying on our stomachs and grabbing hunks of bread and cheese from the wooden tray between us. There are two varieties of cheese, a hard one with crunchy crystallized bits in it that I love and another with a pungent rind that spreads easily on the crusty bread. The wine is sweet, and we drink it straight from the bottle, laughing as we enjoy a moment with zero responsibility. When the plate is nothing but crumbs, and the bottle is nearly empty, Tuii sets the tray on the floor beside the bed and rolls over to me. Her lips are red from the wine, and her kiss is warm and sweet. It takes me only seconds to remove her silken top, and then it is just the two of us and the bed.

KONIDAS

CHAPTER SEVENTY-FOUR
MAELWEN
YEAR 993

My mind is a deluge of twisted theories and unease. I am unable to shake the feeling this bard shares a connection with Caelfry. It cannot be mere coincidence—this man singing a song about the love of a witch and a river of gold. As much as I would love to find Cicerine and lose myself in the lush pull of her body, I will not be able to rest until I speak with the man. From my shadowed seat in the corner I see Shell provide the bard with a key to one of the extra rooms, leading him up the stairs shortly after. I sip my ale, knowing it will only impede my success if I rush into this headlong. The man is likely tired after a day of travel and a night of performance, so I do not wish to wait *too* long to approach him, lest he fall asleep. Shell heads outside, wrapped in a heavy cloak, and I seize my opportunity and head up the stairs silently.

I rap on the door brusquely and hear the rustle of fabric and shuffle of feet before a faint reply sounds out from behind the wooden door. "Can I be of assistance?" the bard says in a voice heavy with wariness.

"I have come to speak with you about your song."

"I won't be playing an encore, and I do not share written copies of my music," he replies.

"That is not why I am here."

He sighs, a long, low, sound of defeat, and I hear the locks on the door unlatch one by one. When the door opens, he is standing in the doorway in his nightclothes, expression guarded, with the slightest tremor in his fingers. "I had hoped it would not be you."

The room is sparsely furnished but homey and warm, located over the kitchen so it does not require a hearth of its own. The bard gestures for me to sit in the single chair off to the side of the room, and he settles onto the edge of the bed with the mannerisms of a deer preparing to flee from a predator. He twists his fingers in his lap while not making eye contact, clearly waiting for me to start the conversation. When I do not, he begins.

"I always wondered if I would run across a witch in my travels, and so far I have not, until tonight. Your kind do not tend to spend much time gathering in drink halls, so I've played mostly for humans for the past few decades." When my brows raise, he goes on. "Yes, I am not as I seem. I met my witch when I was fresh out of an apprenticeship. I began late, and so I was just shy of thirty. I still have absolutely no inkling of what she saw in me, but I was smitten from the start. I've heard the stories, just like anyone else. I know witches aren't known for kindness with their lovers, but she treated me like a king though I was no more than a peasant."

"So she was your lover, then?" I ask, wanting him to continue.

He sighs, the look on his face one of endless longing and heartbreaking sadness. "She was my *love*. The only lover I ever took. I was an untried bachelor when we met, and I haven't laid with a woman since. She ruined me for all others. She ruined me for everything. I began my career as a bard shortly after she left. I wasn't able to hold down a job, only to sing sad songs and keep myself moving. When I stopped for too long, the sorrow crept in and I couldn't handle the weight of it."

"What happened?"

He doesn't reply for a long while, simply stares at the wooden slats of the floor. "I died." He finally says in a near-whisper. "I died and she brought me back."

Though I anticipated this, the effect of his words is not lessened. I suck in a breath and bite the inside of my cheek. I need to know so much more. "When did this happen? How did she bring you back? This is not a witch gift I have ever heard of."

"It isn't a gift," he laughs bitterly. "It's a curse." He stands and begins to pace the small room. He seems tightly-wound, a cord about to snap. "There was an incident. She and I were in Iowain, and I was so wrapped up in her that I was incapable of being a responsible man. I made bad decisions, became involved with worse people, and when my actions caught up with me, I lost my life trying to save a friend. She found me on the plain, bleeding out and nearly gone. I will never forget the look on her face. She was stricken, but full of depthless rage at the same time. The earth shook with it. Even as my life faded, I felt the magnitude of her. I'm not sure what happened, or how she did it, but I awoke to her holding a stone cup to my lips. It was rough, as though she had carved it from the rocks of the plain, and the liquid inside was like molten gold. It hurt. It hurt in a way I cannot describe, but when it was over, I rose and was whole again."

"Ichor. The golden liquid is called Ichor."

"Yes," he replies. "That is also what she called it. However, after I recovered, she called me 'a weakness she could not afford.' I begged her to kill me, to let me die having loved her and lived a life full of that love, but she refused. Said the gift she had given me was too precious to throw away, that I would live a life far longer than that of any mortal. I don't even know if I can die. I've considered it—ending it all—but I'm a weak shell of a man. All I have is my lyre and a story about a witch who loved me once."

"What was her name?" I ask, already knowing the answer.

His eyes are dark with pain when he at last replies. "Caelfry."

I AM CLOSE TO WEARING A HOLE IN MY RUG FROM ALL THE pacing I am doing. After leaving the bard, I returned to my apartment to look at the vessel once again and to see if I could glean any further information from the book. I would like to bash the vessel against the wall, my frustration is so great. I have solved half a riddle, and it infuriates me. I understand this is an artifact of intention, and that a similar one must have been the thing to save the bard. However, I cannot work out why this item was created with the powers of Cicerine and I. Why could we not have crafted an item that would help us destroy Farragen and his Idyth cult? This vessel gives life, when all I want to do is bring death.

Small fingers drum on my door, and I'm pulled from my brooding. Setting the vessel atop my desk, I open the door to find Cicerine, a smudge of flour across her cheek, wearing an apron over her dress and smelling of baked apples. I brush the flour from her face, and she blushes furiously.

"Gods, I'm sorry. I'm a mess. I should have washed up, but I just wanted to see you, and so I came straight away and…"

I stop her rambling, cupping her chin in my palm and running my thumb across her lower lip. Molten heat settles deep within me, and I feel the surge of our combined power as my skin meets hers. A faint spark pops from my thumb to her plush lower lip, and she gasps as it hisses out on her skin. Wordlessly, she rises on hooftip and reaches her hand up to rest on the back of my neck, smoothing my hair over one shoulder as she does. A rough purr rumbles within my chest as I lower my face to hers with aching slowness, reveling in the way her breath quickens. Before our lips can press together, I pull away, eliciting a huff of displeasure from Cicerine. Her hand falls from my neck, and she looks adorably petulant, but it takes me only a moment to kick the door closed and pull the latch before returning my hands to her.

All thoughts of ichor and men evaporate from my mind as her taste hits my tongue. I feel her fumble to remove the apron, dropping it in a heap at our feet. My fingers dig into the soft flesh of her hips and our skin electrifies at every point of contact. My toe catches on the edge of the thick rug beneath my bed, and I growl as I kick my foot forcefully to push it out of my way. I walk her toward my bed without taking my lips from hers, directing her steps with my hands on her waist. When her round ass hits the edge of the bed, she pushes herself onto it, wrapping her legs around either side of me and pulling my body flush with hers. Her round little stomach presses against me, warm and soft against the angular bones of my hips. She giggles and flushes as my fingers skate across it.

"Stop that," she says, her lips smiling against mine.

"I will not," I reply. "You will not deny me any part of you."

With that, she groans and I feel the heat between her thighs intensify. My mouth opens, pulling in a ragged breath, already dizzy with the intoxication of wanting her. *Needing* her. My thoughts are a tangled mess as I struggle to verbalize this need, this devastating claim I have upon her. I want this woman so thoroughly that it feels as though my very cells belong to her.

"I know," she gasps.

Pulling back, I look at her, questioning. "Know what?"

"I can feel what you're thinking, it's in my head. *You're* in my head. This isn't want, Maelwen. It is more, fate? You were made to be mine. Gods, I think I love you Maelwen. Every filament of my soul is yours."

Something clenches within my chest, like the force of massive hands gripping the muscle of my heart. I am fully overwhelmed by an emotion I cannot articulate, so I say the only thing I know to feel right, "I love you as well, Cicerine, my woodborn heart."

There are no more words between us. Her fingers tangle in my hair, and I kiss her with bruising force. My bed is alight with sparks, the air buzzing with the physical manifestation of our connection. My coverlet smokes in places, but I pay it no mind. My only focus is on her. I push her farther onto the bed, her hooves coming up to rest upon the tousled blankets, legs falling to either side of my insistent body. I use a claw to slice down the side of my leggings, ripping them from my skin and throwing them to the ground. I hook that same claw at the fabric between her breasts, raking it down and tearing a line through both her dress and her stays. The fabric falls away, baring her luscious form to me. She shrugs her arms out of the ruined garments and rises on her elbows to plunge her tongue between my lips.

She tastes of honey and home, and I drink her in like a starved beast. I savor her for a moment before pressing my hand to her chest and forcing her back down onto my bed. Pulling my blouse over my head, I am nude and nearly feverish with frenzied desire. I crawl onto the bed, one knee at a time, my hands on either side of her halo of curling hair. Her horns catch the light from my bedside lantern, and I reach for one, pulling her head back to expose the sensuous expanse of her throat. I lick and bite my way down the soft skin, feeling her pulse flutter beneath my tongue. The arousal I feel from her vulnerability, knowing her life force lies just beneath my teeth, has me close to breaking. I grind my hips into hers, moaning against her throat as my body nearly dissolves at the heady rush of sensation. She presses back into me, her slick sex leaving me glistening in its wake. For a few heartbeats we remain like this, moving against one another, my mouth on her neck and her fingers leaving crescent-shaped marks on my shoulders as she grasps me desperately.

I release my hold on her horn and her head falls back against the pile of silken pillows that top my bed. Slowly, with infinite care, I move down her body. My tongue appreciates every inch of her, tasting the salt of her skin across both breasts and their pert nipples, the velvety skin along her ribs. My hands move through the soft brown coat at her hips, and I drink in the sight of the v-shaped space where flesh gives way to a tiny patch of softly curling hair. She wriggles beneath me, small noises tumbling from her lips, her hands grabbing and releasing the rumpled coverlet over and over. I press her legs up, spreading her before me, seeing the darkened fabric beneath where her desire has left my bed damp. I spread her with my fingers, ignoring her soft sound of protest, gazing upon the lush pink of her. I do not linger, lowering my head to press my mouth to her wet heat in a single fluid motion. There is too much intensity in this moment to draw it out. I know her climax is close, laying in wait behind a few deft strokes of my tongue. I allow myself the gratification of a few languid caresses, tasting her slowly. A fluttering noise that sounds wild and untethered ripples through the room, and I cease my teasing, pleasuring her in earnest. She comes almost instantly, her thighs quaking and her body quivering as she pants out my name. *"Maelwen, Maelwen, Maelwen."* I have never heard a more beautiful word.

I rest my head on her still-trembling thigh, closing my eyes and breathing deeply. My bed smells like her, like cinnamon and baking things, like sex and fire. She sits up and strokes my hair as she looks around us. "Your pretty bedcover is ruined."

"I can replace it quite easily," I reply, pressing a kiss to the downy fur above her knee. "Anyway, I think I prefer it this way."

She giggles. "Full of holes and covered in sweat?"

"Covered in you."

"Come here," she says, pulling on my wrist. Her tone is playful, but I hear the note of lust that lies beneath. I shift upward in the bed, coming to rest eye-to-eye with her. The golden amber of her irises glints in the lantern-light like citrine. Her lips are full, with a defined cupid's-bow and a soft crease in the lower lip that begs for my mouth to press against it. Her eyelashes are impossibly long, curling upward and glittering with miniscule droplets of sweat. Even now, messy from work and mussed from sex, she is divine. I watch those sumptuous lips shape her words. "What are you staring at so intently?"

"You are flawless, Cicerine. Each and every bit of you is a study in perfection. You are everything I am not and everything I could ever want."

Her apple-round cheeks blush crimson. "I'm a woodborn faun who makes flowers grow. I'm squishy and doughy and clumsy…"

I interrupt her, wrapping my hands around her waist. "Your mirror is not my vision. If only you had the ability to look upon yourself through *my* eyes."

The joy on her face fades, falling into something I have not seen in her expression before. *"A shattered mirror is but a thousand new mirrors, and they all reflect a different truth,"* she whispers.

"You said that before."

"I feel like I almost had it," she says, looking frustrated. "It's murky, like it's on the tip of my tongue, but I just can't grasp it. I wish I knew what it meant, but there was a flicker just then. That's all."

I run a finger along the curve of her cheek and press a kiss to her chin. "We will find your answer," I reply, "together."

KONIDAS

CHAPTER SEVENTY-FIVE
SHELL
YEAR 993

My bar is being overtaken by pirates, and I'm not mad about it in the slightest. I could've cried with joy when they started showin' up one after another, and I saw there wasn't a single man among 'em. Pirates can be messy folk, and can be a bit o' trouble, but men are a whole different story. Ain't nobody harassin' the girls, ain't nobody pissin' on the floor. They're a raucous group but still respectful, and it feels like a godsdamned dream come true. Their captain is a curious kind of lady, unrestrained and outspoken; she hollers out jokes and jests with a smile a mile wide. Though I can see that beneath her jovial exterior, she knows her shit. She's a solid captain, and clearly the crew respects her in a way that few captains earn. She's dressed like a damn jester: her hat nearly the size of a bar table, boots halfway up her thighs gleaming with massive brass buckles. Her hair looks like she cuts it with a dull sword, choppy and blunt, sitting just above her shoulders. When I drop off a growler of cider, I spot a hairline scar across her mouth. She's a pretty thing in a coarse way, and I feel like she's my kind of person the moment she opens her mouth.

"Aye! My savior!" she shouts in wild joy. "I heard tell that you were hidin' cider back in ye secret cellar! And here it is! Brought forth for me crew!"

I laugh. "Captain, I ain't got no secret cellar, but I do have a new brewer who's been bubblin' up a wicked good cider with the last of the pear crop!"

The gathered pirates pull out their own tin cups and pass the growler around. I head to the bar and grab another two, knowing they're gonna need it. The crew is an odd assemblage of folks. There's a small dark-haired girl who looks nearly like a kid, but I can see from the way she moves and the glint of blades at her back that she's deadly as fuck. She looks like a shadow. A pair who introduced themselves as Briar and Ardelle sit near the captain. Ardelle is blonde and reserved, but she seems to love my whisky. Briar is the kindly sort and makes me want a hug and a warm blanket; they keep ordering breakfast buns—though it's well past breakfast. There's a pair of twins who sit quietly in the corner sipping sour ale, and a girl with thick, black hair done up in a mass of long braids that go from her scalp to below her shoulders. A couple of the city's workin' girls have stopped in, and I see a few of 'em flirtin' with the pirates at the bar. One keeps eyein' the captain, but she ain't havin' none of it. I'm sure by the end of the night the pirates will all be headed to the inn, paired up, with a night of fun ahead of 'em.

The tavern buzzes with energy from folks long at sea, lettin' loose and enjoyin' their time earthside. I can't help but notice Cartwright as he enters, his shoulders broad but slightly curved inward, like he's nervous to be here. I haven't seen him since the night he kissed me, and my own palms have gone a bit damp rememberin' the feel of his mouth on mine. I ain't got time to act like a besotted teen, so I get back to work takin' care of the visitors. The captain, who tells me her name's Ballad, inquires about lodgin', and I assure her that the inn has rooms enough for all of 'em if they don't mind sharin'. Beatrice will be glad for the coin, but Cicerine is 'bout to have her work cut out for her—this crew is *hungry*.

Leita is currently workin' the kitchen and Martine has gone to fetch Agnes to give her a hand with the cookin'. The wee ones can play in the kitchen where it's warm and out of trouble. Losh will be glad for the attention. He clearly feels at ease, but I get a good chuckle when the shadow girl drops to the floor in sheer delight as he passes. She rubs his big head between her delicate hands and smiles at him like he's a sunbeam in the black of winter.

"I haven't seen a cat in *ages!*" she croons. "Our ship's cat died a while back after a long life of rat catching. This sweet boy reminds me of him."

"That's Losh," I reply. "He's a big softie, and once you start pettin' him, you best not intend on stoppin'."

She presses her nose to his and in a baby voice that sounds ridiculous comin' out of her, says, "Never, ever, lovie boy."

Laughin', I brush my hair off my face and quickly twist it into a loose braid. Spoiled rotten cat. I light more lanterns, and the tavern fills with the scent of burnin' oil and stale beer. Cartwright's eyes find me as I putter around the place, fillin' cups and clearin' empty plates. I won't deny the extra swish of my hips when I feel his gaze at my back. I am, after all, a generous woman. As the night wears on, the crew gets drunker and my pockets get heavier. Tonight has been *quite* profitable, and I hope this group stays around awhile. I send a deposit off with Cartwright and don't miss the way his thick fingers graze my hand as he takes it. The last damn thing I need is the complication of a man. It's gotta be a passing fancy, an infatuation. There ain't no damn way this man has been harborin' feelins for me all this time. I can't possibly be *that* daft.

Ballad breaks me from my reverie with a tap to my elbow. Her voice and hand are steady, and I realize she holds the same cup of cider from hours before. She sees me lookin' and slips me a wink. "Someone's gotta be the responsible one—tonight it best be me. Ye can't be sure in a new port, and I needed to make certain me crew were safe and sound-like."

Smilin', I nod. I understand the respect of her crew. This is a captain I'd follow gladly.

"Now that they're all sauced and loosey-goosey, I'd like to have some words with ye, if ye don't mind."

"Of course," I reply. "What's on your mind?"

"Well, we been tangled up in a whole mess on Minos'Idyl, some sort o' somethin' knocked me ship asunder, three of me crew ended up makin' landfall where they found somethin' of much concern."

My heart leaps into my throat as I realize of what she speaks. "Pennyway."

Her eyes widen, nearly imperceptibly, and I notice the surprise that sweeps across her face. "Ye know of it."

"Unfortunately. There's a cult called the New Church tryin' to bring back some sort of man-god named Idyth. They're growin' the stuff to try and get powers."

"Aye, we have a crewmember I picked up a while back from Kanitosh who encountered some of their fuckery. Do ye have any sort of plan? Protection?"

"We got a witch named Maelwen, and she and her kin plan to meet soon. The Crone has some sort of plan to end them—one they won't share with us. The witches look out for the witches, but I suppose it helps us all in the end."

"Have ye had trouble here in Konidas?"

I sigh, vision thickenin' as I recall Godrick's face. "It's quite a tale. You may want another cup of cider."

∽

I tell Ballad the whole story: the bar fight, the mob, the burning of the witch. I tell her of the threats to non-humans and the men we've questioned. We come to the same conclusion that they've got somethin' comin', *soon*. "We planned to be out to sea within the week," the captain says, "but we ain't got a thing more pressin' than this. Would ye like us to stay dockside? We can remain through the solstice."

"I can't ask you to do that. We don't even know what's coming exactly, and I don't want to be puttin' your folks in danger."

"Well, I ain't one to run from danger. Wouldn't be captain if that were the case. We got ourselves a half-nereid, and one way or another, we will get news to you should we be seein' anythin' afoot. We'll stay close to the coast, that way if they come by sea, we'll warn ye."

I toast her, clinkin' my cup of water against her cider. "You have my gratitude."

The door flies open and hits the wall with a resounding *boom*. Cartwright stands in the open doorway, chest heaving and eyes wide. "Where is Maelwen?" he asks, voice low and heavy.

"Upstairs, what is going on?"

"I don't think they saw me, but some of 'em are here. I'm goin' to alert the Brick Union. Keep 'em hidden." His eyes catch mine for another moment, and then he's gone.

I don't bother with explainin' to the captain, headin' quickly for the stairs. I take them two at a time and reach the door to Maelwen's apartment out of breath, but runnin' hot with adrenaline. I knock, and she's at the door in an instant. "What is it?"

"Stay up here, and bar the door. Some of the Idythian fucks are here. Cartwright saw them when he took my deposit."

"I will not hide here as a coward would. Cicerine and I both possess adequate magic to defend ourselves."

"We don't know how many of them are here or why. Don't be runnin' into trouble that ain't callin' your name."

"Shell, any beast is weakened when you chop off its limbs. There is no reason for us to remain hidden other than your fear of us coming to harm. We are capable."

My fingers dig into the wrinkles of my forehead. Why can't the damn witch just be cautious for once? She didn't see the girl in the square. She didn't smell her flesh or hear her dying cries. That image is seared into my mind; I see it in my sleep. "Please, Maelwen."

"I will not promise this, however, I will remain here for now. Is there anyone who can go out? Attempt to assess why they have come?"

"I'll ask someone." I answer, knowin' it's the best I'll get from her.

I jog back downstairs and speak with Ballad. She volunteers the shadow girl, Cenna, to go see what she can glean of their intentions. Another pair walks in as she heads out. The ginger is tall and freckled with hair cut short on the sides and high in the center. They're broad shouldered, with a wiry sort of muscle, wearing a loose ivory blouse and black breeches. Holding their hand is a small woman with hair like midnight. She's dressed head-to-toe in black, and I see daggers at her sides. She's compact, more than a head shorter than the redhead, but her elegantly shaped eyes convey confidence with a single glance. They're clearly together from the way the ginger's arm comes around the girl protectively as they see Cenna run out. The ginger opens their mouth to speak, but their words are silenced with an earsplittin' crack and a low gurgle.

It takes my mind far too long to make sense of what's before me. The ginger crumples to the floor, the dark-haired girl fallin' to her side for an infinitesimal span of time before drawin' her blades and spinnin' in mid-air. A dark robe and a crown of wiry gray-black hair that I recognize as Salvatorre comes into view before tumblin' backward down the steps into the dark night. A cacophony of male voices shout from outside, but are replaced with shouts and the sounds of steel tearing fabric and flesh. The dark-haired girl vanishes out the door, joining with Cenna to fight the horde. One of them lets loose a distinctive whistle and the rest of the crew races out the door while I stand, dumbstruck, before the fallen ginger. Blood trickles from between their wide lips, and their eyes flutter as I drop to my knees.

"Don't you worry; we've got you. I'll get help, I'll be right back—" They grab my wrist and try to speak, but nothin' comes out other than a rattling rasp. "Please, hold on," I beg as I uncurl their fingers from my wrist and run toward the stairs. Maelwen and Cicerine are already descendin', runnin' hand in hand with a look of stoic determination. The three of us run back to the form on the floor. They're pullin' in ragged breaths that sound wet and desperate.

Cicerine's knees hit the floorboards hard enough to bruise. The sound that comes from her is nearly incoherent, but I manage to make out the single word. "Jynn?"

ATHYDIS

CHAPTER SEVENTY-SIX
THE CRONE
YEAR 993

The snare has been set; faith, the wire she shall use to bind them all to ruin. In two weeks' time, the whole of the kingdom will gather in the Cathedral city where she shall sing their end. She has yet to establish the range of her Song of Death, but she will gather power in the days before, gain the strength needed to sing an entire kingdom to their end. The dreams have become more frequent, flashes of faces and realms she has never walked. Something stirs in the great tapestry of time, and when this is done, she shall consult the vast trove of memory that lies within her for answers. Surely the Crones long past can provide some clarity to this murky vision.

The bodies of the King and Queen lie still in their beds. The Queen's dark hair spills over the pillow in a cascade of curls. It grates on the Crone to do so but she brushes their hair, trims his beard, and bathes them with damp cloths. She keeps them appearing as they should, so as to keep the facsimile of their governance believable. No one has yet discovered the truth of their puppetry—she has gone to great lengths to ensure this. Even the crawling creatures of the castle have been kept from this chamber, for even rats have voices. Even mice tell secrets. The Crone hums a song under her breath, a song she once sang long ago when she was lovely and unbound by this endless duty. With each stroke of the ivory-handled brush, the hair of the Queen shines more brightly, a shimmering chocolate-brown befitting a woman of such stature. This moment feels maternal, and the Crone swallows the thought. She is the Crone; she is mother to no one.

She has cast a circle around this room, her magic like a dome of glass surrounding the clandestine chamber. The crack begins slowly, a hairline fracture that is almost too miniscule to detect; but slowly it spreads, and she feels the fracturing magic with the outstretched fingers of her mind. The shattered bits prick at her, sharp and unexpected. She looks up from her task, milky eyes moving to the barred door. The masonry of slightly rounded gray stone, the thick wooden brace across the entryway. The heavy beam begins to move, and she remains still, curious.

The fingers which open the door are too long. A waxy, creamy color that does not belong to human flesh. The nails are overgrown, scratching against the wood like the claws of a bird of prey. The tremendous weight of the stone door swings inward, and the man who is not a man steps inside the chamber; a malicious smile curving the corners of his thin, colorless lips and making his sallow skin wrinkle.

"Hello, Morwenna," he speaks, a voice heavy with hate. "It is good to see you have taken such care with my dear cousin." *He looks at the Queen, and she sees the similarities between them, the shape of the brow, the angle of the jaw.*

She peers at him, that familiarity tingling in the depths of her mind. When it happens, she drops the brush to the bed. The image in her mind settling over the face before her like a mirror from the past. She recognizes the aristocratic tilt of his head, the shade of his hair, and as he unfastens the collar of his long, gray priest's robe she sees the jagged scar across his throat. She sees the line traced by her own claw twenty-three years in the past.

"A man can lose a great deal of blood, Morwenna — but a God can lose a great deal more."

KONIDAS

CHAPTER SEVENTY-SEVEN
CICERINE
YEAR 993

I shake uncontrollably as vomit rises in my throat. My eyes swim with tears, and I lose control of myself; my power shooting into the earth, cracking the wood of the floor. Jynn is here. Jynn is here, and she's dying. I glance around frantically to see the mob fighting just outside the tavern, the pirates' blades clashing with flashes of power from a crowd of robed men. I see Salvatorre dead on the steps of the tavern. I take it all in within the span of a single heartbeat, and then my attention is back on Jynn. Every bit of anger or resentment I felt toward her is gone, replaced by a heart-rending, agonizing pain. I press my hands to her chest, willing my gift to heal her, to find the injury, to fix this; but I don't know what I am doing. I don't even know if I can do this. From the edge of my vision, I see Maelwen run out the open doors. I have no idea where she is going or what she is doing. I cannot let my thoughts linger on Maelwen right now. In every fiber of my being I know with certainty she will not leave me, so I focus on Jynn.

"Jynn, *Jynn*," I sob. "Please wake up, please open your eyes."

Her lids flutter, and I see gemstone green for a moment before they fall closed once more. My hands fly over her body, searching for the injury that has left her this way. Blood leaks from the corners of her lips, but I do not see a wound or contusion—she appears unharmed. Still, she lies dying on the floor of Shell's tavern.

"Jynn, please, for the love of the gods, hold on!" I shake her shoulders, but she doesn't stir. A blonde woman appears next to me, face stricken as she removes a large hat and looks down at Jynn's still face.

"Are they breathing?" she asks.

"For the moment," I reply, voice quavering. "What do we do?"

"Where are they hit?"

"I don't know, I cannot find a wound." Tears fall from my eyes to splatter against Jynn's freckled cheeks. This can't happen. She cannot find me only to die before we've even had a chance to speak. I scream in frustration, the tavern quaking around me with the force of my power.

A small woman with black hair kneels next to Jynn, looking at me with a combination of wonder and rage. "You are Cicerine," she says.

"I am. *Please*, help her. I cannot lose her, please." I sob, wiping my nose on my hand as I shake with sorrow.

"They thought you were dead," she whispers, and my heart breaks as I realize what she says—Jynn didn't leave me. The black-haired woman leans down to Jynn and kisses her face gently, lovingly. This woman loves her as I do—as I did. "Jynn, please come back to me," she whispers. "I need you."

Jynn's eyes open, barely enough to see their peridot green hue, and her bloodied mouth smiles slightly as she looks at me and then at the woman in black. Her hand reaches for the woman's black-gloved hand, and she grasps it tightly. Jynn looks at me once more and closes her eyes.

Her chest goes still and does not rise again.

KONIDAS

CHAPTER SEVENTY-EIGHT
MAELWEN
YEAR 993

I race down the stairs, heart in my throat as I take in the scene unfolding before me. Total chaos has descended upon the tavern, a man lies dead on the steps and a red-haired body is sprawled upon the floorboards just inside. A sharp bolt of agony tears through my chest, and I realize it is Cicerine's magic, pain so intense that it rips through my totality like wildfire. Noises of battle rage from outside, and I watch as Cicerine falls to her knees before the red-headed person, crying out "Jynn?" in a voice I have never heard. I do not have time to contemplate the situation, instead, my mind shutters—the only coherent thought remaining *keep her safe.*

I run. Dropping Cicerine's hand, I run outside, leaping over the body on the stairs and landing on the dusty ground. I sense something inky and vicious, and turn to see a dark-haired woman appearing and disappearing into shadow as she slices into gray-robed men with a blade. There are far too many people here to use the Song of Death, I do not know these people, and I cannot tell friend from foe, so I extend my claws with practiced grace. I *do* know these robes, and I feel as though I can already taste the hot blood of the Idythian cultists on my tongue.

 A man runs at me, his eyes full of malice, and I grin as I swipe my claws through the thick flesh of his neck. He falls, blood spraying and splattering my legs as he does, and I kick him aside. Another man grapples with a woman to my right, and I run toward them, the ground beneath my feet feeling sticky and coarse against the soles of my bloodied boots. The woman sees me, and steps back just a fraction, enough for me to reach between them and plunge my claws into the man's face. I feel a sickening pop as his eye is impaled on my long claw, and when I pull my hand free, the eye comes with it. I flick my wrist, throwing the repulsive bit of flesh toward the earth, and the man screams in rage and pain. His hands scrabble at his face, blood pouring from between his fingers, exposing his throat to me in his frenzy. My claws slide into his neck in a single, clean motion and I close my fist within his neck, ripping his trachea free. His scream is silenced, and he collapses into a gray heap at my feet.

 Spinning, I see another man with his back toward me, raising what appears to be a bowstaff over his head, preparing to strike a tall, broad-shouldered person before him. My hand darts out, grabbing the bowstaff and wrenching his arm backward, breaking his wrist with an audible crack. He whirls to face me, a roar of pain bellowing from his mouth, and I grasp the weapon in both hands, swinging it into his head and crushing his skull. Over and over again, I tear men apart, my face and hands black with blood, its delicious tang bright on my tongue. But that same strike of pained magic rips through my chest again, and I turn to see Cicerine sobbing, bent over the form on the floor. Their chest does not seem to be rising, and the look of absolute desolation in Cicerine's eyes pulls me from the blood-drenched slaughter, and compels me to act.

I know nothing in this moment except the all-consuming need to end her pain, to solve whatever befalls her and fix whatever is happening. My mind whirls, a tangle of thoughts and memories and an idea that explodes in a burst of golden light. I think of Cicerine, the love I feel for her, and I run.

KONIDAS

CHAPTER SEVENTY-NINE
JYNN
YEAR 993

Tuii and I stare at one another in the rumpled blankets of the bed. We've spent the entire evening tangled up together, and the taste of her on my lips lingers as if to tempt me into never leaving. "Come on, Red," she laughs as she rolls over and rises. "I want a drink. You know Ballad's likely up to no good. Let's go party with the crew.

"I just want to party with *you*," I croon, swatting the curve of her bare ass with the edge of the blanket. "Come back to bed."

She laughs as she bends to kiss me. "You're insufferable. Get up, lazy-ass."

"Fine," I draw the word out with mock-irritation. I kiss the top of her shoulder as I grab my breeches from the floor, pulling them over my lanky hips. I pick up the strip of fabric I use to bind my chest and wind it around my ribcage and toss on my blouse. "Are you happy now?"

"Very," she says, and I can see in her eyes there is more to that word than satisfaction with my state of dress.

I swing her in my arms, easily lifting her small frame. "Be mine," I ask her softly.

She smiles up at me and replies, "I am yours."

"No, I mean, forever. Be with me. Be my partner, wife. Whatever pirates call it, I want you forever."

Her eyes widen and her lips fall open. "Jynn, we've known each other for two seasons, not even a year. How can you be sure you want me forever?"

"Tell me you don't feel it too, Tuii. If you feel what I feel, you know it's not going to change. I don't need more time to decide, I decided on you months ago."

Yes," she says. "I'll marry you, you foolish creature, but you owe me a ring."

I kiss her deeply, my tongue sliding against hers in a slow, sensuous motion. I have never felt happier than I do at this moment. I love this woman, and she has agreed to be mine forever. Laughing with the sheer joy of it, I grab her hand and head out the door. She wears head-to-toe black and is as stunning as ever, her silken hair unbound and falling around her in a sleek sheet down to her waist. Our fingers intertwine and she leans her head against my shoulder as we walk, strolling toward the tavern.

A huddle of men in gray cloaks stands to the side of the cobblestone road, tucked nearly into an alley. My skin crawls as we pass them. Their cloaks look far too similar to Farragen's robes, but I shrug it off. It is cold outside and very likely that such a style of coat is popular here. I'm just being paranoid, and I'm not going to let foolish paranoia dull the shine of this night and the joy that fills my heart. I can't wait to tell the crew, to tell Ballad. I've grown close to the captain, and I know Tuii cares deeply for her as well. And now, somehow, I have Tuii, the midnight dream of a woman who rests her hand in the crook of my arm. The woman who tastes like heaven and earth, and whispers my name like a prayer. The woman who accepted me as I am, who loves me without questioning, who easily shifted their view of me from *woman* to just *Jynn*, without blinking an eye. My heart overflows with sheer rapture, spilling my joy onto the street like a cup filled too full.

The tavern is brightly lit from the inside and has a large sign out front painted in a bright shade of blue-green. "Shell's Tavern." I wonder if that's the name of the owner or just a play on being seaside. I move to push open the door, Tuii's hand in mine, when Cenna darts out, clad in shadow. She's gone so quickly I don't get the chance to even call out her name, but I walk through the door in her wake. A woman stands just before me, a tall lady with a full bosom and wide hips. Her corset cinches in her middle and her dishwater-blonde hair is falling out of a poorly woven braid. I open my mouth to greet her, but a force strikes my back, pushing through my chest as it does. I look down, expecting to see my ribs and organs exposed, but I am whole. *Magic.*

I come-to just in time to see Tuii leap into the fray. I hear voices behind us and know I should have spoken up about the men in the alley. This has to have been the same sort of magic that nearly sank the Sea Song. The pain is a dull roar, and I fade in and out of coherence as the force of its damage takes hold.

The blonde woman is speaking to me, but I don't hear her words clearly—they sound like cotton in my skull. I try to grab her, to keep her with me, but she says something and peels my finger from her wrist, dropping my hand. I see fear in her eyes.

I am confused as I open my eyes once again, but then I realize what this is. This must be the next place. Cicerine—my Sunbeam—kneels before me, just as lovely as she was the last time I saw her. Her cinnamon curls are lit from behind, and she looks so ethereal, like a dream in soft focus. I never knew what to believe about life after death, but Mamère told us we would see all those we had ever loved and lost, that they would be waiting for us when we left this plane. I am so glad to see Ceci; this is a gift. I smile at her and try to tell her I'm sorry, that I should never have left her. The words don't come. Tuii's face appears beside her, and

I smile once more. Even through the pain, I feel so loved. She kisses my cheek and asks me to come back. I try to speak, to tell her that I'm still here, but my mouth refuses to form the words.

I feel tears on my face, like droplets of summer rain. I see the green of the glade and feel the lapping water of the creek around my knees, the deck of the ship beneath my feet, and the brisk ocean wind whipping through my hair as I smile. *I'm all right,* I try to say. *It does not hurt, and I have you both with me. If I cannot live forever, at least I was lucky enough to have known real love.* I don't think they can hear me, so I squeeze the hand that rests in mine. *It's all going to be all right. I love you.*

I close my eyes, and all I see are stars.

ACKNOWLEDGMENTS

I could never have written this book without the unwavering support of my friends and family. I could write another entire book with the amount of thanks I have to give, but I'll spare you the details and keep it succinct.

Chris, you unwittingly inspired this whole story and accidentally gave me a world to write it in. I'm sorry we never got to play that campaign, Cicerine would've made a sweet satyr bard though, am I right?

Rachel, I love you forever for all the support and all the assurance that my writing *is* worth sharing. You've always had my back and made me feel like a writer worth reading. Thank you for making me feel worthy, and always being behind me.

Alyson, my biggest cheerleader. You have touched so much of this story and I am endlessly glad to have found you in this world. Thank you forever for loving me and loving my story. Stop living so far away, come back for tacos.

Jess, for giving me the courage to do this. For showing me that it *is* possible, and lighting a fire that had long been extinguished. I'm glad I found you on the internet. I'm sorry that I don't understand computers or the Midwest.

Amber, for giving me confidence in my own abilities. You gave me an amazing opportunity for growth, and made me a better writer by doing so; not to mention all the formatting and publishing assistance. I love you to bits, even when you argue with me about it.

Ambria, for helping me hone my rambling mess of adjectives into an actual novel. You're a light in the dark and I'm so glad to know your radiance.

Elaine, I can never thank you enough for bringing me back to poetry and prose, and for giving life to Jynn. For teleporters, cabins, flannels, mushrooms and all the sleepy eyes.

Olga, for continuing to encourage me to write for the last twenty-one years, your support means more than you know. Also, thanks for the laptop without which I could never have written anything, nor gone back to school. I hope you skip the spicy stuff.

For all my beta readers who made me feel like a real author, I'm so grateful for you all.

ABOUT THE AUTHOR

Heather Nix is the debut author of Woodborn, the first book in the Song of Gods series. Born and raised in sunny San Diego, CA she longs to return to the forests of the Pacific Northwest. She is the mother of two human and three cat children, and enjoys tattoos, tabletop RPGs, and creating feminist art in her limited spare time. Heather is passionate about writing queer fantasy, and strives to create nuanced characters who resonate with underserved communities.

CPSIA information can be obtained
at www.ICGtesting.com
Printed in the USA
BVHW041320210123
656723BV00004B/781